AENIGMA

By

Erus Ludus

Translated by Sharon Heller

ISBN 978-0-9908360-8-7
First Paperback printing Sep 2014
Erus Ludus LLC
Printed in USA by Create Space

To Rossana,
A beautiful sculptress
with magic in her hands.

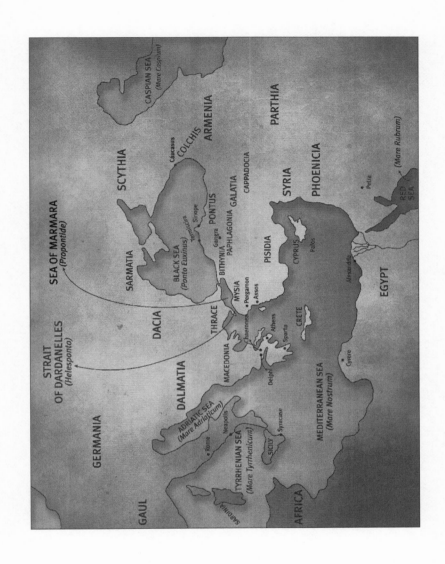

PREFACE

Allow me to introduce myself; my name is Erus Ludus. I was born many years ago in the region of Adria, in the Roman province of Tarvisium. However, a short time later, I moved to Rome, where after learning mathematics, astronomy, geometry, and music, I devoted myself to the entertainment of kings, emperors, lords, and beautiful women, with riddles that combined all the knowledge I had acquired.

May my long white beard, the lines on my face, and my weary step not confuse you. I am much, very much, older than what you might think... And sadly, I believe I will live many, many, more years.

As to why I have lived to such a long age, I do not have the answer. Perhaps history needs simple people like me to attest to the incidents that happen and to convey them in an impartial manner. In any case, the story that I am going to tell you happened such as I tell it, and it is important that you pay attention to all the details, since its fortuitous outcome will bring glory, riches, and unimaginable wonders to both your name and mine.

Erus Ludus

CHAPTER ONE

The young girl loosened the ties of her tunic, which gently slid from her virginal body until it reached the ground, displaying the splendor of her nudity. She walked slowly towards the circle of burning laurel leaves. Waves of thick smoke began to caress her body, purifying and preparing it to receive the prophecies from the God.

After she was draped in white vestments, one of the priests moved her towards the tripod that was on top of the Sacred Crevice in the center of the temple. There, as she breathed the gases that emanated from the aperture, she fell into a trance, just as thousands of other young women had done since the beginning of the oracle, when Apollo, *He Who Strikes from Afar*, killed the Great Serpent.

Her gaze became lost and distant. The images she was seeing were beyond the horizon. Suddenly, she closed her eyes and began to gasp. The gasps turned into cries that were deafening to the priests, who were sitting in a circle around the young woman. She stopped abruptly, opened her eyes, and in a serene voice she began to speak:

The Seventh has revealed himself.
Prepare thyselves! Hunger overwhelms the walled city
and the Red Commander will avenge the Vespers,
bringing desolation and grief to Pallas Athena.
Seven they shall be to save the Treasure:
Athlete without Laurels, Heiress of the Throne of Women,
Sailor of the Goddess, Princess of the City of Stone,
Priest of the Gods, Bearer of the Word,
and Discreet Stranger.
Miserable Traitor! You will appear from the circle of seven.
Only the Word will save them,
only the Seventh will know how to decipher it.

After uttering these words, the Pythia fell into an unconscious state.

The priests remained for a long while without speaking, until Enos broke the silence.

"Hunger is defeating Athens. I do not know how much longer Aristion will be able to withstand the blockade by the Romans," he said, addressing the other priests. "I have heard it said that the Athenians are soaking leather in water to eat it."

"Mithridates should never have incited anger in Rome, and the Athenians made a grave mistake in becoming his allies," Tesseros replied.

"They thought they would be just as fortunate as they were against Xerxes, but Sulla is a magnificent general, and he will not cease in his resolve until he feels avenged for the affront against his people," Pentos said sadly.

"A general without money!" Exos grumbled. "We will be sacked once more in order to pay for the soldiers and the weapons. To finance the death of those who afforded us honor."

"I do not understand why they left us without protection!" Tryos interrupted. "If our riches are so apparent, how is it that no king has put his armies at our command?"

"The Amphictyonic League no longer exists to protect us. The Greek states are weak, and they are taking a position in favor of either Sulla or Mithridates," Duos said. "But many know that, after this conflict, Rome will become the greatest empire ever seen by mankind, and nobody will dare to rebel against her."

"Duos is right. The Pythia has said it; Sulla will be victorious and will come to sack us. We must save our treasures!" Enos said, and then, in a grave tone, he added, "This discussion among ourselves matters not; we will face reality and we will act swiftly."

"On whose shoulders will this task lie?" Tesseros asked curiously.

The question remained hanging in the air for an interminable moment. As if guided by a strong attraction, all eyes turned towards the one man who had kept his lips sealed until right then. All eyes were fixed on the oldest of Apollo's priests.

"I will take the responsibility of such a dignified task on my shoulders. May wisdom enlighten us in the path we must follow!" Heptos said solemnly.

Heptos arose from the circle formed by the priests. While his companions continued heatedly debating the significance of the prophecy, he felt the need to walk alone, to dispel from his mind the ominous predictions that he had just heard. He wanted to see one more time, with his own eyes, the shrine to which he had dedicated his life, and which he knew once his mission began, he would never see again.

A long time ago, Zeus, the supreme Lord of Olympus, wanted to determine the position of the center of the world. In order to achieve this end he released two eagles simultaneously, one from the extreme east of the world and the other from the extreme west. The birds, flying at the same speed, met in Delphi, at the foot of Mount Parnassus. There, the God placed a stone, to which he gave the name *Omophalos,* the navel of the earth. With the coming of time, his son Apollo killed Python, the serpent, taking possession of his wisdom and creating there what would become the most powerful religious center of antiquity, the Oracle of Delphi.

Kings, generals, and villagers alike came from all corners of the earth to consult the oracle and ask for advice. The responses tended to be offered in such an ambiguous manner that they could give way to different interpretations. Like when Croesus, King of Lydia, who before embarking on a war against the Persians consulted the oracle and received the reply: *if you cross the river Halys (which is the border between Lydia and Persia), you will destroy a great empire.* Croesus saw a positive response in the answer, but the empire that fell was his own.

Even Alexander the Great visited Delphi in search of a favorable oracle for his campaigns of invasion. To his surprise, the Pythia refused to receive him, and asked him to return another time. Alexander became furious and dragged her out of the temple by the hair. He stopped when the woman cried, "Let me go, you are invincible!" Alexander immediately released her and said, smiling, "Now I have my answer!"

Heptos thought that the oracle had been ambiguous once again. The other priests had concluded that the chosen ones would be seven, and they had designated him as the one to be the *Priest of the Gods*, because of his greater hierarchy. But who would the others be? Would all of the chosen ones reach Delphi? It would soon be the seventh of *Bysios*, the most important day for the oracle, and perhaps Apollo would further clarify his own prophecy.

The words of the Pythia once again began to resonate in his mind. *Miserable traitor! You will appear from the circle of seven,* cited the prophecy. He would be the leader of a group that had foreseen a traitor ahead of time. Whom should he fear? Will Heptos have enough courage to expose the traitor and accomplish his task perfectly?

While these thoughts swarmed around in his mind, the priest walked along the Sacred Way, replicating the journey that many pilgrims, in devout faith, had made in centuries past. This avenue began in the extreme southeast of the *peribola,* the wall that surrounded the whole enclosure. At the same time as his weary feet staked out the steep stones of the path, his eyes fell one more time on the various *Treasures*, the small shrines bestowed by Hellenic city-states ever since ancient times, which could be found along the way.

Each of these shrines was filled with gold, silver, jewels, and the spoils of war. Treasures that provoked the greed of every new invader, treasures accumulated in a period of peace to finance times of war.

Delphi had been destroyed in the past, but like the Phoenix, it arose from its ruins. *But Sulla wants something more than gold, silver and jewels,* that he knew for sure. *Sulla was looking for the Treasure, the real Treasure. The Treasure that they had to save.* The time to act was now, just as the Pythia had foreseen; it was the moment to save the legacy for future generations.

With these thoughts in his mind, the aged priest finally arrived at the temple of Apollo. He sat down on a stone bench on the terrace that opened into the shrine, next to the magnificent golden statue of the God. His gaze settled once more on the effigy and, after careful contemplation, a doubt came to mind. *Will I be the traitor?*

At last, after having completed his long walk, Heptos arrived at the edifice where his sleeping quarters were situated. He went into his room, and said to the maidservant who took care of him, "Tell Cleantes to come here immediately." The maidservant left in haste; a short while after, a middle-aged man of slight, but sturdy build entered the quarters.

"How can I help you, my Lord?" he asked diligently.

"Cleantes, my loyal servant, the time has come," Heptos said. "I need you to carry a message with the utmost discretion. No one, absolutely no one, must know of your mission. We must alert those who need to be warned in good time, so that they are prepared. I will wait here for those who need to gather together," Heptos paused before continuing, "I trust your discretion and the loyalty that you have always afforded me."

"Lord, you know that you can trust in me," Cleantes said, with a slight bow. "I will give my life for you, because it is you to whom I owe it," and then he asked in a low voice, "Where is my destination?"

And letting out a breath, Heptos said, "Alexandria."

But, my dear friend, not all tales begin where you believe. Stories are not tapestries formed with stitches by chance, rather they are canvasses woven with pinpoint accuracy. Woven by whom? The Greeks believed that they were the Fates - three sisters, blind, deaf and dumb, who, in front of the loom, would weave the lives of wretched mortals, one thread at a time.

I, throughout all these years, believe that the universe is a loom that operates in another way. Gods or not, it is an undeniable fact that the interwoven functions with exquisite precision, and at times some isolated events are, in reality, threads of the same cloth that eventually reflect an exquisite pattern in the fabric.

When the Pythia launched her oracle, the spinning wheel was working tirelessly. Other events had taken place to give rise to her prophecy, and the same prophecy was one more thread that was woven in the loom.

CHAPTER TWO

Zoe walked cautiously along the narrow rocky paths, taking care not to slip and hurt herself on the sharp stones. It was not easy to reach Pontus Euxinus, the inland sea of dark and tranquil waters that formed the northern border of the country. Access from the interior of the continent to the coast was limited, owing to a precipitous range of mountains with narrow valleys that flowed laboriously to the waterline. The region was isolated due to these natural geographic conditions. It was precisely for this reason that her ancestors had chosen this area as their settlement.

The sun would still shine for a few more hours but the moon, its rival, had already appeared over the firmament. *Artemis, the Goddess of Hunting.* When she saw it, she remembered that within one lunar cycle the initiation ceremony would be performed, and she finally would become a true Amazon.

She had attended numerous ceremonies in her lifetime, and she knew exactly what to expect. They would amputate her right breast, which was considered a nuisance when using the bow, then, given her royal lineage, they would place the golden armor upon her, and she would be charged with sounding the Sacred Horn, thereupon leading the corps of female archers, one of the greatest honors that an Amazon could have. After, of course, being Queen. She ought to feel very proud; Hippolyta had high hopes for her. In the coming years, Zoe would be the favored candidate to become Queen.

While she was walking, a bitter feeling was taking shape in her heart. *I do not want to be an Amazon!* She did not want to dedicate her entire life to learning the bow, the axe and the art of combat; to grow old, to have to look after girls who were not her own, and train them in the same arts of war that she did not even enjoy. Furthermore, there was the thorny subject of detaching herself from her male children. Zoe had not yet been a mother, but the thought of separating from her offspring struck her as horrendous, even if the child was considered as belonging to the wrong sex.

A rebellious sensation overwhelmed her; this was not the life she wanted, she yearned for something else, but what other kind of life could the daughter of Hippolyta have?

She was so absorbed in her thoughts that it was not until she looked up that she saw the sea. It was a great blue expanse of calm waters, similar to those of a lake. Timid waves spat foam on the rocky coast. Light-footed, she went down the gentle slope that separated her from the shore, and when she reached flat ground she began to run on the sandy beach. When her feet touched water, she took off her sandals, her short leather skirt, and her *bustier;* she threw them behind her, and she immersed her naked body in the haven of peace that unfolded before her eyes.

She swam for some distance, wishing that the sea would wash away the thoughts that were pounding her mind. She took strong strokes, until she arrived at a valiant and solitary rock in the middle of the sea that defied the superficial flatness of the waters. When her arms began to ache from fatigue, she decided to return to the shore. She stretched out on the sand of that solitary beach and, as the sun dried her moist body, she fell into a deep sleep, induced by the physical exertion.

She was awoken by something warm and humid on her cheek. Her eyelids were too heavy, and so she opened her eyes slowly, but a brilliant light blinded her, and she had to close them again instantly. She kept her eyes closed for some time, while she recuperated. Carefully opening them again, she could finally see what had awoken her.

It was a splendid horse. His coat was a very shiny white that resembled silver. His mane, long and golden, glistened in the sunlight. He was the most beautiful creature she had ever seen.

Every Amazon has a love of horses that runs through her veins and is branded on her skin. She stood up and began to caress the animal's head; all the while he stood very still, rubbing himself against her. Zoe was overwhelmed by an irresistible desire. In one leap, she mounted the horse, and of his own will the creature set off for the waterline.

It started out as a gentle trot, but little by little, it became a dizzying race; the horse was galloping at great speed, his silver hooves leaving trails of foam in his wake. Zoe oozed happiness from all pores. Never, in all of her years of training, had she mounted a beast so fast and strong. Upon his back, she felt like she were flying through the air; she forgot about the troubles that burdened her soul and for a moment she became part of the foam, of the afternoon, of her surroundings. For the first time she felt the joy of living, of being young and carefree, able to do what she really wanted.

Suddenly the gallop came to an end and she found herself in the same spot where she had found the horse, or, rather, where the horse had found her. She was lying on the sand with her clothes spread out next to her.

Still confused, she got dressed. *Had it been a dream?* She looked at the waterline. There were no hoof-prints in the sand. *How strange!* She thought. *It had been such a real experience!* Puzzling over her dream, with slow steps she began to head towards Themiscyra, to the palace, where no doubt her mother awaited her.

Pilomenes was spending time in the company of his wife, Queen Valia, and his eldest daughter, Toula. As he listened to the banal conversation of the two women, paying no attention whatsoever, he nervously pondered the future of his kingdom. He had still not decided who would be his heir.

He was the sovereign of Paphlagonia, one of the first nations in the region of Anatolia. With more than one thousand years of history, it had been named in Homer's Iliad as an ally of Troy. Its lands, strategically located, were an essential path for the armies that crossed from Asia to Europe. Hundreds of years before, the Greeks and the Persians plunged into various battles over its possession. Now, the ambitious King of Pontus, Mithridates VI, intended to begin a campaign to take over the whole region.

Pilomenes had not been blessed with the privilege of having sons; quite the opposite, the Gods had given him six daughters. He knew, however, how to make the most of the situation, marrying his daughters to each one of the princes who were heirs to neighboring kingdoms. It was a very intelligent strategy that would guarantee him a balance of power in the region, it also meant that he could count on influential sons-in-law who would stand up for him, should it be necessary. It was a tactic that his ancestors had used in ancient times, and one that had supported the long-standing survival of the kingdom.

In spite of planning everything to the minutest detail, his strategy had not been quite as successful as he had hoped. The eldest of his daughters, Toula, had been repudiated by her husband. Toula was not an ugly woman, but her unbearable disposition, together with the tone of voice she used to put it into words, were enough to drive any man beside her insane with despair.

The fact that Toula's dowry had been one of the highest recorded in the region was irrelevant. Phelon was not able to bear more than seven years with such a reptile by his side. Although he had to spend the last denarius in his kingdom to pay back the dowry, and aware that his actions could bring disastrous political consequences, he sent her back to her family home under the pretext that she was incapable of conceiving an heir.

Even though he never admitted it in public, Pilomenes understood his former son-in-law perfectly well and there was no enmity between them. The King thanked him for the seven years that he had kept her out of his house, and Phelon took pity on the poor father who had to have Toula under his roof once again. Paradoxically, Pilomenes had his strongest ally in Phelon.

Pilomenes thought about the avatars of destiny; of his six daughters, the eldest, Toula, and the youngest, Rikae, were the only ones who gave him a headache. Toula was ill-raised, possessing the stupid airs of an offended princess. Rikae, his youngest daughter, was ambitious and had no scruples. *Rikae is completely different*, Pilomenes thought, shaking his head. Without any doubt at all, she was the most intelligent, manipulative, and egotistical of his daughters.

A good strategy might be to offer her hand in marriage to one of Mithridates' sons. Perhaps with this alliance, the King of Pontus might quench his thirst for Paphlagonia, considering it as already conquered. He would then direct his zeal for invasion towards other kingdoms in the region. In the negotiation of the nuptials, he would delicately put out the idea that he would name her as his successor, without, of course, putting anything in writing. As soon as they married, the conqueror would think that Paphlagonia was now part of his territory, with Rikae being the future heir. Only he would know that his daughter would never inherit the kingdom.

Pilomenes knew that in times of political turbulence, it was all a matter of waiting. An ambitious sovereign who intended to confront the Romans with violence would not survive for long. He doubted that Mithridates would die peacefully of old age, surrounded by his family in front of the fire. He, on the other hand, without participating in any warlike conflict, would be able to maintain control of his subjects until his death. *But, then, on my death, who will the heir be?* He asked the question for the millionth time.

He was so absorbed in his thoughts that he did not notice the servant coming towards him. He stopped at a distance required by protocol and, trying to call his attention, said in a formal tone, "A messenger is asking to see you, my Lord."

"A messenger? We will receive him in the pavilion in the garden," Pilomenes replied.

He took his wife's arm and they moved towards a great tent of Oriental style, in the center of the palace gardens. This pavilion was only set up in summer time, so that the King could stop for a rest from his walks during the hotter months.

Pilomenes was sitting inside the tent drinking spring water from a jeweled cup when a tall woman of athletic stature entered with a confident stride. She was dressed in silver armor to her waist, and she wore a short skirt made of bands of leather. On her shoulder, she carried her bow and an empty quiver; the guards had disarmed her before she could present herself to the King.

Resolute, and in a powerful voice, she asked, "Are you King Pilomenes?"

Pilomenes assented.

"I bring an urgent message on behalf of my Lady, Hippolyta, Queen of the Amazons."

The ceremony would take place in three days. All the young Amazons were excited in the preparations for what would be the most important day of their lives. All the young warriors were dedicated to the task of polishing their swords until they shone like mirrors, filing axes so that they could split a hair, and preparing arrows to fill every quiver to the limit. Only Zoe walked with her head down, pensively. Only her equipment lay dirty and unpolished, abandoned on the ground.

She took hold of her *pelta*, the light shield in the form of a crescent moon that was used by the Amazons. They spent so much time polishing these shields that, in open battle, the shine would blind the enemies. When she saw the reflection of her face in the shield, she made a decision. With a decisive step, she made her way to the Royal Palace where her mother, Queen Hippolyta, was presiding over the Council of Warriors.

The Royal Palace was a structure that imitated the style of the Temple of Artemis in Ephesus, one of the Seven Wonders of the ancient world, and a monument that the Amazons had helped build. Of lesser dimensions, it conserved the same proportions, and was constructed in its entirety of red marble from the region. The inner chamber was long and narrow, and at the end there was a canopy that held the statue of Artemis, *The Virgin Huntress*, the Goddess worshipped by the Amazons.

The Queen's throne was in front of the statue, with chairs for the Amazons who officiated at the council forming a semi-circle around it. Hippolyta was seated on her throne; the statue of the Goddess behind her giving the Queen an imposing air. Zoe interrupted her, "Mother, I would like to speak to you now."

Every head in the room, irritated, turned towards the inopportune girl.

"This meeting has concluded," Hippolyta said, addressing the women who were around her, at the same time throwing her daughter an angry look because of her lack of formality.

Displeased with the interruption, but without wanting to appear contrary to an order from the Queen, the women all left the enclosure. They passed by Zoe's side, sweeping out of the room arrogantly to show their feelings of disapproval. The girl took the arm of the last of the Amazons who was about to leave.

"No, Lisipe, do not leave, please," she asked, in an imploring tone. Lisipe was an excellent Amazon who had stood out because of her ability in warfare. A contemporary of Hippolyta, from a very early age she had been the strongest competition that Hippolyta had faced to become Queen. Nevertheless, when the Council of Warriors unanimously decided that Hippolyta would be sovereign, Lisipe accepted her defeat in a stoic manner, and with the passing of years, she became her adversary's best advisor.

When they were very young, Zoe and Xanthe, Lisipe's daughter, became inseparable friends. The mischievous girls would escape from their training to eat fruit from the trees, and to plan magical excursions in the neighboring forests. Both enjoyed horse riding, and although Zoe was always faster, she would slow down her mount so that they both reached the finish line at the same time, not making her friend feel bad. Xanthe, for her part, behaved the same way in combat with weapons. Although she was superior in this discipline, she never defeated Zoe; rather they would declare a draw just before the thrust that would give her the victory. Hippolyta was riled by such attitudes, since while this was going on her rivalry with Lisipe was at its peak.

Zoe was sweet, carefree and a dreamer, and Xanthe was disciplined, responsible, and loved all aspects of being an Amazon. Lisipe dedicated a great deal of time in the equal instruction of both girls, giving no preference to her daughter. She was a strict but understanding teacher, she knew how to reward or to penalize, giving neither excessive praise nor punishing her students' egos too harshly.

"Zoe, what can be so important that you interrupt a meeting of the assembly?" Hippolyta asked, still irritated.

Without giving the Queen any forewarning of what was to come, Zoe, looking directly into her mother's eyes, said, "I am pregnant."

Hippolyta was stunned. For a moment she lost her voice. Making an evident effort to remain calm, she asked, "How? Where did you meet a male? It is prohibited to have intimate relations before the initiation ceremony." Hippolyta shook her head in despair. "Besides, an Amazon can only meet a man within the boundaries of our customs. We have agreements with neighboring armies; you can only lie down with a chosen soldier..."

Zoe interrupted her, "Mother, I swear in the name of the Goddess that I have not been with any man..." The feeling of impotence made her want to cry, but she contained herself. Her mother had never pardoned a tear. She wanted her mother to believe her; she had not committed any wrongdoing against the code of the Amazons. She had not lain down with any man.

"Stop your whimpering! Do not shame me!" Hippolyta said, irritated. And then, with a worried look she continued, "This very much complicates your initiation..."

"Mother, I do not want to be an Amazon!" In spite of the deep hurt that it caused her to disappoint her mother in this way, Zoe no longer suppressed her desires.

Hippolyta collapsed in her throne. In a brief moment, her only daughter, her great pride, the one in whom she had placed all hopes for her succession, had told her that she had committed a grave wrongdoing, and furthermore, she was asking for something that would only lead to her expulsion from the community.

"I want to have this child," Zoe continued, with a challenge in her voice. "If it is a male, I will not consider giving him up!" The rebellion that been building up throughout her whole life uncorked, and for the first time Hippolyta saw her daughter defend a cause with passion and strength.

The affront was, however, too great, and she proudly raised her hand to give her a smack, but Lisipe intervened. Holding the Queen's hand in the air, she said, "Enough! Zoe, you can leave. Let me speak to your mother in private."

Zoe left the enclosure slowly, with her head held high and her spirit revived. Lisipe remained alone with a hurt and confused Hippolyta. The two women, sisters in battle, looked each other straight in the eyes.

"I don't know why you are so surprised. You knew very well that this was going to happen, but you refused to see the signs from the beginning." Lisipe walked in circles around the enclosure, trying to shake off the heaviness in the air. "Zoe never

22

showed any interest in weapons. You placed her in atrocious training which she managed to master, but she did not inherit your warrior's blood... nor your ambition," she concluded, gently.

Lisipe had known of the circumstances for several days, since Zoe had approached her in the quest for advice. From that time, she had spent the nights wondering how they could tell Hippolyta the news. Apparently Zoe had not wanted to wait until she had some plan of action, and she had sprung the news on an unsuspecting Hippolyta. Lisipe knew her very well, and she knew that she would try to change her daughter's opinion in any way possible. Ever since Zoe was born, her greatest dream was to make her the successor, and now her own daughter had made it clear that she did not want that destiny.

"And besides, times are changing rapidly; you know that our end is coming. There are more and more kingdoms hostile to us that want to take over these lands. Only the Goddess knows how much longer we can contain our enemies. Maybe if she gives birth to this creature far from here, there will be some hope for us."

Hippolyta let out a breath. Her face did not reflect her customary pride. For the first time, the Queen's expression was one of sadness and disillusion.

"What you say only matters if she gives birth to a girl," she said, bitterly. "And you already heard her; with all her soul she wants what is growing in her womb to be a male."

Hippolyta's lips were pursed; there were many things happening at the same time, her daughter pregnant, the initiation ceremony, Zoe's decision. When had all of this started? Was she the only one who did not notice Zoe's feelings? Moreover, there was the prickly subject of the baby...

"How did she become pregnant?" she asked.

"Zeus," Lisipe replied. "Just as he did with Danae when he transformed into golden rain and she gave birth to Perseus, or when he turned into a bull and seduced Europa. This time he chose the form of a horse. A white horse with a golden mane and silver hooves. A brilliant idea to conquer an Amazon."

When she heard Lisipe's cynical comment, Hippolyta let out an acrid laugh. The cunning Zeus knew how to change his form to best seduce his prey. The problem was that this time the victim was her own daughter.

Shaking her head in desperation, she began to bellow, "But my daughter? Why does my daughter deny who we are?" Hippolyta was unable to resign herself to reality.

"The Fates stitch straight tapestries with twisted threads." It was so difficult to convince someone as stubborn as the Queen of the Amazons.

The silence of the two women pervaded the room. The statue of Artemis shone white and brilliant under the sunlight that penetrated the room from the various crevices in the roof. In this statue, the Goddess was represented as a young girl, strong and athletic, preparing for an evening hunt. Hippolyta fixed her gaze on it, silently asking her for help in dealing with this dilemma. Her countenance began to change slowly as she started to conceive an idea in her head. The furrow on her forehead disappeared; she stood up, resolute, and said, "We have to call the Council. My successor must be chosen right now." Looking straight into Lisipe's eyes, she said, "It is common knowledge that Xanthe, your daughter, is the best warrior out of all of this generation that will be initiated."

Taking the hand of her former rival, she said, "Lisipe, we have grown up together, and regardless of our rivalry, you have become the best advisor that a queen could have. You are the only person in whom I entrust my most prized possession. Let us make a pact: I will make your daughter an outstanding Amazon, and a queen who will take my place when the time is propitious." A promise made. A promise to which she would dedicate her life.

"What do you want in return?" Lisipe asked, well enough acquainted with Hippolyta to know that she never gave anything without receiving something in exchange.

"I will take care of your daughter, and you take care of mine. You leave with her, and make sure that she fulfills her destiny…whatever that may be," Hippolyta said, with a hint of melancholy in her voice. The proud Queen would never cry, especially not in Lisipe's presence.

"Where are you going to send us?" she asked. She had accepted the pact. Lisipe's heart was filled with a deep sense of pride; Xanthe, her daughter, would one day become Queen.

"Where else, if not to her father?" Hippolyta replied.

Pilomenes read the message delivered by the Amazon several times. *He'd had a daughter with Hippolyta!* He could not believe it. A flock of images danced around in his mind; the memories of that night under a full moon, when he was young and just another soldier in his father's army.

From time immemorial, it was a custom in his kingdom to unite the young and strongest Amazons with the most gallant young men in the army on certain nights during a full moon. Nine months later, when the Amazons gave birth, they kept the females and they returned the males to the King. These boys received special care and they were put into fast-paced training from a very young age so that they would form part of an elite army corps.

This was a beneficial arrangement to both parties, since it guaranteed the Amazons their perpetuity, and it provided the King with future strong warriors; furthermore it lowered the levels of prostitution in the kingdom, and it kept the morale of the soldiers high.

Pilomenes met Hippolyta when she was fifteen years of age. She had arrived at the Palace of Gangra in the company of her mother, Penthesilea. He remembered her black, defiant eyes, and her red hair that resembled a fit of fury. She was taken aback by what she saw in the palace; it was clear that it was a new, unknown world that was unfolding before her eyes.

When her mother entered the audience room and she remained alone, without a chaperon, he introduced himself and invited her to take a tour around the palace. Hippolyta looked at him with suspicion while he showed her the reception rooms and other chambers. They arrived at the gardens, and after walking through them for a short while, they sat down to rest under a tall tree.

"Where does the training take place?" she asked curiously.

"The soldiers train far from here. My father ordered the

25

construction of precincts outside the palace for that purpose."

"Where do you train?" she asked, surprised.

"One of my father's generals comes to give me classes in fencing and body-to-body fighting, three days a week. A teacher for philosophy, astronomy, and mathematics comes on the other days."

"Is it the case, perhaps, that the son of the King does not practice every day?" the young Hippolyta made fun of him, condescendingly. "True, you have a light, weak build to be the heir to your father's throne."

Pilomenes' masculine pride had been stabbed to death.

"Weak? Thank the Gods that you are a damsel, and that I am bound by the sacred laws of hospitality; if not, right now, I would give you a beating that would be anything but weak." He spoke with fury.

"You defend yourself under the guise of being a host!" And then, looking at him in a mocking way, she said, "Well, show me that you are a man of combat. I challenge you to a race; this way you will not insult your noble position, and I will show you how weak you are compared with a true Amazon." Hippolyta tossed the challenge into the air.

Pilomenes accepted without giving it any thought. They agreed that they would run from the eastern part of the gardens to the entrance of the stables, a distance that Pilomenes had never covered before. They took their positions at the starting line, and Hippolyta signaled the start of the race.

They had barely set out when Hippolyta took the lead at great speed. Pilomenes was running behind her, appreciating the line of her back and the slenderness of her legs. The young girl was too fast; he knew that he could not beat her, so he made a decision that would leave his male pride in better standing. With all the momentum he could muster, he jumped on her from behind and pushed her to the ground. They rolled one on top of the other until they ended up lying down, Pilomenes on top of her, looking into each other's eyes. He could feel her anger and the softness of her body under his. She began to struggle but he tried to keep her still beneath his weight.

"You cheat, you could not beat me so you chose to knock me

down!" she said, spitting out her words.

"Have you not heard, dear damsel, that all is fair in love and war?"

"What has love to do with all of this?" Hippolyta asked angrily.

"Nothing, perhaps," Pilomenes said, realizing that the idea that had fleetingly crossed his mind would be impossible. She was an Amazon, a woman who would never subject herself to a man. But he could not deny how pleasant it felt to have the soft body of this woman beneath him.

As they talked, Hippolyta remained still, and feeling more confident, Pilomenes relaxed the pressure on her. It was strange to observe this Hippolyta, motionless and submissive. Maybe she, too, was enjoying the contact.

But he was wrong. Suddenly he felt a sharp pain in his gut. Hippolyta had taken advantage of his distraction, and she had dealt him a strong blow with her knee into his private parts. An acute pain invaded his crotch and quickly spread through his thighs. He was unable to resist when Hippolyta pushed him and rolled him aside. The young girl got up quickly. She gave him a steadfast look, her red hair disheveled from the race and the rolling around.

"It is only in *war* that all is fair."

And she walked towards the palace, leaving him on the grass, crying out in pain.

The second time he saw her was on the night of a full moon; the night agreed for the meeting between the Amazons and the soldiers from the army. The encounter between the soldiers and the young girls would take place in a copse consecrated to Artemis, located on the border between the two countries. The most striking of the Amazons would sound the Sacred Horn, and while the notes filled the air, the girls would hide themselves in the forest. When the sound of the horn came to an end, the soldiers would go in and look for the young girls among the trees, with the approval of the moonlight that lit up their path.

Given her lineage and the reputation she had earned with her feats, Hippolyta had sounded the horn, and therefore she was the last to enter the forest. Pilomenes knew he had to look for her. It was a tacit agreement that the daughter of the Queen kept herself for the son of the King.

He began to stalk the land, as though he were preparing for a hunt. He looked for the trail of footprints on the ground and he penetrated into the forest, knowing that finding Hippolyta would not be an easy task. He saw a track of steps and he followed it; the footsteps were fading out at the base of a large tree with a thick trunk. He looked up and, from the crushed leaves, he deduced that someone had been there just a short time before, no doubt spying on him from above, and laughing as he searched for her.

Nevertheless, she could not have gone very far. He knew that she had been the last to enter, and this gave her little time to be able to move far into the depths of the forest. He was also a consummate hunter. He had learned to hunt with his father and a certain instinct allowed him to smell when the prey was close by. He stayed still for a few minutes; if reason did not fail him she had to be hidden somewhere close to here. He began to look around the tree, searching for the girl's potential hiding places. Suddenly he saw it. It was just a tiny glimmer. Artemis, Pilomenes' accomplice, was helping him that night. Hippolyta had moved imperceptibly, but the mouthpiece of the Sacred Horn, carved in silver, gleamed in the moonlight.

Hippolyta immediately realized that Pilomenes had discovered her hideaway. She quickly stood up and began to run, as she had done the time before. Just like on the previous occasion, he began to follow her and, using the same trick that had been so effective, he once again leapt on her from behind and knocked her over.

This time there was no force; the two of them remained stretched out on the grass, Pilomenes on top of Hippolyta, looking intently into her eyes. How she had matured from that time! Regardless of the fact that she was an athletic woman, Hippolyta now possessed a body with more pronounced curves, curves that were once again molding themselves perfectly into his manly body.

"You will take your revenge?" she asked.

Pilomenes plunged into the dark sea of those eyes that he had not been able to get out of his mind, and there he saw fear. *Fear? Calm down, I will not hurt you.* With a sweet smile, he said, "I already told you the last time, my beautiful damsel, all is fair in *love* and war." He began to kiss her softly, while those marvelous legs, that he had dreamed of so often, embraced him.

After that night, he waited nine months for the delivery of the males. They followed the progress of each one of them with great care, but the Amazons had an absolute and unbreakable rule; there were no explanations with regard to paternity. No child carried any mark or sign that would allow recognition of who his mother was, or from which father he had been conceived. As for the girls, it was best to forget; they already formed part of the community and nothing more would be known of them.

None of the boys looked like either himself or Hippolyta. Either the young girl had not been left pregnant, or the fruit of their relationship had been a girl, in which case he would never know her. A short time later, his father arranged his betrothal to Valia, and as time passed and his daughters arrived, the memory of Hippolyta remained guarded in the depths of his mind.

Now Hippolyta had told him that they had conceived a daughter, and she had asked him to host her in his palace. Something very serious must be happening for Hippolyta to break the rigid tradition and ask him to welcome her heir in his palace, he thought, rather worried.

"Another female child," he said aloud. The Gods had denied him a male heir, but he was happy. On that night, under a full moon, he had left his seed in that untamed woman.

Valia and Toula looked at him closely when they heard him. Instinctively he knew that it would not be an easy task, but he would take the girl in and protect her. He owed it to the only woman in his life he had ever loved.

CHAPTER THREE

The moment had arrived; he and the Word would transform into one sole being.

He was completely naked, with his shaven head and his shaven face on the Sacred Stone, waiting for the arrival of the Council of Wise Men. They would begin the ceremony, a ceremony that dated back to the beginning of the world, when the Word had been proclaimed for the first time.

It was a secret ceremony, since few could know the Great Mystery that led to the Word. Only a few chosen ones... to preserve it from generation to generation, across the path of time.

And he was the one chosen to be the Bearer.

He wanted to pluck up his courage and not to cry out. He knew that blood would flow, his own blood... But as the worthy heir of his father, he would not scream, he would not move, he would not display any sign of weakness.

Once the ceremony came to an end, he would have to be stripped of his privileges, his vestments, his servants, and his chambers. A difficult decision. Others would not have withstood the sacrifice implied in being the Bearer, but he most certainly would. He swore to himself upon that Sacred Stone that he would be a dignified heir of the tradition.

He heard the chants from the Circle of Blind Ones who preceded the entry of the Wise Men.

The ceremony had begun.

CHAPTER FOUR

Queen Aruza had been riding her favorite horse across the desert, just like every other morning. She used the pretext that her morning exercise kept her robust, but, in reality, it was the only time in the day when she could be alone with her thoughts; when she could enjoy the peace that the landscape inspired. She had spent more than three hours mounted on her mare. The sun was starting to reach its zenith, and heat blanketed the air. It was time to go home.

On horseback, she swiftly took the trail back through the desert. Aruza recognized a huge mass of rose rock that towered over the silver sand, above the outline that the horizon drew on the sky. The sun shone on the gigantic pink rocks, revealing a dark fissure between them. It was the *Siq*, the tight gorge that gave way to the triumphant entry to Petra, the Rose City of the Desert.

Immense, thick, walls flanked the *Siq*; the lowest part measured three hundred feet, climbing to more than six hundred feet at their highest point. Aruza was indeed an experienced rider; few could boast going through this access at such speed, since at some points in the passage the distance between the two walls was barely seven feet in width.

The reward for the journey was the spectacle of welcome extended by the *Al Khazneh*, the first building that any traveler would see after completing the more than five hundred yard ride through the *Siq* when he entered Petra.

Carved in the beautiful rose stone that defined the city, this temple measured almost one hundred feet wide by one hundred and thirty feet high. The ample façade, sculpted directly into the stone, had six sustaining pillars whose heads were finished with acanthus leaves, like the temples dedicated to the Gods on the other side of the Mare Nostrum. The lintel was the only part that followed local style; rather than the triangular line of the classic pediments, this one split in the center to make way for a circular shrine topped with an urn.

After admiring the building's façade, she set off towards the main thoroughfare that was bordered with buildings also carved in pink stone. *Petra,* she thought, while she looked around with pride, *one of the most beautiful cities in existence, ever.* The color of its stone was indescribable. At first, it could be defined as a light pink, but the inside of the stone displayed veins ranging from blood red to toasted brown, creating an explosion of color that was a delight to the senses.

Petra was beginning to enjoy its greatest era of splendor. Its territories would soon stretch from Damascus to Gaza, and the stone city would dominate all routes for all the caravans that came laden with incense, spices, pearls, and ivory.

Suddenly, Aruza heard a soft sob that was barely perceptible. It took a few minutes to realize its source. Dushara, the God of Petra. The inhabitants of Petra did not represent their God with a glorious statue of a human figure as was done in the West, rather with a block of stone.

Stone was not by chance the very essence of Petra. Then should they not give reverence to it, in the same sacred way that it gave life to the city? It was for this reason that they could see large square blocks of spectacular rose stone in distinct points of the metropolis. The blocks were the abode of the God, and, at the same time, his altar.

Upon one of these blocks of sacred stone, Aruza saw the tiny naked body of a recently born baby. Shocked, she moved towards the little creature resting on the hard stone. *A girl.* For a woman who had given birth to seven males, seeing a recently born baby girl aroused an intimate desire, a repressed wish to coddle, caress, kiss, and breastfeed. A wish that she could never express to her sons.

She wrapped the baby up in her shawl, and taking her in her arms, she held her to her breast. She noticed the chill of her skin. *As if she is made of stone*, she thought to herself. Her white skin also resembled stone; it was an immaculate white, like alabaster. The only touch of color the child had was the black mop of hair on her head... and the eyes. The child opened her eyes and Aruza could see that they were a deep, brilliant green, like jade. With a sweet funny face, the baby smiled at her.

At that moment, Aruza decided to keep her. Surely, the

Goddess Al'Uzza, a woman like her, had sent the baby in response to a solitary prayer that she was never able to say in the presence of her husband, a husband who only wanted strong males to continue his lineage. She had to give thanks to the Goddess Al'Uzza. And to the God Dushara, of course.

"Where did you come from, little one?" She asked, in a sweet voice, as she lulled her to sleep against her chest. "How could anyone leave you, so tiny and naked, on this stone?"

And suddenly, the absurd idea that the stone had given birth to this little one, sprung to mind.

There was no doubt; Dushara, too, had sent her.

Petra had a princess.

CHAPTER FIVE

Mithridates, the sixth of his name, watched how the skin of the poor miser, whom his men had forced to drink poison, continued turning blue. His tongue was starting to swell and it seemed as though his throat was doing the same, as he was making guttural sounds, trying to breathe an air that was apparently not reaching his lungs.

He was in his personal laboratory, a room in the west wing of his palace, far from all the happenings in the court. It was a room without windows, the lintel of the heavy door, with an iron lock that brandished the entrance, constituted the only opening. No one could enter there, only he and the tight circle of his Royal Guard. He wanted absolutely nobody to know his secrets.

On top of a vast wooden table, there was an infinite number of glass and ceramic jars, with distinct herbs, animal fluids and other preparations. There was an antique still near the chimney, and a strange odor of sulfur filled the room.

The victim of the poison, a wrong-doer pulled from the prisons, was at the point of death, but the King wanted to wait until the last minute to fully understand the effect of the poison. When he realized that if he delayed one more second he would lose the opportunity to test the antidote, he raised his hand, and a soldier swiftly moved the body of the dying man to his majesty's side.

Mithridates opened his mouth with his own hands and poured the contents of a glass bottle down his throat. The prisoner started to scream as the liquid burned his throat, but color quickly returned to his cheeks. He took deep breaths as he struggled to trap the oxygen that had refused to enter his body because of the intense contractions in his throat. The struggle lasted a few seconds, but straight away the prisoner, who had fallen to the ground on his knees, was able to sit up and gently control his breathing. He leaned to one side, vomited up the entire contents of his stomach, and collapsed onto the stone floor.

"Give him some fresh water and let him sleep on a straw mattress," the sovereign said. "Don't let him have anything solid until tomorrow."

Mithridates was happy; he had tried seven different potions and each time the victim had died, but this test had been distinct. At last he possessed the universal antidote that he had wanted to acquire so badly.

He still remembered clearly the banquet when his father died of poisoning. He was only twelve years of age, and ever since that time this was one of the recurring themes of his dreams. Every night, as he went to sleep, he could see his father laughing and enjoying the festivities at the large round table, surrounded by neighboring kings and allies, raising his goblet to the dancers who were entertaining the dinner guests.

An ox that had been sacrificed for the royal banquet was slowly cooking in the great brick oven of the palace. Tireless servants served plates of wild venison, recently hunted, and trays of precious mackerel from the Black Sea. Platters of olives, peaches, and cherries flowed swiftly from table to table. Each dish was served individually, but they were all washed down with copious amounts of wine. To entertain the guests, there were magicians from Parthia, snake charmers from India, and beautiful Syrian dancers who shimmied to the sound of the music from the harps, flutes, and drums.

In the jubilation of the party, the King let out a few cries of joy and raised a goblet of wine to his lips. Instantly, his eyes opened wide, like plates, and his chest began to move like a worn-out accordion. He put his hands around his neck in a vain effort to remove the invisible thongs that were choking his throat, and suddenly he collapsed on the table.

The music stopped immediately, and, motionless, the dancers stared at Mithridates V. When his wife leaned over him, it was already too late; the sovereign had died.

Mithridates VI was sitting at a side table, observing the whole scene with the innocence of youth. In the uproar that ensued, a pair of strong hands grabbed him and pulled him out of the royal palace. The boy recognized Dorylaus, one of his father's most loyal generals. He surreptitiously took him from the dining room, and taking advantage of the confusion that had erupted, he put him on a horse and took him far away from the palace. They rode all evening and, in the dead of night, they arrived at a cabin in the middle of a forest in Amasia.

"Why?" The child asked the general. It was the first time they had spoken since they had abandoned Sinope, the capital of the kingdom.

"To protect you, Your Majesty," were the faithful soldier's words.

Mithridates did not respond. He nodded in agreement, and went into the cabin where an old shaman was cooking a stew in a large casserole. He ate what was offered and lay down to sleep on a straw mattress in the corner of the cabin. From that night, and the following nights of his young life, he would always have the same dream, the image of his father laughing while he raised a glass of wine to his lips, and then the look in his eyes when he fell on the banquet table, with the boy's mother leaning over him. The silver goblet was silently spilling the rest of the poison onto the thick carpet.

A short while afterwards, he received news that his mother had proclaimed herself Queen Regent, and had declared his younger brother, Mithridates Chrestus, as successor. No further explanations were necessary. Everything was clear in the boy's mind.

He lived distanced from the court for seven years, in the cabin in the middle of the woods. In this wild environment, he learned to brandish a sword, to fight, to kill wild boars with a spear, to break spirited steeds, and to concoct a substance capable of acting as an antidote against any poison.

The shaman who lived in those woods taught him the art of identifying and mixing the right herbs, to capture vipers and extract the poison from them to make an oil that he would use in his mixtures, and to take small doses of lethal poisons so that his body would become used to them and render him immune. Fascinated with all that he was learning, the young Mithridates dreamed of finding the universal antidote.

After those seven years that gave him courage and strength, he assembled a group of soldiers still faithful to his father's ideals, and he attacked Sinope. The first thing he did when he entered the palace was to look for his mother, Gespaepyris, and his brother Mithridates Chrestus. No one had to confirm it for him; he was certain that the hand that poured the poison into his father's goblet was that of his mother.

He ordered the Queen's and the anointed prince's imprisonment. They were sent to the deepest and darkest cell in the palace. He took personal charge of the foods that were given to them. A short time later, the Queen and the heir died of a strange illness caused by the humidity in the cell, or so the royal doctors said. Nobody would dare to contradict the cause of death of a queen who had fallen into disgrace.

Mithridates organized royal funerals for both, and ordered mourning in the city for three days. When he saw his mother's corpse on the stone slab, the image of his father, asphyxiated and falling on the table, came back to him. *Father, now you have been avenged*, he thought, with the pride of a loyal successor. He looked back at the remains of Mithridates Chrestus that rested by the side of the Queen. Killing his brother had been a matter of survival, his mother had anointed him heir; he had no other alternative than to wipe him off the face of the earth.

Soon afterwards, he married his sister Laodice, to further legitimize his rights to the throne. His heirs would have royal blood that was indisputable. He locked his other sisters up in a tower separated from the palace. He could not take any risks, they had to keep their virginity and remain in waiting. If Laodice did not give him male heirs, perhaps he would need another royal wife, and they constituted the best reserves.

Even after crowning himself King of Pontus, he continued to study poisonous substances and their antidotes; the fear of dying of poison at the hands of a coward, and not in battle like the great warrior he was, possessed him. He resumed the work of his grandfather, King Pharnaces, the first of his name, a sovereign from whom he had inherited the obsession of discovering the antidote to any poison.

He revived his personal garden, where he cultivated all the herbs necessary for his potions. He had a small zoo with different species of snakes, scorpions and poisonous toads, and he purveyed all the essences, crystals and metals that were traded in the rich city of Sinope on the border of the Black Sea.

The King also owned nefarious mines of rare minerals, which gave off vapors so toxic that only the slaves sentenced to death for committing terrible crimes worked in them.

Mithridates focused his attention on the most dangerous one, the mine known as *Sandarakurgion Dag*. This quarry most resembled hell on earth. It was made up of a series of underground passages that went inside the heart of the rocky mountain. By virtue of a lashing, the prisoners were obliged to enter on their knees. None of them lived more than six months after beginning their somber task. The skin of these poor wretches would turn green in a few days. By the end of three months, their reddened eyes would lose vision, and they had to use the sense of touch to find their way around in the caverns. The prison guard would argue with cynicism that, in any case, the sense of vision was useless in dark places not reached by sunlight. The cough that they developed from the early days was one that would eventually end their lives, since the toxic vapors would destroy their lungs.

None of these events generated compassion in Mithridates' soul, on the contrary, his curiosity and desire to discover a potent poison led him to study the composition of the mine in detail. Taking samples of its earth and, one more time, using defenseless prisoners as laboratory rats, he succeeded in isolating a substance that he named *Zamikh*, a colorless, odorless poison that caused instant death. Once he had his new poison, he dedicated himself to the task of looking for its antidote, and he had finally found it.

His devotion to the study of poisons and antidotes had become an obsession, only surpassed by his desire to destroy Rome.

Mithridates left behind him a legend of poisons and antidotes well respected by all herbalists who continued his work. Zamikh would later become known in the West by the name of Arsenic, and it caused many deaths and misfortunes.

Of his two obsessions, to destroy Rome and to distill new poisons, we can say that the first was the cause of his death and, paradoxically, the second impeded that his departure was quick and without pain.

When Pompey, one of the three greats of Rome that he confronted, corralled him in and he realized that all was lost, Mithridates tried to commit suicide, using the poison from the handle of his dagger, but all the years of ingesting its antidote had taken their effect and the King, terrified, could see that his nemesis was very close and would trap him alive. Unable to stand the idea of dying in a Roman jail, he asked one of his most loyal generals to kill him by sword.

However, we are getting too far ahead of ourselves with these events; there is still plenty of the story to be told before we reach this episode.

CHAPTER SIX

Raiko was hoisting the sails on the ship. He looked out at the ocean, where bursts of foam marked the trajectory that they had just made. One more time, thanks to the song of the mermaids, they had fooled the officials, and the cargo of contraband had passed through without inspection by the authorities. He was on his way to making himself extremely rich - richer than he would ever have imagined when he used to wander the ports, hungry and barefoot. Nevertheless, in spite of having chests filled with gold, his heart did not find peace.

Maybe it was because he spent so much time at sea. He had not stayed on firm ground for more than three consecutive days in the last seven years. He was nostalgic for his land, for his home... right now he would have given anything to know what happened to his family. Would his father still be alive? Would he still feel as ashamed of him? Would he have forgiven him? What would have happened to his brother?

Going home to find the answers to these questions was not an option. Perhaps if he consulted the oracle... The idea had been dancing around in his head for months, inciting him. Yes, definitely, he would go to the Oracle of Delphi, he would offer the corresponding sacrifices, and he would try to find out if his destiny was to stay on this ship, roaming the seas. He wanted to know if one day he would be able to face his past.

He looked at Odon, his faithful friend, and said to him, "Turn the ship to the West."

"To the West?" Odon asked, surprised. "The island of Rhodes is in the other direction."

"I want to head towards the port of Kirra. I would like to visit Delphi."

"Do you want to go to the Oracle of Delphi?" he asked, with derision. "Since when did you believe that your destiny is governed by the Gods?"

"Perhaps we'll have the chance to do some business in those lands. It is in times of war that we earn more money. Maybe we can get them to pay a high price for what we have in the hold,"

Raiko lied, turning away.

Odon looked at him directly and did not let himself be deceived. He realized that for the first time in seven years, Raiko wanted to reconcile what had happened.

"As you like. Your wish is my command," he said, sarcastically, making an exaggerated and sardonic bow.

The ship changed direction, while Raiko, from the railing on the deck, looked out over the vast blue ocean. From the water, the mermaids greeted him with a flirtatious splash. Instinctively, he put his hands on the necklace of shells hanging around his neck. The gift from the Goddess.

I don't know where my trade would be without you, he thought, and offering them his finest smile, he waved his hand in the sign of a greeting. Seeing that the ship changed direction and was heading towards the port of Kirra, the mermaids bade farewell with a cry that signified *until we meet again,* and they distanced themselves into the ocean.

CHAPTER SEVEN

The oracle was celebrated on the seventh day of each month, from spring through autumn, to commemorate the birth of Apollo. On a day such as today, the seventh of *Bysios*, the God had come into the world with the help of his twin sister, the Goddess Artemis, who was born one day before him, and who had helped her poor mother Leto with the task of the birth of her brother. The jealous Hera, in the knowledge that Leto's swollen belly was the fruit of her infidelity with Zeus, had prohibited her from giving birth on solid ground. Then, the island Delos emerged from the sea, a shield of water covered it like a transparent cloak, and the wretched Leto was finally able to give birth, to not one, but two children.

As it was a day of great consequence for the followers of the cult, the priests were waiting for a visit from pilgrims en masse. They were stationed on the terrace of the greater temple, since, from there, they had a privileged view over the whole sanctuary. It was an excellent spot to watch people arriving without being seen.

The number of people circling inside the walled enclosure was greater than usual; they were able to recognize the people of Sparta, Thebes, and Phrygia by their dress... only the Athenians were notable by their absence.

"It seems as though today we will receive people of pedigree, as we are accustomed to do," said Enos, as he pointed to a royal committee that had just arrived.

"They have the emblem of Petra," said Duos as he recognized the emblem of the Rose City of the Desert.

"But it is not the King," Exos replied, who, on hearing their voices, joined in the conversation. "It must be someone else from the royal family."

A strong man with long black hair pulled back in a braid, and with a long, equally black beard, got down from a horse that was pulling a carriage. From his muscular build, it could be perceived that he was a robust man, and no stranger to the elements. A beautiful woman stepped down from the carriage; she was tall, with long, black, curly hair and large green eyes. Her most striking feature, however, was the color of her skin. Impeccably white, flawless. She possessed majesty and serenity beyond equal. She walked slowly and silently, as though her feet did not touch the ground.

"Might these visitors have anything to do with the prophecy?" Enos asked curiously, pointing at the entrance.

The priests followed with their eyes to where their colleague was pointing his finger. A man and a woman arrived accompanied by one single servant; they had neither standards nor shields, but by the quality of the horses and their attire, it was easy to deduce their noble pedigree.

On looking at the man, anyone could have believed that the God Apollo himself had come down from Olympus to visit his temple. He was young, blond like molten gold, with clear, bright eyes like rays of sun, and he had perfect physical form. He was wearing a short tunic gathered together on only one shoulder, leaving his chest partially uncovered. His body, sculpted by long hours devoted to physical activity, gave him the same proportionate and perfect appearance as the statues of the God.

The girl was beautiful, slender, and well proportioned. She had hair that was the color of recently polished copper, and gray-green eyes. She did not wear a tunic like other women, but instead, a short *quiton* in the style of the Amazons that exposed a pair of well-toned legs. The two dismounted, and leaving the servant in charge of the horses, they approached the group of stalls that had been set up in the southeast corner of the enclosure.

"It could be that they are the chosen ones." Pentos, who was listening to the other priests, answered the question that had been left in the air. "But remember that we have left the mission in Heptos' hands, and he alone is in charge of carrying it through."

"Are you all certain that Heptos is the right person to fulfill the task of saving the Treasure?" a voice asked.

The voice came from a priest who had stayed inside the temple listening to his companions' conversation. He took a few steps forward and the sunlight revealed his face. It was Tesseros.

He was the youngest of the priests, and the one who had most recently joined the cult. From the beginning of his residency, he had not developed bonds of trust with any of his companions, and he considered this the opportune moment to sound out the loyalties of those present.

"Of course!" Pentos answered immediately. "He is the priest of the greatest hierarchy in the oracle. He is the one who knows the whereabouts of the sanctuary's riches."

What was known as the Treasure of Delphi was not only a group of statues and architectural pieces that decorated the enclosure, it also included the collection of objects of value, works made from precious metals, jewelry, and gold and silver coins that the different Greek city-states had donated to the oracle in the past. Some important Greeks had also used the treasury as a safe to guard their personal fortunes under shrines that carried their family name.

After the holy wars and the invasions of Phillip of Macedonia, Delphi realized that it was not immune to plundering. For this reason, the priests had created hiding places throughout the enclosure and in the adjacent areas, to conceal the pieces of value that could be stolen by future invaders. The guardian of this secret was normally the priest with the greatest hierarchy, or seniority in the position.

The coins, jewelry, and goods easiest to transport were inside makeshift wooden chests in simple carts pulled by mules; they had placed dry straw on top of them so that they would not attract attention. When the seven chosen ones of the prophecy met, they would be responsible for putting this fortune in a well-sheltered place.

Heptos would lead the group of seven to save the Treasure of Delphi. The priests were sure that the oracle would be reborn once more, after the war between Rome and Pontus ended. That was the significant fact that they had interpreted from the prophecy that the Pythia had told them a few days earlier. Sulla, the Red Commander, would plunder them, or at least he would pillage whatever they allowed to be taken. However, they were not afraid. The same had happened in the past, wars came about, and the victors took what they could get on the way. It was only a matter of waiting, and going back to rebuild everything again, but this time they would have sufficient funds.

Tesseros looked suspiciously at the others. He, in particular, never totally trusted Heptos. The old priest was not a greedy man, nor did he display an insatiable thirst for power. On the contrary, he always had a humble and servile attitude, however Tesseros was afraid that Heptos would use the gold for another purpose, even though he himself did not know how to determine what this was. He greatly distrusted him, and even more so that servant of his, Cleantes, who was as agile as a cat.

Tesseros did not feel safe blindly leaving his future in the hands of Heptos. At that moment, he decided he would take the necessary measures to ensure that the oldest priest complied absolutely with the task that they had so nobly offered to him.

CHAPTER EIGHT

Cleantes was at the rail of the ship enjoying the sea air, when he spotted a remarkable white marble building that came into sight on the horizon.

"Impressive, isn't it?" He heard a voice beside him saying. The voice came from one of the passengers who had boarded with him at the port of Kirra.

"Ptolemy I assembled a large number of wise men to build this lighthouse. They call it Pharos, the same name as the island where they built it," he said, pointing to the small mound of land that rose from the sea and formed a tiny island facing the coast. "It is not in vain that it is considered one of the Seven Wonders of the World that we know. The King used all human knowledge available to him to arrive at a mechanism that would constantly maintain the fire seen at the top of the tower," he said, pointing to the magnificent monument that measured more than four hundred and fifty feet high. "The light it emits by night warns the ships that sail this sea of those reefs of limestone bordering the coast, especially that one. Do you see it?" he said, pointing to the northern part of the coast. "They call it the Golden Horn, and it has caused the sinking of many vessels."

Cleantes stared at him, in silence. The passenger continued speaking with the familiarity of an old friend.

"Of course, what Ptolemy did not tell anyone is that, given its height, the lighthouse was also designed to spot the enemy. It is very difficult to reach Alexandria without anyone knowing," and saying this, he turned his gaze away from the small island and looked straight into Cleantes' eyes. Cleantes noticed for the first time that the stranger had one brown eye and the other blue.

"They would have to be Zeus, all powerful Lord of Lightning to know everything that happens under the light of the sun," Cleantes kept looking at him, calmly.

"Not only the Gods govern our destinies. If I were you, I would spend more time worrying about humans," and as he spoke, the stranger walked away.

Cleantes reflected on the veiled threat in the words of the

unknown man, as he watched the approach to the coastline. The island where the Pharos was found was joined to the continent by the *heptastadion*, a man-made causeway that measured the length of seven stadiums and that divided the port in two. This causeway had two immense arcs in the lower part that allowed ships to pass from one end to another.

The eastern port was adjacent to the royal palaces, thus it was known as the Royal Port, since ships belonging to high dignitaries of the city docked there. The ship that Cleantes was traveling on, however, would be tied up at the western port that was reserved for merchants and regular travelers.

Once on the ground, he collected his bag containing his few belongings, and began to stroll distractedly around the streets of the city. Walking lazily, he arrived at the market in the grand square.

His eyes wandered over the different stalls. The merchants displayed the best products that came from all along the coast of the Mare Nostrum and beyond: dates from the Nile valley, olive oil and goat's cheese from Greek lands, wines from the island of Sardinia, and the most precious spices - cinnamon, cloves, and nutmeg - from India.

Cleantes stopped in front of a fruit stall, and as he was handling a date, the hair stood up on the back of his neck; the one who was following him had come too close to his back.

He had suspected this since he disembarked, and that was why he had begun his visit with a brief stroll to explore the city. Agile as a cat, he threw the box of fruit to the ground. It fell with a loud din at the feet of the man who had stopped behind him. He ran away, while the stall owner and his sons seized the individual who had not been astute enough to predict Cleantes' move.

He ran and ran, between stalls and alleys, trying to remember his last time in the city. If he were not mistaken, turning at the next street on the right, there would be a fountain where the carriage bearers stopped to drink water during their journeys. He kept on running, ignoring the cries he could still hear behind him. He crossed to the right and, just as he remembered, and to his pleasant surprise, before his eyes he found a group of servants chatting beside the fountain.

He stumbled into a tall, strong, black man. Their eyes met, and without saying a word, the well-built man lifted the cloth of a palanquin and made signs for him to get inside. He immediately lowered the net curtains and continued the conversation he was having with his friends.

A man appeared, running. When he saw the group gathered at the fountain, he stopped and trying to recover his breath, he asked, "Have you seen a thin man with chestnut hair pass this way? Wearing an old white toga?" he asked the litter drivers.

They all looked at each other in surprise.

"No, nobody has passed by here," one of them replied.

"Are you sure?" They all agreed, indifferent.

The man cast his eye over the scene. Fixing his attention on the carriage with the drawn curtains, he asked, "And, that litter? It seems wide enough to fit a man comfortably. It is the only one that I cannot see inside," he said, with mistrust. "I am going to take a look."

The tall, strong, black man stopped him dead.

"Do you know who owns this palanquin, by any chance?" he asked.

"No, who?" he asked, suspiciously.

"This carriage is the property of my Ladyship, Berenice," he said, gloating over the name. "I do not believe that you want someone from the royal family to learn of the lack of respect that you are about to show."

The Pharoah's niece? He rapidly considered the risks that his action might incur, and unwillingly, he replied, "Well, you know, if you see the man that I am talking about, apprehend him, he is a truant who has stolen from the market. We cannot leave these rats on the loose." He turned around and left.

The carriage drivers, accomplices in the cover up, calmly continued talking until the unknown man disappeared down one of the streets. When they felt that danger had passed, the black man pulled back the curtain of the litter, and with a big smile that showed his white teeth, he said, "Cleantes, old friend, so what trouble have you got yourself into now?"

"Thank you Abu, the Gods put you in my path one more time," he said, with a sigh of relief. "I don't have much time and

I need another favor from you."

"Another? Dear friend, I cannot protect you from all the thugs in the city," he said with a smile.

"This favor is easier. I need you to take me to a place in Alexandria as discreetly as possible."

"Where do you want to go? Is it something to do with a woman?" He asked, with a wink.

"No, not that at all," Cleantes said, in a serious tone. "I need you to take me to the site that history will record as the glory of this city. I want you to take me to the Library of Alexandria."

CHAPTER NINE

Queen Aruza was watching Roxana playing with the potters. The girl, who was already three years old, had turned into a beauty. Her skin was even whiter and more perfect than when she was found and the hair that now touched her shoulders was an intense black that contrasted with her skin. Her green eyes would shine when she was happy, and they kept a fixed and direct gaze on the things she was observing. At first, the Queen came to believe that the girl was dumb, since she did not offer a single sound apart from a gentle whimpering to ask for food, but when she reached three years of age she began to speak fluently, leaving everyone confused.

Roxana was a sweet and tranquil creature. In spite of the Queen's effusive demonstrations of affection towards her, the girl would smile sweetly but rarely return the kisses and hugs she received.

Aruza always took Roxana with her wherever she went. When she would visit the city's residents, the girl accompanied her, always smiling; however, she always put a barrier between herself and the other children. She did not run around or play with them.

During one of these visits to the market, Aruza took Roxana to the workshops of the city's artisans. Petra was famous for pottery work of an exquisite quality, the pieces were so finely produced that the thickness of their walls was barely more than the hair of a camel.

An artisan was seated on the floor on a mat of reeds while his hands worked on a piece of alabaster. From his skilled hands, an amphora began to emerge from the stone, and slowly, as though he was caressing the material, the sculpture discovered a harmonious form. The man's work immediately roused the girl's attention. Roxana looked at it, engrossed, and the man smiled, happy to see the attention he was receiving.

Every afternoon, with a silent gesture, the little girl would ask Aruza to take her to the artisans and she would sit and watch them for hours. They received her with smiles, feeling proud to have such an important visitor.

On one of these afternoons, while she was watching them, an old potter gave her a piece of rose-colored stone, "So that Your Majesty can play," he said. The child looked at the piece, a little afraid, and slowly, as though she was trying to touch fire, her little hand moved closer to the stone. She took it between her fingers and slowly, very slowly, she began to stroke it.

Something is beating inside it, Roxana thought, and she began to feel a warm force emanate from her hands as they came into contact with the material. *I want to transform it, to free the creature inside,* she thought.

She had seen other children play with a likeable, mischievous kitten in the street, and she wanted to have her own cat, but she did not dare to ask for one. With the piece of stone that the potter had given her, she took a tool from the ground and began to work it, just as she had seen so many times.

Little by little, relieving her body of any tension, allowing her fingers to pull the excess material away from the stone, and with her mind fixed on the vision of the animal that she wanted to create, Roxana sculpted incessantly.

With scratches here and there, submerged in a place with neither time nor space, the stone began to take form. First of all, there were the paws, all of the same length, then the curved back, and the little belly hanging down. The neck stretched out as though it was sniffing the air. The tail, she remembered it, tall and alert. Then came the turn of the face. She visualized it perfectly, she saw her little cat smiling at her with its little pink tongue sticking out. And as she modeled the little figure of the animal, she enjoyed her pet as though she were very close to him.

Her hands took from the stone an image of a cat amazingly close to reality. She did not skimp on detail, she could picture the animal clearly in her mind, and her hands succeeded in making an exact replica. When she finished, she supported him on the ground, and she gave him a name. "Cat will be your name," she said in a loud voice. And slowly, very slowly, just as kittens start to move when they are born, the little animal made himself look slender, he yawned, and he approached her with awkward steps. However, after a few strides, he slipped, fell to the ground, and shattered into pieces.

Queen Aruza looked away from what she was doing, curious to know what was causing the little one so much amusement. Initially, she thought her eyes were playing tricks on her, as it seemed she was looking at a cat made of stone that moved on the orders of the little sculptor. But straight away, the image she thought she had seen became sea of little pieces of stone spilled on the ground.

Aruza jumped up. Only she knew where she found Roxana. It seemed to make sense that, being who she was, daughter of the God of stone, she held in her hands the power to give life to the same.

CHAPTER TEN

Pilomenes was nervously walking around the room in circles, waiting for news from the midwife. Zoe had started labor pains hours ago. Curious to know the outcome, Queen Valia and her daughter Toula were by his side, sitting quietly, waiting.

He still remembered the day that she arrived at his palace. An imposing committee of Amazons in silver armor, mounted on exquisite steeds, and carrying shields in the shape of a crescent moon, preceded the carriage in which Zoe and Lisipe were traveling. Pilomenes was anxious to meet her, to see her face for the first time. When the carriage came to a halt and the door opened, his breath stopped. A girl with brown hair and light green eyes, just like his own, stepped out.

The same eyes. Glaucous, like those of the Goddess Athena, according to the songs of the poets. They were very unusual eyes, of a gray-blue shade, with pupils encircled by a golden-colored stain that made them look green when observed from afar. There was no doubt whatsoever - he had fathered this girl, and she was his legitimate child. On seeing her, he forgot the tirade from his wife, who had blurted out that she could not possibly be his child, and that he would never really know if he had conceived her. With these, his own eyes, he was absolutely certain.

Zoe began to walk towards him with a faint smile on her lips, and that was when Pilomenes noticed her swollen belly. She was pregnant! Maybe this was the obscure reason why Hippolyta had sent her to be under his watch. Whatever the reason, he would care for her even more. This girl was his legitimate heir, and soon she would give him a grandson.

Pilomenes was not the only one worried at this moment. Lisipe, who never left Zoe's side, was now watching the girl in labor. She feared for her, she was very thin, and this stomach was larger than normal.

It had not been easy to live in this palace for these last few months, where all the females were so different from the women where they came from. Back there, in her country, the women supported each other, they helped one another, in some cases treating each other like blood sisters. Here, everyone was plotting among themselves, they criticized, ridiculed and scorned each other. In Themiscyra, the Amazons respected those who had achieved recognizable feats; here everything was an absurd competition to get the men's attention, which they depended on for everything. The life of the kingdom was in the hands of men and the women had no voice.

The worst part is to have to live with Toula, Lisipe thought. A few days after they arrived, the King's daughter had entered the small room allotted for the personal needs of Lisipe and Zoe. They used that room to prepare for the arrival of the baby. Without any introductions and without asking permission, Toula sat down in one of the chairs, uninvited, and began to speak in a pejorative tone.

"Where is your Ladyship?" she asked, haughtily.

Lisipe was working on what appeared to be a small bed of wood. Without looking up from what she was doing, she answered, "Zoe is weary; the baby will arrive soon and she tires easily." Calmly, she added, "She is not my Ladyship, she is the daughter of my Queen, and the one whom I swore to protect as though she were my own." There was a chilly threat in her voice.

Toula was looking angrily at the crib that Lisipe was making.

"Zoe is a whore, she doesn't even know the father of the child she carries in her belly." She started to speak with poison in her voice. "You Amazons and your barbaric customs. I, on the contrary, am a decent woman of good breeding and I arrived at my wedding bed a virgin, and immaculate. Men want to marry a virgin, not someone who has slept around and become pregnant by whoever, and who then lies grandiloquently, saying that it was the result of an encounter with a God."

On arrival, Lisipe had a private conversation with Pilomenes in which she explained that Zoe had been left pregnant after an encounter with Zeus. This situation, it seemed, answered an ancient legend that claimed that, in order to save the Amazon race, one of them would conceive a daughter from the God, and she would give birth outside the community. When Zoe told the story of her encounter with the mythical horse, Hippolyta and the Council of Warriors reached the conclusion that Zoe was the girl in the legend and they sent her to Pilomenes' home so that the baby would born under his protection. Pilomenes, in the interest of explaining Zoe's pregnancy in the most fitting way possible, repeated the story to all the members of his palace.

Lisipe looked up from the crib that she was working on, and in a calm, firm voice, she replied, "In the *civilization* that I come from, we worship, and devote ourselves, to the Goddess. For us, God is a woman. Women help each other mutually and we are strong and independent of men, whom we only turn to in order to reproduce. We provide our own food, shelter, and security. We exalt the role of woman in creation, since it is she who creates life inside her own being. To us, it quite simply does not matter who the father is. Our line of succession is by means of the female, therefore we give birth in front of the community, and the entire community is witness to our delivery. No one may question the legitimacy of our daughters, blood of our blood, heirs to our possessions."

Looking directly into her eyes, she continued, "The truly important attribute in a woman is fertility, as without that there is no life, and without life there is absolutely nothing. Your entire tangle of virginity and fidelity in marriage, which is only applied unjustly to the female, is because of the male's suspicion of not knowing if the son that his wife gives birth to, heir of all his possessions and his titles, is really his. You lock yourself up and commit to leading a life of privations under a false moral, to placate the fear of men never being sure that their sons are really their sons."

The speech was too audacious for Toula's foolish mind; stupidly clinging on to one single argument, she repeated, "This is what happens in your land of barbarians. In the rest of the civilized world, virginity is the most valuable attribute in a woman."

"And if that is the most important attribute, why did your husband reject you?" she asked, sarcastically. "It was not enough for him that you were a virgin. Did he not reject you, perhaps, because you were not able to give him an heir?"

Throwing the chair to the ground with a loud crash, Toula retreated, irate, thereby ending the conversation.

Lisipe knew she would have an enemy forever.

"Here he comes, here he comes!" The midwife screamed.

They hurriedly went into the room where Zoe, lying on a bed with her knees bent, was pushing with force. The midwife was leaning over her with her arms extended, waiting for the new life that was struggling to come out. The girl's head was drenched in sweat and she was breathing heavily, meanwhile Lisipe helped to hold her up. Faithful to her rigid education, Zoe neither complained nor cried out, in spite of the fact that the midwife urged her to do so.

Zoe took a mouthful of air and concentrated all her strength on the necessary push that would help the little one be born. Helped by the cries of the midwife, a little head came into the view of the world for the first time. The midwife pulled the shoulders with her experienced hands and in an instant, the whole little body was outside. The woman tied the umbilical cord with a flaxen thread, cut it with iron scissors, and disinfected the wound with a mixture of herbs and wine.

At once, Lisipe held out her arms to receive the little creature who was covered in blood and sebum. Almost instantly, Pilomenes, Valia, and Toula approached with curiosity to contemplate the newborn.

"It's a girl!" Lisipe cried, happily.

The Queen and her daughter smiled with delight when they saw the disappointment on Pilomenes' face. The King could not disguise his dismay; since Zoe had arrived, he had closely followed the pregnancy, hoping that this would be the much longed for heir, the solution to his problems. However, it seemed that the possibility of a male heir of his breeding was not in his destiny.

Lisipe wrapped the baby in a white linen cape and carried her to a nearby table where there was water, perfumed oil and all the necessities to wash the little one. Now that the labor was over, the midwife would be able to take care of Zoe. Lisipe wanted to assure herself that this very special child had a deserved welcome into the world.

"But, what is this?" they heard the midwife cry in surprise. "In the name of the Gods! Just like the persecuted Leto. Here comes another baby!"

Once again, all heads turned in surprise towards the midwife who, showing off her experience in the role, was expertly receiving a little body for the second time.

"Congratulations, Your Majesty!" she said, speaking directly to the King. "It's a boy!" And she placed the second baby, covered in blood and sebum, in Pilomenes' arms.

In a flash, Pilomenes' spirit and expression changed. Not really knowing what to do with the parcel that the midwife had given him, he went out to the balcony with the baby in his arms, and lifting him up high, he showed him to the heavens, the Gods, the people, and anyone who wanted to see him. Finally, the heir he had hoped for so much had been born. At the end of the day, just as Valia and Toula had feared, Zoe was Pilomenes' primogenital daughter, and with no father to lay claim to the boy, by reason of the unique customs of the Amazons, he was able to declare this boy as his heir. He was a prince of noble blood, grandson of a king and a sovereign queen.

With the baby girl in her arms, Lisipe thought of the designs of destiny. Zoe, sweet Zoe, had pleased her mother and her father at the same time. She had given birth to a girl who would continue the lineage of the Amazons, and a boy, heir of the kingdom of Pilomenes.

At times, I wonder if Zeus had planned all of this from the outset

.

CHAPTER ELEVEN

After a long journey by land, Adhara and Dromeas had finally arrived at the Oracle of Delphi. After dismounting, and without noticing that there were priests watching them from a distant terrace, Dromeas had delivered the reins to his servant, telling him, "Wait here and look after the horses. My sister and I have some business to resolve," and they both began walking towards the market that had been set up at the gate of the enclosure.

"Dromeas, I think we ought to buy the goat for the sacrifice to the God," Adhara said. Dromeas agreed, and accompanied her to the spot where there was a small corral displaying goats of various sizes. They tried to attract the attention of the seller, but he was not able to cope, as there were many people waiting to be served. Dromeas, impatient to get to know the site, said, "Adhara, wait here until they attend to you and you can buy a goat. I am going for a stroll. I will not be long," and saying this, he left, without giving his sister time to answer.

Since he arrived, he had felt the burning desire to see the *Stadium* of Delphi with his own eyes.

He began his quest, climbing the Sacred Way. He asked a pilgrim for its whereabouts; the response was that the stadium was even further up the hill, right within the limits of the oracle.

Dromeas hurried so that he would not leave Adhara alone for too long. Following the directions he had received, he reached the end of the Sacred Way, went around the Temple of Apollo, and arrived at the Theater. From there, he could make out the framework that comprised the structure.

The stadium at the Oracle of Delphi had originally been built four hundred years before, following the standard parameters for ancient stadiums. It was made up of an oval track, five hundred and eighty feet long, and surrounded by stone steps that served as seats for the spectators.

Dromeas went down to the track, suffering the effects of a febrile longing to run. He took off his sandals and he pulled his blond hair back in a braid behind his head. He took a lungful of air and did a few small jumps to relax his leg muscles, while he pumped his arms parallel to his torso. He placed his feet on the lines carved on the marble stone that marked the starting line, just as thousands of other athletes had done in the past, and giving himself the signal to go, he tried to imagine how the trumpets of the *agonothetais* would sound.

When he began to run, he reached a pace that he had never achieved before. His feet barely touched the sand, and the force of the wind distorted his face muscles, giving him a strange expression. He ran one, two, three, four, five laps consecutively, breaking his personal record in distance and speed. At that moment, with the wind in his face, feeling that his feet were barely touching the ground, and with his heart racing inside his chest, he felt closer than ever to the Gods.

Breathless, he began to slow his pace, and his tired legs folded, causing him to fall on his knees to the ground. Kneeling in the sand, he looked around the stands. He tried to imagine how it would feel to be here, with the stadium full, listening to six thousand, five hundred people calling his name, congratulating him, carrying the glory to his grandfather's country, and becoming a hero for his own people and for the whole world.

Glory - that was what he pursued. It was to that, that he wanted to dedicate his life to. Very soon he would fulfill the minimum age requirement to be able to compete. On the very day of his birthday, he would enter, and he would start rigorous training in the city of Elis. He was sure that he would be successful, he would win the crown of laurels in the city of Delphi, and he would also win the most prestigious of prizes, the crown of olives of Olympia.

But first, he had to resolve the matters that had brought him here. He had to find answers to the questions that tormented him so badly.

Raiko had finally stepped onto firm ground. Once the ship had docked, he had left a small part of the crew on board with the mundane tasks of doing repairs and routine maintenance. For the others, they had two days off, with the recommendation that they did not spend their entire earnings in such a short time.

Everything was in disarray because of the conflict with Mithridates. With the war in the port of Piraeus, the port of Kirra was overrun with people and ships. He rented the best horse he could find at the inn where Odon and his men would await his return.

While he was on horseback, he could enjoy the spectacular view that the Corinthian Gulf offered when seen from on high. The blue waters shone in the reflection of the brilliant sun. It was the first time he had been alone in many years, and for a strange reason he felt that they were looking at him. A pair of eyes was following the insecure steps of his horse. He pushed those thoughts from his head and concentrated on making his horse move forward more quickly. However, the journey was not as short as he had hoped, in some parts the path turned into a narrow mountain goat trail, making it difficult to pass on horseback. *Perhaps it would have been better to rent a donkey rather than this costly steed,* he thought, with his usual cynicism.

When he arrived at the oracle, the first thing he saw were the merchants' tents that they had put up at the entrance.

The improvised market was abuzz with people selling goats that the pilgrims would have to offer as a sacrifice to the God. There were also stalls of food and wine, and the smaller stalls of artisans that displayed statues of Gods made of clay, or sculptures of stone and, of course, there were the tricksters. Those snake charmers never missed the opportunity to extract some easy money from innocent strangers.

He was weighing up which goat to buy when he heard a voice giving off at the place to his side.

"Today, the day we celebrate the birth of our great God Apollo, we will carry out an unsurpassed act of magic," pointing at a box of wood shavings resting on the table in his improvised booth, he continued, "I have a quantity of wood shavings in this box, chosen by chance. From them, by divine intervention, the number seven will appear, the number consecrated to Apollo."

Pointing at a burly peasant who was watching, awestruck, he said, "Please choose a quantity of wood shavings that is less than the number of fingers on both of your hands."

The villager separated five shavings with his pudgy hands.

"Very good." The charmer, who by that time had attracted the attention of a large crowd around him, replied. "Help me to count the rest." Counting aloud, the audience confirmed that there were fifteen wood splinters in the box.

"Fifteen. If we add the two digits from the number fifteen, we will get six, as one plus five is equal to six," pointing again at the villager, who was red with embarrassment for being the object of so many stares, he asked him, "Now remove the number calculated."

The villager did what was asked of him and took out six shavings, which he placed together with the first five ones.

"As we all know by now, our great God Apollo did not arrive in the world alone. His sister Artemis accompanied him at birth; it is for this reason, my noble citizen, that I ask you to take out two more shavings, one in honor of Apollo, and the other in honor of his twin sister." The villager did as he was told.

"Now, my dear audience, you will witness the miracle accomplished. This noble villager chose, by himself, the initial number of shavings he would take out, the judgment of none of us interfered in his choice. But without mattering which number he or any other person chose, our great God would continue working his magic." Pointing to the box with the rest of the shavings, he said, "help me count the pieces of wood left here." Before an astonished crowd that counted in unison, one-two-three-four-five-six-SEVEN, seven shavings appeared in the box.

"It doesn't matter how many you choose, the God Apollo will always revere the number seven as his own, and this will always be the number of shavings that appears in the box. Would any one of you like to challenge the divine mathematics?"

The people started to applaud, some nervous, and others totally spellbound in the face of this act of God. Meanwhile, his colleague passed around a canvas sack to accept any coin or offering, which, according to him, would be presented to Apollo so that marvelous things like this would keep happening.

Raiko, amused, was watching the man who was collecting the alms; it was clear beyond doubt that these offerings would not reach the feet of the God, but rather go into the pockets of two much less divine beings. The crowd began to disperse, but Raiko noticed that a girl stood still in her place. She was staring at the box, so engrossed that deep furrows marked her forehead.

"This trick would only work if you start with twenty splinters of wood in the box, and not with a number by chance as you claimed," the young girl said in a firm voice. Raiko could not take his eyes off her. She was a young, slim damsel with long copper hair. She was wearing a short toga, and sandals that tied at her calves. Some very well formed calves, in Raiko's judgment.

"What are you saying, beautiful lady?" The merchant asked, warily.

"This trick is only possible if, and only if, the initial number of splinters is twenty. As you establish the initial number to be taken out to be between one and nine, the rest has to be between eleven and nineteen. If you take the sum of the two digits of this quantity, and subtract it one more time from the quantity in the box, you will *always* be left with nine pieces of wood. Then you apply the banal argument of deducting two, because Apollo has a twin sister, and you are left with seven splinters in the box.

"But this is not due to the designs of the God, it is because of the particular quality of the number nine in the decimal system, restricted in that the initial number is twenty, and that you only take out a number of shavings between one and nine," the girl explained.

Why should such a beautiful young woman be so well versed in mathematical problems? The stall owner wondered. *Why was she not at the neighboring stall, trying on necklaces and bracelets from Caria that ought to sit so well on that haughty neck? Or was it perhaps that there was no man around to keep her busy with other things and put her in the place where she belonged?*

"Perhaps you deny the powers of Apollo, right here, in this place consecrated to him?" He asked, wagering on the religious card of the people present.

The villagers, simple people, were not following the mathematical reasoning, and even less did they want to be involved in any form of blasphemy, which helped the swindler.

While the conversation was heating up, Raiko had reached her and he could appreciate that her face was made up of beautiful features and some impressive gray eyes.

"I am telling you that what you assert as magic is nothing more than a distinctive feature in the numbers. This is nothing to do with the God's plans." The young girl didn't change her tone. "They come here to pray and to listen to the oracle, not to be taken for fools."

In a split second, the partner positioned himself behind the girl. With his lips almost pinned to her left ear, he whispered, "It would be better if you kept quiet and didn't continue explaining our tricks to all of these people."

The woman felt his disgusting breath on the nape of her neck and suddenly she realized how alone she was. Out of the corner of her eye, she noticed that the man was putting his hand on his belt and she felt something sharp against her waist.

Suddenly, she heard another voice coming from behind the man who was threatening her.

"I understood that nobody enters the Oracle of Delphi with weapons."

The girl no longer felt the pressure on her back, and she turned around so she was directly facing the partner from the stall. Behind him, there was a tall man with brown hair and eyes, who was restraining the partner's hand behind his back with force, immobilizing him.

"Weapons? Nobody is talking about weapons. I just wanted this lady not to speak so loudly... Dear Lord, you know that everyone has their way to make a living, and she is ruining ours." He replied in a conciliatory voice.

"I am delighted that it was all a misunderstanding. I beg you to let her go and we will call it a day, you can gather up your honorable means of survival and leave." And saying this, he let the man go with a push so strong that it sent him to the ground.

Raiko held out a hand to the girl and they moved away from that spot, as the two rogues gathered up their belongings to leave.

"A woman alone and unarmed should not be calling men of the street thieves," Raiko commented.

The girl frowned.

"Your intervention was not necessary. I am not a weak maiden who needs to be defended. I could have taken care of it alone," she answered, proudly.

As they were talking, they had arrived at the area where goats were being sold.

"Adhara!" A voice shouted. The girl looked around, and a young blond man approached her.

"I have been looking for you everywhere, what did you get into? I shouldn't have let you accompany me, I should have left you at home," he said, angrily.

"Dromeas, nothing happened. I stayed at the market, walking around," Adhara tried to explain.

Seeing that Dromeas was staring at the man by her side with mistrust, she said, "This gentleman was at my side waiting to buy an animal." Adhara lied.

Dromeas gave him a short, but dry, bow of his head, took Adhara by the arm, and pulled her away, not even saying goodbye. As they distanced themselves, Adhara turned her head and looking at Raiko, she gave him a gesture of thanks and, at the same time, apology for Dromeas' behavior.

Raiko was annoyed. *What am I doing protecting the women of others instead of worrying about my own affairs?* He went to the goat stall. The sooner he finished this business and was on his boat, the better for him.

CHAPTER TWELVE

Toula was sitting beneath the window in her private room, sewing a tapestry. She needed all the light from outside to make the intricate knots. Her meticulous fingers followed the line of the different threads, but she was unable to concentrate because of the cries coming from the garden. Her diligent fingers bristled and, frustrated, she threw the tapestry to the ground, as was her habit when something was beyond her control. The commotion from the garden forced her to turn and look outside. *There are those brats making a noise again,* she thought angrily.

Since their unexpected arrival into the world, the twins had changed the lives of everyone in the kingdom. Dromeas had grown into a blond-haired child with honey-colored eyes and a vivacious and restless character. Adhara was a precious girl who had inherited her mother's (and her grandfather's) grayish-green eyes. Zoe loved to spend long hours brushing Adhara's long brown hair that glistened with strands of copper.

From a distance, only Toula, by her mother's side, would watch these scenes of affection with hatred. She was the great loser in this situation. Now that this boy was here, she was an irritant in her father's palace, a single woman who had to be addressed, but not respected. Her husband had scorned her, and the role of heir had been wiped out of her future. Her innate resentment against everything and everyone was growing, while the relationship between Pilomenes, Zoe, and the children strengthened.

She had been the Queen of Pisidia. She was the first-born; one day she would inherit Paphlagonia, at the side of her handsome husband, and she would be respected and loved by all her subjects. That had been her future, but it had all been snatched away from her. She dwelled on this in fury.

Her marriage had been going well, she reflected, while her diligent fingers returned to weaving in mechanical movements. When her husband rebuked her seven years later, she returned to her father's house. At the end of the day, she was the first-born. Her father had not produced a male heir and her mother worshipped her. She would be the Queen of Paphlagonia, it was her right… until Zoe and these horrible brats appeared. Now Zoe was the first-born, and furthermore, she had had a son, supposedly of divine origin. Every night she cried in fury, while during the day she watched Dromeas and Adhara grow.

This blond boy had ended all her hopes; old and with no bequest, it would be even more difficult not to be a burden on the palace. From the window, she watched Pilomenes sitting by Zoe's side and a stab of jealously pierced her heart. *Worst of all, they not only robbed me of my inheritance and my future, they also robbed me of my father*, she thought, sadly.

Lisipe was watching the twins mounted on their respective horses, wielding wooden swords and bamboo shields. The children were listening attentively to the old Amazon's lesson, and were obediently following her instructions.

She had taken the reins of the twins' education when she had judged it appropriate. For her, the training Adhara had to receive was a huge responsibility. Hippolyta would never forgive her if she did not make her an Amazon of the purest stock. But, as the children were inseparable, she had decided that she would train both of them in the same way. Maybe it was a waste spending her time on Dromeas, but this way Adhara would have the companion that she needed for the practices.

"Adhara, sit firmly, hold the rein in one hand and go fast, fast. Take all the breath out of this stallion!" Lisipe would shout. "Now, push the animal's rump with your knees, and let go of the bridle. If you do not have both hands free, you cannot use the sword and the shield."

Adhara had done what she was told, and on the back of the horse, she let her hands go and raised her arms, brandishing the sword and the shield in the air. She kept control of the horse with her knees, all with a look of approval from Lisipe.

Mounted on his stallion, Dromeas laughed, jokingly. He rested his hands on the animal's neck, and in an impulse, he stood up on the saddle. With the horse in motion, and achieving perfect balance, while standing up, he brandished his shield and his sword, just as his sister had done a few minutes earlier.

"Careful, you're going to fall!" Lisipe cried, pretending to be annoyed, though inside she was proud of the boy's skill.

"Don't worry Lisipe," Dromeas shouted from his horse. "I am learning from you. And you, you fight and ride the horse better that the generals of *Pappous*," And, with the offended Pilomenes frowning, the Amazon tried awkwardly to conceal a smile of satisfaction.

Pilomenes was seeing this scene from afar and he was troubled. These children had more of Hippolyta's blood in their veins than he would have liked. If he left Dromeas in Lisipe's hands, all the equilibrium that he had achieved in the region would disappear in little time. Although he was proud of his grandson's physical capabilities, he did not want a warrior as his successor on the throne.

Pilomenes had handled diplomacy well, like all his ancestors, and he believed this was the proper way to rule. He wanted, in some way, to guide the drive for glory and the arrogance of his grandson. He would have liked Dromeas to show more interest in history, writing, and mathematics. These were all useful knowledge for a king who wanted to govern in a peaceful way.

He tried to arouse his interest, bringing a considerable number of teachers to the palace, but none of them provoked the boy's curiosity. As soon as the teacher became distracted, Dromeas would escape and head for Lisipe, to get back to the practice he loved so much. Lisipe was amusing, she taught him to fight, to ride horses, and to make arrows. The boy adored the old Amazon and was only happy when he was at her side.

Frustrated, the teachers would shout and follow him through the garden trying to catch him and force him to return to the classroom, but the little one was demonically fast, and he was impossible to catch.

He ran with the speed of the wind. Dromeas felt in his element when he ran. Running, running, running, to defy the wind, while feeling it humming in his ears and its force on his face. To gallop on fast horses, feeling he was the owner and master of the animal, of nature, of the world. To defy everyone and everything, all the laws of nature, gravity, and his grandfather's authority. To fight, to show the world he was the best boxer, the best horseman, the best athlete. This was what Dromeas wanted, not to sit still listening to old people talk about things he could neither see, nor touch, nor feel. He liked to use his brain to control each one of the muscles in his body, to feel the divine energy that flowed through his veins, and not to dedicate it to abstract ideas that bored him.

For her part, Adhara had benefitted from her brother's education, something that might not have happened in this era when women only learned duties in the home. Pilomenes hoped that by having his sister as a companion, Dromeas might find the classes more appealing. However, it was not so. While Dromeas despised the classroom, and tried to run away the minute he could, for Adhara a marvelous world had opened up in front of her eyes. The love for what she learned competed with the time she had to dedicate to her training, and this bothered Lisipe.

The girl was incredibly intelligent. The teachers thought it a waste that such a brilliant mind should exist in a woman's head. It would bring more problems than benefits, they reflected sadly, shaking their heads. No man wanted a woman smarter than him by his side.

At least she was beautiful, thought a teacher from Athens, who taught her geometry. He looked at her profile as she was leaning over the study bench. Any man would want her as a wife, if she would agree to subject herself to a man, something that no Amazon would be disposed to do.

Maybe I should leave my kingdom to Adhara, Pilomenes thought. Yet, to leave his kingdom to an Amazon was also not in line with the idea of diplomacy held by his ancestors.

Adhara liked all subjects, but she was particularly attracted to mathematics. She spent hours solving problems. In her mind, everything corresponded and made sense. When her mind considered some mathematical challenge abstractly, her thinking went away, traveling to superior levels, where there was neither time nor space, only reasoning. Her mind would navigate and analyze the alternatives; it would wind between the trees of decision, pick up the argument again and, after having floated for a while, timeless, the solution would jump from some obscure corner of her brain. As if for an instant, a divine spark had generated a connection with a greater mind, a mind that knew all, and shared it with her. To solve a problem was entertainment. She understood how Dromeas felt when he won a race or a fight. This sensation of success, of command, of feeling fulfilled, was the same experience she had when she beat her teachers in solving problems.

Pilomenes would look at her, proud of her intelligence, while the cries of Dromeas could be heard from the garden, and his empty chair reminded him of the little interest that books aroused in the boy.

How do you control the children of Zeus and an Amazon? Pilomenes wondered.

CHAPTER THIRTEEN

The sun shimmered on the streets of Pergamon. All of the inhabitants were running hurriedly to the Theater of Dionysius in the Acropolis, to celebrate Mithridates' first great victory over Rome.

Since early morning, the theater, with a capacity for ten thousand people and with the steepest tiers in the world, had been crammed with villagers who had risen at dawn so they could attend the great event. A tide of people, frustrated because they were not able to enter, thronged the outside of the building,hoping to at least hear what was happening inside.

Mithridates had sent his spectacular solid gold throne to be placed on the platform designated for actors. A marvelous silk canopy protected the King and his entourage, made up of his sons and daughters, his generals, and some of his concubines, from the sun.

Mithridates wore a long white linen tunic in the Greek style, and dark purple-colored pantaloons, rolled at the ankles. On his waist, he wore a sash of cloth, also purple, wound around him two times; this is where he carried his inseparable dagger. The iron leaf dagger had a pronounced curve, measured ten inches long, and had both edges sharpened. The handle was carved in gold, encrusted with precious stones. Rumors abounded that the knob was a cavity, and that the King used it to carry the lethal poison he had discovered in his mines. A gold ring shone on his hand, inset with an agate, just like the ring Darius of Persia wore on his hand a long time before. His eyes were made up with kohl, and his face was shaven like the western generals.

Facing an exalted public, who were shouting out his name from the stands, the happiness on Mithridates' face was unparalleled. He had demonstrated his strategic expertise to overwhelmingly defeat the allied armies of Rome and Bithynia in a magnificent manner.

Blinded by ambition, the allied armies of Aquillius from Rome and Nicomedes of Bithynia had invaded the kingdom of Pontus in haste; Nicomedes settled in a flatland near the River

Amnias ready to give battle, with Aquillius and his troops near Mount Escorobas. Unaware of the colossal supremacy in numbers of the army that Mithridates had at the ready, they were positioned in precisely the most convenient location for a victory on the part of the King of Pontus.

As the supreme commander of his armed forces, Mithridates settled on a hill that allowed him to have an ample view of the battlefield, a flat valley along the side of the River Amnias. He placed his throne there, and seated upon it, he supervised the contest. His son Arcadius would command the cavalry and he had posted his two best generals, the brothers Neoptolemus and Archelaus, to command the infantry.

The army of Pontus responded to the schemes of the great Persian commanders, from whom Mithridates felt he was such a proud descendant. His brother-in-law, and most loyal ally, Tigranes of Armenia, supplied the cavalry with monumental stallions, ridden by his swiftest horsemen. The infantry was made up of Hoplites, who were generously equipped with forged bronze helmets and armor, brilliant spears, and shields with lustrous jewels. Following the tactics of Darius, the second line was comprised of archers on foot, carrying large bows and poisonous arrows; behind them were the men with slingshots and lead projectiles, skilled never to miss their target, and the *peltast,* fighters with light shields and javelins.

Mithridates did not leave any detail to chance, and to assure victory he put his naval fleet of three hundred ships in place to protect the Black Sea coasts. More men could disembark from the north, should they be needed at the peak of the battle. In total, Mithridates had three hundred thousand men: two hundred and fifty thousand infantry, and fifty thousand horsemen.

For his part, Nicomedes had succeeded in uniting fifty-six thousand soldiers, who had received intense training, and six thousand horsemen. Aquillius' army had only forty thousand men, and both leaders, ignorant of the might they were facing, were confident that the number of soldiers would be sufficient to dispose of the forces of Pontus.

The sun was showing its face over the horizon; its warm rays reflected over the babbling waters of the river that continued on its way through the valley, indifferent to the events around it. The silence of dawn was broken by the sound of trumpets with the call to battle. In step with the impetuous drumbeat, Nicomedes' men stood in perfect formation and they began to beat their spears on the ground, keeping in time with the drum roll. Perspiring faces under the masks of the helmets preserved a rigid expression; at this moment, the will to live was paramount.

On hearing the calls to battle from their leaders, Nicomedes' men moved quickly and systematically towards the hills to attack the enemy. They marched at a quick pace, and their shields, tightly wedged together, reflected the sunlight like infinite mirrors. The extended spears formed an impenetrable forest of sharp points, hungry to be rammed into the chests of the enemies.

But Mithridates had astutely divided his infantry into two groups, commanded by the brothers Neoptolemus and Archelaus respectively.

The infantry commanded by Neoptolemus was the first to be charged by Nicomedes' army. The men of Pontus had gone down the hill where they had been posted, and they clashed violently with the phalange formed by the Bithynian army they met on the plain.

The first encounter was a brutal one. The might of the first lines was put to test, as was the order and determination of each one of the armies. The instant a Bithynian fell, he was replaced at once by a soldier from the next line, preserving the compact alignment. As soon as spear points were broken on shields and human chests, the soldiers drew their swords. The blades clashed with each other as they pounded shields that put up a solid defense. The robust discipline of the Bithynian phalange contained the ocean of soldiers that attacked them, but soon Mithridates would resort to the distinct variety of resources in his possession.

The Pontic archers, who were behind the fifth line of combat, began to throw their poisonous arrows that went arcing through the air, penetrating from above the compact group that was advancing. The men with slingshots drew again and, launching their lethal lead projectiles, they succeeded in gravely wounding the soldiers in the center of the formation. They quickly raised their shields to the sky and continued their advance, forming a shining bronze canopy that moved slowly across the plain.

When the Bithynians found themselves in the heat of the battle, Arcadius, the first-born son of Mithridates, made a surprise attack on the mass of troops at the rear. Due to their superiority in numbers, as well the strength of their horses, they finished off Nicomedes' cavalry in a humiliating flash. Then, from the back, they began to charge at the group of soldiers defending themselves on foot.

Straight away, without giving them the time to breathe, Archelaus and his men moved in from the right side. This finally accomplished the scattering of Nicomedes' army. Although the soldiers were brave and well-trained, they suddenly found themselves defending three fronts at one time. The compact formation came apart, and the men of Bithynia had to fight back to back against the various sides that were opening in front of them. Each Bithynian had to fight against three enemy soldiers at the same time if he wanted to come out of the battle victorious.

Mithridates' army attacked the opposition army from three different positions in harmony, like a well-orchestrated melody. It was more of a triumphal march than a melody, one that would hit the highest note *in crescendo* with the entry of the scythed chariots.

The scythed, or war chariots, which had been made famous in the poems of Homer, were very light vehicles with two large wheels, tied to feisty steeds that pulled them at an incredible speed. Their place in battle had been long forgotten, and they were only used in races in the Roman Circus.

Having studied the battles that liberated his Persian ancestors, Mithridates ordered the construction of one hundred and thirty carriages replicating those used by Darius III in the battle of Gaugamela. Mithridates' chariots were very similar to those that competed in the sports in the circus, but they had a demonic difference, a sharp blade that stood out over three feet perpendicular from each one of the wheels.

When Mithridates saw, from his privileged position, the disorder that had unfolded in the Bithynian army, he gave the order to Craterus, the Auriga leader of the scythed chariots, to enter the battle.

Craterus raised his whip into the air, this signal giving his men the order to attack. One hundred and thirty whips lifted into the air at the same time, and, with raging cries, they cracked on the ardent horses, invading the only flank left to assail the enemy.

The blades going round in ferocious circles on the wheels hurtled into the crowd of disorganized soldiers like the hungry teeth of a wild animal. The carnage defied description. The sharpened blades sliced human parts with such speed that some soldiers continued in battle without realizing that their left arm, still brandishing the shield, was lying on the ground, detached and bloody.

In the face of the terrorizing spectacle of seeing their comrades cut in half while still breathing, as well as pieces of humans stuck to the wheels of the enemy's carriages, panic took over Nicomedes' lines, and many soldiers fled in terror, abandoning the battlefield. A few brave men remained, resisting the pounding of the enemy, but exhaustion, disorder, and the oppressive avalanche from all four sides made victory impossible.

Mithridates had won the battle.

As soon as he realized his defeat, Nicomedes fled to the camp of Aquillius on Mount Escorobas. But even there, defeat did not pretend to wait. Filled with frenzy by the recent triumph, Archelaus and his men attacked the Roman army, in a overwhelming assault.

In the confusion of the brawl, Nicomedes and Aquillius tried to escape from Anatolia. Nicomedes was able to reach Rome, but not Aquillius. Mithridates swept the region with his powerful army in search of him, taking kingdoms along the way.

Aquillius fled with Mithridates on his heels. Evasive, he managed to reach Greece, but when he found himself in Mitilene, ready to set sail for the Italian peninsula, the hands of traitors, loyal to the King of Pontus, handed him over.

Mithridates was overjoyed. In this campaign, he had succeeded in extending his kingdom over all of Asia Minor, and he snatched control of Pergamon from the Romans. And now here he was, in the theater of Dionysus, surrounded by a large crowd to celebrate his triumph.

With the taste of victory on his lips, he stood up from the throne on the stage and, showing his excellent skills as an orator, he began his speech.

"Citizens of Pergamon and all Anatolia, I, Mithridates, the sixth of my line, stand before you victorious," he paused, and the crowd shouted unrestrainedly, applauding and praising him. "We had the opportunity to decide whether or not we wanted war, but Rome invaded our kingdom, leaving us with no alternative."

The crowd shrieked with joy. They had been under Roman rule for many years, at a costly price. All of the occupied territories had to pay high taxes to the Republic, and if they failed to do so on time, they were taken as slaves. The oppressed population was tired of this situation, and they all began to see in Mithridates the leader capable of freeing them.

"I have proven to you that Rome can lose battles and that we are strong enough to confront her. Rome is not invincible! We have defeated Aquillius and his ally Nicomedes. This is only the beginning; under my rule, all of Anatolia will be free from Roman oppression.The Romans hoisted their emblem with the Royal Eagle, of which they feel very proud, but their true founders, Romulus and Remus, suckled from a predatory she-wolf. The Romans are not eagles who fly majestically across the sky, they are no more than greedy wolves who want to take all our riches!"

Shouts and applause could be heard all over. The whole crowd, in one single voice, supported Mithridates' speech with a cry.

"On the contrary, I can talk about my ancestors," the proud King continued. "From my father, Mithridates V, I have inherited blood of the Greats of Persia, Cyrus and Darius. My mother was a princess descended from Alexander the Great. I, successor to the two cultures that unite Anatolia, will end Roman oppression!" He spoke in an ecstatic voice. "I am the Savior, the Messiah you have been waiting for!"

His words resonated powerfully in the most remote parts of the theater. The spectators were drunk with the victory of Mithridates, which they saw as their own.

The crowd, roused, was roaring out of control. Taking advantage of the collective hysteria that Mithridates' speech was generating, Archelaus, the supreme commander of the army, addressed the public. With his arms raised in the air and speaking in his magnificent voice, he said, "Since Rome began her campaign of invasion more than two hundred years ago, with disastrous results for those conquered, prophets from different religions and kingdoms have announced that a Messiah will rise up from the East and will come to free us from Roman oppression. The prophecies all coincide with each other. He will be a king among kings, and the apparition of a comet in the skies will mark his birth."

With a majestic gesture, he drew his sword, which gleamed brilliantly under the ardent sun that bathed all the spectators.

"It is true, the Savior King has arrived! Listen to these wise words," and pointing his sword at the King of Pontus, he said, "You are the Messiah we have all been waiting for!" Without taking a breath, he continued. "All of the divine signs have been present in your life. During your birth, a brilliant star plowed through the heavens, and its tail could be seen for seven days, shining in revelation, with tongues of fire that illuminated the skies," he said, pompously.

He pointed at Mithridates' forehead with one hand.

"The scar left by a flash of lightning that hit your crib when you were still an infant is visible on your forehead. Not only did you survive, the mark on your forehead resembles a crown, an unmistakable sign of the great plan that the Gods had for you."

"Who else but you, born in the East, descendant of kings, announced by the skies and touched with the divine sign on your forehead, could liberate us of the ills that trouble our region?" Archelaus cried, jubilant, opening his arms to add a dramatic effect to his words.

"All praise the Savior King!" he shouted, frenzied. "Mithridates is the One chosen by the Gods to free us!"

The power of the general's voice was staggering. The audience had gone quiet for a moment, as they absorbed the revelation they were witnessing in silence. The soldier's claims were more than convincing, and with the memory of Mithridates' victories fresh in their minds, the citizens accepted the statement, that the King was the much-anticipated Messiah, as the only truth.

"Long live the Savior King!" Archelaus cried.

And the public responded in unison, "Long live the Savior King!"

The soldiers positioned around the stage began to tap their javelins on the ground, while, exalted, they continued crying, "Long live the Savior King!" The loud voices and the rhythmic blows resounded in the theater. The echo, like a divine voice, affirmed that Mithridates was the Chosen One announced by the prophets.

Archelaus, addressing the other generals, said, "You, go back to your soldiers and spread the good news in all the occupied territories. The Savior King has finally arrived!"

And the fanatical crowd continued shouting, "SAVIOR KING, SAVIOR KING!"

Mithridates opened his arms, and with a smile on his face, he turned from right to left, looking at the steps. This was, without doubt, the best moment of his life!

However, there was still something missing. He wanted to display another example of his supremacy to his subjects. He wanted to humiliate the Romans in such a way that all of Asia Minor would witness the power he had over the destiny of his enemies.

Then, the King turned to his soldiers. "The time for justice has arrived. Bring me the prisoner," he said, with an authoritative gesture.

A donkey appeared, and on it was Aquillius, the Roman Consul, dressed in rags, gagged, and with his hands tied behind his back. The people booed as he passed, throwing rotten vegetables and stones at him. One of them hit his face, producing a wound from which a narrow stream of blood started to trickle.

To the side of the platform, where Mithridates and his committee sat, there was a cauldron on a pile of dry straw. On Mithridates' command, a soldier lit the straw with the flame of a torch. The flames grew quickly, lapping around the pot and heating it. One of the soldiers lifted his head towards the King and Mithridates gave a nod of approval. The soldier then began to throw gold coins into the pot and started to stir the contents with a wooden spoon.

While the gold turned into liquid, Aquillius arrived at the royal court. Brusque hands took him down from the unhappy beast and directed him to Mithridates' side. The King received him with contempt and, showing the wretched Aquillius to the crowd, he said, "Here you have him. A Roman who invades our lands to rob us of our riches - riches that belong only to us." The crowd booed Aquillius. The cries were deafening.

"Romans, you will pay greatly for your greed," he shouted.

He gave a signal to the soldier who was beside the bonfire, and acknowledging it, the soldier put leather blacksmith's gloves on his hands and carried the burning pot to the king. Inside, the gold coins had already melted, and a shaky smoke exuded from the hellish stew.

The King also put on some thick gloves, with all the parsimony he could manage, while the exhausted Aquillius had opened his eyes wide in terror, trying to understand what his cruel destiny would be.

Mithridates then took the pot from the hands of the soldier and placed it in front of the unfortunate prisoner. One soldier restrained the weak Aquillius, while another brusquely opened his mouth.

"You have an infinite thirst for gold, Manius Aquillius," the King said with hatred in his voice, "so I will relieve you of your greedy ambition once and for all."

And, saying this, he poured the molten gold into the forced open mouth of the Roman general. Mithridates did not stop until he had emptied the whole pot into Aquillius' entrails.

After this brutal punishment, Aquillius, unable to cry out, unable to move because of his tethers, fell to the ground. From there the inhabitants of Pergamon witnessed his death as the molten gold burned his insides.

The proclamation of Mithridates as Savior King had not been a random speech. On the contrary, the king of Pontus had met with his generals, and they had discussed how they could reap even more benefit from the catastrophic victory.

Mithridates was a very vain man, but at the same time, very intelligent. He knew that a publicity campaign in his favor would facilitate the task of expelling the Romans from Anatolia.

Now, for a long time, various prophets from different religions had foretold the arrival of a Savior, a Messiah who would free the world of Roman oppression. Mithridates took it upon himself to personify this prophecy, and personally I believe that he started to believe it himself, since the signs really coincided with his persona. However, history tells us that it was not he who finished off Rome, but Rome who ended him.

But, for the intentions of this moment, Mithridates achieved his purpose, and after his first victory, many began to believe that he was the Savior King, the Messiah announced by the prophets.

CHAPTER FOURTEEN

"Bring me more warm water, the bath is getting cold," Rikae ordered her servant in a demanding voice, while a slave massaged her back with a sponge doused in essence of jasmine. She was soaking in a tub made of bronze and embossed with complex designs that resembled geometric flowers traced with a compass and a triangle, rather than the free hand of an artist.

In the kingdom of Pontus, Rikae enjoyed all the advantages of being the wife of one of Mithridates' sons. Her quarters were immense, her clothes made of the finest silks from the orient and linens from Egypt, she owned jewels from beyond the ocean, and she had tens of slaves to attend to her every minute wish.

Submerged in the warm water, she closed her eyes and smiled. She was happy for Mithridates' recent triumph. *The Kingdom of Pontus is growing considerably*, she thought, as she opened her eyes again, admiring the new ring from Caria that sparkled splendidly on her finger.

Just as Pilomenes had planned, Rikae had married Pharnaces II, one of the sons of Mithridates VI, King of Pontus. *My father must be pleased with me, of all my sisters I am the one who has acquired the best husband*, she thought with pretentious happiness. *Moreover, my father has me to thank for my father-in-law not setting his troops on Paphlagonia in the horrific way he did on Bithynia.*

"My father is an astute old fox," she said aloud. The slaves continued massaging her back, keeping their heads down, with the attitude of persons who did not exist. This princess was unpredictable and nobody dared to displease her. "Survive, that is all the very fearful ones had always tried to do."

So different from her father-in-law, she thought, with affected voluptuousness, remembering the night before he left for the battle against the Romans and their allies. He had arrived in her quarters unannounced; it seemed as though the nerves of battle had aroused his carnal desires. She was reclined on a divan, dressed in a white tunic, with her long, dark hair falling down her back, right to her waist. Desire glistened in the King's eyes. She approached him with a provocative smile, and without looking away from Mithridates, she took off her tunic, leaving herself completely naked in front of his eyes.

The King was a passionate man, but his tastes were not very different to those of other males. *In the end, all men have the same needs*, Rikae thought, with a voluptuous smile. *The art of the nymphs.* It was an art she had practiced from a very young age.

In this perfumed bath that caressed her whole body, she remembered discovering her sensuality when she was very young. She had escaped from the care of her nursemaid and had gone to the gymnasium where the young soldiers from her father's army trained. Hidden in a corner, she watched them, naked and smeared in oil, fighting each other. With the image of these muscular bodies writhing together, a fire awoke inside, a stirring desire possessed her, a thirst that demanded to be satiated.

When it got dark, she escaped from her quarters and, without a sound, she entered the bedchambers where the youths slept. She approached the first cot where a young man was sleeping, naked, covered with a well-worn woolen cloth. Rikae lifted the cloth to the side, and releasing her tunic, she lay down beside the youth, awakening him with a sultry kiss.

This gesture immediately stirred the soldier's desire, and without being very sure what to expect, Rikae delivered herself into the arms of her young lover. That night she discovered how she could use her body both to feel pleasure and to provoke it... and she became addicted.

Every night she would escape from her room and go to the barracks that were filled with men. She could not help herself. She needed to satisfy this fierce urgency that clawed inside her. She was insatiable.

After those many nights, she became a very experienced lover. She was open to trying whatever entered her imagination, or that of her companions. She discovered that she could use her body as a weapon, and that men had weaknesses. She knew that she had great power over men, a power that allowed her to get anything she wanted from them, while at the same time plunging herself into oceans of pleasure.

She played at making them suffer; she undressed in front of them, she danced gently, swaying her hips, and she would not let them take her until they carried out some task that she would impose. She manipulated them like slaves. She knew that they had to obey her because, at the end of the day, she was the King's daughter and they could not force themselves upon her. On the other hand, the pleasure she had learned to give them turned them into docile lambs, ready to do whatever it took to make her theirs.

Mithridates was an ardent and experienced lover. He loved to take pleasure to the limit, and to venture in the search for more sophisticated pleasures. But Rikae was the best, and she knew it. She knew how to take the sovereign to the boundaries of ecstasy, she knew she was better than his wives or his concubines... and best of all he, in return, gave her pleasure. In his hands, she felt satisfied, at least for a brief moment.

But of all the pleasures she had experienced, the greatest was to lie in his arms afterwards, exhausted with passion, and hear him talk about his plans to conquer the world. It amused her when he recounted his experiences, and she laughed voraciously when he would describe the effect of some poison on his victim. Nothing excited Rikae more than Mithridates' power, of the sword or of the potion. He was the Lord and Master of the rest of the mortals' lives.

Mithridates was definitely more interesting than his bore of a son, Pharnaces. Rikae had to do the impossible not to fall asleep in his disappointing arms. His conversations were always lacking in ambition. Her husband reminded her of Pilomenes, little disposed to weapons; he preferred to solve conflicts through agreements. *Like cowards,* she thought, with disdain.

On the other hand, her father-in-law was a warrior, he would conquer all of Asia Minor and, on his death, she would be the Queen and Lady of all of Anatolia, she said to herself, with exaggerated anticipation. To offer him a little pleasure was a very small price compared to all she would obtain in the future. That was her scheming thought.

She got out of the bath and another anxious slave wrapped her in a linen towel. She dried her gently, and started to apply perfumed oil to her voluptuous, full body.

A maid brought her a saffron-colored tunic and very gently put it over her head and fastened it at the top of her shoulders. Rikae's prominent chest stretched the front part of the dress, and on placing the belt on her waist to complete the outfit, the slave noticed it was holding her in with difficulty. Someone needed to tell the princess that she should avoid eating so many pastries with honey and almonds, but the poor girl could not imagine anyone would be capable of telling Rikae that she was getting fat, not even Mithridates.

Rikae realized that the slave was having difficulty closing the belt and her smile did not go unnoticed. Irritated, she asked, "What are you laughing at, stupid?"

The slave paled in fear, nervously lowering her gaze. A messenger entered the room and unknowingly saved the poor devil from the embarrassing situation.

"Your Majesty, correspondence." The herald delivered two parchments to Rikae.

The two missives came from Gangra. *What did her father want now?*she wondered. Always so noble and correct, always so meticulous, he had written her thousands of letters, asking her to speak to her husband so that he would intervene with Mithridates to stop the provocation against the Romans. But Rikae ignored these communications; she would say yes to her father and, in reality, burn all his letters.

Please Gods,it was not from Toula either, complaining about Zoe and the children, she thought, aggravated. Rikae had not had the opportunity to meet them. *Who wanted to go to Gangra when she could be in Sinope, the capital of the Kingdom*? Here, she had interests to protect, and in her father's house there was nothing of consequence.

Notwithstanding, the subject of the little boy in the court and the excessive attention that Pilomenes showered on him irritated the kingdom of Pontus. Pilomenes would do well to remember his promises.

Frustrated, she saw that her worst fears had been confirmed; there was a letter from her father, and one from Toula. The parchment her father sent was an invitation to three days of festivities in commemoration of his years of life. The second was a letter from Toula, in which she said that at this party, her father would proclaim Dromeas as his future heir.

Pilomenes must be very deranged because of this child. Did he not realize that by naming him as his heir, he would put both Paphlagonia and Dromeas himself in danger? Mithridates had paid little attention to Paphlagonia, since he considered it already conquered. If Pilomenes continued with this nonsense of pompously naming an heir, the King of Pontus would see it as a provocation and a mockery of the alliance that they had made in matrimony. Rikae would have much to lose, her power in this court came from the legacy she brought with her. Without Paphlagonia as a dowry, her authority in Sinope would be diminished. She must go to this party for the good of Pontus, and for herself.

In her mind she recreated the list of guests. All of her sisters would be there with their husbands, Zoe, whom she would finally meet, the brats, Toula, and of course her husband who had rejected her, Phelon. When she thought of him, a sensual smile formed on her lips. Pleasant memories returned to her mind.

Now that Mithridates was in Pergamon, she would attend the ceremony in his name. She would go to this party and enjoy the circus.

CHAPTER FIFTEEN

The caravan of camels traveled slowly across the desert. The sun shone splendidly on the sand; its reflection could have blinded other eyes less accustomed to such landscapes. But not them, they were men of the desert.

He had joined them a while back, when his hair and his beard were already grown. After completing the initiation ceremony that had made him the Bearer of the Word, the Wise Ones had taken him to the caves, and they had left him alone with a few jars of spring water and some pieces of dried meat. There, his wounds had formed scars, and he had regained his strength.

He roamed the unknown desert alone through seven moons, seven solitary moons without the company of another human soul. When the seventh moon rose in the sky, his eyes distinguished a group of errant travelers coming towards him.

He arrived like a stranger among them, but they received him cordially. They gave him the nickname *the Silent One*, because he hardly ever spoke, he only said what was necessary. His reserve was considered his weakness, since this was a race that appreciated eloquence above all other human qualities. However, he thought that not only did he not have much to say, what was of real importance would be said soon.

He had joined them because he needed the desert. He needed his hands to become sensitive, and the contact with the white, gleaming sand helped. He spent long hours sitting on the ground, sifting the sand through his fingers. He had already got used to its texture, its temperature, and its sound. His hands worked like infinite hourglasses; when the last grain slid through his hands to the ground, his fists would fill once more with the precious material, and it would begin the journey through his purifying palms.

Many years had now passed since he met them, since he had enjoyed their camaraderie, the long treks on the back of a camel, hearing marvelous stories by firelight on cold desert nights, but today was the day to abandon them.

She had been born one more time, at the same time the

ceremony took place. The connection between them came from afar, when the Word was pronounced for the first time, and every time that it was uttered. Her essence was the same as that of the Word, and destiny mandated that they set forth on the journey together. She had to be ready now, waiting for him. The time had arrived to look for her.

Delphi. That was the only word the Blind Men said to him after the ceremony. *Delphi.* Only this word and nothing more. He knew that after meeting her he would have to go to Delphi. There, where his destiny awaited.

Queen Aruza was with Roxana in one of the rooms in the palace. Many years had now passed since she first found her on that stone, tiny and unclothed.

Roxana was by her side and, in her usual way, she was carving a piece of stone. Since she was small, since she saw her giving life to her own toys, the Queen never ceased to marvel at the magic her daughter had in her hands. Only she could extract marvelous forms from ordinary pieces of stone.

Roxana felt the caring eyes of the Queen over her and she was afraid her mother would suffer when she departed. And the day was getting closer, she knew it. She did not know exactly how it was going to happen, but she would have to go.

Her thoughts were interrupted by a servant, who entered with a message. Bowing in front of Aruza, he said, "There is a man asking for the Princess, my Lady."

"Let him come in," the Queen answered.

A man, with long black hair gathered in a braid, and a long beard of the same shade of black, entered the room. His skin was weather-beaten from the desert sun. When he entered the room he looked for Roxana's face, and when he saw her he addressed her, "I have come to look for you, my Lady," he said, respectfully.

"I was waiting for you," Roxana answered gently, her voice showing no surprise.

The man got down on one knee in front of her.

"I am Ammos, from the tribe of the desert. In me you have

your most loyal servant," he said, with his head bowed over his knee.

"Stand up," Roxana said, as she held out her hand, "you know very well that I am the one who should be serving you."

Aruza was watching the events with concern. Deep down in her soul, she had always feared that one day Roxana would leave. Apparently she was witnessing the scene of her departure.

"Mother," Roxana said, addressing the Queen, and Aruza was waiting for the fated words, "I have to go."

A tear rolled down the Queen's cheek.

"So soon?" she asked in faint voice.

"I have already spent a lot of time with you," Roxana said. "Thank you for having me in your house."

"Thank you for having lived with us," and she took her cold hands into her own, and kissed them.

She ordered her servants to prepare a royal carriage, and to fill it with jugs of water and hides filled with food. Her beloved daughter would leave the palace as a princess from high ancestry.

When Roxana got into the carriage, with Ammos at her side on a lively horse, the Queen approached her. For the first time Roxana hugged her strongly, knowing that she would never see her again.

CHAPTER SIXTEEN

It had been a long journey from Petra, but they had finally arrived in Delphi. Roxana was enjoying observing the statues and buildings that comprised the oracle. In Petra, her city of origin, the buildings were carved in the wall of rock, literally having been sculpted into them. This was her first journey away from home, and for that reason, she was surprised to learn that, in other places, stone was torn from its crib, worked, and then elegantly arranged to form buildings.

However, more surprising was the perfection of the Greek sculptures; these were carved in solid blocks of marble, brought from their original quarry. She moved her hands gently over a statue that represented a young man who was preparing for a competition. She knew that by brushing her fingers over the stone, her hands would soak in the knowledge and skill of the artist who had produced it. This was her unique way of learning.

The figure was in perfect proportion, the muscles were exceptionally well depicted, and even the robust chest appeared to be inflated with a powerful breath. On the head, too, meticulous care had been taken in every detail: the curly hair, and the serene face, illuminated by a faint smile and a melancholy look.

She had worked with stone and clay before, and hence she admired these works in front of her eyes. These statues were so well made that they gave the impression of human beings that had been rendered motionless by a spell, encased in a prison of stone. Being here and seeing these creations, she understood the mission that she had to complete even more, the mission that had brought her here.

The mission that made her reborn... An old consciousness, that at times looked down on her, brought memories of other lives. Other existences that she had lived before, vague memories of other pieces sculpted, the vision of her hands revealing secrets. At night, in her dreams, she would see a pair of eyes watching her. A pair of warm eyes that looked at her with curiosity, but at the same time urged her to find the others and fulfill the prophecy one more time.

She took a deep breath and went towards a temple whose columns had the form of maidens. The women sculpted there seemed to be enjoying their role of supporting the temple's structure. Facing them, she passed her fingers over them again and, startled, she seemed to feel the statues moving. No! In reality, it was the ground that was moving! She was so absorbed in contemplating the effigies that she had failed to notice a tremor had started.

The clamor that came from the entrails of Gea was heard all over the oracle. All the pilgrims who had come to their meeting with the God felt the ground beneath them shake. The shrines shook, some statues were balancing on top of each other, and rocks of all sizes were rolling down the hillside. A cloud of dust was blinding eyes and drying throats, and the entire crowd was running in all directions, screaming wildly as they looked for refuge.

Pulling Roxana by the arm, the man with dark hair forced her into a small shrine on the Sacred Way. They could die in the open, crushed by one of the rocks that were rolling down the hill.

Raiko, who was a few steps away from them, had watched what Roxana and her companion were doing, and he followed them through the cloud of dust that had formed. Having a quick look around, he understood why that man had chosen this building: it was robust and it was not supported by columns, but by solid walls.

The noise that, between the cries from the people and the bellowing of the earth, had become deafening, lessened on entering the temple. After his pupils adapted to the different light, Raiko started to move around. The inside of the temple was completely empty; it seemed that there was no firm arch under which he could find shelter.

The surroundings suddenly turned dark; a statue had fallen at the entrance of the building, preventing light from coming in. This was making his experience a little more sinister.

Fortunately, the tremor did not last long. The earth stopped growling, the buildings remained standing, and dust began to settle on the ground. Inside the temple, two shadows began to stand up slowly. As he had followed them in, he was not surprised to see the woman with long and curly black hair and her companion.

The two figures stood gazing at the entrance where the statue obstructed the way.

"We must look for another passage," Raiko remarked.

They started to look around, searching for an alternative way out. The three of them turned around at the same time and they saw that, towards the center of the temple, a hint of light could be sensed. They went to the circle of light and noticed that there was an opening in the roof allowing the entry of the sun's rays, which were projected onto a mosaic built on the ground.

On their right, two other shadows came forward cautiously. This time, Raiko was pleasantly surprised to recognize Adhara and Dromeas; apparently they, too, chose to enter the temple for protection from outside.

The five figures converged on the center, unintentionally forming a circle.

"Stay calm! Do not worry about this earthquake." A voice was heard from the other side of the temple; they followed the sound of some footsteps that were coming towards them, and the figure of a man began to emerge from the darkness.

"In Delphi, tremors are frequent... Moreover, a negative effect of nature is not always a bad omen. In this case, the Gods have used this peculiar method to unite us." As he was saying this, he had moved into the middle of the circle that the others had formed. The beam of light formed a magical cone around him.

"But first, allow me to make the requisite introductions." Pointing to the blond man and the woman with auburn hair, he said, "Dromeas and Adhara, grandchildren of a great King and a brave Queen. They say that their mother conceived them with a God," he said, sarcastically.

Siblings? Raiko felt a pang of joy in the knowledge that this couple's relationship was purely fraternal. He did not yet want to ask himself the reason for his happiness.

The man's tone and his gaze softened when he approached the woman with white skin and black hair.

"I bow before you, my beautiful lady. Roxana of Petra, Princess of the Rose City of the Desert. You have the gift of giving life to stone, a gift that your ancestors possessed since time immemorial," taking a pause, he added, "With her, Ammos, her most loyal companion," saying this, he stared into his eyes. "Do you have anything to add?"

A too quick and too strong "*NO*" was his reply.

Looking at Raiko, he said, "Do not believe that I do not know your story. You are Raiko, only Raiko for now. Descendant of the great merchants of the Council of Zion of ancient Phoenicia. Your ship has sailed all known coasts of the Mare Nostrum... thanks to that, and to your encounter with a particular Goddess, you managed to amass a certain fortune. Yet, after that, family complications caused you to lose what was rightfully yours," he was silent for a moment.

"My name is Heptos," he introduced himself, "and I am the oldest of Apollo's priests," and he took a small bow. "Do not think that this meeting has been by chance, the Gods have brought us together. Just as the prophecy predicted, finally, the seven chosen ones have been united."

Then he said, pompously, "The mission for which you were born is about to begin."

CHAPTER SEVENTEEN

Flavia took her son out of the brass tub with a protective movement. It was the first bath she had given the little one since he was born, and the child had put up a good resistance to the immersion in water. With the care that only a mother could give, she brought him to her chest and sat down near the chimney so that the fire would warm them.

She and her husband had arrived in Pergamon from Rome one year before. They were part of a group of merchants who had started to do business in the area when the city became a Roman province. They lived in a neighborhood for the most part populated by Roman citizens like them, who enjoyed their lucrative activities.

While she was drying the baby with a wool blanket, the flame in the chimney went out. Flavia looked at the extinct fire, worried. As a good Roman, she knew that her duty as a woman was, above all, to protect and maintain the sacred fire in her home. This was a deep-rooted tradition among Italians. The chimney in the home was not only for cooking food, it was the altar where the head of the family offered his prayers and his sacrifices. It was a bad omen when the fire went out.

She put the child into his crib and, from a chest that was leaning against the wall, she took out the concave mirror that she would have to use to light the fire. The task was tedious and difficult. With a frustrated sigh, she opened the window; she needed to reflect the sunlight to the mirror, and from there to the splinters of wood to make fire. This was a technique that her mother had taught her when she was very young. It was the most important lesson that any Roman woman would learn, if she wanted to be the woman of respect in her own home.

A fierce noise was sounding through the open window. It was strange to hear such cries in this quiet neighborhood, where only the cats called a fight. When Flavia leaned out to see where the confusion was coming from, the shout from a man stopped her.

A slave, tall and muscular with a tattooed face, was holding his head down, waiting respectfully until Flavia gave him permission to be able to speak.

"What's happening?" Flavia asked.

"A crowd of people are entering houses by force, *domina*."

A cold hand embraced Flavia's heart. She glanced at her son's bed and, after being reassured that the boy was safe in his crib, she went swiftly up to the terrace. From there, she looked attentively at the streets of the district where she lived.

Just as the slave had said, there was a crowd armed with sticks, broken swords, kitchen knives, and improvised weapons, beating and tearing down the houses that surrounded them. The noise was a cacophony of yells, insults, and threats that would turn into cries of triumph when they would finally overcome the resistance in one of the homes.

Flavia shook with fear in the face of the spectacle she was seeing. Her husband was not with her; he had left very early to deliver an order, and she was alone with her little son, and Livio, the slave. She ran down the stairs, back to the main room where she had left her baby.

The slave who had given her the news was there, waiting for her orders. Flavia had to think quickly.

"Oh, Livio! What can we do?"

"We must flee, we cannot confront the crowd. I blocked the main door with some furniture. It will take some time to break it down, *domina*."

"Well done, Livio! We will escape through the back door."

Without stopping to think, Flavia took the child in her arms and went towards the kitchen where there was a door that gave access to the back exit of the dwelling.

The three figures left through the back alleys that joined the houses. These were still partially empty of the people who were shouting in the main streets.

As she ran through the narrow passageways, with her baby in her arms and her faithful servant in front of her, Flavia tried to understand what was happening. The city was under the rule of Mithridates. Who could be attacking them? The crowd that was carrying out the attack looked like the ordinary residents of Pergamon, and not soldiers of any foreign army.

As she ran behind the protection of Livio, she began to notice that not all the houses appeared to have been destroyed by the mob. The crowd was methodical, and was not damaging every one of the houses of wealthy lords. On the contrary, many were ignored, and the owners were calmly watching what was going on in the streets from their windows. Only the houses of Romans were being invaded and sacked.

Like a bolt of lightning it dawned on her what was happening. *They were the target of the attacks*, and before she became paralyzed with fear, she knew what to do.

"The sanctuary!" Flavia shouted with all her strength, so that the slave would hear her. "We must go to the Sanctuary of Asclepius." Their only hope to be saved would be if they reached the temple and asked for *asylum*.

The temple of Asclepius in Pergamon was a pilgrimage site for the followers of the Gods of the Greek pantheon. Asclepius, son of the God Apollo, and a high-ranking man with the status of God because of his expert cures, owned the most beautiful temple in the city. Nobody would dare touch them if they asked for asylum in this temple. They would be safe there.

As she ran, her skepticism grew; the corpses she saw on the ground were dressed in linen togas and old-fashioned Roman sandals. When she reached the center of the city, her suspicions were completely confirmed. Under the cry "Death to Romans!", the crowd was sacking renowned establishments of Italian origin and, as soon as they were empty, burning them. A group of youths was beating an old man and his wife with venom, as they tried in vain to protect themselves from the ground with their hands.

Flavia held her son even more tightly against her chest and the boy started to cry.

"Hush, quiet, little one," she said to him, while tears of fear and pain ran down her face. Her vision was clouded but she was able to move safely between the crowds because she was following Livio, who was so corpulent that he acted like a shield, defending both her and her child.

Finally, she could see the silhouette of the temple of Asclepius in the distance. She realized that many people were running from different directions, seeking help under the same

94

roof. Less than six feet away, a group of three armed men with spears confronted them. Livio stood his ground.

"Be happy, slave. Today you will be free. Today we will wipe from the face of the earth all the Romans who live here and exploit us. Join us, kill this bitch and her child, and you will be rewarded."

Livio stopped in silence as he stood looking at the men, as though he were evaluating the offer. Only these three men separated Flavia from the temple.

Livio turned around to the woman and gestured toward the temple.

"Run, *domina,* save yourselves," and as he said this he took out a small dagger that he had in his belt and attacked the man closest to him. The man moved back, but not far enough, and the dagger wounded him in one side.

Livio was a strong slave, who came from the region of Thracia. He had learned to live in the streets, and he knew how to defend himself. This was not his first fight and it would not be his last.

Flavia summoned her strength from wherever she could, mentally thanking Livio for his bravery, and blindly running towards the building. Her arms were numb from carrying her baby all over the city, but the idea of finding shelter gave her the energy she needed to cover the distance that still separated her from the building.

She ran as fast as she could, while Livio confronted the two men who were still standing and, without looking back, she climbed the stairs of the temple and entered the enclosure shouting, "ASYLUM!"

The picture she found inside was desolate. The majority were woman and children of all ages. The sobs of the frightened children overlapped the weeping of the women and the few old men who had managed to reach there.

Flavia recognized two or three of the women who were there and she went to them. Instinctively they all hugged each other.

"What is happening?" she asked.

Nobody knew the answer. Nobody understood why the crowd was attacking Roman and Italian civilians. People with no military training and without arms, who lived their lives like normal citizens among other races.

"But we are safe here," she said with conviction, trying to inspire all those who had reached the temple in a vain attempt to save themselves. "It is taboo to kill anyone in a sacred temple. Nobody will dare to touch us."

But not enough time passed to allow her voice to echo in the walls of the sanctuary when her worst fears turned into reality. A group of armed men with pointed swords entered the enclosure, shouting slogans of hatred and death.

"No!" the women shouted, clinging onto their children in a hopeless effort to protect them. The old men started to offer their lives to their Gods.

Flavia maintained a stoic calm, looking her executioner in the eyes, daring him to kill her while she sustained her gaze. But there was no compassion in them, those dark pupils reflected only hatred.

The man raised his sword and, with one single thrust, crossed through Flavia's heart and that of the child at her breast. Straight away, many other swords joined in and, shining in the air like a badly synchronized choreography, they lowered violently to cut short the lives of everyone, absolutely everyone who was there.

It mattered not if you were a man, a small child, a defenseless woman, or an elder asking for mercy. All were guilty of being Romans; they all had *Death* written in their future. And in this way, the Temple of Asclepius, known and respected in ancient times for possessing the strongest tradition of asylum, came to know the blood and hatred of human beings.

It was the year 88 Before Christ. Rutilaos Rufus, a Roman who lived in the region, was one of the few survivors of the massacre, and he related the events with the luxury of details.

Mithridates carried out his plan in an incredibly perfect way. The massacre took place on the same day and at the same time across all of Asia Minor, without any suspicion on the part of the executed. No one would ever know how he was able to achieve such perfect synchronization.

The only necessary requisite for death was to be a Roman citizen. Everything they owned was seized; their properties were confiscated, their credit cancelled and their slaves freed and quickly incorporated into the army of Pontus. Not even their sullied bodies received any form of respect; their remains were delivered to beasts and vultures in a macabre feast. Whoever dared to protect a Roman, or tried to at least give him a dignified burial, would be cruelly punished.

Historians do not have a concrete number, but the lowest estimates were 80,000 to 150,000 lives. This infamous deed is written in the pages of history as the Asiatic Vespers, when all Romans were wiped off the face of Anatolia under the orders of Mithridates, later known as "Mithridates the Great".

CHAPTER EIGHTEEN

When news of the massacre reached Rome, the Senate, the army and the people erupted in a fit of rage. Such an affront would not go unpunished. Although there was an internal war in the Republic, they drew straws to decide which of the two consuls, Marius or Sulla, acrimonious enemies, each one a leader of the factions in dispute, would go to Asia Minor to reconquer the kingdoms and give Mithridates his just reward.

To the King of Pontus' misfortune, the chosen one was Sulla.

Lucius Cornelius Sulla was tall and well-built, with white skin, blond hair, and defiant blue eyes. His face had red marks, and it was not known it if was for that reason, or for his strength of character, that he was known as the Red Commander. Although of Patrician origin, his family had fallen on hard times and the young Sulla had grown up on the streets, among artists, musicians, and dancers. However, clever like no other, the astute Sulla, with his handsome face, managed to find a wealthy prostitute who fell madly in love with him. She left him all that she owned in her will, and soon, with this money and his good family name, he was able to join the army.

From the moment of his arrival in the army, Sulla shone like the great leader and strategist that he was. One after another, his victories ensured that he was crowned one of the most admired military and political figures of his time.

He and his armies had barely set foot on Greek soil when the Hellenic villages, which had united with Mithridates in the massacre of the Asiatic Vespers, surrendered to his army without them lifting a sword. The force that this man emanated from all his pores was that imposing. Sulla retook many of the Greek territories in his path without lifting a weapon, but with his presence alone. Only one city rebelled against the Red Commander. Only one, Athens. And she was paying very dearly for the consequences.

Lucius Cornelius Sulla looked at the walls of Athens in front of him. These walls were damned strong! They had been built a long time back in the era of Themistocles, when proud Athens had confronted Persia, and they were made of solid limestone from the local area. Surrounding the whole city, the walls measured twenty-five feet high, with a thickness of seven feet.

In the frenzy of construction, they had used all the stone available. The Athenians had taken headstones from the cemetery, and columns that should have belonged to the temple of Zeus. The citizens thought it was a more sure form of protection to use the stone in the wall than in the construction of the temple, confident that Zeus would approve of their intentions.

At certain distances, they had built towers that were fifteen feet wide and that stretched ten feet above the top of the wall. Soldiers from the Athenian army were posted on top of these towers; they constantly monitored every movement of the Roman troops outside.

The Romans had tried to demolish them using battering rams, but they had not been able to make the slightest dent. They were going to need their best engineers to construct equipment that would destroy these walls.

At least he had time, Sulla thought, resigned. He knew that the Athenians were weakening due to lack of food. He had blocked all the supplies that might come from Piraeus, and by now there should neither meat nor grains left inside these arrogant walls.

Sulla was in the central pavilion of his encampment, meeting with his centurions. For the umpteenth time, Lucius Licinius Murena went over a map that showed the perimeter of the city. Impatient, Sulla lifted the flaps of the door, stuck his head outside the tent, and, in an authoritarian voice, he said to one of the soldiers who was standing guard, "Call Cassius. Tell him to come this instant."

"Yes, my Lord," and the soldier hurriedly went to look for the chief engineer.

Only a few minutes passed before a short, stout man, loaded down with papyri, entered the tent where the Roman Consul awaited him.

Without waiting for any greeting from the man who entered, Sulla addressed him.

"Cassius, I need a way into the city," he spoke to the engineer with urgency.

"I know, my Lord," and with a smile he went on, "I have been spending time working on an idea, and I believe I have an answer to your request."

Cassius unrolled a papyrus that he had brought with him on top of a folding table in the center of the tent. Once he had secured the corners with weights, he began to explain his design in detail.

"At present, we have catapults that can launch five pound projectiles a distance of two hundred and twenty yards. When we make these catapults, we imitate the tension generated by an arrow, taut in a bow." Cassius stopped his explanation, looking at the faces of the generals in the meeting to confirm that they were following the details.

Sulla gave a slight nod of affirmation, forcing him to continue.

"So then, if we want to launch heavier projectiles with superior impact, we must succeed in making the force stored in the rope that launches the projectile much greater."

Pointing to the sketch of his catapult, he continued, "I have designed a catapult capable of launching projectiles of at least ten pounds. If we launch a constant shower of projectiles of this weight onto a concentrated area of the wall, we will succeed in creating the impact we need," he took a breath, and while he was tracing his fingers over the plans, he explained, "To be able to achieve this torsion we will tie mules to the machinery."

Sulla was following Cassius' explanation and a smile appeared on his face.

"Excellent! Good work, Cassius," he said euphorically.

The engineer was brimming with poorly hidden pride. He

took out another papyrus and displayed it.

"I also want to show you this." He spread out the second papyrus and began to explain, "These are light, but very resistant, towers. We could build them high enough, and with enough capacity to support more than one hundred soldiers at a time. This way, when we move this structure to the ramparts, we will be able to reach right to the top, and because of our numbers, we will overcome the few guards watching that stretch."

Sulla laughed, exalted.

"Excellent, excellent!" and with a pressing voice he said, "Start construction immediately."

At that point, Cassius felt embarrassed. He looked down and, in a worried voice, he said, "My Lord, we still have many catapults to build if we want to accomplish a true avalanche over the ramparts. There are many supplies we need - rope, tools, mules...."

"That is not a predicament; many cities have surrendered on our way." Turning to his first in command he said, "Murena, take a legion of your men and go to all the regions we have passed through, and demand that they give you the supplies and mules we need. Thebes surrendered too, demand weapons and metal from them, anything they have left over. This way we will ensure that they do not use them against us."

"Yes, my Lord," his loyal soldier replied, and he swiftly left the tent to carry out his task. Nobody could allow himself the luxury of making Sulla wait.

Amazed, Cassius continued.

"My Lord, we are going to need wood too, a lot of wood. Where do you think we can find it?"

Sulla kept looking at the engineer, his hands were on the folding table and, once more, he looked at Cassius' plans. His eyes were delighted with the engineer's meticulous designs. Punching the table, he went out of the tent and crossed the encampment. He headed for the forest that surrounded Athens. The generals and the engineer instantly followed his footsteps, without saying a word.

Sulla pointed at the immense olive grove behind his encampment.

"From there," he said, pointing with his finger. "We'll take the wood from there."

The men looked at him in surprise, nobody daring to answer. Plucking up his courage, one of the generals said, "But my Lord, this is the sacred forest of the Academy and the Lyceum. It is a forest consecrated to the Goddess Athena, and it is part of the glory of Athens. Socrates, Plato, and Aristotle gave classes under those olive trees. Cutting those trees would be considered sacrilege!"

Sulla listened to him with his eyes riveted on the trees. Without turning around to look at him, he answered through clenched teeth, "It would be a sacrilege to go home humiliated by defeat. That is the only sacrilege that we cannot allow!" He turned to Cassius and he gave an order. "Gather a group of the strongest soldiers, give them axes and tell them that I, Sulla, do not fear the anger of the Gods."

Fearful or not, Sulla awoke the fury of one Goddess in particular. From above, Athena went into a rage when she saw what Sulla's soldiers were intending to do. How dare this mortal touch her sacred trees! That forest was created the day she won the joust against Poseidon, and she delivered the olive tree as a gift to the Athenians. She would not allow this arrogant foreigner to insult her dear forest. Rapidly, Pallas Athena went to Zeus. She was his favorite daughter, her father had to listen, to support her legitimate complaint, and to help her to stop this happening, the Goddess thought.

Mortals and Gods never knew which side of a dispute Zeus was on until it was over. Able like no other, the great God managed both sides out of the corner of his eye, until he decided who the winner would be, and moved the balance in his favor.

Zeus received Athena and, trying to placate his daughter's anger, he heard her complaint and agreed to intervene in the conflict.

From his temple on Olympus, Zeus looked towards the forest of the Academy. A group of soldiers, with recently sharpened shining axes, was moving towards the grove. The men stopped in front of the trees and looked at one another. One of the men moved forward valiantly, lifted his ax, and nailed it into the trunk of a twisted olive tree in the first row.

With his daughter's gaze fixed on him, Zeus put out his right hand, moved his fingers in the air and, with a whistling sound, a flash of lightning appeared in the palm of his hand. The bright, electric flash began to emit sparks that burst into the air. He lifted his arm, and with a precise aim, he shot it at the poor soldier. After suffering the impact of the divine shot, the poor wretch dropped to the ground, dead. Athena smiled with delight.

However, I, who know how this story unfolds, can tell you that Zeus, in this dispute, was not sympathetic to the cause of the King of Pontus and his allies, even though the allies were Greeks. The Romans were always among his favorites. While he let his daughter see that he was fulfilling his promise with his right hand, sending the sudden and fatal ray, what Athena did not realize was that with his left hand he manipulated the position of the body of the fallen soldier, sending a message of confidence to Sulla's army.

When Sulla's camp heard the flash and saw the poor man lying on the ground with an ax in his hand, a sense of despondency overcame the troops. Sulla approached the corpse and called his augur.

"Calcas, can you tell me if this is a bad omen?" He spoke in a loud enough voice for all his men to hear. "Have we awoken the anger of the Gods by cutting this tree?" He looked straight into the eyes of his fortuneteller. Calcas looked back bravely, knowing that his answer could change the disposition of the army. He was aware of the responsibility that rested on his words.

The augur took his time to answer. He looked at the corpse meticulously, went to it, walked around it in circles, and then said with a smile, "No, my Lord, on the contrary, it is a good omen," and pointing to the man's head he continued, "look, when he fell to the ground his head rested in the direction of Piraeus," and he went on in a triumphant voice, "that means you will win the battle in Athens just as you will in Piraeus."

"Then get to work immediately," Sulla shouted at his

soldiers. "I need these devices to be ready as soon as possible."

And before the stunned eyes of Athena, the soldiers swiftly took up their axes and started to cut down the trees.

Most of the woods had been cut down, and squadrons of soldiers were building the infernal war machines under Cassius' precise orders. The engineer estimated that they would be ready in a few weeks. Sulla had sent a squadron to go around the perimeter of the walls one more time, and now he saw them approaching him.

"Sir, we have circled the walls and we still have not found any sign of a fracture," they said, regretfully.

Time, Sulla knew it was only a matter of time. When the Athenians began to soak leather in water to be able to chew on it, when they had eaten the last rat, when the cramps in their stomachs started to blur their vision and their frame of mind, that would be the moment. And he would wait. *Yes, in the name of the Gods he would wait!* He would take revenge against the Greeks for having united with Mithridates' cause against Rome, and moreover he would make off with the treasure he sought.

The Treasure. He had known of its existence since he was a child and, now that he was a man, he still dreamed of finding it.

He remembered when he was a young boy wandering the streets in the poor part of Rome. They were not the same streets where his father and his ancestors had grown up. After his family had fallen on hard times, Lucius Cornelius Sulla, his mother, and his siblings had moved to the run down part of the city, which was crammed with brothels, taverns, and markets for the working class.

He remembered, as a child, running through these streets that smelled of pork fat and urine. Together with other children, he would throw stones at the windows of the brothels. The windows were shut even after midday, as they protected the prostitutes from the sunlight, and let them regain their strength after the previous night's work.

Due to the incessant throwing of pebbles, one prostitute in a nightgown stuck half of her body out of the window. Shooing them away, she gave them a chance to see a breast that escaped from the woman's flimsy clothing, as she bent over to yell at them and pour the contents of the chamber pots on their heads.

How different those streets looked by torchlight!

At night, those streets transformed into passages of magic and entertainment. The roads were filled with artists, jesters, magicians, clowns, dancers, charmers, and prostitutes. The jubilation of music, the smells from meat frying on small stoves on the street corners, the laughter of the passers-by, and the occasional drunken brawl were all common features in the evening landscape in this quarter of Rome.

But the attraction that most caught the young Sulla's attention, after the prostitutes of course, was the aged Locutius. Locutius was an old, toothless troubadour who had pale white eyes because of cataracts. He would sit at a corner, his usual corner, with his back against the wall, wrapped in his old cape that had at one time been red. For a coin, he was able to recite any poem the spectator requested. His miserable expression transformed as soon as he started to speak, since the power of his oratory was such that he captured the attention of his entire audience when his voice gave life to one of his narrations.

Sulla listened to him from afar, and carried himself to fantastic places in the company of Heroes and Gods, Kings and Amazons. By listening to him every night, he had learned the verses of the Iliad, the Odyssey, the Aeneid, and many other works by famous authors and philosophers. Among the diversions of the night, there was always one soldier, one drunk, or one rich shopkeeper, who would toss a coin in the little clay pot that Locutius kept at his feet, and he, like a festival robot, would systematically begin narrating and not stop until he had recited the complete work. The older troubadour was the closest that the young Sulla came to going to school.

The clay pot became a temptation for the bullies in the neighborhood. After a particularly lucrative night for the old man, a couple of boys approached the corner where the old man was sitting. They were two loud-mouthed brothers, very tall and with scars on their faces. The older one had a nose bent from the many breaks it had suffered in street fights.

This was the one who closed in on Locutius, and, giving him a surprise kick in the stomach, he shouted, "An old man like you with no teeth does not need so much money. You couldn't even chew the food that you would buy with these coins," he said mockingly, while his brother quickly went to take the money accumulated during the night. The old man began to sob and, covering his face with his hands, he cowered to avoid another kick from the big youth.

Sulla was watching the scene from the other side of the street, and a deathly fury unleashed in his chest. He ran across the street and, with a head start, he knocked over the good-for-nothing who was trying to take the money from the pot. Taken by surprise, the lad could not respond to the quick punch from Sulla that landed on his chin. He felt the acrid taste of blood on his palate. The knock was strong enough to displace a tooth. He put his hands to his mouth, and he started to scream with the pain coming from his bleeding gum.

The big kid, who was standing, started to tackle Sulla who was still on the ground, kicking him from his advantageous position. Sulla, light and slim, rolled in circles so quickly that he was soon out of reach of his enemy's feet. He got up nimbly, and placing himself behind his adversary, he grabbed the boy's neck with both arms and pulled it back, using his whole body weight like an inverted noose. As the boy sensed he was becoming asphyxiated, he opened his mouth and began to let out guttural sounds, trying to breathe and speak at the same time.

Sulla, still behind him, put his lips to his ear and said in a threatening voice, "You and your brother get out of here and never come back to this street again, deal?"

The overgrown boy's eyes were popping out due to lack of air and, with a faint nod, he agreed. Sulla then released his arms from around the boy's neck and let him go. Both boys took off running down the street. In the meantime, the old man had sat up straight, put the cape back on his shoulders, and looked at his savior with his milky eyes.

"I am indebted to you, boy," he said in a soft voice. "How can I pay you? Would you like me to recite any particular poem? The glory of Achilles, perhaps?"

"No," Sulla said, catching his breath. The fight had sucked all the energy from his young body, and he sat on the ground beside the old man to rest for a moment before going home.

"No, I know. Someone like you wants poems to be recited in your name. You are not the one to listen to the feats of other heroes," he said, with the smile of an omniscient one. "You will become someone great, with absolutely no doubt."

Sulla smiled. How he would have liked the words that the old man said to become true! He dreamed of joining the army, of returning glory to his family name, of no longer being a street child, and becoming part of the group of noblemen who governed the city.

"I am going to tell you a secret," the old man said in a low voice. "I am in debt to you and I always pay my debts."

He was quiet for a long moment, and Sulla thought that he had fallen asleep. In a hoarse voice, he resumed the conversation.

"There is a Treasure waiting for a man of valor like you. A Treasure that will give great power to he who owns it. A Treasure for which the wise men would give their lives. A Treasure that has been waiting for years for someone to find it. "

And the young Sulla, sitting on the dirty street, listened to the old troubadour's words, captivated.

Just as the old Locutius had predicted, Sulla had accumulated triumphs and successes, returning glory to his family. But all throughout his military career, he had never forgotten the confessions that the old man had related that day. During all those years, he had never let up in his resolve to find the Treasure. He had followed various clues, and finally one of them had revealed the name of Apellicon of Teos.

He knew that Apellicon had taken refuge in Athens, under the protection of Aristion. He stared at the outline of the city in front of him. *So near and yet so far*, he thought with apprehension.

The words of the old Locutius came back to resonate in his ears. As soon as he took the city, he would take Apellicon prisoner and force him to hand over the Treasure.

Meanwhile, he had to end this war, and that was no easy task.

CHAPTER NINETEEN

Pilomenes saw the horses and their riders leave, and a sadness from the depths of his heart overwhelmed him. A tiny voice in his mind told him that it would be a long time before he would see his grandchildren again. Dromeas and Adhara, Zoe's twin children, had just set out on a long journey.

Dromeas had come to him a few days before, and informed him that he would leave in search of a teacher with a renowned reputation, who would help him to train for the Pythian Games, the competitions that took place in Delphi. He still had not reached the required age to start training, but he wanted to prepare himself in good time; that was what he told him. Pilomenes knew him well enough to know that it was not the truth. One year after the tragedy, neither Dromeas nor Adhara had been able to recover.

Before getting on his horse, Pilomenes called Dromeas to his side. He placed around his neck a fine gold chain with a pendant that proudly displayed the steed of Paphlagonia on a blue background. This was the emblem of his kingdom, and only the King of Paphlagonia could wear this pendant. Pilomenes handed it over then, without pomp, without witnesses, and without grand ceremonies. All very different from how he had planned it the year before.

He hugged Adhara tightly; she was the most intelligent creature he had ever known, and he felt very proud of her. *If only there were not so many women in the line of succession,* he thought, with a sense of unease.

"Look after your brother," he said and, with a mute gesture, she promised that she would.

Seeing their silhouettes disappear into the horizon, his heart began to fill with pride for his descendants, since nobody could deny their noble stature and their proud demeanor. Zoe would have been very proud of them – and Lisipe, too.

How Pilomenes wished that things had stayed as they were forever! That his only problems were related to the education of his grandchildren. However, destiny is something unpredictable, and when least expected, misfortune returns like an unwanted visitor.

Such a celebration should never have taken place, he now thought. It was an arrogant act to display his happiness so blatantly. The Gods considered it an affront, and they punished him.

The day after the banquet, the King got up early with a strange feeling of anxiety in his chest, and he headed for the pavilions that had been set up in the garden. While he was having a cordial conversation with his guests, a servant arrived with the news.

"Your Majesty, you must come immediately," he said in a whisper, without looking up from the ground.

"What is happening? " He heard himself ask.

"Dromeas, my Lord," He said, almost without a sound.

"What has happened to Dromeas?" he asked, concerned.

"I beg you to follow me to the stables."

Pilomenes hurriedly followed the servant to the stables, and then the scene exploded in front of his eyes. Dromeas was on the ground, hugging Zoe who was bathed in blood. The woman's chest had been pierced with an arrow, and seeing the vacant expression in her eyes, he knew that she was dead.

The boy had remained silent and motionless, but he was squeezing his mother's corpse to his body forcefully, and the frightened servants were trying in vain to separate them.

Pilomenes approached him.

"Dromeas, please let me help you," he said.

"No, go away!" Dromeas cried. "All of you go away!"

Various servants tried one more time to help him. They approached him timidly, reaching out their arms, but Dromeas, shouting with all his strength, separated himself from them without letting go of his mother's body. His look of madness frightened them.

Stepping between the crowds that had now formed around them, Adhara arrived. Perplexed, she stopped in front of her brother, and her eyes filled with tears when she saw the scene. She immediately understood what was happening. With a gesture, she ordered everyone to be silent, and she slowly approached Dromeas. She gently hugged both him and the inert body of her mother. Feeling the contact with his sister, Dromeas began to cry. Adhara pressed her lips to his temple, and she comforted him with a shushing sound. She whispered a few words in his ear, and finally, between cries of pain, Dromeas let go of his mother's body. Pilomenes went to him and, giving him a strong hug, he led him out of the stable.

Meanwhile Adhara had bent down beside Zoe's body, which was now stretched out on the floor, and an expression of horror altered her face. It was a few moments later that a servant read the girl's mind, and turning his gaze in the same direction as Adhara's, he shouted, "In the name of the Gods, the arrow that stabbed her heart belonged to Lisipe!"

Zoe's heart had been pierced with a red arrow with three rooster feathers, an Amazon arrow, the same type of arrow that Dromeas had learned to make with Lisipe when he naughtily escaped from his teachers' classes.

The spectators let out a collective cry. Everyone looked around, trying to find the figure of the Amazon, but she was not to be seen anywhere. Pilomenes ordered an exhaustive search that day, and for many days afterwards, but there was not a trace of the woman to be found.

Pilomenes never knew what tormented the twins more, the fact that their mother was dead, or that Lisipe was her assassin. Lisipe, the woman who had raised them, who had sworn to protect her mother and Adhara above all else. Could Hippolyta have been so wrong? Pilomenes doubted it. What could incite Lisipe to kill Zoe and disappear? It did not make sense.

More than a year had passed, and in all that time, they had never been the same. Since the death of his mother, Dromeas had abandoned his weapons. The idea that one of the arrows that he himself had made had caused Zoe's death was something he could not bear. He could not hear Lisipe's name mentioned without a fit of murderous fury overwhelming him. But conflicting emotions thrashed around inside his soul. Dromeas had adored Lisipe, the old Amazon was his teacher, the model he followed, and the very thought that she had ended his mother's life tormented him. The boy devoted himself to running, and more running, in the hope that physical exhaustion would allow him to sleep at night.

For her part, Adhara also put her weapons to one side for a while, for the same reasons as her brother. She concentrated more and more on her abacus, her sand box, and her impossible circles. She had a sad and distant expression; she neither had understood what had happened. The palace of Gangra, so accustomed to hearing screams and laughter inside its walls, had turned into a silent mausoleum where every whisper echoed.

Dromeas had stopped under the shade of a large tree. He was breathing hard as he tried to get his breath back after the run he had just finished.

Running was the only way to break free from his demons. At night, he was unable to sleep, because of the urge for revenge flooding his soul. His mother had died by cruel and cowardly hands. Who would have wanted to end her life? Zoe was a sweet and inoffensive woman, a woman who had renounced being an Amazon so that she could raise her children. Worse than the feeling of revenge, was that of impotence. He did not know who the coward was. Everything had pointed to Lisipe, but neither he nor Adhara could believe it. But where was she? Why had she disappeared without the slightest trace? If he confirmed that Lisipe was his mother's assassin, would he be capable of killing her? The more these thoughts remained in his mind, the more he needed to run to release himself from them, and to find some comfort.

A voice distracted him from his thoughts.

"Drink some water, you'll have a headache if you don't," a young man said, as he approached with a goatskin flask of precious liquid. He held it out to Dromeas, who drank the whole contents in one go.

The young man who had come to him was Dimitri, the teacher who had come from Athens to instruct the children. He walked around the palace with nothing to do, as he could not fulfill the mission assigned to him. There was nothing he could teach Adhara, and Dromeas spent the whole day out in the open, either running or on horseback.

"Do you know that the way you run, you could attain great victories in Olympia or in Delphi? " he said, with admiration.

"What are you talking about?" Dromeas asked, without interest.

"About the games in Olympia. It is a custom in the Greek city-states to celebrate every four years with athletic competitions, singing, and poetry to honor our greatest God, Zeus." Seeing that he had captured the boy's attention, Dimitri continued. "A few months before, they proclaim a sacred truce, and messengers go to all the cities looking for athletes ready to compete. All wars are put on hold and, for one week, the representatives of each city compete fairly, without arms, and without death, to obtain the victor's crown of olives."

He paused, and looking the young man in the eyes, he said admiringly, "I have seen young people compete in races, and I am sure you could beat them all."

It bothered him to see this boy with such physical ability exhaust himself every day for a senseless obsession. Dromeas needed to recover from his loss, heal his wounds, and get on with his life. He could not remain locked in a routine without meaning.

"Anyone can participate?" Dromeas asked, curiously. Dimitri smiled. For the first time, the boy was listening to something he was saying with interest.

"No, to compete in Olympia you have to first complete the mandatory training in the city of Elis," he paused and continued, "but there are also games of this type in the city of Delphi. They are called the Pythians and you don't need such rigid training to take part. The stadium is inside the Oracle of Delphi."

"You said oracle? " Dromeas asked.

"Yes, inside the oracle," Dimitri replied. "The faithful go to the oracle to consult the God Apollo, about their future, their past, and their present. They go to look for answers to their doubts and advice for the future."

An idea began to form in Dromeas' head.

Yes, just as you can imagine, to say that he was going to Delphi to train for the Pythian games was only a half-truth on the part of Dromeas. The real reason for his departure was related to the questions he wanted to ask the Pythia. But this proved, one more time, that there is no such thing as coincidence, and that it was the twins' destiny to meet with the rest in Delphi.

CHAPTER TWENTY

The mission for which you were born is about to begin. The words of Heptos lingered in the room for an indefinite time, as they tried to seek approval in the mind of each one of the individuals present. Incredulous, shocked, and wary looks fell on the priest's face. He took advantage of the silence that his words had generated to repeat the prophecy that the Pythia had made a short while before:

> *The Seventh has revealed himself.*
> *Prepare thyselves! Hunger overwhelms the walled city*
> *and the Red Commander will avenge the Vespers,*
> *bringing desolation and grief to Pallas Athena.*
> *Seven they shall be to save the Treasure:*
> *Athlete without Laurels, Heiress of the Throne of Women,*
> *Sailor of the Goddess, Princess of the City of Stone,*
> *Priest of the Gods, Bearer of the Word,*
> *and Discreet Stranger.*
> *Miserable Traitor! You will appear from the circle of seven.*
> *Only the Word will save them,*
> *only the Seventh will know how to decipher it.*

Heptos spoke, bathed in the ray of light emanating from the roof that made his white beard shine in the sun. Specks of dust mingled with the light, creating the effect of frost around him. The same words, spoken again, echoed wisdom, legend, and magic.

They were still stunned by the effects of the tremor, by the appearance of the priest, and by the strangeness of his speech. They looked at him, without making a sound, until someone broke the silence.

"Treasure?" Raiko asked. The merchant in him came to light. "We will save the Treasure of Delphi? Who is the Red Commander?"

"Yes, Raiko, we will save the Treasure of Delphi," Heptos replied, smiling in the face of the man's enthusiasm. "But it is not as easy as it seems. Life, and prophecies in particular, present many uncertainties."

"Lucius Cornelius Sulla, known as the Red Commander, is facing a horrendous battle at the gates of Athens and, at the same time, his enemies in Rome have unleashed a cruel war against his followers. He has run out of money, and he knows that reinforcements are not coming." He paused, shrugging his shoulders, and continued, "You don't need to be a great clairvoyant to foresee that he will come to strip us of our treasures. We are very close, we have plenty of gold, and we have no defense. It is not the first time we have been sacked, nor will it be the last." He ended with a sigh.

With a complicit smile, he continued, "We, the priests of Apollo, have taken precautions, and therefore specific chests, filled with gold, silver, and jewels, are waiting to be placed in a safe shelter before the Roman troops arrive," and clicking his tongue, he said, "but that is not the treasure we want to save. That is not the Treasure in the Pythia's prophecy. There is a greater treasure, a treasure for which the wise men would give their lives. That is the Treasure we will save."

Heptos took a deep breath, crossed his hands on his chest, and began a speech that he had prepared some time before.

"Many, many years ago, man began to become conscious of his own existence, he began to become aware of his surroundings, he began to realize that he lived in a universe governed by certain laws, of which humanity was ignorant. At the same time as their minds awoke from their long sleep, a group of thinkers, philosophers and scientists came into being.

"While a great majority of individuals believed that nature was governed by capricious Gods, who moved the stars in the sky at their whim, or caused miseries and calamities to humanity, these men dedicated themselves to understanding and studying the beauty and order of the Cosmos. They tried to deduce the laws that governed the stars in the skies, the working of the body, and our very being. They made this quest for knowledge their religion.

"The Word was revealed to this group of men, and then they understood. They understood that what exists is the Universal

Mind. This is a live subject, capable of thought, and filled with creative energy that is always searching for more life. This Universal Mind possesses all knowledge that governs our existence, it is here, in the open, waiting for us to discover it.

"Some human beings succeed in gaining access to it, and obtain knowledge that offers help, progress, and evolution for humanity. But it is not an easy task. It requires work, concentration, compromise, and much humility."

Ammos and Roxana looked calmly at the priest while he was speaking; Adhara was looking back at him with suspicion. It was clear by their furrowed brows that Raiko and Dromeas were finding it difficult to follow Heptos' sermon.

"Do you not believe me? Is it hard to follow my talk?" he asked.

He then looked at Adhara. Heptos continued speaking, to her only.

"Before our time, there were mortals who succeeded in mastering their thoughts, who had control over their minds, who had the vision to be something more than what they were, and, thus, they were able to exploit their full potential. Who were they? Men of science, philosophy, astronomy. Men who knew how to use their minds in a magnificent way. How do you think someone like Eratosthenes was able to calculate the earth's diameter without moving from Cyrene?" With a slow nod of her head, Adhara agreed.

"Those wise men left us a legacy, an inheritance that we must treasure, carry on, and share… when the time is right." Heptos paused, and in an emotional voice, he said, "The Treasure, the real Treasure, is composed of five manuscripts produced in the handwriting of five great wise men. Five wise men who knew how to gain access to the Universal Mind, and to take immense amounts of knowledge from there. In them lies the key to deciphering the Word and only through the Word can a human being access Supreme Wisdom."

Dromeas broke the listeners' silence.

"Books? That's it, the great Treasure?" Dromeas asked, disillusioned. When he heard the word 'Treasure', he had imagined riches, adventures, power, and not the boring books in which Adhara was always absorbed.

"Yes, the real Treasure is in the knowledge that these books contain, and not in the gold or silver that we have stored here. If I wanted to save the gold of Delphi, I could do that by hiring three hefty men, burying all the gold possible in one of those places in the wilderness, and then killing them, so that they could not divulge the hiding place. I would leave in writing the exact location of the place in question, and try to pass the secret on to the next generation of priests. I am sure that, on the way, greed would corrupt some heart, and the gold would be wasted, used as fine brass sheeting for some individual's whim. It would be nothing but a mineral that passed through the hands of different generations, creating futile benefits only for the person who owned it.

"Knowledge is something different." Heptos continued with delight. "As soon as you share it, it never lessens, it multiplies. It finds fertile land in the right minds, and there it grows. It helps other brilliant minds to connect through Universal Intelligence, and it continues the process of evolution through humanity."

Adhara interrupted him, curiously.

"Which are those five manuscripts?"

Heptos smiled.

"That's the question that thousands of men have asked since the beginning." Trying to explain himself, he said, "the existence of the Treasure is known by many, but no one, absolutely no one, knows which books are the ones that will lead to deciphering the Word. A secret war has been unleashed to find them, a web of schemes and spies has been woven, but, until now, there is only conjecture with regard to which manuscripts belong to this select group."

"Secret?" Raiko asked in surprise. "Why does it have to be a secret?"

Heptos looked at him, amazed.

"Don't you know what happened to Socrates, one of the most brilliant minds that has graced the face of the earth? The greats of Athens made him drink hemlock for publicly doubting the existence of the Gods! We still live in a society where our

118

religion is not accepted, it has no place," he said, sadly. "On the other hand, the knowledge of the Word gives such a great power to he who proclaims it, that it is a huge temptation for men of great ambition."

"If no one knows which the five manuscripts are, how we will know?" Raiko asked suspiciously.

"Because we have him," said Heptos, pointing at Ammos.

Six pairs of eyes turned to Ammos. A man with long hair tied at the nape of his neck, and a thick black beard that covered half of his face. It was very difficult to interpret his expression. He stayed in his place, quiet and upright, listening as the priest described him.

"Ammos is a descendant of the first men who became aware of its existence, of the first men who received the Word." With a respectful gesture, Heptos continued. "He is the only one who can discern which the five books are. He is the Bearer.

"To be the Bearer, he has taken a personal decision, not without sacrifices." He looked into his eyes, and Ammos surreptitiously agreed. "To carry out his mission, he has to rely on Roxana, a magnificent creature, who was born at the same moment that Ammos made his sacrifice. Without her, he would not be able to achieve his undertaking. Every time a Bearer is anointed, she is born again, of the most pure, authentic matter on earth. She is reborn to give strength to the Bearer, to make it possible that the Word be proclaimed again."

Roxana was listening impassively to Heptos' words. She approached Ammos and gently took his hand in hers.

Heptos walked around the room and stopped talking for a moment. The listeners were staring at the priest, who was enjoying the attention he was receiving.

A silence, generated by six pondering minds, pervaded the shrine that was still full of dust and debris from the tremor. He knew he had to give them time to think, but he wanted them to join his cause so badly that he interrupted their silence, saying, "I have wanted to embark on this adventure because I believe the path to wisdom is such that it makes each person a better human being, at the service of understanding nature, the universe, our very species. To choose this path is, in my view, what makes man great, and what gives meaning to life. But this is, simply, my humble way of looking at things," Heptos concluded.

Another long pause followed the priest's words. Those present were digesting the long discourse that Heptos had given.

Ammos and Roxana understood that they were connected by a distant bond, a bond that was established in the beginning of time, when the Word was proclaimed for the first time. They had to make this journey together, their natures were powerfully united, and they needed one another to achieve their mission. There was no doubt on their faces.

Raiko was weighing up his situation. He had come to the Oracle of Delphi in the search of an answer to his destiny. Apparently, the God had answered, without sacrificed goats or ambiguous prophecies by the Pythia. He was presenting him with a unique opportunity. If the old man had as much gold as he said, he would be able to gather enough money to go very, very far away, and start a new life. He had heard talk of some islands famous for their breeds of dogs, beyond the Pillars of Hercules in the confines of the known world. Perhaps there he could leave behind his past, his family, his bad reputation, and truly start a new life. Yes, Raiko thought, he ought to feel pleased, having come to the oracle to look for an answer, and having obtained it. He just needed to clarify the tariff that he would charge.

"For such an ambitious undertaking as this, you need resources. Who is going to finance this?" Raiko asked, disdainfully.

"The gold of Delphi. Given my hierarchy, I have access to it and, as I told you before, I believe the correct way to use it is in the endeavor that I am proposing to you. Gold has limitations, knowledge does not. Gold is constantly being extracted from the earth, but the time comes when the mine is depleted. Conversely, the possibilities of knowledge are infinite."

"If you pay me a fair price, you can count on my ship, my Lord." For Raiko everything was reduced to simple negotiation. "I do not share your ideals. In my case, I am just someone you are contracting to provide a service. I warn you, the price will be high."

"I will pay," Heptos said.

Adhara was absorbed in thought. Of everyone in the room, she was the one who best understood the priest's motives. To know the Word tempted her. How many marvels to discover, having access to the fountain of Universal Wisdom! For her, it was a stimulating thought, to know that she was going to have contact with the work of so many wise men, new manuscripts to read, new problems to solve. Moreover, the idea of getting to know the world was an attractive one. She did not want to go back to Gangra, where everything oozed so much sadness. The change would be good for them, especially Dromeas.

She turned her gaze to Raiko. The only thing she was not sure about was the thought of sharing a journey with this man.

She put her fears to one side, and looking at Heptos, she said, "You can count on me for this endeavor."

Only Dromeas was not convinced. He, too, like Raiko, had come here with the hope of finding an answer to his questions, but he had found none. He would leave there before consulting the God, and he would set out on a mission of which he understood nothing, and which would be of no help to him.

"Why would you need me?" Dromeas asked. "You have Raiko's ship, Ammos and Roxana will help you decipher the books, and I am sure that Adhara will be of help in the selection of texts. She has spent her whole life among them. But I, I have no role to fulfill in all of this."

"You will have," Heptos said, solemnly. "We need you for this assignment and I guarantee you that you, too, Dromeas, heir of Paphlagonia, will have an important role to play. It was not in vain that the Pythia named you in the prophecy. We are all threads in this cloth that the Fates are weaving."

"But I have not found answers to my questions here in Delphi," he huffed, irritated.

"You will not find them in Delphi, you will find them on the way," Heptos promised.

Dromeas gave in, and lowered his head in a sign of consent. With a happy smile on his face, Heptos concluded, "Seventh, silence is consent. Your silence is the approval that you have joined our mission."

With a pragmatic gesture, he added, "Very well dear friends, we will prepare ourselves to leave." Addressing Raiko, he said, "Our first destination will be, with no doubt whatsoever, the site that has accumulated the greatest quantity of knowledge in our time. The city of Alexandria."

CHAPTER TWENTY-ONE

"Dear disciple, if such an assertion about the movement of the stars were true, it would discard the work of all the astronomers that have passed through this institution," Zenon said.

"Master, I believe I am right about this, even when it goes against the very fundamentals of this center of learning," Ignatius replied.

You cannot imagine the emotion I feel in my soul as I recreate this scene. Ah, the Library of Alexandria! If you could see it as I did in all its splendor... it was a temple dedicated to knowledge, dedicated to the magnificence of the human mind.

On the death of Alexander the Great, all his conquered territories were divided among his generals. One of them, Ptolemy, consolidated his position as King of Egypt, and formed a dynasty of Greek blood that would end with the suicide of Cleopatra VII, the Cleopatra of Julius Caesar and Marcus Antonius.

Under the Kingship of Ptolemy, he ordered the construction of what would become the greatest center of knowledge in antiquity: the Mouseion, a sanctuary dedicated to the muses, the Goddesses of art and the sciences. It was this King's intention that all knowledge in the world would be concentrated in his capital, Alexandria. They did not spare any type of resources, and the most brilliant minds in the whole world gave their time to work between these walls.

"In any case, I believe that Aristarchus of Samos was wrong when he said that the Earth moves around the Sun," Zenon replied, convinced that the heliocentric theory was completely absurd.

"But, have you seen his declarations? They are perfect. His observations are meticulous, his hypotheses, flawless." Ignatius did not want to end the discussion. "The only problem is that we do not have the original text. I have only been able to work with a few comments on his postulations."

A servant interrupted the heated conversation.

"Excuse the interruption, my Lord. There is a man here who wants to speak to you. He says it is very important," the servant said.

"Who shows up without having asked for an audience in advance?" Zenon asked.

"He did not want to say his name," the servant continued. "But he arrived in a carriage belonging to the niece of the Pharaoh."

"Berenice?" And turning around, giving his pupil a sardonic smile, he asked, "Another member of the royal family who wants to learn geometry?"

With the joke still in the air, Zenon ordered, "Let him come here immediately."

The Temple of the Muses, or the Mouseion, had been built following the classic lines of the Greek temples, in contrast to the palace and the royal buildings that had marked Egyptian styles. Doric columns of beautiful simplicity supported the temple. Inside, the nine statues of the muses, the Goddesses of art and the sciences, adorned the small chamber. The buildings, including the library, were annexed to the sanctuary. There were private conference rooms that connected through an open patio. Each one of these rooms was dedicated to the study of a particular subject: zoology, anatomy, astronomy, philosophy, philology, physics, engineering, and mathematics. There was also an observatory in the upper terrace, as well as dissection rooms, and a great dining room where the wise men enjoyed discussing the ideas to which they had devoted themselves. The sanctuary was surrounded by fountains, statues, a botanical garden, and a zoo of exotic animals brought from all corners of the world. More than fifty scholars were working in the sanctuary, under the management of Zenon, the present librarian.

There were two entrances to the building. The first was a large series of arches that joined one side of the temple with the main passage in the library, and continued to the garden. The other access was a direct path from the street, through a small room that served as a vestibule to the building. Cleantes was waiting in this room to be received by Zenon.

A short time later, the servant who had attended to him appeared again.

"Please follow me. The Director will see you immediately."

Cleantes followed him down the long passage to which the various rooms joined. At the end of this passage there was a double door that, when open, gave access to a large circular room of immense height. The walls were covered with shelves that supported the hundreds of papyri, carefully stacked on top of each other, from the floor to the towering roof. There were various movable ladders leaning against the shelves to enable access to the volumes that had been placed out of reach.

In the center of the room, there were various work tables with their respective chairs and essentials for study. Some papyri, unrolled, denounced the detailed analyses that the two people in the room had generously performed.

The first of the figures was a middle-aged man, whose gray hair had started to reveal his years, and whom Cleantes recognized as Zenon. The other person in the room was a young man. Cleantes deduced that he had to be one of the students of the library.

"Zenon of Alexandria?" he asked looking at the man.

Zenon replied, "Yes, that is me. And what request of the young Pharaoh should we address?"

"The reason why I arrived in a royal carriage is a story I will tell you after having completed my mission. The message I carry is from much further away. It comes from Delphi."

"Delphi?" Zenon asked curiously.

"I bring a message from my Lord, Heptos, priest of the Oracle of Apollo," Cleantes said as he delivered a sealed papyrus.

Zenon took the message that Cleantes delivered, but before reading it, he asked, "Have they deciphered the Word?"

Ignatius was staring at them, without understanding anything of the conversation that was taking place.

"No, my Lord, not yet. But the Seventh has appeared."

Cleantes replied.

"I can perceive that," he said, after a pause. "Only he can help us," Zenon breathed in relief.

CHAPTER TWENTY-TWO

Four cycles of the moon had gone by since they had settled outside Athens. The winter had been cold and wet, and the constant rain had turned the camp into a bog. Although they were well-trained soldiers, the morale of the troops was in decline. Besides, Sulla needed money to pay their salaries. He was waiting for reinforcements from Rome, both resources and more men, but this response was also taking time to materialize.

"My Lord, a merchant who sells oil is asking to speak to you." The soldier guarding his tent had approached him with the message.

"A merchant in oil?" Sulla asked, surprised. "Why does the head of supplies not deal with him?" he said, annoyed.

"My Lord, he insists that he can only speak to you. It seems he has come a very long way with his oil," the emissary said respectfully.

"From afar? There isn't enough oil in Greece for...?" The question stayed in the air. With a worried look, he headed to his tent.

When he entered the pavilion, he found a young man, thin and athletic, dressed in a long brown tunic that covered him right to his feet. Sulla's suspicions were confirmed. This could not be an oil merchant; all merchants were bland and chubby.

On seeing him, the young man bowed his head and greeted him, "Hail, Lucius Cornelius Sulla, Roman Consul!" he said, respectfully.

"You are not an oil merchant," Sulla challenged.

"No, my Lord, I am a soldier at the orders of your son-in-law, Quintus Pompeius Rufus," the man replied. He looked directly at the Red Commander and continued.

"I am afraid I do not bring good news, my Lord," the messenger said, and he delivered an amphora filled with oil.

Sulla took the jar in his hands and emptied the contents onto the floor of the tent. The oil trickled slowly from the clay urn, and, when only a few drops remained, Sulla smashed the pot against the ground. It broke into a thousand pieces, uncovering a type of deflated globe. Sulla lifted it from the ground and shaking it off, he held it with both hands. What he really had in his hands was the bladder of a pig.

In his campaigns in Africa, the Red General had designed a way to send secret messages. He took the bladder from a pig, which was very flexible and tough, he dried it in the sun, and then he wrote the message that he wanted to send on it. He would put the bladder in a clay amphora and fill it with olive oil. The liquid would make it expand, and it would stick to the walls of the pot, making it almost impossible to see the message.

Now, with the bladder in his hand, Sulla read the message that had been sent from Rome.

"What is written here is true?" He asked, incredulous.

The emissary nodded.

"Marius and Cinna have created a revolt in Rome, taking advantage of the fact that you are not there. They have arrested your friends and followers and they are displaying their heads in the Roman Forum for all to see. They have declared you Public Enemy of Rome, and they have put a price on your head," the emissary said, somberly.

"And my wife and children?" He asked, apprehensively.

"You still have good friends. They have put them under protection, and they are traveling in this direction. Nobody knows their whereabouts, not even I, my Lord. They were afraid they would intercept me and, by torturing me, they would obtain the information."

"Cursed bastards!" Sulla yelled. "And the wages for the troops? The reinforcements?"

The emissary remained silent. He summoned his courage and, looking directly at him, he said,"I believe they are wagering that you will die here, or that your defeat will be so great that you will not dare to return to Rome ever again, my Lord."

Sulla slammed the table in front of him with his fist and it broke in half, sending everything on it flying. The emissary cowered and withdrew to a corner, fearful of the disagreeable reaction that his message had provoked.

"Damn, damn, damn!" Sulla shouted. "I should never have trusted Marius' word. Never, never, never again!"

As he said this, he lifted the flaps of the tent door and went out into the open air. He walked around the encampment without direction, blind with anger and anxiety. A cold hand covered his chest. He was thinking about his family, his wife, and his children. In these times, they were some place on the way to his encampment, in danger of death or something worse. The secret message had warned him that they would arrive by land. They had left Rome by the north, and they were waiting until they could cross the sea to Dalmatia. They were taking a longer but more secure route. On asking the messenger, he understood that only his son-in-law and he knew of the journey they were taking. May the Gods not allow them to fall into the hands of his enemies, or he would find himself completely vulnerable! What type of general was he, that he could not protect his own? What sort of leader was he, that he could not generate due respect from his enemies? Rambling around, he ended up in the forest that had been cut down. He stayed there, looking at the empty spaces that were once filled with sacred trees, while a myriad of thoughts thronged his head. What should he do? Go back and defend his friends and abandon the soldiers who had given their all in this battle? In any case, how would he finance the return? Would he go back, exhausted and defeated, to a divided Rome? To continue fighting among themselves, while the enemies of Rome were gaining strength? Was this perhaps a punishment by the Gods for having reaped the sacred forest of Athens? Desperation filled his heart and, for the first time in his life, he did not know what to do.

Confused, he sat down at the base of a tree that had been cut and turned into a war machine, under his orders. He put his hands to his head and breathed deeply with his eyes fixed on the landscape in front of him.

He looked up, and a majestic eagle appeared in the sky. Her magnificent extended wings measured more than six feet long. She glided powerfully over the clouds, defying all the laws of nature. She opened her beak and squawked, making it clear that she feared no other living being, because she was above any creature on the face of the earth.

The Imperial Eagle, the symbol of Rome, Lucius Cornelius

Sulla thought. Seeing her fly in the sky, something shook inside the chest of this man of steel. Love of his homeland. He was, above all, a Roman, and his duty was to avenge the humiliation to which Mithridates had subjected his citizens. No man could crown himself as leader of his people, without bearing the intrinsic responsibility of defending them, of protecting them from their enemies. He knew that he would not respect himself, he could never sleep again, and he would never be able to give an order again in his life, if he did not seek revenge for the deaths of the eighty thousand innocent souls who had died only for being Roman citizens.

The spirit of Rome was like this eagle, grandiose and above all other creatures on this earth. That was when he found the answer that he was seeking. His duty at this time was for his men, for his homeland. He had to finish this war successfully, and only then could he return to Rome to confront the internal conflicts.

He trusted his family to the Gods, swore solemnly to avenge his massacred friends, and with a firm stride he returned to the camp. His mind was working rapidly, looking for tactical solutions to the problems he faced.

He would immediately send a message to his deputy, Lucius Licinius Lucullus. His deputy would have to leave straight away for Alexandria and draft a fleet of ships with enough force to face the fleet of Pontus. He knew that Ptolemy Alexander was sympathetic to Rome and would help him. This was the time to test his allies.

As for the money he needed, he already knew where he would acquire the resources that his enemies in Rome had denied him.

"Call Caphis, the Phocian," he said, in a loud voice.

The news of the revolt in Rome spread quickly through the camp, and the generals watched their leader's face with apprehension, hoping for a plan of action. Caphis instantly appeared in front of Sulla.

"Caphis, prepare a squadron of men and leave straight away for Delphi," he said, in a commanding voice.

"Delphi, my Lord? What task requires my presence in Delphi?"

"I want you to bring me enough gold so that we can end this war and return to Rome victorious," the Red Commander said.

"You want us to sack the Oracle of Delphi, my Lord?" the confused soldier asked.

"Better to look on it as though we are asking Apollo for a loan. It will be repaid at the right moment," he said, with a grim smile on his lips.

CHAPTER TWENTY-THREE

They decided to take advantage of the chaos that had arisen because of the earthquake to leave without the knowledge of anyone at the oracle. They agreed to meet at the port of Kirra, at the place where Raiko's crew had spent the night. They would each depart separately, so as not to arouse suspicion.

Heptos would take the old cart with the chests covered in straw, pulled by a mule. It was a risky plan that only one man, and an old man at that, would transport these riches alone, but the streets were full of soldiers, and an old peasant driving a worn-out wagon would not attract attention.

Raiko would be the first to leave the enclosure; he needed time to prepare his ship for the long journey, followed by Heptos. Ammos and Roxana would leave next, and the twins last.

"What is the name of your ship?" Heptos had asked.

"*Aphrodite*," Raiko answered.

"Well chosen," the priest replied, with a smile. Raiko grimaced by way of reply.

Adhara and Dromeas arrived at the port of Kirra on horseback, together with their servant. It had been easy to find the tavern that Raiko had named, since it was a very small port with only three inns for travelers.

The twins went directly to the dining room, a large salon with different tables and chairs place around a great stone hearth. The room was full of guests waiting to be served. Heptos, accompanied by Roxana and Ammos, was waiting in a corner, removed from the hustle and bustle. A maid brought them slices of warm bread, goat's cheese marinated in olive oil, basil and rosemary, and a jar of wine diluted with water.

"The crew is ready to leave," Raiko said, as he entered the tavern and sat down at their table. The precious chests had been securely stowed and were safely resting in the ship's hold.

Dromeas and Adhara said their farewells to the servant they had brought with them, asking him to tell Pilomenes that they had accepted Heptos' hospitality. The message was very vague as, for thetime being, they did not want him to know of the mission they had undertaken.

They left with the sun directly overhead. It was midday, and the port was full of sailors preparing their ships. Walking along the wooden pier, they saw different ships docked in the quay, but they did not see the name that Raiko had mentioned on any of them.

The *Aphrodite* was anchored at sea, very close to the coast. It was a merchant ship of medium size, with a rounded hull, and one single sail. A small boat was grounded on the sand, waiting for them.

"Please meet Odon," Raiko said, pointing to the hefty man on the boat. "He is my first man on board, and he is known as a great sea wolf. But don't be confused, it is not because of his skill, but rather his breath."

"It's a pleasure," Odon said, in a humorous tone, and with an exaggerated bow. "But it is better to be known for emissions from the mouth than from the behind."

Just as he said this, he realized there were two women in the group. Seeing Adhara and Roxana, his face reddened and, by way of an apology, he said, "I am sorry. You get covered in mud spending so much time in bad company," and he looked at Raiko.

Roxana and Adhara concealed a smile and together with Heptos, they got into the boat, with the solicitous assistance of Ammos. The four men pushed the boat to the water, and when it began to float, they jumped in. Dromeas and Ammos sat behind Roxana and Adhara. Raiko and Odon, in the third row, took the oars and began to row in the direction of the anchored ship that awaited them a short distance away.

It was a truly precious day, perfect to take pleasure in the open air, sailing the seas. The sunlight sparkled over the surface of the water, creating silver flashes that played with their sight. Amidst these flashes, they started to discern female figures, who were enjoying swimming and romping around with each other close to the ship.

Dromeas squinted to focus his view better. He was delighted to discover that the figures, which at first he had not recognized, were beautiful women with long hair, swimming and playing together, naked. He was leaning forward to enjoy the spectacle better, jeopardizing the boat's balance, when he heard a cry coming from Odon's deep throat.

"Keep still, lion cub!" the hefty man said in a bossy voice, "It's best you stay seated where you are, or you will make this small boat capsize."

"I wouldn't mind getting lost in these waters with such good company!" Dromeas replied, smiling and pointing to the shapes who were still dancing, adding, "They are beautiful."

"To you they are, because you still haven't heard them sing." He stopped rowing for a moment and gave him two pieces of wax. "You ought to put these in your ears. And you too," he said, giving other pieces of wax to Heptos and Ammos. Then, looking at Roxana and Adhara, he said, "You, beautiful ladies, will not need it."

Dromeas stood staring at the pieces of wax in his hand with interest. He looked up again at the women who were swimming around the ship, and then he understood. One of them went underwater and a shining fish tail shone on the surface of the sea, like a flirtatious farewell from its owner who entered the deepths. They were mermaids.

"Mermaids?" Dromeas asked, inquisitively. "What are they doing so close to the ship?"

"They, dear friend, are the ones who make this ship the most profitable business on the whole of the Mare Nostrum. They sing for the customs officials and we pass through with all the merchandise we want, without paying one single denarius in taxes to any kingdom."

"Why don't you succumb to their charms?" He asked, curiously.

"Who told you that we are immune to their charms? All the men in the crew have to use wax in their ears if they want to avoid being victims of the insanity of their charms," Odon said. Gesturing to Raiko, who was still rowing, he explained, "He is the only one of us who can listen to them and not fall victim to their magic."

"Under what heavenly design does he fall, that makes him immune to this ancestral magic?" Dromeas asked, and then, Odon told him the story.

Raiko was a young lad who was starting to learn the family business. His father was a rich Phoenician merchant who distributed his goods to every coast on the Mediterranean Sea. It was in the interests of his powerful family that Raiko started to learn the business at an early age, and his father decided to send him on a voyage to sell cedar wood on the nearby islands.

His ship stopped at a port near Paphos, on the island of Cyprus, and the sailors swiftly unloaded the cargo and delivered it. It was one thing to learn how to sail a ship, and a very different matter to load wood like a lowly laborer. Given his family background, he stayed at the seashore, waiting for the crew to return. Bored, with nothing else to do, he started to walk along the edge of the beach. It was a windy day and huge waves were crashing on the shore, creating a mass of spray.

He sat down for a moment to look at the sea. He saw that a wave of very large proportions was forming in front of his eyes. With momentum from the wind, this wave crashed against a rock, creating a rain of white, dense foam. From this foam, a beautiful woman, in all her splendor, emerged onto the glistening sand.

The woman had long blond hair that caressed her perfect body, barely covering her nudity. Her eyes were green like the sea behind her, and her full lips had a flirtatious pout. Still ankle-deep in water, she approached the spot where Raiko was sitting and said, "What is a young man as handsome as you doing alone on this beautiful beach, without any female company?"

"I am not alone," the young Raiko replied. "I am with you, that's like being with all the women in the world at the same time, beautiful Aphrodite," Raiko had recognized her straight away; a woman like this could only be a Goddess.

She let out a burst of laughter.

"Ingenious reply," she said, and then she moved slowly to where he was sitting on the sand, and started to trace her index finger over his chest, drawing incomprehensible shapes on his skin. Raiko endured the caresses, holding his breath while a myriad of sensations exploded in his body. He was secretly grateful that he had not kept quiet, and that he had been able to articulate an answer that she found amusing.

"They say that sailors are good lovers," she said, with a wolverine smile. "I think I am going to dedicate my entire immortal life to testing the theory."

She gently approached him and put her lips to his. Raiko remembered having stayed silent, spellbound, and entranced by the charms of such a magnificent creature. She smelled of the sea, of foam, of seventh heaven.

Aphrodite intensified her kiss and took the boy's hand, putting it on one of her voluptuous breasts. With a sensual gesture, she tossed back all of her long hair, exposing her superb nudity. With awkward excitement, Raiko embraced this perfect body with both arms and buried his face between the breasts that parted in front of him.

Only the gulls were witness to the encounter between the boy and his divine lover on that beach, where she had come into the world at the beginning of time.

While Raiko was sleeping off the exhaustion of love, Aphrodite looked over him, satisfied. His body was still young, but already developed and muscular. The smile of satisfaction displayed on his sleeping face.

"You have served me well, young man. You will make many women happy, and for that I will repay you." She leaned on him and planted a soft kiss on his neck.

When the boy woke up, he looked for her, but she had already gone. He put his hands to his eyes and then scratched his head to clear his mind a little, and he noticed that he had something around his neck. It was a short necklace made of small white shells, round and flat, very tightly strung together. He never used any adornments and this necklace was without any doubt a gift from the Goddess.

With time, he discovered that when he was wearing the necklace he was immune to brews, curses, love potions, or any other love spell. He knew the intentions of any woman who approached him in advance. He happily drank from any glass that any young girl offered to him, with an obvious desire to make him fall in love. None of those love potions worked.

The adornment proved just how valuable it was when one day the ship was sailing along the coasts of Sorrento. On its way to the Roman port of Ostia, the ship had skirted around the south of the island of Sicily, to avoid the dangerous waterway where the monsters Caribdis and Escila lived, and it had entered the beautiful waters of the Tyrrhenicum Mare from the west.

The beauty of the Italian coast was breathtaking. The coast, made up of high cliffs of limestone and quartz, formed an impregnable wall that rose up proudly in front of the sea. At the top there were small houses, built between wild orchids and lemon trees. They were tiny and innocent, defying their altitude. To one side the great volcano, *"He that Gives More Light"*, stood up like the proud guardian of these lands. The waters, a brilliant emerald green, were transparent and warm, pleasant to bathe in all year round.

Nevertheless, these beautiful waters were known for the large number of mermaids who inhabited them, and who forced sailors to fling themselves against the rocks.

The ship had diverted towards Naples when, on passing alongside the island of Capri, a sailor gave the alarm call. "MERMAIDS!" he yelled.

On top of three sharp rocks that stuck out defiantly over the transparent waters, three mermaids were sitting grooming their long hair with combs made of mother of pearl. They were three beautiful creatures. The first had half of her body in the water; she had light brown hair and blue eyes, her beautiful face with uniform features smiled invitingly. Across the shimmering waters, one could see that she had a tail of shiny silver scales.

To her side, there was a mermaid with blond hair and large honey-colored eyes. Her tail, of beautiful reddish tones, moved against the rock, shaking off little drops of seawater. The third was sitting on the highest rock, and she was the most beautiful of all. She had bluish black hair, and large green eyes. Her pearly tail shone ostentatiously in the sunlight, with iridescent pink and lilac reflections. These reflections emanated from scales encrusted with small flat pearls that were of uneven shapes.

As soon as the three mermaids saw the ship approach, they immediately took out their combs, and with provocative smiles, they began to sing their seductive songs, reaching their well-toned arms to the sailors in an attempt to entice them closer.

The sailors, who had already experienced the insanity that their songs would generate, had put wax in their ears. They were trying not to look at these beautiful creatures who had tossed back their hair and were shamelessly showing their naked breasts to the men.

Raiko ignored the warning; he did not cover his ears. Resolute, he climbed up to the railing of the ship to get a better look at these fascinating creatures. He brazenly took off his shirt and threw it on the ship's deck, and dressed only in pants that reached his knees, he dived into the water and swam quickly to the three rocks. When the captain of the boat saw him, he began to shout, begging him to come back; his master would flog them to death if anything happened to his youngest son. But Raiko, unaware of the fears that were tormenting the poor captain, swam to the spot where the mermaids were. He nimbly jumped on one of the stones and sat down next to them.

The mermaids continued singing and opened their arms, making gestures to tempt him, but Raiko was immune to their magic. Seeing that they had no effect on this mortal man, the mermaids became quiet and looked at him, confused.

Raiko spoke to them with a mocking smile on his face, "Hail, beautiful ladies! What are your names?" he said, beguilingly.

The mermaid with black hair was staring at him in amazement. Her deep green eyes reflected her surprise and curiosity. She looked over that face with handsome features, and then stopped at the choker he was wearing on his neck.

"You have met the Goddess, have you not?"

"Yes," Raiko replied.

"Well, I see that it was a very lucky encounter. You have given her great pleasure," she said, with a pleasant smile. "My name is Radne, she is Ligeia," she said, pointing at the mermaid with blond hair, "and she is Teles," she continued, pointing at the mermaid with brown hair.

Raiko stayed there talking to them for a while, establishing a friendship that would last for many years. When he realized that the ship would have to continue on its way, and would not be able to wait for him, he said goodbye and swam back to the vessel, where the sailors were looking at him in shock. From that day, it was known by all that there was a mortal man who was immune to the charms of the mermaids.

Raiko was listening to Odon relate his own story while he rowed towards the ship. It sounded strange coming from another person, and after so many years. He had to acknowledge that this necklace had been very useful throughout his life. This necklace had helped him not fall under the spells of the Serpent-Woman, he thought to himself. Still, all the help of the Gods had not prevented her from ruining his life.

When they were approaching the *Aphrodite*, the group of mermaids swam towards them. Flirtatious and bold, they approached the boat, to the delight of Dromeas who, even though he had filled his ears with wax, had not stopped looking over at them. The mermaids stared curiously at the people on the boat.

"Ready to board?" Ligeia asked, looking at Raiko.

"Yes," Raiko replied. "How have you been in my absence?"

"Bored," Radne answered, as she came out of the water, supporting half of her body on the boat deck. Staring at the passengers, she asked, curiously, "Who are they?"

Roxana turned her eyes to the beautiful mermaid with black hair, she returned the stare and a chilly current disseminated between them. The face of the stone princess assumed a serious look, like an unspoken warning.

"They are a few passengers who contracted me to take them to Alexandria," Raiko replied.

"Alexandria? That's a long trip," Teles commented from the other side of the raft.

Radne kept looking at Roxana with an arrogant air, and then her green eyes fell on Adhara. She looked the girl up and down with displeasure. It seemed she did not like what she was seeing.

139

"I don't think these stupid women will be able to survive the journey," she said, rudely.

"RADNE!" Raiko caught her attention with a poorly disguised smile on his face. He knew that the mermaids were capricious, that they wanted all the attention of the men for themselves, and that, above all, they hated mortal women. It was evident she was jealous of seeing him in the company of other women for the first time, boarding his ship.

The mermaid pouted her lips whimsically, turned around, and submerged her woman's body into the sea, leaving her fish tail protruding from the water. By way of farewell, and vengeance, she angrily slapped the fins of her tail against the sea, sending a stream of water over the boat and directly onto Adhara, soaking her. Her wet clothes clung to her body, and the chilly wind made her shiver. The girl was red with anger. To make matters worse, the others, unable to avoid it, had started laughing. Only Roxana kept staring at the spot on the water where the mermaid had disappeared, and a worried expression appeared on her face.

Finally, the boat arrived at the *Aphrodite*. The crew was leaning over the deck to welcome them. Ammos and Dromeas were the first to board the ship. They helped Heptos up first, given his age. From the boat, Raiko helped Roxana to climb up. When it came to Adhara's turn, Raiko offered his hand, and she replied condescendingly, "I told you before that I don't need your help. I am an Amazon," and, in her mind thanking Lisipe for all the training that she had subjected them to in the past, she pulled the rope that her brother was holding and climbed up to the railings of the ship.

"What that fickle mermaid did is not my fault," Raiko shouted, but Adhara was already on the deck.

"What an arrogant woman!" he said to Odon, who was smiling with pleasure at one of the few slurs his friend had ever suffered in his whole life.

140

CHAPTER TWENTY-FOUR

The catapults designed by Cassius were ready. The soldiers were gathering together stones and debris to make an embankment where they would get into position. The engineers wagered that, from a higher position, their range would be further.

Sulla looked at the ramparts from the outside, and began to walk around them one more time, unaware of the two pairs of eyes that were watching him surreptitiously. Two pairs of eyes that hated Aristion and were tired of the hunger and harassment of the citizens of Athens. Two pairs of eyes belonging to the dregs of society: two sets of eyes belonging to slaves.

Sulla was walking, with frustration visible on his face. There had to be some weak point in the walls; he had to get into the city as soon as possible, the concern for his family and friends had incited in him a hatred like he had never known before.

Suddenly a small missile hit his face. He turned to the right and to the left, but did not find any explanation for the attack. A few minutes later, another missile hit his head again; he looked up, and then understood that they were coming from the top of the wall, where two timid heads appeared over the edge.

"Bastards!" he cried. "Do you think those tiny pebbles could put a dent in me?" he said, lifting his fists in the air in anger. The two faces stayed still, staring at him without reacting, without moving, and so he understood. If those two individuals had wanted to harass him, they would not have thrown small stones; they would have sent arrows, or used a stronger weapon in their assault. Then, he realized that what they really wanted was to attract his attention.

He focused on the ground trying to find the missiles. The grass was tall, but sparse, and the soil was thinned due to the traffic of soldiers throughout the siege; there was more sand than vegetation, and moving his foot in the space around him, he found them instantly.

They were not stones, as he had thought. They were two iron pellets that had a small message wrapped around them. Sulla picked them up from the ground. He freed the small piece of papyrus and read the brief message.

KERAMAIKOS.

He looked up and two heads appeared at the surface. From their skin, Sulla realized that they were foreign slaves, probably from North Africa. Smiling, he waved at them.

"I will not forget you," he said, and he walked quickly to his quarters to meet with his centurions.

Sulla and his men surprised the Athenians on the first night of March in the year eighty-six B.C., almost eight months after leaving Rome. The date immediately preceded the Ides of March, when the Roman military corps would take their new oaths.

The catapults were lined up, one beside the other, in perfect formation. Thousands of soldiers whipped the mules that were laboriously pulling the ropes that bent the arms backwards. As soon as they were within reach, the arms were fixed to the ground with taut ropes, while the men placed very heavy pieces of stone bathed in tar on top of them. Under Murena's instructions, they put torches to the projectiles and the stones were set alight. On the cry of *Fire!* the ropes that restrained the burning projectiles were cut. The catapults, like an armada of machines, spat a shower of balls of fire onto the walls.

The tired and hungry Athenians were sleeping peacefully when they heard the pandemonium as their city was being thrashed. The first to realize were the residents of Keramaikos, since that was where the wall came apart in the wake of the feat of Cassius' powerful catapults. It was the weakest part, just as the slaves had informed Sulla.

The opening they made was big enough for all of Sulla's army to enter easily. Panic hit the souls of the Athenians when they heard the noise of trumpets from the Roman troops, announcing the capture of the city.

The Romans, tired of waiting such a long time outside the wall, launched themselves with doubled fury on Athens. Their swords ended the lives of everyone in their path. Fathers killed their wives and children, terrified at the idea of them succumbing to Roman vengeance. Sobbing women surrendered submissively to the soldiers, hoping that in exchange they would pardon their lives, or the lives of their children. The hungry and weak Athenian soldiers were no defense whatsoever in the face of Sulla's battle-hardened centurions. They were finally seeing the affront by Mithridates, and the long winter that they had spent outside the walls, avenged. Historians tell of rivers of blood that flowed down through the Agora, and of colossal damage to public buildings.

Sulla, who had led the capture, gave his soldiers a free rein to turn to pillaging, and he went to the government palace, where he was sure to find Aristion and his close followers.

The tyrant had been awoken by his guard as soon as they heard the first sounds of the attack, and he had escaped with a small committee to the Acropolis, at the highest part of the city. He had taken certain precautions and had hidden some supplies and weapons in the citadel. On his way, he burned the Odeon of Pericles, fearful that the Red Commander would utilize the wood for more weapons to use against him. Aristion was still confident that his great ally, Mithridates, would save him from this plight.

A group of soldiers informed Sulla of the tyrant's movements. However, he calmly told them that it was only a matter of time. Aristion could not escape from the Acropolis, and the supplies he had there would not last long. Now, no one would come to his aid. Athens had fallen.

Right then, he wanted to catch one other person. A person who had shown himself to be extremely elusive, but who was not going to get his way this time. With a determined stride, he climbed the steps of the government palace and went into the abandoned audience chamber. If he were smart enough, he would negotiate his life in exchange for giving Sulla what he had obtained in the Troade, and so jealously guarded.

The echo of his steps resounded on the marble pavement. His eyes had a momentary delay as they got used to the shade, and then he saw him. A solitary figure on one of the chaises longues along the side. Hearing Sulla's steps, he looked up, and their eyes met.

"Apellicon of Teos, finally we meet," the Roman Consul said. "You have something I want and you know it. You obtained it with intrigue and ill-gotten money. You have astutely hidden in Asia, and now behind Aristion. The time has come to give me what I so greatly covet."

CHAPTER TWENTY-FIVE

The anchor had been raised and the *Aphrodite* had set off on her voyage, accompanied from afar by the mermaids. Following Raiko's orders, the crew had put the boat in a sure wind, in the direction of Alexandria.

The ship passed by the large island of Crete, and sailed into the deep waters of the Mare Nostrum. Here, the journey became more difficult as it required great skill to sail the open seas. At the same time, the voyage would be at a more rapid speed, as they could count on the Etesian winds that raged with force towards the Egyptian coastline.

The days passed peacefully on those waters.

A pleasant camaraderie had developed between the crew and the chosen ones. Dromeas and Ammos willingly helped Raiko and Odon with tasks on the ship, which they did with much laughter. More so, Dromeas. The boy had recovered the jovial disposition he used to have before Zoe's death, and the memory of his mother was not clouding his mind all the time. Surrounded by companions, and busy with work all day, he was enjoying better times.

Ammos, with his strength and his ability to tie knots, had become indispensable on the ship. He too, seemed to enjoy the company of the others, but he was a person who kept quiet most of the time; he only spoke when it was absolutely necessary.

As for Adhara and Roxana, they had also become good friends. Raiko had put his narrow cabin at their disposal, and he was sleeping on the deck with the rest of the men, under the starlight. In the calm of the night, the two girls held long conversations; for being so different, they soon realized that they had much common ground.

Heptos was on the deck of the *Aphrodite*, looking at the great blue mass of water in front of him. His heart overflowed with happiness, he found himself on the path to fulfilling the dream of his father and his grandfather. In truth, it was the dream of a long line of his ancestors.

He was from a family of scholars; his father, grandfather, and others before them, had applied themselves to the study of astronomy, anatomy, and philosophy. He had always had an insatiable thirst for knowledge that flowed from the genes of his ancestors. A desire to learn.

Heptos was a boy when his father introduced him to the world of sciences; he explained to him that the universe was not governed by the fury of Zeus, or the skill of Apollo. Rituals and human sacrifices were meaningless offerings; the universe did not answer to the whim of the Gods, but to pre-established rules. The Cosmos responded to precise laws that had been designed, laws that had been planned by a Universal Mind, and his purpose in life was to engage in it, and to understand its magnitude.

Such scholars worked in select circles, separated from society. Their knowledge only carried weight as entertainment for kings, or, in some cases, as practical solutions for the construction of buildings or weapons. At no time could they take the place of Gods. Socrates was one exception, and he paid for it with his life.

Among that community, there was a well-known secret that there was a way to communicate with the Universal Mind. The Great Wise Men had already connected with this source of infinite wisdom, and they had left in their writings the clues as to how make that bond: The Word. And he and the chosen ones would soon decipher it. He was sure, he could already sense triumph.

From a very young age, he had tried to find out which were the five manuscripts that were judged to be the Treasure. He made contact with many centers of knowledge, he sent emissaries to analyze the work of other wise men, or to evaluate manuscripts that were for sale. It had been an arduous task, but he had succeeded in creating a map of the great works that had been produced in the known world. This endeavor consumed many years of his youth.

The day he heard the Pythia's prophecy, his heart burst with joy. In between her fervent words, he immediately recognized what the real treasure that the oracle spoke of was, and he felt happy that, by a strange twist of fate, it was he who found himself leading the group that would reveal the Word.

He gazed at the group of chosen ones. They were scattered around the deck; the men helping with the tasks on the ship, and the two women sitting in a corner talking to each other. *Anyone who saw them would think they were happy to complete this mission, but, who would the traitor among them be?* Heptos wondered.

Adhara was on the deck, smoothing wax on her wooden tablet so that she could start working. Roxana was sitting besides her, looking out at the sea. Some mermaids in the blue waters were trying to attract the attention of the sailors. Since they started the journey from the port of Kirra, it seemed that Radne had called on more of her species, and they were steadfastly following the ship, never letting her out of their sight. This situation pleased the men of the crew enormously, and especially Dromeas, who did not mind putting up with wax in his ears so that he could admire these beautiful half-women. It created a great many complications for Odon, as he had to lead a crew of deaf men, only able to communicate with them using signals. On top of that, the men were very distracted.

Roxana was looking at them with a troubled expression on her face.

"Why are you so worried?" Adhara asked.

"I don't like the mermaids, I don't trust them. They are ancient creatures with primitive, wild sentiments. Raiko is immune to them, but their souls, if they have any, are indomitable. They respond to their most basic instincts. They are egotistical and capricious."

Adhara frowned, she had had a bad experience with the mermaids and always tried to avoid them; every time they came around she moved away from the others and hid herself in a corner of the ship.

Roxana turned to look at her with a sad smile, while she watched her writing on her tablet.

"I feel strange without a piece of stone to sculpt," she said.

"Why don't you try with wax?" Adhara said, and gave her a small piece of the wax she had in her hand.

Roxana took the wax and began to mold it. Her fingers started to work quickly and diligently, and in a short time Adhara saw that Roxana had succeeded in creating the figure of a tiny swan. The girl was staring at the figure in her hands as though she was expecting something from it. Confused, Adhara asked her, "What's wrong?"

"I feel a power in my hands, a force that pushes me to take figures out of stone, or any other material, but I cannot give life to my pieces," she said with frustration. "I succeeded one time when I was a child, with a little cat that I sculpted, but it did not last long, and it smashed into pieces. Ever since then, none of my figures has had a life of its own."

Heptos, who was passing close by and had heard the conversation, approached the girls, and addressing Roxana, he said, "Don't worry Roxana. This power will come to you as soon as we are nearer to the Word. It will work the magic in your hands, you just need to be in contact with the five manuscripts," he was speaking in a whisper. "But, in the meantime, keep working, don't let the energy stop flowing through your fingers."

Heptos then turned to Adhara and to the tablet she had in her hands. He smiled, as a master would smile at his most outstanding student.

"Working as usual?" he asked, beaming.

"It is a problem *Pappous* and I were working on before I left, and I still haven't found the answer," Adhara said. The girl looked at the priest, puzzled. There was something she had wanted to ask him ever since that day at the oracle, but she had not dared. However, doubt was torturing her and, resolute, she addressed him.

"I have had a question to ask you ever since we met in Delphi."

"What dilemma pounds your mind, Adhara?" Heptos asked.

"Since that day at the oracle, when you recited the prophecy to us, you talked of the seven chosen ones, but I only see six of us, Roxana, Ammos, Dromeas, Raiko, you, and me. We are six, and not seven."

"Adhara, it is you who asks me?" Heptos shook his head despondently. "You still haven't realized who the Seventh is? Perhaps your mind is so wrapped up in questions of reason that you do not notice certain subtleties."

He turned his head to Roxana who had been listening to the conversation. The stone princess acquiesced with an imperceptible nod. She got up and, walking in the direction of the stern, she went towards Odon so that they could continue talking in private.

Heptos looked at Adhara again.

"The Seventh is a very special person. Even though it is true he appears to be someone who is wrapped up in himself, I do not doubt that when the time comes, he will fulfill his role in this adventure."

Adhara looked at him, both confused and guilty for not being able to understand, or to know more about what was being asked of her. Heptos felt sorry for this girl. She was too young to be put to the test the way he was doing it.

"Stop worrying, little one, when it is time I am sure the Seventh will act appropriately, and then you will know who he is." Heptos pacified her.

Meanwhile, Roxana had quietly approached Odon.

"Excuse me, do you have a piece of stone available on this ship?"

Odon, looking at her with a dazed expression that he could not disguise, answered, "No, my Lady, I am afraid that you will not find any of that material on this ship. If you don't mind my asking, for what purpose do you want it?"

"It's just that I feel the need to sculpt something," Roxana said softly. Her tone of voice was always serene and calm.

"I can find a piece of wood for you, if you like."

"Wood? I have never used wood, but perhaps it would work."

"I will attend to it straight away," Odon answered, diligently.

Odon went hurriedly to the stores to fulfill Roxana's wishes. As he took hold of the railing that led to the lower level, he met with an amused smile from Raiko.

"What a sweet tone of voice! I will go straight away, my beautiful lady," he joked, sarcastically. "I don't recognize you, you old sea wolf."

Odon was not in the mood for jokes. He hung his head with humiliation and, in a sad voice, he answered, "She is a beautiful, serene, majestic woman. Unattainable, like a Goddess."

"But there are Goddesses who are attainable," Raiko replied.

"Not for men like me, my Lord," he said, shaking his head. "Anyhow, she is far beyond that. She is not like you or I. Or like anyone I have ever known."

To dispel the weak moment that he should never have allowed, Odon responded to the affront.

"My feelings towards the lady are strictly platonic, but I see nothing platonic in the way you look at that one," he said, pointing at Adhara, and he continued walking towards the store, where he hoped to find a piece of wood for Roxana, and some tool that she could use to sculpt it.

Raiko followed Odon's gesture with his eyes and he saw Adhara leaning on the balcony, lost in her thoughts. Since he had boarded the ship, he had been too engaged to be able to establish a conversation with her. Moreover, she was extremely evasive, or was avoiding him for some reason he did not understand. He decided to go and speak to her.

"What are you thinking of so zealously?" he asked.

Adhara turned around and saw the tall figure of Raiko, with his amused smile permanently painted on his handsome face. Without wanting to, Adhara glanced at his neck where he wore the choker.

She had also heard the story that Odon told Dromeas, about Raiko's encounter with the Goddess. She did not know why, but an angry flame surged inside her as she thought how no mortal woman would come out well when compared to Aphrodite.

"I was thinking about the Seventh," Adhara lied.

"The Seventh?" Raiko asked.

"Yes, the Seventh. It is assumed that this mission will be carried out by seven people, but until now I have only seen six of us. I have asked Heptos and he told me that, in time, I will know. My brother doesn't even know who the Seventh is. Do you know?"

Raiko shrugged his shoulders.

"No, and in truth, nor do I care. Remember that I am only in this for the money. Heptos and I have agreed a fee for the use of this ship, and my duty is to take you safely to Alexandria or wherever you need to go. I do not believe in treasures, nor in legacies that need to be saved. I differ from Heptos' opinion, gold does *not* have limits. When it is yours, you are the Lord and Master of everything and everyone," he said, bitterly.

"You speak like a mercenary. When Heptos introduced you, he said you came from a noble family of the Council of Zion. If that is the case, why are you devoting yourself to piracy?"

"It's a very old story and I don't want to discuss it. I am Raiko, and only Raiko. A man without stupid ideals and with his feet firmly on the ground. A merchant who has made his fortune, thanks to his skills and his charms," he said, putting his hands to the necklace he was wearing.

As soon as he finished speaking, he regretted what he had said. He did not even know why he had said that. Maybe he wanted her to know that he was immune to love. He wanted to make it clear that he could dominate the power she exercised over him every time he saw her.

Can I, really? He wondered, now that he had her so close. *Perhaps this trinket no longer works*, he thought, frustrated, because what he really wanted to do, right then, was to kiss her. When he lay down at night, he could not erase from his mind the image of Adhara with wet clothes clinging to her body, looking at him defiantly. There was something in this woman that attracted him, that forced him to think of her all the time. He wanted to

151

hold her in his arms, to take her to a secret place, under the full moon, and whisper in her ear....

His thoughts abruptly came to a standstill when he saw the look of disdain in Adhara's eyes.

"I have never seen a man so full of himself," she exclaimed, indignant. "I imagine you must be anxious for this mission to come to an end. I am sure there will be some fickle and foul-smelling hake awaiting your return from this voyage that will make you rich and important. If it weren't for money, I do not understand how any woman could put up with you," and she walked away, bringing the conversation to an end.

CHAPTER TWENTY-SIX

The regiment was marching along the narrow paths that lead to Mount Parnassus. Caphis, the Phocian, had Sulla's order to plunder all the riches possible from the Oracle of Delphi. Behind him, there were fifty empty wagons, pulled by mules. Sulla had made certain that they took enough resources with them so that they could bring back all the gold they could find.

Caphis had met Sulla a long time back, when he was a young soldier starting out in the Roman army, in Sulla's campaign in Africa against Jugurtha. Since that time he had shown him absolute loyalty. He had no hesitation in joining him in this battle against the Greeks, his blood brothers. He adored Sulla, and his sympathies were with him. However, fighting humans was one matter, provoking the anger of the Gods was another. He was not feeling comfortable with this idea of robbing Apollo of his possessions.

Caphis was born in the region of Phocia, in Asia Minor, in a small village with sea views. He lived there throughout his childhood, until the time when his father, a prosperous merchant, decided to move his business to Rome. The young Caphis wanted to try out his chances in the army and he was soon under the command of Lucius Cornelius Sulla.

The Phocians were famous for their precision in business; it was not an accident that they had been the first people in humanity to mint coins and use them as a method of payment more than five hundred years earlier. Sulla trusted the skills the accountant had inherited from his father, and, for that reason, as well as his unconditional loyalty, he always held a special place among his troops. Now, on his way to the Oracle of Delphi, he had orders to weigh each piece exactly, and bring a complete inventory of the riches they were taking.

The horsemen arrived at the entrance of the precinct. There was no market with its unique sounds to liven the entrance for the pilgrims. In Delphi, there was only a sepulchral silence; the whole sanctuary was in a deep sleep. The soldiers were bewildered; the oracle seemed like a ghost town. The news of

Sulla's victory had spread rapidly throughout the region and no Greek dared to defy the Roman army. That, at least, was a relief, Caphis thought. It will not be humans who confront us, he mused; but once again, he was shaken by the fear of facing the Gods.

They set forth on the climb along the Sacred Way. In passing, they looked at the various shrines that they would soon relieve of their riches. But first, Caphis wanted to introduce himself to the priests and explain his assignment. He wanted to make it clear that he came on Sulla's behalf, and not for his personal gain.

Caphis dismounted in front of the stairway that led to the terrace of the temple. He entered the vestibule with heavy footsteps that resounded on the marble floor.

"Who lives here?" he asked, aloud.

Six figures dressed in white appeared from the *Adyton*, the rear section of the temple, and they stopped in front of him in silence.

"We are the priests of the oracle," Enos said.

Caphis glanced at them. This mission was going to be much easier than he had first imagined. Only six old men to defend the God.

He spoke in a thunderous voice. "I have orders from Lucius Cornelius Sulla to take any object of value that could be used for the cause of liberating the Greeks from Mithridates' control," he said, trying to believe his own speech. "My soldiers will begin to load the pieces we consider necessary, and everything we take will be measured and labeled perfectly."

The priests looked at each other in despair. They were the only ones there to defend the pride of the temple; at least Heptos was in a shelter with part of the treasures.

"You have come, with no shame, to steal from us," Tryos said, in a fury. "Sulla is not coming to free the Greeks from Mithridates' control, he is coming to seek revenge against Greece, and us, for having united with his cause," and pointing his finger at him in anger, he asked, "You would dare to rob the God?"

"It is not a robbery," the Phocian replied, calmly. "Sulla says he will put these riches in a safe place, because he fears that with

154

so many wars, vile hands will take all of this treasure, and it will never be returned."

"Nonsense!" Pentos said. "In the past, the Roman Generals who invaded these lands always showed respect for this divine temple. Even though they were conquerors, they came with gifts for the Gods. You are the first Roman who sacks our possessions in such a brazen manner."

"This only proves that Sulla's kingdom is founded on terror, and on a lack of respect for the Gods," Exos said, dejectedly.

Notwithstanding the priests' anger and frustration, it was clear that they possessed no resources to match the Red Commander's men.

"We will not put up any resistance," Duos said, speaking for all of them with resignation. "At least allow us to help with the selection and the transportation of the pieces. I want to leave a very clear inventory of what you take from here. And I hope that you will truly return it, as if you do not, you will have to answer to someone greater than us. You will have to settle with Apollo himself."

Under the mandate of Caphis, and the strict supervision of the priests, the soldiers began to take objects of value and place them methodically in the wagons that had been brought for the purpose.

In spite of the previous robberies, and the gold that Heptos had been able to take, there were still many riches in Delphi. Caphis had decided to begin by emptying each of the shrines that had been established, in a dignified and orderly style, along the Sacred Way.

The first to be pillaged was the Treasury of Sifnos, the most luxurious in the whole sanctuary. The shrine was in the Ionic style, with two caryatids - columns in the form of a woman - sustaining the two frontons and the long frieze. Sifnos was a small island in the Aegean Sea that had possessed rich mines of gold and silver. While these were producing precious metals, Sifnos had contributed one tenth of its wealth to Delphi each year. Now this fortune was going into Sulla's wagons. Caphis was standing by, diligently annotating on a papyrus the exact quantity he had taken.

They continued with the Treasury of Athens, which held one tenth of the bounty of the glorious battle of Marathon. The heavy bronze weapons and silver breastplates, stolen from the Persians by the Athenians, were weighed precisely, documented, and loaded onto the mules.

The sanctuary had also benefitted from gifts from the richest man in the ancient world, King Croesus. Among the fabulous bequests that this sovereign had made to Delphi was a huge statue of a lion, made of yellow gold, and weighing six hundred pounds. This statue was supported on a pedestal of white gold ingots of such weight that it took all of Caphis' men to lift the base into the largest wagon. In accordance with the detailed list that the Phocian was meticulously completing, Croesus had also donated one hundred and seventeen gold ingots that together weighed one hundred and sixty pounds, four silver urns, two golden pitchers, one golden effigy measuring three cubits high, and a silver urn that could hold three thousand gallons.

While the soldiers were carrying out their operation, sweating in the midday sun, the sound of a lyre playing permeated the oracle. The mysterious melody came from the interior of the temple. The men stopped work so that they could hear better. The six priests who were beside them, taking care of how the objects were being loaded onto the wagons, ceased what they were doing and looked up into space. A smile of delight appeared on their old lips.

With a defiant air, Exos said, "It is Apollo who is sounding his lyre in disagreement with what is happening here." The soldiers had a look of panic on their faces. They turned their heads left and right. The six priests were here with them, and all the troops were around the wagons. Who could be playing the lyre inside the temple?

The hair stood up on the back of Caphis' neck. He had never liked the idea of this mission. With the mules half-loaded, and overcome with fear, he decided it would not be a good idea to defy the God. He promptly called his youngest horseman, a young chap who would be able to make the journey to Athens in the shortest time, and take a message to Sulla.

"Marcus Ateyus," he shouted. The youth appeared immediately. "Take the fastest horse and leave for Athens straight away. Tell Lucius Cornelius Sulla that we have heard Apollo's lyre being played inside his temple. That we await his orders."

The young lad acquiesced and ran like the wind to mount the fastest mare so that he could leave immediately for Athens.

Ateyus arrived a few hours later. The distance between Delphi and Athens was short, and Ateyus did not let his horse rest until he reached the city. As soon as he was there, he asked to see Sulla straight away. At the audience, he told him what had happened inside the temple. Seeing the fear on the young man's face, Sulla threw his head back and let out a roar of laughter.

"Don't you see that Apollo himself is happy to support our cause?" He exclaimed, amused. "If not, why would he play an instrument that is so precious to him? Take a well-rested horse and go back immediately. Tell Caphis to bring me that treasure once and for all." He spoke with authority.

Ateyus related this in the presence of all the troops and the priests. The response from the Red General was enough for the men to get back to work, loading the wagons with the precious bounty and ignoring the music that was still being played. The Roman Consul had already shown them that his interpretation of the will of the Gods was the right one.

The immense silver urn was becoming a serious challenge for Caphis. It was so big that it was impossible to place it in the wagons that they had brought, not even by joining two together. The Phocian decided that the only solution would be to break it into pieces.

"Bring me a hammer and a saw," Caphis shouted.

Exos answered, irate. "Are you going to break up this cup? This urn is used in Apollo's spring festivals of Theophany to mix

157

wine with water!" The priest's consternation was beyond comparison. "Did you not say that you were taking our treasures to keep them safe? If you destroy it, it will be very difficult to mend it."

Caphis was tired of the complaints from the priests who were hovering around his soldiers. With an imposing wave, he ordered them, "You have already helped too much; go to your quarters right now!"

With their heads down, the priests went slowly to their quarters. Desolate, they dragged their feet as they walked between the empty buildings of the sanctuary.

Caphis was absorbed in the operation of breaking up the great urn when he heard a voice that said, "There is a treasure greater than what you found here."

The Phocian turned in the direction of the voice that spoke, and recognized that it came from one of the priests who, to tell the truth, had appeared very calm and had not spoken until now.

"What Sulla really wants has been elegantly removed in front of your eyes and he still does not know," Tesseros said.

Tesseros, the man who never trusted Heptos. He had followed the trail from the beginning, and he knew the intentions of the old priest very well. However, Tesseros had taken his own measures, and he knew exactly where he was now. Tesseros had also interpreted the prophecy, and he had not let himself be deceived by Heptos. The priest was burning with a thirst for vengeance. His companion had betrayed the trust that had been put in him. He had betrayed his God, and his own.

"I know who the thief is. And I know very well that Sulla would give anything to get his hands on that precious Treasure."

Caphis was staring at him in silence, weighing up the truth in his words. He did not exactly understand what this priest meant. *Another lunatic*, he thought to himself.

"What are you talking about?" He asked, confused.

"I am talking about the Treasure that Sulla has been looking for his whole life, and that he was hoping to find when Athens fell. But it is in another place and I can help you find it," Tesseros said, full of promise.

"Do you know where I can find it now?" Caphis asked. He still did not understand what the priest was saying, but his general would not mind getting his hands on more riches.

"I lost the trail in Alexandria, but I can pick it up again quickly. I believe I know his plans, I can smell his steps," Tesseros said, confidently.

"Good, I will take you to the Red Commander, but if you are lying he will not think twice about giving you the punishment you deserve for wasting his time."

The wagons were already crammed full and, according to the Phocian's count, they had at their disposal the riches of a king. He gave the order to his men to secure the pieces and prepare to depart. Sulla would be happy with his work.

CHAPTER TWENTY-SEVEN

Sulla was standing on the Acropolis, looking down on Athens. The city was plunged intoa chaos of waste, weapon debris, and dried blood. There were traces of smoke from already put out fires, and many public buildings had been damaged and robbed of their articles of value. After having broken down the wall, the Red Commander had given a free rein to his generals to loot to their hearts' content.

Aristion survived only three days confined in the citadel of the Acropolis. He and his companions could not resist for long. The cisterns were empty of water, because of the drought the city had endured. Dying of thirst, his guards and the men who accompanied him, surrendered. Sulla took the Acropolis, and with a wave of his hand, he ordered Aristion's execution. Athens had been taken.

As the tyrant's head fell, the skies opened, and the rain, much longed-for for many months, began to bathe the vexed city, washing the blood and stench from the streets.

Now, at the top of the Acropolis, his thirst for revenge satiated and soaked in fresh rain that fell on his tired muscles, he had decided to pardon Athens. His initial orders had been to burn the city until nothing remained but ashes. But from this zenith, with the Parthenon to his side, and appreciating the greatness that this city had brought to humanity, he changed his mind.

"I will pardon the living in respect for the dead," he said, in a solemn tone. This compassion for the people of Athens would be one of the deeds that this man of war would boast about for the rest of his life.

He ordered his men to cease looting and killing. He organized his troops, and without letting the moment of his victory go cold, he took his catapults, battering rams and watch towers, and mounting his white warhorse, he lead the capture of Piraeus. The Roman fury surprised Archelaus, who fled the port city with his ships and his ten thousand men. Sulla had already shown that his infernal war weapons were invincible.

Lucius Cornelius Sulla relished his jubilation. He had achieved victory over Mithridates in Athens and Piraeus, in spite of the few resources at his disposal and betrayal by his own people. His coffers were full of Athens' gold, and would be even more so when Caphis arrived with the bounty from Delphi. However, what he celebrated most of all was that he had obtained what he so badly wanted from Apellicon of Teos.

He remembered the night when the Greek handed it over. They were in the dark audience chambers, and Apellicon, pale in the face, begged him, "Pardon my life and I will give you what you desire."

"How do you know what I want?"

"You are not the only one looking for this Treasure. You know very well that all of us who follow it know each other, one way, or another."

He took a package of damp, stained papyri from a canvas bag that was hanging on his shoulders.

"I will give them to you in exchange for my life," he said, somberly. "These are the writings of Aristotle." As he spoke, he handed over the package with an anguished look on his face.

Shortly before his death, the great philosopher had bequeathed all of his work to his pupil Theophrastus, for whom he had great respect. He, in turn, passed them to his nephew, Neleus of Scepsis. He was very possessive of these works, and in order to avoid the librarians of Pergamon obtaining them, Neleus hid them in his country of birth, in clay pots under the ground in the Troade. His descendants finally found them, more than one hundred and fifty years later, and realizing their great value, they decided to put them up for sale to the highest bidder.

The news traveled like wild fire among all circles of wise men and scholars. Many centers of learning and individual patrons sent emissaries to bid for them. However, Apellicon outdid all the offers presented, and he obtained Aristotle's works by paying a large sum of money.

Sulla took the papyri in his hands and, with great delight, he began to read the writings of Aristotle. Unable to hide his emotion, he asked, "Do you think that one of the five manuscripts might be among these pages?" Apellicon shrugged his shoulders

161

and, with a sad smile, he said, "If Aristotle is not included in the group of five wise men, I cannot imagine who would be," he spoke sorrowfully. He was delivering the fruit of his life's work to Sulla.

Sulla looked up and stared at Apellicon with his penetrating blue eyes.

"How can I know if it really is one of the five manuscripts? How can I decipher the Word?"

"For that, you need the Bearer."

"And where will I find him?"

"I don't have the slightest idea."

Sulla understood that he had only taken a small step in his quest. He looked at the ordered writing of Aristotle again, frustration overwhelming his soul. At least he had one of the five books in his hands, but he still had to find the rest and the Bearer. Patience, he advised himself, patience. He knew that the Gods favored him and that eventually he would find them.

He always achieved what he wanted.

Caphis arrived in Athens with the wagons overflowing with gold, silver, and valuable objects that he had taken from the Oracle of Delphi. Lucius Cornelius Sulla gave orders to melt everything immediately, to mint coins with his emblem, and to use them to pay the soldiers their wages. The victory should remain fresh in their minds, and he wanted to compensate them generously for their absolute loyalty. He knew that although Archelaus had fled, Mithridates was regrouping his troops to the north, and he was preparing a regiment of colossal dimensions to confront him as soon as possible. He had won this battle, but he still had not won the war.

He was approaching Caphis to congratulate him for his mission when he saw that a man wearing a white toga accompanied the Phocian.

"I did not ask you to bring me another bite to eat. You could have left this priest in his sanctuary," he said, amused.

Caphis, stunned, replied, "He insisted on talking to you, my Lord." And as he spoke, he walked away to organize the melting and distribution of the plunder.

"What do you want?" Sulla asked.

"Just a little of your time," the priest answered.

Sulla moved to one side to get away from the ruckus his men were making as they offloaded objects from the wagons. He signaled to the priest to come to him.

"Sulla, I know what you're looking for," Tesseros said, without qualms.

The Roman looked at him suspiciously. How many people knew about the manuscripts?

"What are you talking about?" he asked, with distrust.

"A treasure for which the wise men would give their lives..." Tesseros replied, repeating the phrase Locutius had stated.

"It seems there are more people than I thought after it," he answered, mockingly.

"Oh yes! Many more than you think. But I am not one of them."

Sulla looked at him, puzzled, urging him to explain. Tesseros began his account.

"When you were camped outside Athens, the Pythia unveiled a prophecy. In it, she talked about a Treasure that had to be saved, and that you desired. My companions interpreted from it that you would sack us, and they appointed one priest to save part of our riches, to be able to reconstruct our sanctuary once you left. However, I am sure that the priest we appointed is not thinking about saving our gold to return glory to Delphi. Oh no! He has his own agenda. He is going to use the riches that were entrusted to him to find these five manuscripts for which all of you are fighting."

"Does he know which ones the five manuscripts are?" Sulla asked, avidly.

"No," Tesseros replied, and Sulla looked disappointed, "But the Bearer is with them."

"The Bearer?" Sulla asked, astonished.

"Yes, the Bearer has finally appeared, and his stronghold with him. There are other young ones accompanying them, and of course, the Seventh."

"The Seventh? The Seventh has appeared too?"

Anxious fevers overcame the Red General. The initial disillusion of his meeting with Apellicon was fading. He was very close to possessing the Treasure.

"Where are they? Who are they?" He asked, commandingly. He wanted to get his hands on those manuscripts without delay.

"As you will appreciate, I don't have as many resources as you," Tesseros replied, calmly. "However, I have been following their trail, and I know that they are now in Alexandria."

"Alexandria?" Sulla said, and he put his hand to his forehead. "Of course! The Library of Alexandria. Where else would you look for the five manuscripts? Many suspected the intentions of Ptolemy in accumulating such a quantity of books."

"Let's make an agreement," Tesseros said, "I have a spy who is on their trail and who can locate their whereabouts. For my part, I have seen all of them and I can give an exact description of each one."

Sulla looked at him with distrust. What were this priest's motives?

Tesseros interpreted the expression and quickly clarified his position. "I don't want the manuscripts for myself," he said, in a conciliatory tone. "But on the other hand, I want the riches that Heptos has taken with him."

Sulla mentally weighed up the offer, and with a nod of agreement, he sealed the pact. A satisfied smile appeared on Tesseros' face.

The Roman turned to where Caphis was still organizing the items he had brought from Delphi. A small gold effigy of Apollo, made with exquisite skill, rested on a table. It was smaller than a thumb, and around the crown of sunrays on its head, a leather cord passed through an opening. Sulla went to the table, took the pendant, and kissed the sculpture. He took the leather cord and put it over his head. The image of the golden God shone on his chest.

From that day, he consecrated himself to the God Apollo. This God had given him victory over Athens, a bounty fit for a king, and now the prospect of the Treasure he had searched for so badly.

You may wonder why Lucius Cornelius Sulla wanted this treasure so desperately, he who was a man so close to having absolutely everything: power, money, prestige, the woman he desired...

Well, he was a very ambitious man, like the rest of the Romans, and his dream went beyond his persona. He wanted to leave the bases of a great Rome cemented, an empire that would stretch to the limits of the known world, a civilization that would prevail forever... and he knew that he would not achieve this with arms and money alone. No, he knew that the size of a man goes hand in hand with the reach of his mind, with his aspiration to learn, and no empire would be great, nor last long enough, if it were not grounded upon the endless pursuit of wisdom.

In order that civilizations endure, prosper, are respected and recognized, they must be absorbed in the intellect of their people, and they must be obsessed with the supremacy of their war machines, with the utility of their construction, and with the beauty of their monuments.

A man can accumulate power, glory, and riches, but it all dies with him. The Treasure was the greatest legacy he could leave to his country... And to be the greatest civilization ever known was his dream for Rome.

CHAPTER TWENTY-EIGHT

The *Aphrodite* docked at the Western port of Alexandria, also known as the Port of Good Return, and the same one that had recently welcomed Cleantes. Heptos asked them to hurry to disembark; he wanted to meet the Director of the Library as early as possible. He had a bad premonition, an uncertain feeling that perhaps they had arrived too late.

After having spent so much time on the ship, they were all ready for some exercise, so they decided to walk to the Library. Heptos, who knew the way very well, having visited the city before, guided them through the streets of Alexandria.

Alexander the Great founded Alexandria on the Egyptian coast, but because of his premature death, the great conqueror was never able to see her in all her splendor. With the vision that was characteristic of him, Alexander wanted this to be the capital of his empire, a modern and efficient city, and for that reason he had entrusted the design to the architect and urban planner, Dinocrates of Rhodes. He selected a grid plan, that is to say the city streets were in the form of a crisscross, with parallel streets crossing perpendicular streets. The Via Canopica that ran from the east to west, and the Soma Avenue that lead from north to south, were the two principal arteries of the city.

With the passing of centuries, the orderly city of Alexandria had turned into a cosmopolitan and multicultural metropolis; this could be appreciated while wandering through the streets. Macedonians and Greeks lived in the city, occupying the elegant Bruchion quarter where the royal buildings were situated. The Jews lived in the east of the city, and the Egyptian population in the west, in a settlement named Rakotis.

The Temple of the Muses, where the library was housed, was very close, to the east of the Western Gate and therefore, after meandering through a few streets, they finally reached their destination.

On arrival, they were taken to the same room where Cleantes had delivered his message to Zenon. He was there waiting for them, together with his student.

"Heptos, dear friend," Zenon of Alexandria greeted him, giving the priest a strong hug, and planting a kiss on each cheek. They had known each other for a long time, and although they rarely met, there was great respect between them.

"Your eyes are even wiser, dear Zenon," Heptos said, and looking at Ignatius, he asked, "Who is the target of your criticisms and teachings these days?"

"My name is Ignatius of Catania," the boy said, proudly. "I have been working at this institution for barely a year."

Heptos turned to the people who had arrived with him.

"Let me introduce my travel companions." And looking at each one of them he said, "Roxana, Adhara, Dromeas, Raiko, and Ammos. The voyage from Delphi has been long and we are all somewhat tired."

Zenon received them with a huge smile.

"Welcome! I see that this group of seven chosen ones is nourished and diverse. I hope that you will accept my hospitality," Zenon said, warmly. He gestured to a servant, who came with trays of figs, honey pastries and jugs of spring water.

As they quenched their thirst and helped themselves to food, Cleantes entered the room and bowed by way of greeting his Lord.

"Cleantes, my loyal servant. I see that you expertly completed the mission I entrusted to you. How have they treated you here in Alexandria?" Heptos asked.

"Very well, my Lord," Cleantes said. "But I have to warn you, they followed me."

"Who? Were you able to recognize who was following you?"

"No. He boarded the same ship when I left the port of Kirra. I can say for sure that he is Greek, and that he has one brown eye and the other blue. But I can say no more."

"Were you able to trick him?" Heptos asked, anxiously.

"I think so. I lost him in the market, and no one has followed me since I arrived here. I have not left this enclosure since my arrival. "

Zenon and Heptos exchanged a meaningful look.

"Thank you my dear friend, for helping my emissary."

"It couldn't be any other way," Zenon replied.

With the conversation about the incident with Cleantes over, Heptos asked, "Were you able to read my message?

"Yes," the librarian replied. "Since we received your message, Ignatius and I have focused on the task of separating those manuscripts we consider may hold the key which would lead to deciphering the Word."

"But it has not been an easy undertaking," Ignatius impatiently interrupted his master. All eyes fixed on the young student who started to explain himself.

"How do we know that one manuscript contains more wisdom than another? It is like asking a mother to save only one of her children. Do you know how much time and effort it took to gather a collection of Enlightenment like this?" And, as he spoke, he gestured to the shelves with thousands of rolls of papyrus. At its peak, the library had accumulated more than seven hundred thousand manuscripts. "This center of learning was founded on the belief that all knowledge merited consideration. Every ship that arrived was seized, not for its contraband, but for its books. The books were retained by the authorities, and the *amanuenses* made a copy, which was returned to the owner, keeping the original for the Library. Not satisfied with the texts that reached Alexandria, the dynasty of Ptolemy set out on the mission of looking for manuscripts in different cities. They spent incredible sums in the search of books, but the kings, who considered knowledge to be the greatest treasure, paid no attention to the huge amount of money they were spending."

Heptos stared at him as he spoke. He looked with understanding at that young pupil who would devote his life to this institution.

"I know that it is not an easy task, Ignatius," Heptos said. "But we do not have much time to complete our mission."

Heptos looked at the manuscripts that had been carefully piled on a side table.

"Zenon, Ignatius, tell me, in your expert judgment, if you had to save only one of them, which one would you choose?"

Zenon smiled and said, "I have devoted time to thinking of this and, the way I see it, the greatest work accomplished until now is this one," and grabbing a thick manuscript from the pile on the table, he showed it to Heptos.

"The study of astronomy by Hipparchus of Nicaea. This great wise man explains to us the beauty of the celestial dynamics. The Earth is the center of the universe, and the other planets and the Sun revolve around it in a harmonious dance. It is a hypothesis that has been supported by all the great wise men of this institution."

Ignatius could not disguise a look of disapproval, but he did not dare contradict his master in front of his guests.

Heptos turned around, and handing the papyrus to Ammos, he said, "Ammos, the time has come."

Ammos made an imperceptible gesture to Roxana, and they both moved to the center of the room, facing each other. Roxana reached out her hands with her palms facing upwards.

Ammos looked at Heptos and, in a deep voice, he said, "put the book on Roxana's hands."

Heptos did as he was asked. He laid out the manuscript on the woman's hands and Ammos, facing her, placed his hands with his palms down on top of the manuscript, searching for Roxana's hands with his own. The tips of their fingers were separated only by the fine material.

Ammos looked into Roxana's eyes, breathed deeply, and the two remained staring at one another. A sepulchral silence possessed the room, as all attention fell on them.

Absolutely nothing happened.

Heptos' face showed deep disappointment. He looked with apprehension at the two people who were in the middle of the room, waiting for something to happen. Something that did not materialize.

Ammos shook his head and said, "This is not one of the five manuscripts."

Everyone present heard a scream of delight, and a smile appeared on Ignatius' face.

"I knew it, I knew it! Hipparchus was wrong. Hipparchus was wrong!" the youth said euphorically.

Zenon looked at him, annoyed. His student ought to show more respect for his master's opinion, even if it were in error.

169

Heptos looked intently at the master and the student and, with a knowing smile, he asked the boy, "Which one do you think could be one of the manuscripts that will lead us to the Word?"

"My Lord, if I had to save only one of all the papyri in this library, I would save this one," and pointing with confidence at the pile of books that were on the desk, he took one of them. It was evident that it was a very old manuscript, and that it had been consulted many times. The edges were worn, and the ink was beginning to fade.

"The Elements by Euclid. All the learning we have of geometry is concentrated in this book."

My dear friend, Euclid of Megara, recognized as the Father of Geometry, was born in the year 325 B.C. As he was a brilliant mathematician, Ptolemy I, the founder of the library, called on him to create the chair of mathematics at the young institution. With time, Euclid became the director, dedicating his life to the role, until he died in Alexandria at the age of 70. Euclid was not only dedicated to geometry, his work also covered the study of optics, whole numbers, and conical sections.

I remember one time that, curious for knowledge, the sovereign himself had asked Euclid to instruct him in the marvels of geometry, which the mathematician did with aplomb. However, after a few lessons, Ptolemy asked him if there was not an easier way to study The Elements, to which the Wise Man replied, "There is no Royal Path towards geometry, Your Majesty." This was a huge insult, worthy of capital punishment, but not even the Pharaoh would have dared take the life of such a brilliant mind, and with his royal sense of humor, he let out a roar of laughter at the response.

Yes, like Ignatius, I also believe that Euclid should be considered among the five books. If not, whom? You also studied his ideas when you were in school, do you remember? But let's get back to our story...

On hearing the name of the book and its author, Adhara could not help but intervene.

"Excuse me, may I see it?" she asked. With a perceptive smile, he handed it to her.

Adhara took the manuscript in her hands as though it were the most precious object in the court of a king. She put it on one of the tables and began to unroll it. Her fingers traced over those axioms and postulations she had learned every since she was small. She continued running her eyes over the manuscript until she found proposition forty-seven: *In a right triangle, the square of the hypotenuse is equal to the sum of the squares of the other two sides.*

"It's true!" She said, showing her audience. "Euclid included Pythagoras in his book. The Pythagorean School affirmed that *everything is mathematics*. This is, without doubt, the most exquisite of the equations."

Ignatius looked at her, awestruck. How could someone as beautiful as her share his love for mathematics? Adhara smiled back at him, and together they began to look at the pages of the manuscript while they discussed the postulations.

Raiko, annoyed, interrupted their conversation.

"We must hurry. We came to look for a book, not to receive classes."

Heptos was looking at the scene, amused. If this book generated such confusion, perhaps the boy was right, and it would be worth the effort to have Ammos take it in his hands.

"There is only one way to know if this book is one of the ones we are looking for," Heptos said.

Heptos took the papyrus from Adhara's hands.

"Are you sure that this is the original manuscript?" he asked Ignatius. "The clues can only be found in the original writings."

"In his own handwriting. Euclid wrote it in this room more than two hundred years ago," Ignatius replied.

Heptos placed *The Elements* on Roxana's extended hands and, once again, Ammos diligently stood in front of her with his palms down. Only the manuscript prevented them from touching each other.

They looked deep into each other's eyes and slowly, very slowly, they began to emit a muffled sound. It was a simple melody; it seemed more like a lament or a solitary plea. In unison, the two voices began to grow louder, and their notes filled the whole room. The chant became stronger and its rhythm quickened. The notes danced in the air, and the music that came from them did not seem to have been created by human voices, it was more like the symphony that must have sounded at the beginning of creation.

Excited by the sound they were producing; Roxana and Ammos closed their eyes and sang louder.

Their hands began to shine and, to the astonishment of those present, the papyrus began to send out rays of light that pierced the fine depth of the material. The light, which began as a glimmer, transformed into a myriad of shining sparkles. A group of these sparkles rose above the others, and began a vertical ascent into the emptiness. The glints, in a harmonious dance, settled in the open space, in a shape delineating a phrase of light that shone splendidly in the antique room.

Two Pearls for Two Mermaids, Two Pearls for One Mermaid.

The statement remained above them long enough for them to read it, and then it disappeared, leaving small lively flecks of light that danced in the air, refusing to disappear completely.

Roxana and Ammos slowly eased their chanting, until silence once again filled the room. Roxana gave Ammos a satisfied smile. This was one of the five manuscripts.

The first clue had been freed in the Library of Alexandria, the greatest center of knowledge known to humanity.

"He is the Bearer!" said Zenon, looking at Heptos in amazement. He had heard talk of the Bearer before, and he knew the reverence bestowed on the Word, but nothing had prepared him for the scene he had just witnessed.

"And she is his rock," Heptos said, pointing at Roxana. "Your pupil is correct, *The Elements* of Euclid is one of the books we are looking for," he said, with great satisfaction. His life's dream was being realized. He knew he was on the right path.

Ignatius also had a smile of satisfaction, he was very proud of his knowledge, especially in front of this girl with the auburn hair.

172

Heptos, happy with this first victory, addressed Zenon's pupil straight away.

"Tell me Ignatius, which other book do you consider should be included?"

Ignatius stammered. "I think you should consider the works of Aristotle. The problem is, we never had his writings in Alexandria. After he bequeathed his personal library to Theophrastus, and then he to Neleus, the trace was lost."

"Aristotle. Yes, you are right. I have not discounted his works. Everyone knows that Apellicon of Teos bought those manuscripts," Heptos said. "But apart from Aristotle, are there any other books that you would consider worthy of forming part of this group?"

Ignatius looked at him, overwhelmed. He was looking at Zenon with fear, and then he looked down in shame. For the first time he felt that his ideas were being heard, and that his knowledge was really receiving credence. Embarrassed, he looked at Zenon again and then, decidedly, he spoke to Heptos. "Just before your servant arrived, I was having a discussion with my master. Although it contradicts all the wise men in this institution, I believe you should look for the manuscript of Aristarchus of Samos!" He finally said, in a fit of bravery.

"What manuscript do you refer to?"

"It is a book that presents a completely absurd theory," Zenon replied. "Ignatius is referring to the manuscript in which Aristarchus states that the Sun is in the center of the universe, and not the Earth. According to his postulations, the Earth revolves around the Sun and not the reverse."

"Interesting theory," Heptos said, pondering the thought. "And where is this manuscript?"

"No one knows," Ignatius replied. "It was lost in the war that took place between the two libraries."

Ignatius was referring to the war of knowledge that erupted between the Libraries of Alexandria and Pergamon. The Ptolemy and the Attalids fought to see which of the two libraries, of which they were so proud, would rise up with the greater quantity of accumulated knowledge. The rivalry reached such a point that the Alexandrians pushed for the ban on exporting papyrus to Asia

Minor, hoping, in this way, to slow the growth of the rival library due to lack of material to make their copies. In response, the inhabitants of Pergamon invented parchment, a material made from the treatment of animal skin, which in time turned out to be more resistant, and had the added advantage that both sides could be used.

The rivalry brought with it an increase in contraband and the traffic of books. A ring of merchants sprung up, and they began to sell manuscripts to the highest bidder. However, because it contained such ludicrous ideas, Aristarchus' manuscript had languished in the library of some frustrated merchant, who, having stolen it, had not been able to find a buyer.

"I have followed his postulations from some letters that he had written to Archimedes of Syracuse. Although we only have a few statements, I believe his theory is correct," he said, defiantly, while looking at Zenon.

"I see," Heptos was silent for a moment and then said, "I believe I know who might have it."

Suddenly they heard footsteps running quickly towards the chamber. The door opened violently and Abu, Cleantes' friend, barged into the room. Making an effort to get his breath back, he said in an alarmed voice, "I have come to warn you that a unit from the Royal Guard is on its way to apprehend you. You have to flee this very moment!"

CHAPTER TWENTY-NIGHT

Lucius Licinius Lucullus had arrived in Alexandria on the previous day. He was in the quarters designated for high-ranking visitors in the Royal Palace, as the guest of the Pharaohs, Ptolemy Alexander X and his wife Cleopatra Selene.

A slave was helping him dress, carefully placing the bronze-forged suit of armor on him. Underneath, he wore the skirt made of bands of leather, typical of Roman attire. Another servant was adjusting the greaves on his legs. He would carry the helmet with the crest under his arm, and he would wear the short red cape, thrown back over his shoulders. Lucullus wanted to enter the audience hall like a great victor, and he knew that appearance would help. He had arrived in the city on a mission on behalf of Sulla. He had to ask the Pharaoh for a fleet of war ships to confront Mithridates' navy in the Aegean sea.

The first kings of the Ptolemaic dynasty had brought prosperity and prestige to the city of Alexandria. Under their reign, the city had glistened like a diamond in the Mediterranean Sea. It was a model of culture, business, abundance, and greatness. However, since the reign of Ptolemy VI, corruption within the royal family and intrigues to gain power had placed Egypt in a very thorny situation.

The present regent, Ptolemy Alexander, openly sympathized with Rome, to whom he wanted to leave Egypt as a legacy. Not so his mother, Cleopatra III, who was a candid supporter of Mithridates. In the past, the capricious Queen had alternated her two sons on the throne at various times, until Ptolemy Alexander, tired of his mother's manipulation, put a price on her head.

The Queen fled to the island of Kos, from where she promptly went to declare her support for Mithridates, with such glorious gifts as the cape of Alexander the Great, an article that her family had treasured. But the astute Cleopatra III had gone too far in her passion to demonstrate loyalty to the King of Pontus. She had delivered her grandson, the son of Ptolemy X and Cleopatra Selene, so that he could be raised in the court of Sinope, with Mithridates as his guardian.

This was a situation the Romans could use in their favor - the support of the Egyptian fleet in exchange for returning the boy to his parents as soon as they defeated Mithridates. Lucullus was preparing his speech when a servant interrupted him.

"A man is asking to see you," said the servant, looking at the floor. "He says he brings a message from Sulla."

"Let him come in this instant," Lucullus replied.

A man dressed in a smart white tunic entered the room. He had a brown beard and very distinct eyes, one was brown like his beard, and the other was blue.

"Hail Lucius Licinius Lucullus!" the man said parsimoniously, and he handed him a papyrus sealed with the stamp of Lucius Cornelius Sulla.

Lucullus took it in his hands and, parting the wax seal, he opened it and read the contents. When he had read the entire message, he looked up.

"What has all this got to do with the war against Mithridates, and the mission that brought me here?" He asked, confused.

"My Lord and yours have sealed a pact. You must continue with the task your general entrusted in you, and reach a favorable agreement for the mission against the King of Pontus. Once you have signed the agreement and you have secured your ships, we must ask the Pharaoh to give us access to his library as a personal favor. "

CHAPTER THIRTY

Abu had barged into the room and screamed in a loud voice, "I have come to tell you that a unit of the Royal Guard is on its way here to capture you. You must flee immediately!"

He glanced around the whole gathering and, when he saw Cleantes, the tension lifted from his face. He breathed deeply to replenish his lungs with air after the frenzied sprint that had brought him there and, incoherently, he began his story. Abu was a simple man who related the facts with few details.

"I was in a corner of the audience hall waiting for my Lady, Princess Berenice, to ask for her carriage, and I heard what they said. The great Roman General had sent a commander, whom I believe is named Lucullus, to ask the Pharaohs for a navel fleet to attack Mithridates. In exchange, he offered to free a child, the child of the Pharaohs, who is captive in Sinope. The Pharaohs accepted the agreement and they sealed it with pomp, giving him a gold ring with the serpent of the Ptolemies, set on a brilliant emerald. When the ceremony was over, a man who accompanied Lucullus moved forward in front of the King, and I saw that this man was the one who had followed you in the market, the man with one brown eye and one blue eye," he said, looking at Cleantes. "It seemed Sulla was looking for a group of seven individuals, who have stolen some manuscripts and who intended to sack the Library of Alexandria to augment the bounty they already had. The Pharaohs were grateful to have been warned, and they accepted help in finding the thieves of the books. Immediately, they called the Royal Guard to come here. I remembered that Cleantes was still in hiding, and I came as quickly as I could to inform you."

For a moment, the room was steeped in a sepulchral silence.

"I have brought a carriage but I don't think there is enough room for everyone. I did not realize there were so many of you," he said, apologetically.

Raiko instantly took charge of the situation and asked him, "How many men are coming?"

"Atis and the Royal Guard. A group of at least twenty-five men."

Raiko weighed up the situation with a worried look on his face.

"They are too many for us. We need to bamboozle them, if not we will be easy meat to capture."

Looking at the coachman, he asked another question, "How many people do you think could fit in the carriage you brought?"

"Five in total. Four in the cabin and one in the coachman's seat," Abu replied.

He looked at the twins and said, "Do you know how to ride?"

"Yes," they replied straight away.

Raiko devised a quick escape plan in his head.

"Where is the carriage you brought?"

"It is parked in an alley behind this museum. I did not want the guard to know that I was here in case they arrived before I was able to warn you," Abu said. He was truly showing himself to be an expert in confusing his followers.

Raiko nodded in approval.

"Good judgment, Abu." And as he said this, he gave him a pat on the back. Abu smiled with pleasure, showing his perfect teeth.

"Ammos, Heptos, Cleantes, and Roxana, you will go in the carriage with Abu. Leave right now." Addressing the driver, he gave him precise orders. "Use the streets with the least traffic. Try not to attract attention, as much as is possible. When you arrive at the port, head straight for the *Aphrodite* and tell Odon to prepare the crew to leave for the high seas as soon as possible. Do you think you can do that?"

Abu nodded in agreement.

"Nobody knows the streets of Alexandria better than I."

"Leave now through the back door. Walk steadily," Raiko said. "We will wait here for the soldiers and we will try to confuse them until you reach the ship. Remember not to rush, try not to attract attention."

Ammos, Roxana, Cleantes, and Heptos went towards the exit, following the coachman. Raiko took the priest's arm and said in a low voice, "If you see that after a certain time we have not returned to the ship, order Odon to leave. We will find a way to reunite with you later on."

Heptos nodded in agreement. With the manuscript still in his hands, he walked to Adhara and handing it over to her he said, "It's not a good idea that Ammos and Roxana are captured with the book. We will be handing over our treasure to our captors if they detain us. It is better that the manuscript is united with the Bearer when we are all safe."

Adhara took the manuscript in her hands and smiled.

"We will see you on the *Aphrodite*," he said and he left hurriedly behind the others, who had already abandoned the room.

Raiko addressed Zenon and his student.

"You will receive the soldiers as though nothing happened. Try to keep them in this room as long as possible. By doing this, we will give the others more time to reach the ship."

Looking at the servant he said, "Take us to the stables, and not a word of this to anyone," The servant acknowledged his agreement, and he solicitously led them to the stables.

The stables were a separate structure, made of wood and supported by one of the lateral walls of the building. They did not have room to keep more than twenty horses since they were designed to shelter only the animals used for service, or to pull the carriage that brought supplies to the Library.

They were reached through a small alley that led off the main street and stopped in front of their gates. There was only one floor, but the high gable roof had a loft that was used to store the bales of hay used for feeding the animals. At that moment, the stables were completely empty.

Raiko looked around the room, trying to find a hiding place.

"Get into the straw," he said, pointing at the loft that could be reached by a ladder leaning on a beam in the center. They climbed the ladder, and as soon as they were up, Raiko threw it to the floor. They lay face down on the floor of the loft and covered themselves with hay.

Abu had arrived just in time, as not five minutes passed before they heard the sound of horses' hooves on the cobbled street.

A servant entered the chambers in the circular tower, where Zenon and Ignatius were working, and announced, "General Atis is asking to see you, my Lord." He spoke in a calm and parsimonious voice. Before he could finish speaking, a tall guard with a gaunt face entered the room abruptly. He was a soldier from the Royal Guard. He was wearing golden armor of small embossed horizontal plates over a white linen toga, with a broad belt displaying the effigy of Amon-Ra. The *Jepesh,* the curved dagger, was attached to his belt.

Pushing the poor servant to one side, he said, "I have orders from the Pharaoh to seize any visitor found in this enclosure." He added, with authority, "We have been assigned the task of watching this library zealously. From this point on, no one may enter without our permission, and no book may be taken away." He pointed to the piles of manuscripts on the tables and shelves.

Zenon looked at him with deliberate confusion on his face.

"I understand your orders, but as you can verify, only my student and I are in this room. The other wise men are working in their respective rooms," he said, opening his arms with a gesture that spanned the whole hall.

The guard looked at him mistrustfully and replied, "That's not what we have heard. We have a detailed description of a group of seven bandits who hope to rob this center of learning. I will have my men check every room."

He turned towards the soldier who had entered with him and ordered, "Close all the doors and entryways to the Library and put an armed guard at each one of them. Go outside and have all the men we brought with us come in. Leave only two of them in charge of the horses. This is bigger than I thought," he said, walking to the door and pointing at the gallery that opened out onto all the study rooms.

The soldier walked away quickly to honor the command, and soon they heard the echo of heavy footsteps on the stone floor. The soldiers violently opened every door where peaceful scholars, ignorant of what was happening, were calmly at their

180

work. They opened armoires and turned over tables in an effort to come upon the seven characters that they had to bring before the Pharaoh and his Roman guest.

"I beg you to act with great care," Zenon said, in the face of the little respect that the soldiers were showing for the Library's possessions, while he tried to follow their aggressive inspection. "We have very delicate manuscripts. Also, I beg you not to cause so much chaos in your search; the scientists here need silence while they are working."

Zenon was closely following the soldiers who had spread to every corner like a swarm of bees. The birds and other exotic animals squawked as they moved about in their cages when they heard the ruckus that Atis' men were making.

"Be careful with the laboratory, and especially the animals' cages. We have species there that cost us greatly to bring them from every corner of the earth, and they are very sensitive to loud noise or any distress..." the sentence on the librarian's lips died away.

A clamor of horses' hooves, neighing, and cries came from outside. The same soldier who had received Atis' orders came in, shouting.

'My Lord, they have taken three horses and they have scared off the rest of them."

"Damned ones, after them!" Atis roared.

CHAPTER THIRTY-ONE

The arrival of the Royal Guard was clearly heard in their hiding place. The captain banged the hard wooden door and, soon after, a servant let him in, along with one of his men.

Raiko, Adhara, and Dromeas heard this as they crouched down, holding their breath, watching through the straw and beams as the soldiers were dismounting and starting to bring their horses into the stables. Inside the stables there was great confusion; the space was too small for all the men and their mounts, and the creatures whinnied nervously as they had sensed the presence of the three strangers hidden in the area above them.

Not much time had passed when Atis' envoy returned with orders for his companions.

"Idut, Heikab! Stay here and look after the horses. The rest of you come with me, we need you to check the Library." The soldiers immediately responded to the order from their superior, and the troops entered the enclosure. The two men who stayed behind took the bridles of the tangle of horses and began to lead them into the covered shelter.

They tied up the steeds with loose knots, and they began to fill the heavy wooden buckets with water to let the animals drink. The two soldiers were focused on their chore and they did not notice the three people spying on them from above.

Raiko judged it to be the exact moment to attack, and he signaled to Dromeas. Swiftly, Raiko and Dromeas jumped onto the two men with their full body weight. The assault took them by surprise and it was very easy, once they were on the floor, to stupefy both of them with a heavy thud on the head.

Adhara also jumped at the same time and landed on a pile of hay. The horses that had been tied with very loose knots began to fidget because of the racket around them. Swiftly, while Raiko and Dromeas were dragging out the unconscious bodies of the two men and tying them to a joist, Adhara took three horses by their bridles.

"Well done," Raiko said, relieving the soldiers of their weapons, and with a shout he began to beat the remaining horses on their hinds. They ran outside, stunned, in a disorderly mess. Without wasting time, they mounted the three horses and galloped toward the main street, taking care to take the opposite direction that Abu had taken the carriage just moments before.

The neighing and clipping of horseshoes alerted the soldiers inside the Library, and they rushed out to see what was happening at the exact moment that the twins and Raiko passed by.

"Damned ones, after them!" was the last they heard, as they quickly distanced themselves from the Library.

Following Atis' orders, the soldiers caught some of the horses that were going astray, mounted them, and began the chase.

Adhara, Raiko, and Dromeas rode as fast as they could, trying to acquaint themselves with these unknown streets. Raiko was trying to use the position of the sun to orient himself and get to the Western Port by making a detour, but as they tried to reach the dock the streets became more congested with pedestrians. They heard cries from angry villagers who were pushed back by the force of the horses passing them at such speed.

A man, laden with sacks, was about to leave the doorway of his house when he had to step back, stunned, in order to avoid the three crazy horses stampeding him. He raised his hands in the air, shouting a crude insult, but only the dust raised by the creatures' hooves heard his threats. He bent down to pick up the belongings he had dropped, but straight away he had to step back again, this time to dodge the horses of the Royal Guard.

Raiko turned his horse to the left, with Adhara and Dromeas following. To his bewilderment, they crossed one of the principal streets that led to the main square where the market was located. The street was full of heavy wagons laden with merchandise that moved slowly, pulled by tired mules. They desperately tried to weave through the traffic, but the little empty space available forced them to slow down. Dromeas turned around and realized that the soldiers were close. They were losing ground and the distance between them and their captors was decreasing. If they continued at this pace, the soldiers would catch them in no time. They would not escape if they stayed on horseback. The best strategy would be to split up and try to get to the *Aphrodite* by different routes.

Without thinking twice, he shouted at Adhara, in a determined voice, "Give me the manuscript!"

Adhara turned to her brother, and she, too, saw the threat behind them. She understood Dromeas' fear, and she threw the manuscript with all her strength. The boy caught it in the air, put it inside his toga, and tied it to his body with his belt. In a split second, he jumped to the ground and buried himself in the crowd. His horse kept running alongside Raiko and Adhara, without its rider.

Raiko cast a worried look at Dromeas and tried to shout out to stop him but Adhara, smiling, said, "The manuscript is safe. No one can run as fast as Dromeas, I promise you. And they cannot pass through this crowd on horseback."

She had barely spoken when the soldiers realized the boy's maneuver.

"Damn!" the one who was the leader of the small group said. Addressing three of his men, he ordered, "Dismount and follow this boy!"

The soldiers got down from their horses to follow Dromeas. As they ran behind him, they began to push villagers out of their way in pursuit of their prey.

Meanwhile, Raiko had also realized that they could not continue on these busy streets on horseback. His mind was racing, trying to find a way to escape that would give him a sure advantage over the guards who followed.

Raiko and Adhara had arrived at the marketplace, the same spot where Cleantes had duped his persecutor. In front of them, there were wagons with fruits, spices and other products, all positioned next to each other and serving as an obstacle in their path. There, Raiko saw his opportunity.

"Jump!" He shouted at Adhara and, on his horse, he cleanly overturned a cart full of bananas, while the owner bent down and protected his head with his arms. Adhara followed him, and her horse jumped over the cart in pursuit of Raiko's, but when the horse put its hooves on the ground she lost her balance, and she fell to the ground, with all her body weight on one side.

A sharp pain hit her shoulder and she had to clench her teeth to stop from shouting. Her face, hair, and entire body were covered in dust, and she struggled to get up because of the discomfort in her left side. In agony, she rolled onto her right side and sat up. The piercing pain in her left arm lingered. *I have dislocated my shoulder*, she thought, grimly. From the ground, she saw Raiko running towards her.

After having jumped over the fruit cart, he had turned around and he saw Adhara fall. He got down from his horse and went to her rescue. He knew, however, that the guards were very close, and would soon realize that they had abandoned the horses.

He approached her and pulled her by the arm that was not in pain, forcing her to run down a small side street. He saw a house with open doors and, without dithering, they went in. Huddled in the hallway, they saw how the soldiers had dodged the banana cart and were trying to follow in the direction of the horses that were now running free.

"In no time they will understand that we are not on the horses, and they will come back to look for us," Raiko said. "Let's go, we need to find another way to reach the port."

The owner of the house came out of the one of the rooms, and she started yelling at them to get out of her house. Raiko offered her money, and he bought two discolored striped blankets that were drying in the sun in the entryway. When she saw the money the women agreed, satisfied, and with a wide smile that revealed missing teeth, she handed them the blankets. They put them over their heads, covering their hair and their upper bodies, and they went into the market that was still bustling with the chatter of the chase by the Royal Guard that had just been witnessed.

Adhara started to walk with her left arm pegged to her body, but her face was contorted, showing her pain.

"Have you hurt yourself?" Raiko asked, attentively.

"Just a little. I think I have dislocated my shoulder, but I am fine," Adhara said, clenching her teeth to endure the agony. How she hated showing any sign of weakness in the presence of this man!

"You can't run like this," Raiko said, worried.

He looked around the market, and he saw a man who had obviously just sold all his wares and was concentrating on tying a mule to his empty wagon.

"Greetings, good man!" Raiko said. "Where are you going?" he asked him.

The man looked Raiko up and down, and answered in a dry tone, "I have sold everything I brought, and now I'm going back to the port to pick up more merchandise."

"Could you take me and my wife there?" he asked, showing some silver coins in his open palms. The man stared at the coins that they offered and gave his silent agreement. He diverted his gaze to Adhara, his eyes stopping where her *quiton* ended and her long legs began.

Damn! Raiko thought. *Why can't this woman wear a tunic like the others?*

CHAPTER THIRTY-TWO

The peaceful carriage rambled slowly through the lesser-known streets of Alexandria. Abu knew his city very well, and although he was taking the longest route to reach the port, the streets they transited were calm and uninhabited, far from the typical hubbub that was characteristic of the city. Inside the carriage, they all traveled nervously, and they were attentive to any noise from the outside. They would not dare to raise the blinds for fear that inquisitive eyes might recognize them and raise the alarm.

Finally, they heard the sound of gulls, along with the distinctive sounds of the port: the cry of the sailors, the movement of merchandise, and the sea beating against wooden crates.

The plan had worked to perfection, and they had arrived safe and sound at the ship. Abu finally stopped the carriage as close as he could in front of the *Aphrodite* and, opening the small door, he helped them down.

Heptos moved close to him and said, "Dear Abu, I know that you have risked your life for us and I thank you. After what you did today, you cannot continue living in Alexandria."

He took a small velvet sack from his belt and put it into Abu's large hands.

"You have enough here to lead a dignified life in any other city. I hope that fortune always accompanies you. Know that, in me, you will always have a grateful friend," he said, while he took the big hands in his own.

Abu accepted the package, and a smile lit up his face when he felt the weight of it. There had to be a good amount of silver to weigh this much.

"Nothing would make me happier than to go back to the town where I was born. It might be a bit boring," he said, looking at Cleantes, "but I believe I will tolerate that."

Cleantes went to him and gave him a strong hug.

"Thank you my friend, one day I, too, will pay you for your favors."

And with a smile, Abu said, "Who knows if we will ever see each other again? But the next time, try not to let the Royal Guard follow you," he said jokingly, and as he spoke he climbed into his carriage and set off.

The four figures walked along the dock until they reached the *Aphrodite*. Odon was waiting for them anxiously.

"You have lingered too long," he said, and seeing that Raiko was not with the group, he asked, "Where are the others?"

"They will arrive soon," Roxana replied. The answer did not satisfy Odon and he said, worriedly, "There is quite the pandemonium on the docks. Soldiers from the Royal Guard started to arrive a short while ago, and they are prowling around the ships. Apparently, they are looking for a group of seven thieves of manuscripts. The Pharaoh has just issued the old command to search all ships for books. I do not like the way this is going."

Heptos then passed on Raiko's message; they should board and prepare to set sail straight away. If more soldiers arrived, or if one of them tried to approach the ship, they ought to leave immediately.

Dromeas secured the manuscript to his body with his belt one more time, and he began his crazy race through the streets of Alexandria. He ran through the crowd, pushing villagers, dodging wagons, and evading mothers with small children.

"Stop in the name of the Pharaoh!" The guards shouted, running behind as they tried to catch up with him. "Stop the thief!" They hollered, trying to get the attention of the passers-by so that they would stop the boy, but he was quicker than the orders imparted by the soldiers.

He ran and ran, like he had never run before, trying to hoodwink the three soldiers who followed him. His legs started to ache, and he did not know how long he could keep running at this pace.

Dromeas wondered if Heptos had had enough time to get to the *Aphrodite*. He asked himself if this would be the time to change direction, and make his way to the port. Suddenly, a strange feeling overcame him. It was as if someone were speaking to him, reassuring him that his companions were already there, and that he could return any time now. The image of Heptos, Ammos, and Roxana talking to Odon on the deck of the *Aphrodite* appeared in his head, giving him the assurance that they were safe, and that he could return any time now.

He decided to take heed of this premonition and he started to evaluate routes to try to change direction, but he could not work out how to do this with three soldiers on his heels.

He looked back and noted that the guards had stopped at a corner and only one of them was still following him. What had happened to the other two? Dromeas analyzed the actions of his persecutors, and immediately he understood the strategy they had planned. Most likely, one of the other two men was running along the streets parallel to this one, hoping to catch him at the next intersection.

As he ran, he tried to think of a solution to his imminent capture. What could he do? He glanced at the houses on the sides of the street. They were only one floor high, made of mud baked in the sun, and whitened with lime. The roofs were flat and the inhabitants used them as terraces. Some houses had steps built onto the exterior wall, allowing the residents to reach the terraces of their homes.

Dromeas headed to one of these houses and quickly climbed the steps to the roof. From there, he could see the blue of the sea. Only five blocks separated him from the port. From this height, he confirmed his suspicions; the soldiers were running down three different streets at the same time, hoping to reach him at the intersection with the street along which he had been running.

Smiling in the knowledge that he was confusing his followers, Dromeas began to move across the rooftops in the opposite direction. They were built so close together that it was very easy to jump over the gaps that separated them. There, from on high, running and jumping with the adrenalin flowing through his athletic body, Dromeas felt in his element. Although he knew that his life was in danger, he was enjoying this moment like no other. He felt the wild beat of his heart pumping energy through his entire body, and his legs, pushed to their limits, responded magnificently to his desire to flee.

The soldier who was pursuing him closely saw him disappear onto the roof of a house, and he followed him. When he reached the steps he looked up, and he saw Dromeas jumping between the roofs of the city. He had no way to alert his companions, so he made a decision, he climbed the steps and began to follow him across the terraces of the houses. But as he moved from roof to roof behind the young man, he lost his balance and fell to the ground. Badly bruised, he was not able to continue the pursuit.

Dromeas kept on running from house to house, roof to roof, until he reached the last of the streets which, if he followed it to the north, would allow him to reach the ship. He went down the steps and, demanding a final effort from his legs, he arrived at the port. He saw the *Aphrodite* anchored in the middle of the dock and with the breath he had left, he headed to the ship.

However, as he sprinted, he caught the attention of the soldiers positioned at the end of the quay. When they saw him running, they called the alarm and ordered him to stop, but Dromeas ignored the orders. He aimed for the ship and he climbed the plank that joined the *Aphrodite* and the port. He ran rapidly along the short flat timber and threw himself on the deck, while the sailors quickly pulled back the piece of wood to make sure that no other unwanted passenger boarded.

Odon saw the movement of the Royal Guard and, following the precise orders that Raiko had sent, he gave the command to leave. The crew quickly raised the sail and the oarsmen guided the ship towards the high sea.

Dromeas sat down on the deck of the ship, taking deep gulps of air as he tried to recover his breath. As his breathing became more regular, he looked around for his sister. When he did not see her, he asked, "Where is Adhara?"

"She and Raiko have not arrived yet," Roxana replied.

Dromeas got up straight way, and walking towards Odon, he said anxiously, "We cannot leave without them."

Odon looked at him with a serious air and said, "I have orders from Raiko to leave. If we stay here they will capture us, and all that you have done will be in vain."

Dromeas was about to reply, when they heard voices from the other side of the dock. They saw two figures running towards the ship, followed by another group of soldiers, but the *Aphrodite* had already set off and her hull was entering the high sea.

CHAPTER THIRTY-THREE

Raiko and Adhara had finally convinced the merchant to take them to the port.

"You can sit in the driver's seat with me," he said, looking at Adhara's legs again.

"We are fine in the back," Raiko answered in a dry tone of voice. They sat down in the back of the wagon with their backs to the driver. Adhara pulled the blanket over her head in an attempt to hide all of her hair and most of her face.

They must all be on the ship by now, Raiko thought to himself. He would not dare to say anything out loud to Adhara for fear that the driver would hear them. The wagon traveled along, jolting through the cobbled streets. For Adhara, the journey was taking an eternity, her shoulder was hurting more and more, and not being able to complain was making matters even worse.

After what seemed a very long time, the wagon stopped, and Raiko hastily got down.

"Many thanks for your kindness," he said to the man and he handed over the sum of money they had agreed. He helped Adhara step down from the wagon, and they began to walk towards the ship, trying to avoid the group of soldiers who were patrolling the area. In the eyes of the guards, they were only an inoffensive couple walking between the vessels.

While Raiko and Adhara walked along the harbor with a false sense of calm, a strong breeze came up from the sea and, taking them by surprise, the force of the wind blew the blanket the girl was wearing off her head. Her shining red curls were exposed, waving defiantly around her face in the sunlight like tongues of fire. One of the soldiers recognized her and gave the alarm.

"Stop them!" he said, pointing at them. "They are the thieves who were in the Library."

When he heard the soldier, Raiko started to run.

"Run as fast as you can!" He shouted at Adhara.

In response to the alarm, every guard at the port was running towards them from every direction. Raiko saw the silhouette of the *Aphrodite* which had taken off from the port and was moving slowly in the direction of the high sea. His worried gaze turned once more to the soldiers; they were many, and they were getting close.

A couple of guards had managed to reach them. Quickly, and acting on instinct, Raiko and Adhara drew the short daggers they had taken from the guards at the Library, and they assumed a defensive position.

Raiko was ahead of the intentions of the closest man, and he launched himself forward, not giving him time to attack. With the skill that he had learned on the streets, he slashed the wrist that brandished the sword. The soldier put his other hand to the bleeding wound, looking like he was in agony. Raiko took advantage of the situation and he pushed him down with both arms. The man fell to the ground, taking a heavy knock on his head.

For her part, Adhara confronted the guard facing her. With the dagger in her right hand, she tried to dribble her enemy. The situation was much trickier because her other arm was in so much pain. The man threw himself at her, and Adhara, fast on her feet, evaded him by jumping to one side. The guard recovered quickly, and bouncing on the tips of his toes, he closed in on her again. This time, Adhara guessed his intentions, and she let the man come at her in full force, with the intention of jumping her. Adhara hopped to one side again, and she quickly pinned her short sword into the soldier's unprotected side. It was not a deep wound, but it began to bleed profusely.

They had been able to dodge these two soldiers, but many more were coming at them, alerted by the commotion they had created. There were too many men, and they could not confront them all. It was an impossible situation, and Raiko decided to take desperate measures. Filling his lungs with air, he started to shout, "Radne, Ligeia, Teles, I need you!" He screamed with all the force of his lungs.

While Raiko shouted at the top of his voice, the guards kept closing in. When he thought that their capture was inevitable, a group of heads with long hair emerged from the water. When he saw them, Raiko yelled, "SING, SING!"

It was very unusual to see the mermaids so close to the coast, but faithful to Raiko, they immediately answered his call. Instantly, complying with his orders, the mermaids took deep breaths and began to harmonize their tunes.

When they heard the voices, the soldiers immediately slowed down. Their feet began to drag, as if their ankles were pulling a heavy weight. Their eyes, wide open, were seeing fantastical images in the air.

A collective madness took over all the guards. Uncontrollable mutterings and meaningless phrases fell from their lips. Some of them dropped to the ground and, on their knees, they covered their ears with their hands while heartrending screams came from their throats. In others, the delirium that overwhelmed them touched fibers deep in their souls, hidden secrets and repressed anxieties.

"Come to me, come to me, my love," a young soldier said, with his arms stretched out, and the forlorn expression of a lover who had lost his sweetheart.

Another guard, in a fit of fury, took his sword and blindly cut the air while he cried, "I will avenge the death of my own," as the blade of his weapon passed dangerously close to his companions. "I am the real Pharaoh."

Even the proud captain of the guards said, "Don't touch my gold, it is mine alone," as he kneeled down on the dock, and moving his arms towards his body, he splashed his clothes with seawater.

The mermaids, with half of their bodies out of the water, continued singing with satisfied smiles on their beautiful faces. They sang louder, using all their ancestral magic on the precarious sanity of the poor soldiers.

Adhara watched the scene, confused; it was bizarre to see all these men succumb to a sound she could not hear. Apart from the cries of madness from the soldiers, and the order to *sing* from Raiko, she had not heard anything else.

Radne sang from the water, obeying Raiko's orders, but she did not take her piercing eyes off him. Now that the soldiers were under the influence of the mermaids' spell, Raiko went to the edge of the dock, taking Adhara with him. The mermaid swam towards them.

Raiko looked at the *Aphrodite* with frustration. There was a distance between them, but it was still very close to the coast.

"Do you know how to swim?" he asked Adhara.

"Yes, but I don't think I can swim like this," Adhara said, feeling helpless. She had tried to hide her pain and she had managed to deal with the guard as best she could, but it would be impossible to swim with a dislocated shoulder.

From the water, Radne interrupted the conversation, saying, "I can take her on my back. My sisters will follow us, singing, until we reach the ship."

"Good idea!" Raiko said.

Raiko jumped into the sea and helped Adhara down from the dock. He took her by the waist and, once she was in the water, he put her on the mermaid's back. The careful gesture that he had afforded the girl did not go unnoticed by the mermaid. Adhara supported her chest on Radne's back and put her right arm around her neck.

Raiko began to swim quickly towards the *Aphrodite*. He was a good swimmer; all those years of experience near the ocean had not been in vain. Close by, Radne moved her beautiful, swift tail with Adhara on her back. Adhara thought the mermaid was swimming too fast, but she did not dare complain. She kept her head up in an effort to avoid filling her mouth with seawater, and to be able to breathe. Behind them, the mermaids continued their songs.

The others were on the deck of the ship, leaning on the railing and watching the scene from afar. Finally, Raiko reached them, and Odon hurriedly threw down a rope ladder so that he could climb aboard. Meanwhile Radne, with Adhara on her back, slowed down and stayed a few yards away from the ship.

From the *Aphrodite*, Roxana had not stopped looking at the water. She noticed a change in the expression on Radne's face.

The mermaid had stopped, and she was waiting impatiently for Raiko to turn his back on her. Roxana could read her intentions.

"She is trying to drown Adhara!" she shouted. Roxana had never trusted the mermaids and, from the first day, she had been watching Radne's movements. Raiko turned around when he heard Roxana's cry and he could see that Radne was going down to the depths of the sea with force, trying to take Adhara with her. The girl had let go of Radne's neck, but unable to move her shoulder, she was staying afloat with only the effort from her legs.

Underwater, Radne was pulling Adhara's feet in an attempt to drag her down and drown her. Adhara could no longer resist the force that was pulling her, and from the ship, they watched her head disappear into the sea as she tried to let out a cry that was unable to leave her throat.

Raiko let go of the ladder and immediately he dived into the water again. Taking a deep breath, he swam towards the spot where Adhara had disappeared. Moving his arms, he went down to where the mermaid and the girl were wrestling, and he saw how Radne was pulling Adhara with all her strength to the depths of the sea. The girl was kicking in an effort to set herself free, but the mermaid was a strong opponent and she was winning the struggle.

Raiko went to them and tried to separate the hands that were holding onto the girl's ankles, but Radne, crazy with jealousy, held on to them even tighter and would not let go. Raiko was losing the battle. In the middle of the water, he could not see clearly and his screams did not penetrate the dense waters. In desperation, Raiko bent his knees and using his feet for pressure he kicked her in the chest and pushed her back, at the same time pulling Adhara towards him.

With the impact, Radne let go of the girl's ankles and set her free. The angry mermaid looked at him, full of hatred and reproach, and then called her sisters. They came quickly and together they entered the deep waters where they lived.

Raiko guided Adhara to the surface. When their heads appeared above the water, Adhara opened her mouth and began to cough, releasing the water that she had swallowed. He swam together with her to the *Aphrodite* and taking her to the ladder, he held her until she was able to climb up to the ship on her own.

CHAPTER THIRTY-FOUR

Mithridates was looking at the remains of his statue, devastated. He had commissioned his best artists to build an immense statue of Victory, with wings open wide, that would be placed in the center of the hall in the Palace of Pergamon. It was the King's wish that the sculpture should glide through the roof of the hall, simulating his triumphal flight over Anatolia.

The artists built a huge sculpture in white marble, representing a beautiful young woman with wings, with a crown of laurels resting on her hair. They designed a complicated mechanism in the ceilings of the throne room that allowed the sculpture to move through the dome in such a way that it seemed like it was flying. During the trials, the mechanism had functioned to their satisfaction, but on the day of inauguration, and in front of his army and the royal committee, the device could not support the weight of the statue, and it fell to the floor with a raucous thud, smashing into smithereens.

Mithridates ordered the immediate evacuation of the hall. Furious, he demanded the beheading of all the artists who had participated in the work. While he watched the servants pick up the remains of the marble that were scattered over the floor, an emissary from Greece arrived. The sovereign felt the hair rise on the back of his neck. Superstitious as he was, he had interpreted the incident as a bad omen, and his suspicions were confirmed when the ambassador told him how they had lost Athens and Piraeus.

The King, however, did not waste time lamenting and, enterprising like no other, he organized an army of more than one hundred thousand men that was dispatched to Thessaly, under the command of his son Arcadius. This army was to meet with Archelaus near Chaeronea, north of Athens, to go to battle one more time with the Roman troops.

Two moons had not yet passed when Mithridates realized that his bad luck had not ended with the defeat in the two important Greek strongholds. A short time after his firstborn had left with his troops towards Greece, he contracted a strange illness in the encampment in Macedonia. The fevers finished off his young, strong body less than two weeks later, near Mount Tisaion.

Mithridates had not felt such profound pain since the death of his father. Now he was in front of the embalmed body of his son, ready to observe the royal funeral, anguish and grief weighing on his heart. Arcadius, his firstborn, his beloved son. A young man who had shown his bravery and sound judgment in the army, in spite of his young age, and who had died in his bed of vomiting and diarrhea, and not in battle like the great hero he was.

Pharnaces II had arrived in Pergamon immediately, accompanied by his wife, Rikae, to attend the funeral rites of his brother. The death of his brother had been a fortunate incident for him. Pharnaces was now the heir, and he had arrived quickly, not only to offer his respects to the remains of Arcadius, but also to make clear his position with regard to the throne.

Mithridates looked from Arcadius to Pharnaces, gazing at the second with scorn. Pharnaces had never shone in the use of weapons, or leading troops. So different from the brave Arcadius, the King thought. Why did the Gods take the son in whom he had the most pride, and instead leave him with this slimy, firebrand creature? Mithridates did not understand. His gaze once again caressed the motionless profile of his firstborn, as though he were trying to give him back the breath of life.

He looked up from Arcadius and, once again, he looked at Pharnaces. What would happen to his kingdom if he left it in his hands? Pharnaces was a coward, and his weapons were intrigues and dishonest pacts. The Gods would have to give him many years and more male heirs so that the throne would never be left in his hands, Mithridates implored.

He looked again at Rikae who was next to her husband. The beautiful, voluptuous princess, as always, was looking at him out of the corner of her eye, and with her lips in an inviting pout. The only good thing about his son was his wife, Mithridates thought, with anguish.

That night, while the palace slept, a slave entered Rikae's chambers and, beckoning her, he urged her to follow him. He put a dark cloak, which reached the ground, over her head, and he guided her along the dark, narrow passages used by the servants in the palace. After walking for a while, Rikae found herself in Mithridates' royal chambers.

She had barely entered when Mithridates took off her cape and the tunic she wore underneath, and he took her with fury. He was releasing, in her, all the anger and impotence he felt on seeing his favorite son die. After the first charges, and without being able to satisfy his carnal desire, the King broke down, put his head between her breasts, and started to cry.

Rikae rocked him in her arms and, with a sweet whisper, she tried to comfort him. Mithridates passed a long time in her bosom, letting the tears, that he had never permitted in front of his subjects, finally flow, and releasing his soul from so much pain.

Exhausted, he fell into a deep sleep. He woke at midnight. He immediately saw Rikae's large, dark eyes that veiled his sleep. He caressed her face with his hands.

"How are you feeling, my Lord?" Rikae asked.

"Well." The King did not want to talk about the moment of weakness that he had demonstrated a short while before. His face once again was determined, and in an imposing voice, he asked Rikae, "Tell me, are the rumors I have heard true? That Pilomenes is thinking of naming the boy that his eldest daughter had, the one who died the same day of his birthday, as heir of Paphlagonia?"

Mithridates had once again become King of Pontus, the Lord and Master of Anatolia. He started once more to take the reins of matters of state. He had not given credence to the rumors that had arrived from Paphlagonia, since he smugly believed that he was already the owner of Asia Minor and Greece... but now with this defeat, it was not the time for the smaller kingdoms to rebel.

"My father is getting old, and at times he forgets the promises he has made," Rikae said, with precaution. "But do not worry, my love. I have the situation under control. Until now, there has been no official announcement and, from what I know, the boy and his sister have left for Delphi to train for the Pythian Games. They are no threat to someone as great as you."

Her voice had a sweet affectionate quality, and it reflected a security that Rikae was far from feeling.

"Sister? Now that you say that, you are right, I remember hearing that that woman had two children. Two offspring of his firstborn daughter."

He looked at Rikae with the same look he gave his generals before a battle. The look of a king who did not admit defeat.

"Can I count on you to take care of the situation?" He asked, bothered. "I don't want uprisings in Anatolia. The youths always awaken idealistic dreams in the villages, and I need to be sure that the whole region is under my control."

Rikae chuckled with amusement.

"Count on me. Paphlagonia will always be yours. As I am, too."

As she spoke, she fell into his arms again.

CHAPTER THIRTY-FIVE

Dromeas helped her climb the ladder, and Roxana brought her a blanket so she could dry herself. Adhara vomited up all the seawater she had swallowed. She sat down on the deck of the boat, exhausted, while Raiko quickly climbed up behind her.

"Are you all right?" he asked.

Adhara nodded, as the color started to return to her cheeks.

Raiko leaned over her and softly said, "Let me see your shoulder." Adhara was unable to suppress a look of pain.

"I am sorry," he said, as his experienced hands moved over her body. "This is going to hurt a little, but only for an instant. I have to put the shoulder back into its correct position."

Adhara tacitly agreed. She would rather have felt pain instead of these strange sensations that were trickling through her body with this man's hands on her. She felt weak and dizzy; Raiko's breath was very close to her face and his smell bewitched her. For a moment, she wondered how she would feel lying down between those strong arms and feeling those lips on hers.

Raiko was focused on what he was doing, and he did not notice how Adhara was looking at him. With great skill, and taking her by surprise, he immobilized her shoulder with one hand and he brusquely twisted her arm with the other. Adhara let out a scream, but immediately she was able to move her arm normally again. She was secretly grateful for the roughness of the moment that shook her out of her state of bewilderment.

"Thank you," she said, looking straight into his eyes. Raiko buried himself in the gray-green sea that was Adhara's eyes. They stayed that way for a too long moment, looking at each other and speaking without words. For an instant, she was not a proud Amazon of noble ancestry, and he was not an outlaw who plowed through the oceans doing dubious business to survive. They were only a man and a woman who had had the good fortune to meet each other.

"You don't have to thank me for anything," Raiko answered, in turn. "I should have foreseen how Radne would behave, and I should never have put you in this situation." It seemed as though his voice was stroking Adhara's face.

Heptos' voice broke the magic moment that had transpired between them.

"I am happy that you are well, Adhara," the priest said.

Raiko got up and moved away from the girl, giving the others the chance to speak to her. In an effort to conceal the feelings of confusion that he had just experienced, he addressed the priest and said, "You never told me that we were going to play with our lives on this mission." He resumed his usual banter. "I am going to have to raise my price."

In spite of what had happened, they were all happy, especially Heptos. It was real! It was happening! They had already obtained the first book, and they had proven that the legend of the Bearer was certain. He did not know what the phrase of light signified, but he was sure that the Seventh would be able to decipher it.

However, although he was satisfied, Heptos was not content. The story that Abu had told was swimming around in his head.

"How could Sulla know that we were in Alexandria?" he asked aloud.

Odon was close by the few who were chatting, tying the sail in a complicated knot. The burly man looked up and, talking to the priest, he said, "While we were waiting for you at the port, I started to talk to a Greek sailor and I found out the news. It appears Sulla has taken Athens and Piraeus, and I am sorry to tell you," he said, looking at Heptos, "that the Red Commander took all he could from your former home. They say that he took *one thousand* wagons, fully loaded with all the treasures he stole from Delphi."

The priest's eyes were overcome by a deep sadness.

"The first part of the prophecy has been completed to perfection," Heptos said. "Sulla has avenged the affront against his own people, and he has fiercely punished Athens for allying with his enemy. But how could he know that we had set off on our search for the Treasure?" he asked.

He also knew that Sulla, like many others, was in pursuit of the five manuscripts. But the Red General had sent his soldiers to Delphi to look for the gold and silver he needed to pay his army.

How could he know, by a strange coincidence, that a committee had departed from the oracle to look for the other Treasure?

The picture of the Roman army robbing the treasures of Delphi appeared clearly in his mind. His heart was overcome with sorrow, and the memory of the other priests, with whom he had spent so many years, awoke a doubt in his mind.

"I wonder what has happened to my companions. I am sure that they did not offer any resistance. What could have become of them? I hope that they have been treated with respect, and that nothing bad has ensued. Of the seven priests dedicated to Apollo, I am the only one who is free," he said, with a sigh.

He had barely finished speaking when his eyes widened, his face took on an expression of shock, and he began to speak into the empty space.

"Seventh! Why didn't you warn us? You were the only one of us who could have known, and you have done nothing to alert us." He carried on, in fury. "I expected more from you."

Heptos was truly upset. The Seventh should have been aware that someone from the oracle must have informed the Roman Consul of this mission, but he had done nothing to warn them who the traitor was, or to alert them to Sulla's intentions. He knew that his intervention was only necessary to decipher the Word, but Heptos was expecting more commitment from one of the chosen ones.

Everyone around the priest was looking at him, confused. They did not follow the thread of his conversation. Dromeas was the first to express his concern.

"What warning are you talking about?"

"Miserable Traitor! You will appear fro the circle of seven. The prediction of the Pythia spoke of a traitor who would appear among the group of seven. I always thought that one of you was the traitor, and I racked my brains, asking myself who could it be? But now, I understand everything, the traitor does not belong to this group, the traitor comes from the circle of seven priests of the Oracle of Delphi: Enos, Duos, Tryos, Tesseros, Pentos, Exos and Heptos."

Heptos put his hand to his head.

"Of course, it all makes sense now." Heptos was speaking rapidly, making gestures with his hands. "The pursuit of Cleantes. He himself told me that they had followed him from the port of Kirra. Someone inside the oracle knew of my mission to find the Treasure, and knew, as many others did already, that Sulla was also hunting down the five manuscripts."

"Once again, the ambiguity of a prophecy has deceived me. One of the priests is the traitor, and he has made Sulla aware of our mission."

Heptos was furious; no one had ever seen him like this. Nervously moving around the deck of the ship, he looked at all the others frantically.

"Now that I sense the betrayal could do us much more damage than we predicted, I believe we should hurry in our quest for the rest of the books, because at this stage we have the Roman army behind us."

"Which one do you think we should look for?" Roxana asked.

"Although nobody knows for sure which ones are the five books, all the wise men agree that one of the books of Aristotle should belong to this group. When the descendants of Neleus went about selling his manuscripts, I sent Cleantes to evaluate the texts. The price they were asking for them was exorbitant, and I did not have that sort of money at the time," he said, pausing, with a guilty expression appearing on his face. He shook his head to relieve himself of any possible remorse, and he continued, "My faithful Cleantes confirmed that the manuscripts, apart from being damaged by moths and humidity from being locked up, were not complete, isn't that right Cleantes?" he said, looking at his servant.

Cleantes respectfully approached the people who were talking and answered, "What my Lord Heptos says is true. The manuscripts were in a bad state, but that was not what called my attention. I was able to leaf through them for a long time, and I noticed that one of the papyri had only the annotations of what the philosopher wanted to convert into a book, in other words, it was only a work in its beginnings."

Heptos interrupted him.

"I have analyzed Cleantes' observation and my instinct tells me that the book that belongs to the group of five is the last manuscript that Aristotle was working on before his death."

"Why do you think this? Why this book in particular?" Adhara asked, curiously.

"Because the notes begin with the argument, *All men by nature desire to know*," Cleantes replied.

"Could a book that is trying to reveal the Word start with a better statement?" Heptos concluded.

"Where is this book?" Roxana asked.

"Unfortunately, absolutely no one knows. I believe that the only one who knows is Aristotle himself."

"But Aristotle is dead," Dromeas reminded him.

"We will have to go to Hades to ask him."

CHAPTER THIRTY-SIX

It was the summer of 86 B.C., and Sulla's legions, with a little more than thirty thousand men, were marching towards the north of Athens to face the troops from Pontus. The Romans settled in an abandoned fortress in the city of Parapotami, on the Chaeronea plateau.

The army from Pontus had arrived from Tesalia, and had set up camp on a rocky hill with a view over the plateau, looking down menacingly at the Roman encampment that showed no signs of wanting to enter into battle, yet.

Mithridates had gathered an immense army composed of one hundred and twenty thousand men and a further ninety chariots of war. This imposing force comprised soldiers from the most diverse origins: Greeks, Macedonians, Scythians, Armenians, and Persians. Each cohort spoke its own language and was under the command of a leader of their own race, all of whom were subordinate to Archelaus, the Supreme Commander.

Sulla's soldiers were looking at the enemy camp from the distance. The number of tents, covering the whole mountaintop, was intimidating.

Murena, Sulla's right-hand man, looked at the general, cowering.

"They have more than three times the number of men," he said, worried.

"I know," Sulla replied, as he stared at the enemy.

To take the edge off the fear that he could see in his men, Sulla sent them to cut trenches and ditches around the flat terrain in front of them. Aside from preparing the land for battle, Sulla was hoping the physical toil would divert the soldiers from their fear, while giving him time to devise a plan of attack.

Archelaus had united a colossal force, the Roman General thought, but it would also be very difficult to control so many men from such different cultures, who had not fought together before. Sulla had sent spies to the area, and they found out that a group of the army had robbed some of the peoples of Boeotia while they were waiting for the call to battle. Lack of discipline and insurrection were two of the greatest scourges that a commander had to face, with such a great number of men under his control.

Archelaus' men were nervous and they wanted to get on with the action. The Supreme Commander knew this, and he was trying to provoke Sulla and lead him into a battle in open field, where his superiority in numbers would be in Archelaus' favor. However, Sulla, who had still not defined his action plan, had faked a retreat, closing himself in behind the walls of Parapotami.

The God Ares was mounted on his chariot pulled by four black stallions, black like hatred, black like the last vision you see before death. He looked back towards the plateau of Chaeronea; he glanced over Archelaus' troops first, and then at the Roman encampment. A vulture appeared in the sky, flew towards the God, and rested on his shoulder with a caw. The God stroked his neck, smiling.

"Stay calm, my friend, dinner will soon be served," he said, with emotion in his voice.

He knew that in a short space of time, a cruel battle would break out in this wilderness, and the thought pleased him enormously. Lucius Cornelius Sulla and Mithridates, two men to his liking, and two men who revered him, although they did not know it.

His father, Zeus, had despised him, saying he only suffered him because he was the fruit of his marriage with Hera, but Ares would show him what he was capable of, he would use these two men to teach everyone his greatness.

Lucius Cornelius Sulla had proven himself a man of ingenious tactics, and he never began a battle without having precise knowledge of the ground where he would operate. An old rival had said that Sulla was cunning like a fox and had the courage of a lion, and this had been the most exact judgment that anyone could have made of the Red General. Showing off this very special astuteness, he had given a few copper coins to some local peasants so that they would accompany his men on a reconnaissance of the area. The goat herders, happy with the payment, showed them a narrow path that led through the rocky mountain, passing above the enemy camp. A plan occurred to Sulla.

He ordered that the trenches that had been dug should be widened to protect the flanks of his army, and he ordered his soldiers to prepare for battle at dawn. He sent a group of his men along the path that they had discovered, and ordered them to launch heavy rocks over the encampment at first light, while Archelaus' camp was still sleeping. Sulla was relying on this attack to take them by surprise.

The men of Pontus fell into the ridiculous trap. When they felt the heavy rocks falling on the canvas roofs of their canopies, the soldiers rushed out of their tents half-clothed, and they ran towards the slope of the mountain in a haphazard way, to meet the army of Sulla that awaited them, ready, in solid formation.

Confusion and chaos reigned in Archelaus' army; the men of different origins, speaking different languages, were mixed among each other, and they could not understand the diverse commands issued by their leaders. It was a Tower of Babel that was toppling down the slope of the hill; the men pushed each other in search of their dispersed companions, and soldiers on top of soldiers fell dead on their own spears.

This was the mayhem that Sulla had expected. His well-organized troops, with their shields in narrow formation, brandishing their spears, stood up to this disorganized mass that was coming down the hillside to a field they had under control, and that was delineated by the trenches they had dug.

Archelaus ordered the launch of the cavalry against the Roman army, but they, too, did not have time to organize themselves, and they received a brutal onslaught from their Roman counterpart, commanded by Sulla himself, mounted on his inseparable warhorse. The beautiful horses of Sarmatia were pushed back to the walls of rock, where animals and horsemen died, flung against the sharp stone.

In desperation, Archelaus ordered the ninety war chariots to enter the battle, trying to achieve the same success he had had at the battle of the Amnias River. However, for the scythed chariots to be effective, they needed flat ground, as well as the element of surprise. Archelaus had neither of these. It was impossible for the vehicles to roll with enough speed, due to the stony conditions on the ground and the trenches that scarred the plateau. Furthermore, very few had boasted taking Sulla by surprise. The Red Commander, who knew this strategy of the Pontus Army, had already warned his men to remain in formation, and that when a scythed chariot with its lethal blades approached, they should move over in an organized way and let it pass; the same strategy that Alexander the Great used in Gaugamela against the war chariots of Darius.

The soldiers did as their leader advised, and as soon as the chariots passed by their side, subjected to the jeering and mockery of the Romans, they pounced on them from behind, killing their drivers with javelins, and applauding their victory with shouts of *"Bring us more!"* as though they were in the chariot races in the Roman Circus. The drivers were massacred, and the horses, now free from their reins and scared, made their way back to the Pontic phalanges, creating even more confusion in their lines.

Archelaus regrouped the last lines of his infantry and ordered them to form a closed line to confront the enemy. When the Romans saw this unit ahead of them, they realized by the tattoos on their faces that they were Roman slaves who had been freed by Mithridates on that fateful day of the Asiatic Vespers, when more than eighty thousand Roman citizens had been massacred in Anatolia.

The simple memory of this disgrace filled their hearts with a fury beyond equal. Throwing their shields to the ground and taking their *gladius*, the short swords they carried in their belts, they confronted them, man to man, unleashing all the thirst for revenge that had brought them to these lands in the first place.

The death toll was staggering. Of the one hundred and twenty thousand men that Archelaus had conscripted, only ten thousand managed to flee with their lives back to their general. The other one hundred and ten thousand died in the frenzy of the battle, or after it, when Sulla ordered the execution of all prisoners. The Roman army mourned only twelve deaths.

This was without doubt one of the most admired feats attributed to Lucius Cornelius Sulla throughout history. The Red Commander ordered the construction of two victory monuments, one of large proportions in the center of the battlefield, and another smaller one in the exact place on the rocky path from where his men had launched the first rocks.

From that day, Lucius Cornelius Sulla added an epithet to his name: Felix, the lucky one.

CHAPTER THIRTY-SEVEN

The spring flowed from the innards of the earth, its transparent waters babbling down to a very beautiful pond surrounded by brilliantly colored flowers. The animal would certainly come here to quench his thirst, since the love that this magical beast had for the fountains was well-known.

Roxana was alone at the bank of the small lake, awaiting him. They had decided she should be the one to make contact. She was the only one who could touch this special creature and not alarm him. Given her own substance, the animal would not be afraid of her. She was like him, part of nature. Roxana had been created from the essence of the most ancient element, she existed before anything, she would remain after everything, he would know this instinctively, and he would trust in her.

A white patch in the sky gave away his imminent arrival. Roxana looked up, conscious that the moment was near. Descending from the expanse of sky, the creature put his hooves on firm ground, pulled in his immense wings, and went to the fountain to satisfy his thirst, as was his custom. On the crystal waters of the lake, there was a reflection of the beautiful figure of a horse. Pegasus.

Pegasus was created from the blood that was spilt when Perseus cut off Medusa's head. He was the only winged horse known, and after serving Bellerophon to end the Chimera, Zeus had sent him to his stables to help the Lord of Lightning with his work. Pegasus, with his marvelous flight, was the only way they had to reach Mount Taygetos as quickly as possible.

The horse was satiating his thirst in the water when Roxana approached him, walking slowly. The creature did not feel any strange body; she was an extraordinary creature, just like him. She stopped by his side and began to caress his neck, transmitting all the peace and serenity that was customary from her body. The horse stood still at her touch, enjoying her caress.

"Pegasus, I am Roxana," she whispered in his ear, "and I need your help." The horse moved his head up and down in a clear gesture of agreement. With an agile jump, Roxana mounted the creature. When he felt the girl's weight on his back, he spread out his enormous wings and climbed to the skies.

"Take me to Mount Taygetos," Roxana whispered in his ear. The horse moved his head again and turned around in the air, changing direction to the region of Laconia.

His immense wings glided through the air, and while he was flying he moved his legs in the empty space as though he were galloping on the ground. From his back, Roxana watched the beautiful spot where they had met disappear, and saw the sea pass below her at a dizzying speed. They crossed the great patch of blue, and shortly afterwards they rose over Sparta. Once they were in this land, it was easy to find the mountain range, since the highest point was in the form of an easily recognized pyramid.

Pegasus flew around this highest peak several times, and when he found a flat surface, he landed cleanly on the ground.

As she dismounted the mythical animal, Roxana whispered to him, "Wait for me here," and she gave him a gentle pat on the neck.

Mount Taygetos towered almost eight thousand feet over the region of Laconia, scarcely one hundred and sixty miles from the south coast of the country. From the top, one could admire the beauty of the Ionian Sea and the seven islands that rested on it.

This remote mountain peak was used by the Spartans to dump children born with deformities, left to fend for themselves. Sparta was a nation of warriors and physical disabilities were not tolerated. When a child was born, he was examined by the elders of the city and if any physical defect was found that would impede the infant from becoming a valiant warrior, he was abandoned there until either hunger or predators ended his life. The earth had retained the desolation of all those innocent ones who had died in this spot, and who had nourished the soil with their tears.

Eager to leave this place as soon as possible, Roxana focused on finding the object of her search, the *Onyros*, a small plant that fed on the grief of these victims. Then she saw it. It was a tired bush with a solitary gray flower that with its very existence defied the lack of life around it.

It was only Roxana, who was all and part of nature, whom the plant would not harm. She took two stones that turned into soft, malleable putty in her hands and, using them like gloves, she picked the flower. She put it in a cloth sack that she had put on across her chest, and flying on the back of Pegasus, she returned to where the others awaited her.

Pegasus hovered over their heads for a moment, until he saw an empty space, and then he landed skillfully in the clearing. Roxana dismounted, caressed the animal, and whispering in his ear, she set him free.

"Thank you, you have served us well." The horse whinnied and, spreading his wings, he set off for Olympus.

"Were you able to find it?" Adhara asked.

In response, Roxana took out a flower from the bag she was carrying. The *Onyros* was a flower that, if ingested, would produce a heavy lethargy in its victims; they fell into such a state that they appeared dead, although they were not really. Thus, without being completely dead, only appearing to be, they would be entering Hades.

"Which one of us will begin the voyage?" Dromeas asked, anxiously.

"Roxana cannot go. It is not in her make-up to come into contact with death," Heptos said.

"I will not part from her," Ammos said. He spoke so little that the deep sound of his voice made an impression every time that he did. He placed himself by her side as though he was her loyal guardian, and he looked at everyone defiantly.

"I am very old," Heptos said. "Why should I go down now, if I will soon go down forever? I don't want to have a preamble of what is going to happen there."

There was, however, someone in the group who wanted to make the journey. Someone who did not fear contact with the dead, on the contrary, he desired it.

"I will go," Dromeas said, decidedly.

"I will accompany you," Adhara said, immediately. She feared for him. She believed she knew the reasons for his decision, and she was afraid that he would go too far in search of the answers.

Heptos looked at Raiko, imploringly.

"I will accompany them," he said, offering relief to the priest.

They therefore agreed that those who would undertake the journey would be Dromeas, Adhara, and Raiko.

"Very well," Heptos then said. "We will put two obolus with you, one under your palates for the journey there, and the other in your navels for the return. You should give these coins to Charon, the rower of the river Acheron. We will care for your bodies here; they will appear dead after you take the infusion of *Onyros*."

Roxana had taken spring water and had prepared an infusion, introducing the flower and adding a little honey. She served a little in three cups, and she offered one to each one of them.

"Before you drink it, remember!" Heptos said, pointing at two glass funnels through which sand was flowing in synchronization, "these clocks measure the time you are allowed to stay in Hades. Not a moment longer. If you pass this point," he said, signaling at the last grain of sand that passed through the narrow glass and settled on top of the rest at the bottom of the clock, "you will stay there forever."

Addressing Dromeas, he said to him, "Don't do anything foolish. We have not come all this way to die here. What's more, you will not really die; you will remain forever in limbo, between life and death. Drink now, and may fortune accompany you."

Following the order of Heptos, Raiko, Adhara, and Dromeas sat down on the grass and began to drink from their respective cups. They immediately fell asleep. Heptos turned the clocks so that the established time would begin its course, and he placed one of them in Adhara's sleeping hands. Ammos took out his large knife and put himself in position to watch over them. Heptos held the other sand clock in his hand and did not take his eyes from it.

CHAPTER THIRTY-EIGHT

Adhara, Dromeas, and Raiko woke up from what seemed to have been a bad dream. In truth, they did not know if they had woken, or if they were still experiencing a bad dream. They were on the banks of a river of dark water, at the mouth of an entrance to a great cavern. The sunlight had dwindled significantly, and the air was the color of gray lead. A multitude of souls wandered along the banks, the souls of those who had not had a proper burial and were destined to wander forever in a limbo between life and death. There were many warriors there, as well as peasants and common citizens. No doubt, the many riots and wars that had recently precipitated in the world of the living had augmented the number of people on this riverbank.

Raiko gestured to Adhara and Dromeas to go towards the only boat that was anchored on the riverbank. Charon, the boatman, received them. He was a figure covered with a long black hooded cape who extended his hand and demanded the corresponding payment to make the journey.

Raiko took out the obolus he had in the roof of his mouth, and delivered it into the bony hand that stretched out in front of them. Adhara and Dromeas followed his actions. Finally, the three of them got into the boat, which then began to enter Hades, the land of the underworld.

To the sound of rowing, they crossed the River Acheron, the River of Sorrow, and a deep sensation of grief overcame them. The raft, that was no more than a floating platform of intertwined trunks, slowly entered a very large cavern with an arched ceiling. Everything was completely gray, the stone walls, the poisoned water, and the ground that seemed like a swampy hodgepodge invaded by other rivers: the Cocytus, the River of Wailing, the Phlegethon, the River of Fire, the Lethe, the River of Forgetfulness, and the Styx, the River of Hatred. Adhara trembled. When he saw this, Raiko put him arm around her shoulders.

They arrived at the other bank, and following the signs of the boatman, they got down from the raft. No one had spoken a word since they had taken the potion.

"Here," Raiko said to them. He had no idea where he was, but he acted on instinct.

They were walking blindly through marshes, when they found the arched entrance to another cavern with a wider opening to the interior. The growl of a dog startled them. They turned their heads to the right, where they had heard the snort, and their eyes fell on a huge black dog with three heads. The three heads began to bark, foaming at the mouth as they brandished their fangs, while its uneasy body got ready to pounce on them.

"CERBERUS, STOP!" A woman's voice shouted. Obeying the command, the animal immediately stopped moving, though his three pairs of eyes looked furiously at the intruders.

A beautiful young woman appeared behind the animal. She had a pale face and withered flowers in her hair. With a click of her fingers, the beast went through the arch and disappeared into the darkness.

"What are you doing here?" She asked.

"We are strangers who come in search of an answer," Dromeas replied, proudly.

"I know who you are, and I know who your father is. Only because of that, my consort has turned a blind eye and let you pry around for a moment." It was Persephone, the wife of the God Hades, the God of the underworld. "I know whom you seek. Wait here and I will bring him. You cannot enter beyond this point."

The air was heavy and murky. Dromeas and Raiko were fidgeting, impatient to get the task over, and they plainly did not like the place. Only Adhara stayed still, with her eyes fixed on the sand clock that Heptos had given her.

Persephone soon returned in the company of an old man. Aristotle was as elderly man, with white hair and bright eyes.

"Who dares to disturb my rest?" He asked, curiously.

"I am sorry for the interruption," Adhara said, "But we are here because we have a question to ask you. We need to know where to find one of your books."

"These are strange times, when those who are alive come as far as Hades to visit the dead," he said. Looking into her eyes, he asked her, "Why do you want to know the whereabouts of my works?"

"Because it will help us reveal the Word," Adhara replied.

At this reply, Aristotle let out a roar of laughter and shook his head.

"Humanity is still devoted to the task of finding the Word? Nothing is so elusive, nothing as ambiguous and frustrating as its revelation." With a disenchanted air he said, "I spent my whole life trying to find it and I had it in my hands so few times..."

Aristotle was silent for a moment, reminiscing on old times, and then he continued, "Who sent you?"

"Heptos, a priest from the Oracle of Delphi," Adhara replied.

"I know who he is. Heptos is a scientist and, as such, he thinks that the search for the Word will bring the goodness he foresees at once. But at times, the Word brings more questions than answers... yet I will not be the one to hold you back in this search of knowledge. I cannot stop anyone who is doing the same as I did throughout my entire life... We must be immortal to the extent that it is possible for us." He said this as though he were in his familiar classroom, surrounded by students.

Aristotle continued, "*All men by nature desire to know.*This was how I began the manuscript that apparently Heptos is looking for so desperately." Nodding in agreement, he continued, "I have to recognize that he is right, that was my last manuscript, and it is likely that it will help him decipher the Word. The copy I gave to Theophrastus only had a few initial notes; it was not the complete work. That was the book I dedicated my life and soul to before I died. On my deathbed, I asked a faithful servant to hide it because I was not entirely proud of this work." In his eyes, he was reliving the last days of his life. He paused, but resuming his speech, he confessed, "I had not reached any concise conclusion and I needed to work on it more, but by then I had no more time."

He stopped for a moment, offered a faint, sad, smile and looking into her eyes, he said, "Go back to your world, and continue with this beautiful task. Who knows? Perhaps the Word can be discovered and understood for the good of humanity."

With a wink, he continued, "I asked my servant to hide it in a place very special to me, the little city of Assos. That was where I founded my school after Plato died and I left Athens. The book is hidden in the Temple of Athena... Isn't she the Goddess of wisdom?" He made a gesture of respect.

"Once inside the temple, look to the west, wait until all the evening light bathes the temple, and the hiding place will be revealed to you," the wise man finally confided.

Adhara smiled broadly. She finally knew the whereabouts of Aristotle's manuscript. The philosopher saw the expression of joy on the girl's face, and finding her happiness contagious, he asked, "Thank you, little one, for giving me some more life... but why have you taken on this mission alone?"

Adhara turned around; neither Raiko nor Dromeas were by her side. She had been so engrossed in the conversation that she had not noticed them disappear. Her eyes turned immediately to the sand clock and she saw that little time remained to get out of this ghastly place.

Without saying goodbye to Aristotle, Adhara ran, retracing the path that had brought her to this spot. She ran and ran, desperately looking to the right and to the left, trying to find Raiko or Dromeas. Which path had they taken? She found only shadows and fear as a response.

She started to call their names, but she realized that the air was so heavy that her shouts did not echo. She arrived at the bank of the Acheron River and stopped to take out the obolus that they had placed in her navel.

Raiko appeared from nowhere and, running, he pushed her onto Charon's boat that, oddly, was stopped at this edge of the river. They both handed over their respective coins. Charon took them with astonishment, he had never taken anyone across the opposite way, but if the clients paid, he was not objecting to the voyage.

In tears, Adhara yelled Dromeas' name, but her cries were subdued by the laments that came from the dark waters under the boat. Charon started to row and the boat took off from the quay.

Suddenly, from the deep darkness, the figure of Dromeas appeared. Running with all the force that his athletic legs could give, the boy unleashed a wild sprint to reach the inner bank of the river. Seeing that the boat had already started its crossing, he took a running jump and leapt toward the raft. Raiko grabbed him in the air and, with Adhara's help, they pulled him on board.

CHAPTER THIRTY-NINE

Jubilation reigned in the streets of Gangra, the capital of Paphlagonia. Peasants, merchants, laborers, and housekeepers had dedicated the preceding days to preparing the city for the celebration of Pilomenes' fifty years.

Pilomenes was a king who was very much loved by his subjects. His policies of harmony and justice, together with his diplomatic skills, had made his small kingdom a haven of peace in the midst of the ever-turbulent Asia Minor. The inhabitants were grateful for the King's wisdom.

The entire nation had been devoted to sweeping the streets, cleaning the fountains, and putting up garlands of flowers on all the doors and windows of their houses. They wanted to show the guests, who would file through the streets to attend the celebration, how proud they were of their city.

The festival would consist of three days of celebrations. The first day, after the welcome, there would be the royal banquet, and on the following two days the Paphlagonia Horse Races would take place.

The country's stallions were known across the whole of Anatolia for their quality, beauty, and spirit. Kings, Amazons, soldiers, and wealthy merchants came from all corners of the known world to acquire the magnificent stallions and beautiful mares that were raised on this land. Some legends told that these animals only fed on some flowers that grew on the slope of Mount Olgasys. These flowers, with large petals of a brilliant blue color, lacking in odor and difficult to chew, gave the horses the qualities of beauty and strength unique to the region.

The Paphlagonians, proud of their horses, had devoted themselves to the job of meticulously braiding all the manes and tails of their steeds with colored ribbons. It did not matter where the visitor looked, his eyes would always meet with a beautiful, carefully adorned horse.

The royal palace did not escape from this collective joy. Its walls had recently been whitewashed and repainted with an ochre yellow, typical of the region. They had adjusted the devices in the

221

fountains, and new statues were peppered throughout the gardens. A gigantic standard that proudly displayed the crest of Paphlagonia - an elegant stallion on a blue background - had been hung over the main entrance.

Pilomenes was positioned on the steps of the entrance of his palace to personally receive the caravans of guests who had started arriving hours before. He wore a long cape of the same blue color as the standard, held on his shoulders by two brooches in the form of horse heads. His beard, still brown, had been curled with hot tongs, and his feet were shrouded in boots of soft calf leather.

The welcome committee was made up of the King, the Queen, his closest family, and some court officials. Branco, the commander of his army, was to his left, richly attired in his war uniform, with his sword in his belt. He looked nervously to the right of the King; Lisipe was there, behind the twins, always attentive and upright.

Guided by the master of ceremonies, the recently arrived guests filed in, a long line made up of neighboring kings, dignitaries, and ambassadors from other kingdoms.

Rikae was the last of his daughters to arrive. She arrived in a *Harmamaxa*, a pompous golden carriage with four wheels, pulled by six beautiful stallions. The cushions were of golden brocade, four wooden columns supported the roof, and the canopy that covered it was of a thick purple fabric. The bridles of the horses were also golden, and their crests were of white feathers. An entourage of eunuchs followed the cortege and, when the carriage stopped, they moved forward swiftly to help the princess down. A dwarf quickly moved close to the door, he got on his knees and put his hands on the ground, as though making a footrest in front of Rikae.

Rikae stepped down from the carriage with deliberate calm, in order to make her appearance a spectacular moment. She supported one foot on the back of the dwarf who gritted his teeth to endure her weight. She looked at the entourage to make sure that everyone there was looking at her. She wanted to ensure that they all knew of the importance and power that those of the kingdom of Pontus enjoyed.

Three soldiers from the Royal Guard of Sinope walked ahead of her, and two solicitous slaves adjusted the excessively elaborate dress, adorned with gems, that she was wearing. She went walking slowly to Pilomenes, with her arms, covered in gold bracelets, extended to him.

Pilomenes, ignorant of the fact that Rikae knew his plans for inheritance, approached his daughter and kissed her on both cheeks. Queen Valia did the same.

Rikae deliberately greeted her sister Toula first, with displays of affection that were far from how she felt. After having given a prolonged hug to the rejected princess, her gaze turned slowly towards Zoe.

"Well! Here is the sister we have not met," she said, disrespectfully, as she looked her up and down.

Straight away, she looked at Dromeas and Adhara.

"And these must be your... children." She left a gap long enough so that everyone would understand that the word she really wanted to say was "bastards." The result was an uncomfortable moment that Pilomenes tried to divert, asking her about the news from the court of Sinope.

While the King spoke, Rikae's eyes were looking around at the people positioned behind Pilomenes. She locked eyes with Lisipe. The Amazon was behind Adhara, just like a shadow. The woman withstood the stare firmly, and Rikae, surprised by such a show of courage, turned back to look at Pilomenes. Interrupting the conversation the King was trying to initiate, Rikae said, "The journey was so long and I am tired. Show me my quarters. We will see each other at the banquet," and without waiting for a reply, she walked into the palace as she spoke, followed by her servants.

Zoe was bothered; she had never met a woman like Rikae. Her attire was splendid, as were her jewels, but beyond the ostentatious richness that undoubtedly placed her in royal standing, she had an attitude of being the Lady and Master of the world. Powerful and contemptuous at the same time. She made the people by her side feel as though they were not worthy of her company. Zoe did not have time to give it much thought as the master of ceremonies announced the next guest.

Three mares with short red blankets and golden stirrups stopped in front of the welcome committee. The horseman at the head quickly dismounted, and with a confident stride, he walked towards Pilomenes. He was a handsome man, tall, with broad shoulders. His black hair was tied back, and his blue eyes seemed uncomfortable. The other horsemen were two robust soldiers who formed his only escort. With military bearing, he approached the awaiting committee.

The man made a gesture of respect to Pilomenes, he also greeted Valia with respect, and he gave Toula afurtive, cold look. That was when Pilomenes turned to Zoe.

"Zoe, my daughter, I present you Phelon, King of Pisidia."

Phelon bowed in front of her, and when he looked up the expression on his face relaxed; his eyes remained fixed on her for a long moment, and an electric current passed between them. Zoe, little accustomed to contact with members of the opposite sex, immediately smiled, and a silly grin appeared on her face. Confused, she looked away, and then met with a pair of eyes that radiated fury and poison - Toula's eyes.

She then realized the delicacy of the situation. *In the name of all the Gods, it was her sister's husband!* Seeing Toula's expression, she felt that the proximity to this man could bring her many problems. She would try to avoid him for the duration of the celebrations.

A Fate, in front of her spinning wheel, was laughing at her intentions.

The banquet would take place in the vast dining hall of the palace. The enclosure had also been meticulously prepared for this celebration. The slaves, on their knees, had cleaned the floors, and waxed them until they reflected images like a mirror. Large bronze candelabras with five arms were placed between the tables, and valuable incense smoldered in the burners, its delicious aroma scenting the air.

Pilomenes would preside over the dinner from the head table

that was set on a platform. Two large side tables would accommodate the guests; these tables were topped with linen cloths and silver bowls filled with hazelnuts, plums, cherries, and pears.

Zoe entered the banquet hall hastily. She had spent too much time in front of the mirror preparing herself for someone she was apparently going to avoid all evening. When she arrived there, she went to one of the side tables where her children and Lisipe were already seated. To her consternation, she discovered that the only free chair was the one next to Phelon. With a feeling of apprehension in her chest, she went to the empty place and sat down.

Hurried servants entered with trays full of meat from the hunt Pilomenes had ordered a week before, offering his guests the most exquisite specimens from his woods. Casseroles of venison, wild boar, and pheasant, cooked in olive oil from Greece and the best spices from the East, were served onto the diners' plates. The King had spared no expense in this celebration. Large jugs of wine were poured to fill the glasses of the seated guests.

With the effects of the wine and good food, the atmosphere had lightened; the guests were laughing and, once in a while, they would raise their goblets to toast Pilomenes. With all the wars and events that were taking place in the region, this party offered the dinner guests the chance to relax, enjoy themselves, and forget their problems for a short while.

The sound of musical instruments was heard, and a group of dancers entered the dining hall. Slim young girls and agile youths dressed in transparent tunics began to dance between the tables, recreating in their movements known episodes of the history of Heroes and Gods.

In the first dance, the young noblemen, adorned with the arms and shields of Paphlagonia, detached themselves from the girls who reached out their arms to them, pretending to cry. This was a scene in the history of Paphlagonia when, after losing the war by the side of the Trojans, a large group of Paphlagonians emigrated to other lands towards the West, to territories bathed by the Adriatic Sea. Pilomenes watched these scenes with tears in his eyes. The exodus had taken place many years ago, but it was a recurring theme in the nostalgic songs that had been heard forever all over the kingdom.

From the opposite side of the dining room, Rikae was watching the spectacle with contempt. She was seated next to Toula, sisters united in the same hatred. They were staring at the neighboring table, while the eyes of the dinner guests were fixed on the dancers.

"It seems as though our half sister has a new admirer," the poisonous Rikae said, looking innocently into Toula's eyes.

Toula signaled to the servant, who quickly filled her goblet with more wine.

"Every minute that she and her children have spent among us has been cursed," she said, angrily pushing her plate away from her. Rikae watched her sister's pathetic reaction with pity, this idiot who had let her husband be stolen.

"Is there any certainty in the message you sent me? Do you really believe that our father will name Dromeas as his heir?" she asked curiously. "The way things are in our region right now, it is the least diplomatic decision he could take. It doesn't seem like a choice that is in tune with how he governs."

"Since that boy was born, our father has changed," Toula said sadly, as she swallowed all the wine she had been served in one gulp. "It's a fact, I know it. He will name him as his heir. He is just waiting until the brat wins the horse race and, in the ceremony to present the trophy, he will announce it." She made demanding signs to the servant who was pouring the wine. Solicitously, he filled her goblet again.

Rikae was pensive, analyzing her sister's words, while tapping her finger rhythmically on the border of her cup. The announcement that Pilomenes was about to make was not agreeable to her in the least. She kept a persistent eye on Dromeas. An idea started to form in her mind.

Suddenly the music changed, the harps and flutes moving from a sad, melancholy tune, started to play music of a faster rhythm. Some men with long beards, wearing silk capes, came into the dining room carrying tambourines and drums in their hands. The musicians started to play faster, and smiling dancers spread out a string of flowers. They began to pass through the

226

dinner guests, wrapping the flowers around their necks, while the rest of the invitees shrieked with laughter and applauded.

A slim dancer with large, dark eyes approached Dromeas and flirtingly wrapped her ribbon around him. The boy got up straight away and went with the maiden to the center of the room. They began to dance to the very fast beat of the instruments. A young nobleman did the same with Adhara. The girl also got up, with a smile on her face, and moved with her partner to the center of the dance floor where they joined her brother.

Lisipe watched them from the table; the children were happy and joyful as they danced, far away from all the events that were happening around them.

She looked at Adhara again. She was precious; apart from Phelon, who did not take his eyes off Zoe, she was the focus of attention of all the men in the party. She had left aside the *quiton*, the short skirt she usually wore, and instead she wore a blue tunic, a blue that reminded her of the sky on a sunny spring day. The dress was fastened at the shoulders with silver brooches, and the cloth fell gently on the chest of the young girl who moved as she was roused by the rhythm of the music. Her long auburn hair was put up, with thick waves that fell down her back in an unruly way. The servants had interlaced silver ribbons between her locks of hair, and the belt that hugged her trim waist was also of silver.

Lisipe was confused. She had sworn to protect this girl and help her to fulfill her destiny but she did not know how. *How could she protect her in this world with such different rules?* Suddenly an idea came to mind. Pilomenes might promise her hand in marriage! Until now, Adhara had enjoyed a freedom unique for women of the palace. She could ride a horse, fight, and brandish a sword. She had had the opportunity to learn to read and write, but now she was getting close to the age of marriage. What would happen if they promised her to a king from an allied country? She was an Amazon. Amazons did not subject themselves to a man! Lisipe had to be by her side to make sure this did not happen.

"You must be very proud of your children. The girl is beautiful." Lisipe heard what Phelon was saying to Zoe. "She looks like you, but you are much more beautiful. More beautiful

227

than any other woman I have known in my life," he said, gallantly, while his blue eyes locked on Zoe's lips. She lowered her head, blushing.

Lisipe threw her a grim look. What was happening to Zoe? Where did all this blushing and these stupid smiles come from? She had never behaved this way; she was shouting to the four winds that this man was affecting her. Would Zoe consider getting married? To her sister's former husband?

Her eyes settled on Toula, on the other side of the room. It was clear that Toula was annoyed, but Lisipe did not understand why. Phelon had rejected her. Why did these women need to have a man by their side? Her eyes followed the line of guests and met with the mocking look of Rikae. *I do not like this woman at all*, she thought to herself. She assumed she was the Lady of the whole world, and she had spent the whole night looking intently at Dromeas. This was something that did not please the Amazon by any means.

A servant put a plate in front of her, on it there was a good piece of wild boar cooked with plums. The old Amazon adored the taste of this meat. With an appetite, she cut a chunk and put it to her mouth, while she watched the celebrated one, who was laughing happily from his table.

Lisipe also thought that Pilomenes was making a mistake by announcing Dromeas as his heir. The Amazon knew Mithridates, and she knew that he was a fierce warrior. Paphlagonia would not have a chance against him; Pilomenes had neither a strong army nor the disposition to face a war.

What is happening here? Why is everyone being carried away by emotions? Zoe and Phelon were unable to disguise the desire they had for each other, Toula could not hide her jealousy, Pilomenes could not hide his pride with regard to Dromeas, and Rikae... *What was it that Rikae could not hide?* Lisipe wondered. She had always been a good interpreter of human weaknesses, but this mocking princess escaped her. One thing she was sure of, Rikae was capable of anything. An ambitious woman, without a doubt.

There it is again, Lisipe thought. *She can't stop looking at Dromeas*. It was that same look of a tiger in the bushes stalking its prey. *Does she not realize that he is too young for her?*

The music came to an end and the guests applauded the performance with euphoria. Breathless, but in fits of laughter, the twins returned to their seats at the table. Dromeas had noticed that Lisipe was looking at Pilomenes' youngest daughter with distrust, and he turned to look at Rikae, trying to understand the cause of the preoccupation on the face of the old Amazon. His eyes took in her dark eyes and sensuous lips. Without doubt a beautiful woman, he thought to himself. A youth of sixteen, like him, could not help feeling attracted to such a voluptuous woman.

Rikae turned her head and their eyes met. She made a flirtatious face and smiled at him. With slow deliberation, while keeping her eyes fixed on him, she took a solitary goblet that was beside her and poured a little wine. Taking both cups with her two hands, she got up from the table and went to Dromeas' place.

She walked slowly through the space that separated them, giving the young man time to appreciate the swaying of her bulky breasts as she approached. Dromeas stared at her like a rabbit hypnotized by a predator.

"I have heard it said that you are very able with horses," Rikae said, closing in on the boy.

"So they say," Dromeas stuttered, not taking his eyes off her full lips.

"I am sure tomorrow you will win. You are the favorite," Rikae said, praising him. "I propose a toast for tomorrow's champion!" And as she said this, she gave one of the cups to the boy, raising her own, encouraging him to drink the wine.

Dromeas took the goblet she offered in his hands, with a dazed look on his face, not taking his eyes off the woman's lips.

"I don't think it's a good idea to drink wine before a race," Lisipe interrupted, taking the goblet from Dromeas' hand. "It dulls the senses and exhausts the limbs." She did not like this woman's attitude, and something deep down urged her to protect Dromeas.

"Besides, you have to be rested for tomorrow if you really want to be the victor," Lisipe continued in an imperative tone.

Dromeas looked at her grudgingly; Lisipe was making him

feel like a stupid child in front of this spectacular woman.

"I am perfectly capable of winning this contest without needing much rest," he said, arrogantly.

"That I toast!" said Lisipe, and lifting the goblet that she had taken from Dromeas into the air, she drank the whole contents in one gulp. "But now, we are all going to bed." And she put the empty cup on the table with authority.

"Good night to all!" the Amazon said, like a hen protecting her chicks, and she retired from the dining room, pushing the twins in the direction of their respective bedrooms.

Rikae's face had turned into a mask of stone as Lisipe had drunk from her cup. She had made a vain attempt to stop the Amazon from drinking, but she had ingested the wine so quickly that it was impossible to stop her. She kept looking at her back, as the Amazon left the dining hall behind Dromeas and Adhara. When she was alone she shrugged her shoulders, pursed her lips, and made sure she took the empty goblet with her.

Meanwhile Zoe and Phelon, far removed from what was happening around them, continued their enjoyable conversation.

"I know that the Amazons are excellent judges when it comes to horses. I would be delighted if you would meet mine. His name is Toribus and I'm going to ride him tomorrow." He moved closer and whispered softly in her ear, "If I win the race, I will dedicate it you, beautiful Zoe."

Phelon had courted her all throughout the dinner. He used any excuse to touch her, and his knee looked for hers under the table. The young Amazon, inexperienced in receiving the attentions of such an attractive man, was barely able to taste a bite the whole evening and, to her regret, she had taken in more wine than she realized. She felt happy and relaxed, wanting to shout out to the world how content she felt in the company of this man.

In the face of Phelon's remark, Zoe looked down with emotion.

"You are very kind," she answered, timidly.

"Why don't you come by the stables early in the morning

before the race, and that way you will wish me some luck?" he asked in a hoarse voice.

The idea of being alone with him was such a great temptation that it was impossible to resist. To hell with Toula!

"I will be there," Zoe promised.

Although she spoke in a low voice, this answer reached the wrong ears.

It was a gloriously sunny morning. Zoe left her room in a hurry, heading for her date in the stables. She had butterflies in her stomach, and had not been able to sleep all night.

The palace was unrecognizable, with the colorful pavilions in the gardens. The guests walked around all over, and rushed servants were taking care of the preparations for the race.

Zoe was happy, happy, happy.

She stumbled into someone she knew as she headed for the stables.

CHAPTER FORTY

Dromeas had been unsettled beside Raiko and Adhara, waiting for Aristotle to arrive. He had not gone down to Hades to talk to the philosopher. He wanted to find here the answers that he had gone to find in the Oracle of Delphi in the first place. He saw Persephone come back accompanied by an old man and so he took the opportunity to set off on his own search. He wanted to find Zoe; he wanted to know who had murdered his mother.

Since her death, he had not been able to sleep at night. The doubt and the unsatisfied desire for revenge relentlessly eroded his soul. He knew that his mother had given up being who she really was and had renounced many privileges for his sake, not to give up the male child she suspected she was carrying inside her... and he had not been able to vindicate her death.

But what hurt him more was the thought that his mother's murderer had been Lisipe, as the whole world suspected. Lisipe had been his teacher, his model to follow. For Dromeas and his sister, she was synonymous with love, dedication, and loyalty. He did not know which would be more painful, to kill Lisipe, or to leave his mother's death unavenged.

He entered the lateral caverns that formed that macabre labyrinth, hoping not to meet that terrifying dog again. Strange and deformed figures approached him, trying to cling onto him, but he shook them off with firm movements, first asking, *Have you seen Zoe, the daughter of Hippolyta, the granddaughter of Penthesilea?* But all he received in response were cries and groans.

"Dromeas! What are you doing here?"

Dromeas turned to the voice and Zoe's figure appeared, like a vague memory.

"Mother," he said.

"Dromeas, what you are doing here?" Zoe repeated, angrily. "This is not the place for you. Besides, I am not permitted to talk to you, leave from here, leave right away!"

"Who ended your life? Was it Lisipe?" He asked, anxiously.

232

He remembered the morning he had found his mother's corpse, during the celebrations for Pilomenes' birthday. Zoe had one of Lisipe's arrows through her breast. Lisipe had disappeared and the rumors had concluded that the old Amazon was the murderer.

"Lisipe? No, Lisipe is here with me. She gave her life for yours," and her image slowly began to dissolve.

With a cry of anger and pain, and seeing that the image of his mother was inevitably disappearing, he set off at a furious pace for the riverbank.

Heptos, Roxana, and Ammos watched over the bodies of their companions. Lying there, they looked like three children steeped in sweet dreams. In the clearing where they were lying, the setting was completely different, the sun was shining brilliantly, and the air was filled with the smells of summer. Roxana decided to sit in the meadow. Her movement disturbed a swarm of brilliant butterflies which, with the fluttering of their wings, created a cloud of color that passed speedily over their heads.

Heptos followed her movement and sat on the grass by her side. Ammos walked around in circles uneasily with his knife in his hands, near the sleeping ones, zealously guarding their slumber.

"There is something that I have wanted to say to you," Roxana said, addressing Heptos.

"Tell me, Roxana," Heptos replied.

"I think that you have been slightly tough in your treatment of the Seventh, when you reprimanded him for not having warned us of the traitor. It is not easy for him to warn us," Roxana said, trying to speak in a soft enough tone so that she did not sound like she was scolding him. The girl understood the attitude of the Seventh; she imagined that deep inside he questioned whether he should interfere.

"Do you know who the Seventh is?" Heptos asked, shocked.

Roxana answered, "Yes."

233

Heptos looked at Ammos, expressing the question in silence. The man nodded in agreement.

"But even I do not dare to speak to him," Roxana continued.

With a wave of his hand, Ammos interrupted the conversation. He made signs to Heptos so that he would look at the clock that he had in his hands. Heptos looked down; the last grains of sand were falling and the three bodies were still stretched out on the grass, pale and motionless, as though they were asleep.

A look of concern took over the three faces. There were very few grains of sand and the three sleeping bodies showed no sign of wanting to return to life. When the last grain of sand had fallen, Adhara opened her eyes and came around violently, followed by Raiko. The last to awaken was Dromeas.

Adhara got up like a coiled spring that had been released, and she began to scream at her brother.

"Dromeas, what did you think you were doing? Why did you leave me alone in such a miserable place as that?"

Dromeas did not even look at her. Moving away from her quickly, he walked angrily towards Heptos and like a raging lunatic, he rebuked him, "You promised me that I would find answers to my questions and that's not how it was. I saw my mother in the depths of that horrible place and she was not able to tell me who murdered her. Even worse, she told me that Lisipe is there with her."

"Calm down now Dromeas! You dared to do something that is not permitted for any mortal, to go down to the land of the dead to speak to your mother. That violates all the rules!" Heptos raised his voice in anger. "Furthermore, you received an answer. Lisipe's honor is intact. She was not Zoe's murderer. At least you can let go of any resentment towards that woman who devoted her life to your mother and you, and try to make something of your life," Heptos opened up his heart.

Dromeas remained quiet. Angry tears ran down his cheeks. In spite of having descended to Hades, he still did not know the name of Zoe's assassin. Even worse, his mother had told him that Lisipe had given her life for him. What was she trying to tell him?

"Did you see our mother? Is Lisipe dead, too?" When Adhara heard these words from Dromeas, two heavy tears began to roll down her cheeks and a deep sobbing came from her chest.

Adhara had not cried when her mother died. She had been strong for Dromeas, so that he would not break down, she had been strong for her grandfather, to prove to Toula that they were people of more robust substance, she had been strong for everyone, but suddenly the dam of emotions she had pent up inside, opened.

In the depths of her soul, she had held out hope that Lisipe would one day return with her mother's murderer and explain what had happened. But now, knowing that the old Amazon was also dead, she could not overcome the sorrow that swamped her heart.

The rest of the group was paralyzed, finally seeing the twins cry. No one knew what to do. Raiko went to Adhara and hugged her; she broke down against his chest and sobbed loudly, letting out all her grief. Raiko hushed her, holding her tight. He was moved to see this side of Adhara. The proud princess cried like an inconsolable child in his arms, and seeing her vulnerability aroused both his sadness and his desire.

His was a fraternal gesture, but he had acted on instinct. He had wanted to hold her in his arms ever since the day he saw her, displaying her pride at the oracle, since the day when she was coughing on the deck and he had been relieved that Radne had not harmed her. He put his lips gently on her forehead and kissed her hairline. A deep hatred overcame him, whoever could make Adhara cry like this would pay for it very dearly. He looked up, his eyes met with those of Dromeas, and in a silent conversation he swore he would help them find their mother's assassin.

After having released her grief, the memory of Lisipe emerged in Adhara's mind again, while she felt Raiko's arms around her. The image of Lisipe with her spear in her hand and her defiant attitude slapped her in the face. She was an Amazon, she had to repeat to herself, and she was not any one of them, she was the Last of the Amazons. Adhara could not look for comfort in the arms of a man, she had not been born for that, she had another destiny. She could not allow herself to fall in love with

235

Raiko; it went against everything her teacher had instilled in her since she was a little girl. She should never have allowed this moment of weakness, and wiping the tears from her face, she broke away from his arm and turned her face to Raiko. In a cold tone, full of reproach, she asked him, "You disappeared too. What were you looking for in the underworld?"

The connection that had grown between them and that had strengthened during the last part of the journey disappeared, and Adhara was once again the proud, haughty girl who would not show her feelings. Raiko instantly reacted. He once again assumed his jovial manner, and the body language that said he could not give a damn.

"My reason was more prosaic and mundane. I wanted to obtain this," he said, showing an object that had made the return voyage with him. It was a shining helmet with arcane letters written on the back part. With a smile, he added, "I always wanted to have the Helmet of Invisibility of Hades; the truth is, I don't know why he needs it in such a horrific place."

CHAPTER FORTY-ONE

Rikae was in her quarters in the palace of Sinope, reading the message the emissary had just delivered. Contrary to all predictions, Lucius Cornelius Sulla had won the battle of Chaeronea. Delivering a humiliating and devastating defeat. The Roman, with little more than thirty thousand men, had reduced the army of Pontus to ten thousand fleeing cowards, when before there was the roar of one hundred and twenty thousand swords. Matters were not going well for Mithridates.

Rikae had returned with her husband to the court of Sinope, and Pharnaces had taken it upon himself to watch over the occupied kingdoms. She was sure that her father-in-law must be livid, sitting on his throne in Pergamon. The image of the Savior King was breaking down, and her husband had told her that those small territories, like those of her father, that had accepted submission to his supremacy, were now not showing the same respect. Now, more than ever, it was a political question that Paphlagonia stayed subordinate to Pontus, Rikae thought.

Reading this missive, she was sure that there had been more shifts in loyalty, after the news of Sulla's victory had arrived in Asia Minor. A few months before, after the fall of Athens, the residents of Galatia had secretly allied with the Romans. Pharnaces had many spies in the region and he had advised his father of the undercover movements that were taking place. Mithridates was furious and he decided he would make an example of them to his neighboring kingdoms.

The King of Pontus had planned a magnificent banquet in Pergamon for all the princes of Galatia. As was customary in his court, he did not skimp on expenses. He brought jesters, dancers, and musicians from every corner of his territories, he filled amphorae with the best wines, and he placed the most tempting feast on the tables of his guests. Needless to say, the meats were dipped in the powerful *Zamikh*, the poison for which the King had such affection, and to which he owed a great deal of his power.

The dinner guests were dying, foaming at the mouth, before they reached dessert. But not everyone had fallen for the trick, to be precise, three princes who did not trust the King of Pontus had not touched a bite and were able to flee. The noble Galatians hid in Ephesus, where the rich lords who had supported Mithridates in the massacre of the Romans debated whom they should support.

The state of affairs in the region was tense, and all the minor kings anxiously awaited the development of the war between Sulla and Mithridates, unsure of which opponent would bring the lesser suffering to their people.

Circumstances had become so tense that Rikae wondered if it would not be better for her father to die sooner. Pilomenes enjoyed good health, but she had loyal subjects in the court of Gangra who followed her orders. Given his age, it would not surprise anyone if her father died.

If her father passed away, she would immediately take power. Toula had no support to put herself in the position, and Zoe had died. Only those two little ones bothered her, she said to herself. Since they had left, she had not been able to follow their trail. *What were they meddling in?* She wondered. *Those two, I need to find both of them.* Until now she had focused on Dromeas, but she could not forget that Zoe was Pilomenes' first born, and in turn, Adhara was hers. If she finished off the boy, Adhara, too, would continue to be a problem.

She had used her husband's spies all over the region and had promised a great reward, but so far her efforts had been to no avail; it seemed as though the earth had swallowed them up.

CHAPTER FORTY-TWO

The *Aphrodite* once again sailed the Aegean Sea, but this time in the opposite direction, towards the north. The town of Assos was situated on the east coast of Anatolia, south of what had once been the great city of Troy. The voyage was slow, because this time the winds were not in their favor. The passengers, however, were in good spirits after the revelation that they had witnessed in the Library of Alexandria, and knowing that they were close to finding the second book of their mission.

They arrived at the port and disembarked, yearning to stretch their legs. They decided to walk to the village. Assos was a beautiful town, built on a hill facing the sea, and from there they could admire all the facades of the important buildings, temples, and theaters built on the hillside.

They walked through the port cautiously, as they did not know if Sulla's spies knew that they were there. But after wandering for a while in the pleasant summer sun, their mood became less tense. It was highly unlikely that anyone would dream of finding them here. They were the only ones who had been able to contact the great philosopher. The whole world took for granted that all of Aristotle's works rested in Sulla's Roman villa, under the attentive care of his librarian, after he had seized them from Apellicon of Teos in the sacking of Athens.

After crossing the city walls without arousing suspicion, they walked towards the Agora. It was midday and the roar in their stomachs reminded them that they were hungry. They stopped at an inn and a solicitous maid brought them lamb stew baked with rosemary, wheat bread, a tray of dates with honey, and a jug of wine diluted with water. They sat down peacefully to enjoy the well-deserved lunch. They knew that they had plenty of time to climb to the Acropolis where they would find the Temple of Athena before sunset.

They finished their lunch, paid the account, and slowly walked up the hill to the Acropolis. There, in the center, the Temple of Athena rose majestically over the city. It had six Doric columns that flanked the entrance, and thirteen columns on either side that supported the structure. The frieze on the front represented centaurs running through the forests of Attica, chasing nymphs and fauns. The temple was painted in bright shades of green, red, blue, and yellow that glimmered magnificently in the sunlight.

The sanctuary had been built on the highest part of the city and, from the steps of the entrance, there was a view of the island of Lesbos, bathed in the Aegean Sea. They sat down at that spot, appreciating the beauty of the landscape and looking to the west, waiting for the sun to set on the horizon.

A short while later, they saw the dazzling circle of the sun start to go down in the distance. The rays of light began to change color and the skies were tinged with a golden-orange tone. The reflections produced little slivers resembling frost on the waters, as though it were a magic path of silver stones that guided the King of Stars.

The sun touched on the horizon and the sky transformed into a canvas painted in various shades of pink. The scenery was so beautiful that they stood, overcome, as they watched the spectacle in front of them. For a moment, they forgot that they ought to be looking for the manuscript.

When the sun had almost disappeared they heard the worried voice of Heptos saying, "Darkness is approaching and we have not found the whereabouts of the manuscript."

The others woke up from the stupor that the beautiful atmospheric effect had produced, and they began to look around for some sign to guide them.

Heptos began to despair. The last rays of sunlight bade farewell and nothing around them indicated any place where the book could be hidden.

Helios drove his carriage of fire into the horizon and finally night covered them with his cape. The moon filled the empty space that the King Star had left behind, spilling its light on the landscape. Dusk was over.

Then, Roxana said, "Listen." They stopped talking, holding their breath to hear whatever Roxana had heard. They remained silent, their ears pricked. It was the timid hooting of a small owl.

From between the branches of a neighboring tree, a tiny owl with gold and black striped plumage flew into the inner chamber of the temple. As Aristotle had said, they had to wait until *all* the light of dusk glowed, and when that ended, the night birds were ready to come out. Athena had sent her favorite bird, the owl, to show them the hiding place.

The little bird flew over the great statue of the Goddess in the center of the temple, taking care to avoid the large copper incense burner where the sacred fire was dancing. He flew around the room twice in an unhurried flight. Seven pairs of eyes followed the path of his wings, and finally the little owl settled on a bronze sculpture in a corner close to the terrace.

Raiko went to the fire and lit four torches; he gave one to Heptos and another one to each of the twins. They followed Roxana to the statue where the owl had perched. It was the image of a centaur sitting on the ground, reading some incomprehensible characters from a shield. Roxana moved over the statue. She stroked the little bird on the back of its neck, and the animal shut its eyes in delight, emitting a pleasant sound. He opened his eyes, hooted again and flew off towards the outside.

Roxana passed her hand over the sculpture and moved it to one side with ease, as though it were a sand castle. There, below it, they found a leather sack with a manuscript inside.

"The last work of Aristotle," Heptos murmured with emotion. He began to unroll it with care. The papyrus displayed the writing of the great philosopher. The book began with the statement, "*All men by nature desire to know*".

Heptos put the manuscript in Roxana's hands. She received it with her palms facing the ceiling. Ammos stood in front of her, and with his palms facing downwards, he put them close to hers. Once again, the book prevented any contact between them. Raiko, Dromeas, Adhara, and Heptos formed a circle around them with the flaming torches. Roxana and Ammos closed their eyes, breathed deeply and began to chant.

But if the scene in the library of Alexandria had impressed them, here it was simply out of this world. On the terrace of the Temple of Athena, with the moon shining over the dark sea and the light from four torches, Roxana and Ammos looked like two Gods who had descended to earth to give a lesson to humans. This time, their chants were deeper. It reached the point that it was impossible to distinguish which voice belonged to whom, as it seemed as though a third, distinct, voice filled the temple.

The game of lights that had arisen in the manuscript of Euclid once again came alive. The playful sparkles filled the air in a crazy chase, its brightness overshadowing the flames from the torches as well as the moonlight. Dancing in front of their eyes, they formed the statement:

One sun, two comets, two blue planets, and two rays of brilliant light.

Just like the last time, the phrase hung in the air long enough to be read, and then disappeared into a cloud of sparkles.

Roxana put the statue back in its original position. Heptos carefully rolled up the manuscript and they started walking slowly back to the city.

That night they slept at the inn in the village. The crew also needed to rest and Odon had taken advantage of the day to stock the ship. They met at the dining table to share a frugal dinner. They were emotionally drained by the spectacle they had witnessed, and sitting around a fire whose flames were dwindling, they did not dare to speak.

The exhaustion of the day overcame them and soon the women went to bed, followed by Ammos and Dromeas. Only Heptos and Raiko remained in the dining room, in front of the remains of the dinner that were still on the table.

Raiko continued drinking from the jug of wine that had barely been touched. Heptos stared at him and with some sarcasm he asked, "Are you happy that you joined this mission?"

Raiko traced his finger around the goblet, he took a drink of wine, and took his time before answering, "I can't complain. You have paid me well. I hope that things don't get more violent because my life is valuable, especially to me."

Heptos, not taking his eyes off him, smiled, "You know very well that I am not talking about money. I am sure that you have never sailed such turbulent waters," the priest replied.

Since they had returned from Hades, Adhara had openly avoided him and was trying as far as possible not to speak to him. This state of affairs affected him deeply, but he disguised his wounded pride with cynical comments, and by making fun of everyone around him.

Raiko made a gesture to indicate that he did not want to talk about it.

"As soon as this mission is over, I will take my crew as far away as possible and I will never return to these lands." He said, forcefully.

He preferred to change the subject. Staring at his glass and without looking up, he asked Heptos, "What is the fate of the manuscripts once we discover the Word? What are you going to do with them?"

"Very good question," Heptos replied. "My intention is that the knowledge of these manuscripts and the very Word reach as many people as possible." Seeing a sign of doubt in Raiko, he continued. "My dear friend, the enlightenment is hidden in temples, museums and other places of learning, and what those manuscripts contain can only be appreciated by kings and wise men. As I said before, I believe knowledge is infinite, by sharing it, it grows and multiplies. All human beings should have the opportunity to be able to access it. The same with the Word, it should be known by everyone." He shuddered in frustration. "I do not have enough money, or resources, to hire thousands of copiers to share this Treasure with all the thinkers in the world. But I am sure that a time will come when it will be possible, and then these manuscripts will reappear because we have preserved them."

CHAPTER FORTY-THREE

Year 1482 A.D.

The fireworks lit up St Mark's Square, to the delight of Venetian onlookers who were enjoying the games of light and color that danced in the sky of *La Serenissima*. The carnival had officially begun, and with it came the hubbub of people with masks and costumes, celebrating, drinking, dancing, and laughing in the alleyways surrounded by canals.

The Grand Canal, with its sumptuous palaces and high-ceilinged halls with crystal candelabras of thousands of candles, spilled its light through those windows. In rhythm with the music from the parties, it imitated a serpent of light and joy that was born again each night.

In each *campo*, music sounded in the air, competing with the laughter and voices of the crowd who happily celebrated days of revelry, the "farewell to the flesh". Days when the men and women of Venice could forget themselves, their social status, how much money they had, and could assume the personality of the costume they had chosen. Days of freedom, days of new beginnings.

On the edge of all of this commotion, a solitary gondola slid along a side canal. The gondolier stopped at each corner carefully; he could not send out the customary calls used to advise one gondola of the presence of others at crossings. They did not want to be seen or heard. If they were caught, they would pay dearly for their pride.

The canal on which this gondola was floating was dark and desolate, leading to the artisan workshops of *Sestiere di Canareggio*. There, a small *palazzo* awaited the arrival of the boat and its precious cargo.

The journey seemed even longer for Marco, who was hidden inside the *felze*, the closed cabin in the center of the gondola. If any indiscreet look fell on the boat, it would only be able to attest to one solitary gondolier who was navigating at those late hours in the night.

Finally, they arrived at a small canal where about twenty small *palazzos* rose up one next to the other, cramped close together. The boat stopped in front of a dark wooden door that did not permit access from the canal to the house.

"Who lives there?" they heard voices asking from inside.

Marco ventured out of the *felze,* and addressing the voice that had asked the question, he replied, "It is me, Marco."

The door opened slowly, and the gondola entered the private enclosure that the Venetians had beneath their palaces, by way of stables, that allowed the gondolas and the other boats to enter their houses. There, an old man was waiting for them, standing by the side of the wooden deck where the steps that led to the first floor of the dwelling began.

"Have you brought it?" he asked, anxiously.

"Of course," Marco replied, with a knowing smile. "Come here."

The old man got into the boat and followed the youth to the cabin. There, inside, was a large lump covered with a black canvas. Marco theatrically pulled off the black covering and, before the expectant eyes of the old man, a book press was unveiled.

"Finally they will awaken from their long sleep!" The old man said with emotion.

They were not aware that, very close by, a solitary figure was watching them. A figure who was dressed in a long black cape and, with the excuse of the carnival, had his face hidden behind a white mask.

CHAPTER FORTY-FOUR

"I think we should follow Ignatius' advice and look for the book by Aristarchus of Samos," Heptos said.

They had gone back to board the ship. Aristotle's manuscript was already in a safe place along with that of Euclid, among the wooden chests in the hold.

"Why is their so much debate surrounding that book?" Roxana asked.

"While all the astronomers of renowned fame, such as Hipparchus of Nicaea, and even Aristotle, assured us that the Sun revolves around the Earth, Aristarchus stated that the Sun was the center of the Universe, and the Earth and the other stars revolved around it."

My great friend, Aristarchus, was an astronomer born on the island of Samos. Euclid, he, and I used to have the most amenable conversations about astronomy, a subject very dear to Aristarchus' heart. By night, he dedicated virtually all his time to studying the stars, and during the day, he would write down his philosophies, leaving very little time for us, his friends. I cannot deny that he wrote important works regarding the position of planets in the canopy of heaven. His writing, "On the Sizes and Distances of the Sun and the Moon" was an obligatory reading in the Library of Alexandria.

His most important work, however, was that one in which he maintained that the celestial dance was not centered on us, the Earth, but on that star that we admire each morning when we awaken, the Sun. A theory that no one believes, and a theory that will still cause a stir a very long time after this adventure...

"Why was that manuscript not in Alexandria?" Adhara asked.

"Just as Ignatius told us, a valiant rivalry broke out between the libraries of Alexandria and Pergamon. Unscrupulous men began to rob books all over the known world, in an attempt to obtain large sums of money from kings. But the kings were not ready to hand over a high sum for every book, and some of them lingered in personal libraries as they had not been claimed by the highest bidder."

"As you have seen, to Zenon's great disappointment, Hipparchus' manuscript did not form part of the five books, which made me think that Ignatius was right."

Raiko grimaced. He had not taken a liking to that know-it-all who looked at Adhara awestruck, and it bothered him that Heptos praised him so much.

"Notwithstanding the fame of Aristarchus of Samos, that manuscript in particular was one of the group that remained without a bidder. In theory, it should not be difficult to obtain a book that nobody valued, but to our misfortune, it is in the hands of a truly despicable person."

Heptos had heard talk of this work in his youth and he put his network of spies to task, making the necessary enquiries in case this book was one the five, a fact that most of the other philosophers had dismissed.

In accordance with his investigations, he came to believe that the manuscript was in the hands of a rich merchant, who had delusions that he was an aristocrat. He lived in the region of Mysia. His lands were a short distance from Pergamon, and he was almost sure that in some not quite honorable way, he had acquired the book.

After having accumulated a fortune as a loan shark, he swindled a ruined aristocrat so that he could buy his lands and marry his only daughter, therefore, in this way, he could inherit the family honor in full. The unhappy wife drowned herself in the Macestus River on her wedding day, preferring death to sharing the nuptial bed with such a monster.

"We must go to Mysia, to the residence of Innoel Hammorib," Heptos said. "I have to warn you that this man is a scoundrel who does not know the rules of honor. He had devoted his entire life to stealing money, lands, honor, and even knowledge, from his victims. His methods are infamous and treacherous. Therefore, I ask you to be very, very careful when we are in his presence. Do not let his insults obscure your judgment." This last comment was for Raiko's benefit.

Looking at Adhara, he said, "You, Adhara, will be the key to the negotiation."

The *Aphrodite*, sailing the Aegean Sea, facing the coasts of Assos in the Troade, took the easterly direction, towards the region of Mysia. The palace of Hammorib was near the northern coast of the area and therefore they had to cross the Hellespont, the stretch that separated the Aegean Sea from Propontis. The crew knew these waters, and the passage through the narrow channel was an easy task.

While the ship plowed through the calm waters of the strait, they could see to their sides the two coasts of Asia and Europe at the same time. Between these two coasts, years back, Xerxes I, King of Persia, had built a bridge of boats, tied together strongly and placed alongside each other, to allow his troops and cavalry to cross from one continent to the other in his march to conquer Greece.

The mermaids had not reappeared since the incident in Alexandria, to the delight of Adhara, and Dromeas' despair. However, a group of dolphins had shown up behind the ship and Odon called everyone to look. The playful dolphins jumped on top of each other, and from their smiling mouths they let out squeals that resembled the laughter of mischievous children.

Roxana smiled happily. She loved those creatures, she undoubtedly preferred them to mermaids. She quickly took a piece of wax and started to mold the figure of a dolphin with her hands. Her eyes were fixed on the animals while her fingers quickly gave form to the material.

Soon, a dolphin, very similar to those swimming in the ocean, appeared. Roxana held out her hand and showed it to Adhara. The girl looked at her friend's work, impressed.

"Very good. The similarity to those ones is really amazing," she said, pointing at the animals that were playfully swimming around them. Suddenly the wax dolphin started to move its tail, and with a jump, threw himself into the water as though he were answering a call from his companions. The two girls watched in surprise, and started to chuckle. Heptos went over to them; he was curious as to why they were laughing.

"What happened?" He asked.

"The dolphin that Roxana made took life and jumped into the sea," Adhara replied, delighted.

And looking at Heptos, Roxana said to him, "You are right, every time I touch one of the books, I recover the power in my hands to give life to my creation."

"I knew it," Heptos said with a knowing smile on his lips.

The voyage continued peacefully, and the warm climate made it very pleasant. They entered Propontis when dawn had barely broken and they reached the coast of Mysia as the sun reached its zenith.

Dromeas saw the coastline and his heart was overwhelmed with nostalgia for his homeland. They were so close to Paphlagonia! How would his grandfather be? He was burning with desire to go and tell him what he knew. He wanted to arrive at the palace gate and scream to everyone that Lisipe had not murdered Zoe. Now he was itching, longing to avenge the death of his mother, and his teacher as well.

What had Zoe meant when she said, "She gave her life for you?" He had kept this information to himself. He had not been able to tell anyone else, not even Adhara with whom he shared all his secrets. Someone had wanted to kill him and Lisipe had intervened? It did not make any sense. He tried to remember the last time he had seen the Amazon, and the only scene that came to mind was the image of the dinner at the Palace in Gangra. Lisipe had forced them to go to bed early and she had said goodnight to him at the door of his room. He never saw her again after that night. Another doubt came to mind, if Lisipe had died, where was her body? So many questions and so few answers, Dromeas thought.

When Heptos had all five books, he would return to Paphlagonia to seek revenge for Zoe's death. And Lisipe's too. It was most likely that the same person who killed his mother was

249

the murderer of the old Amazon. He did not believe his mother had any enemies, but perhaps Lisipe had. Who could it have been? He pondered on this, as the voices of the crew tying up the boat at the port distanced him from his thoughts.

Once at the dock, Heptos had sent Cleantes to make the mandatory introductions and ask for hospitality at Hammorib's home. The servant returned a day later with a positive reply and with horses for the journey.

They went on horseback all the way from the port to the residence. They passed through a forest, dense with luscious trees, and finally they arrived at an open land where there was one unusual building. It was a small palace with so many annexes to the main building that the construction lacked any defined style and was of very bad taste.

The servants were waiting for them and helped them to dismount. Without anyone realizing, while the servants were taking charge of the luggage and showing them inside, Heptos bent down and took a stone from the ground at the entrance in his hands. He covertly placed it in Roxana's hands and whispered "You already know what you need to do."

CHAPTER FORTY-FIVE

The servants accompanied Adhara and Roxana, escorted by a matronly woman, who led them to the western part of the hodgepodge of buildings. As they walked, they could see a great number of statues, fountains, and colonnades in the paths and the gardens, all displayed in a disorderly manner. It was clear that the owner of the house wanted to show the world that he was a connoisseur of art.

A small sitting room with a view over the garden connected Adhara and Roxana's rooms. Bizarrely, the windows were covered with a lattice of thick wood in the form of bars. In the room, there were fruits and drinks for refreshment; they also had two slaves at their disposal. The soft beds were a delight to the girls who had spent their last days in a cabin on Raiko's compact ship.

After they bathed in perfumed water, they brushed their hair and got dressed. An attentive maid asked them to accompany her, and she guided them to a hall where the rest of the group was waiting. It was evident that Heptos, Ammos, Raiko, and Dromeas had also bathed and changed clothes. Adhara was pleased to notice Raiko's poorly disguised look of admiration. Frustrated, she realized she was deceiving herself, she had decided she would eradicate this man from her life but in reality she could not.

A swarm of people was present, giving the impression of a makeshift court. The hall was of very large proportions, and it had an immense dome, painted with over-elaborate scenes of Gods and fauns. The walls were painted in dark colors that gave an affected and decadent air. Innoel Hammorib sat pompously on a kind of throne of solid gold, and he had two slaves who were cooling him down with fans of ostrich feathers. In spite of this, he was sweating profusely.

Their host was a man of approximately fifty years of age. His prominent stomach kept the purple silk clothing he was wearing in a state of perpetual tension. His face had a double chin, and his bulging dark eyes resembled those of a large hungry frog waiting for an innocent insect that would soon be swallowed. He had a tray of food by his side, from which he constantly served himself. When they were about to be introduced by the highest-ranking servant, the large frog belched. Everyone around him laughed, as though it were a little child joking, but in their eyes one could see the fear he provoked in them.

Hammorib made a few signs and Heptos took several steps forward. With a bow, he said, "Hail, Innoel Hammorib! We are most thankful for the hospitality you have shown us. Allow me to introduce my party."

"Dromeas and Adhara, grandchildren of the King Pilomenes of the neighboring kingdom of Paphlagonia." The twins bowed. Hammorib stared at the pendant that Dromeas was wearing on his neck. It was the one that Pilomenes had given him before he left.

"Roxana, Princess of Petra, the Rose City of the Desert, and Ammos, her faithful servant," This time it was the turn of Roxana and Ammos to bow.

"Enough!" Hammorib said. "No more of this baloney; I know exactly who the seven of you are."

"You," he said, looking at Raiko, "Are you still the disgrace of your family?" And after this rude comment, he brought a bunch of grapes to his mouth, which he started to chew without closing his lips, much to the delight of those present.

Raiko gave him a terse look, but at the motion of Heptos, he remained silent.

Looking at Dromeas, he said, "The pendant you are wearing around your neck is the emblem of the King of Paphlagonia. Why are you wearing it, when the whole world knows that Mithridates will reign through his daughter-in-law? It is understood that Rikae is the heir to the throne," he paused, scratched his private parts, and continued, "it is also understood that he was prevented from naming you his heir after that bastard daughter died during the celebration... a celebration to which I was certainly not invited," he concluded, annoyed.

"I am surprised you know so much," Heptos interrupted. Dromeas had clenched his fists at Hammorib's insult to his mother. Heptos, however, contained him with his glare. He had already warned them, this man really irritated people if he thought there was any benefit to him.

"You know then, who I am," Heptos said.

"Of course, you are the priest of the Oracle of Delphi" he said, with the remains of the fruit in his beard. "How did you manage to save yourself from the sacking?"

Heptos looked at him at length.

"Everyone knows that Sulla robbed the nearby oracles of their riches to pay his soldiers and finance the war he would face on returning home. It is my job to know." He replied, petulantly.

And your means of survival, Heptos thought.

"What brings a priest without a temple to my humble abode?" he asked.

Heptos focused on his mission, they had come to look for a book, he had to leave any personal feelings aside and concentrate on the task.

"I want to make you a proposal. I know that in the vast collection that forms your personal library, that has served to nourish a person of such wisdom as yours, there is a book that is dear to me. More than anything it is a sentimental matter, since the manuscript in question has no value because it contradicts all the great scholars of our time. I come to make you an offer for the manuscript of Aristarchus of Samos."

"What you can you offer me?" Hammorib asked, interested.

"I am a priest without a temple, but not a priest without resources. I intend to offer two talents of gold for the book."

The audience let out an exclamation; it was a very high sum for a forgotten manuscript.

Hammorib remained pensive for a moment.

"The Treasure of Delphi. You kept part of it, isn't that true?" Looking at Dromeas, he said, "or did the idiot Pilomenes give some of the treasure to this lad he was trying to make his successor?"

You are aware of absolutely everything that is going on in the region, Heptos thought to himself. This man was to be trusted even less than he thought. It was not safe to stay under the same roof for very long. Hammorib picked at a tooth with his fingernail and extracted a piece of fruit.

"The amount you are offering me is considerable. However, you know the love and attachment I have for wisdom. I myself, a humble and great wise man, must think about your offer. Let us rest our heads and tonight, under the beneficial influence of the land of dreams, we will find an answer convenient to both of our needs," Hammorib said, and leaning forward in the chair he made a gesture to the servants and continued, "Enough talk of money matters! I do not want you to leave without having enjoyed my hospitality. Don't say that Innoel Hammorib does not know how to behave as a host!"

They sat down around the throne and the servants began to offer fare to the dinner guests who were sitting on cushions on the floor. During the dinner, Hammorib did not take his eyes off Heptos, whom he was evaluating like an opponent. Heptos withstood the stares with a serene calm. Roxana and Ammos moved away and sat in different corners of the room, trying not to call attention to themselves. The mood remained tense until after some clapping of hands, Hammorib announced, "The dance is about to begin, call Zarin!"

A beautiful woman with black hair and dark eyes, dressed in a transparent tunic, came into the center of the enclosure. At the sound of music played by four men with wind and percussion instruments, the young woman began to dance.

Her slim body moved to the rhythm of the music and her light legs sketched arabesques on the ground. Her long toned arms moved around her head, making her look like a Middle Eastern Goddess.

Dromeas stared at her in awe. His eyes did not leave that marvelous body that danced to the sound of the music. The girl shimmied, showing her navel, her defined muscles, and her skin gleaming with perspiration. During one of her circles, she looked at Dromeas and, for a brief moment, their eyes met.

"This little bird is my new acquisition," Hammorib said, winking at Heptos. Dromeas heard the comment and clenched his jaw tightly. The thought of this disgusting man caressing this soft body turned his stomach and aroused the fury of an assassin in him.

Raiko, sitting next to Dromeas, whispered, "Be careful! She is giving you the eye and that is our host's mistress." The comment only increased the fury that had awoken in Dromeas.

Raiko thought he understood what was happening to his friend. He gave Zarin a look of approval, he had to recognize that the girl was a beauty and it was not hard to understand why Dromeas was so enthusiastic. He felt someone's eyes on him; he looked around the room and realized that Adhara was gazing at him. Jealous? He wondered. The eternal sardonic smile appeared on his face. The idea amused him.

Night finally fell at the palace and it found all of its inhabitants facing great dilemmas. Hammorib walked around his chambers nervously, not knowing which decision to take. On the one hand, two talents of gold was a very great temptation for a man as greedy as him, but he wondered what made this manuscript so valuable that a priest from the Oracle of Delphi offered such a fortune for it. There was something he still did not know, and perhaps, if he knew the reason, there would be the possibility of getting even more for the book.

An idea was forming in his head. The way he saw it, Heptos was an unfortunate old man, accompanied by a few silly youths, who had money, talents of gold, to squander. If the plan that occurred to him worked, he would end up with the gold and the book, and he would make that old man look like a fool, and all his youngsters along with him.

Now that he was remembering the dinner, he did not like the way the young blond lad was looking as his new dancer, and she at him. It was not that Innoel doubted his own good looks; he had a large number of servants who reminded him daily of how handsome he was, but it bothered him the slave had looked away towards the young man.

He had wanted to try this sweet feast ever since the day she arrived at his palace. He had bought her from a seller of fine slaves a few weeks before, but ulcers in his private parts had prevented him from consummating his desire. He would have to double the guards in the slaves' quarters. He did not want any young lad having her before him.

Adhara was in her room, annoyed; the attention of all the men on that woman had been excessive. Next to her, Roxana was absorbed, working the stone that had been picked up on the way there.

"Do you think that woman is beautiful?" Adhara asked.

"Yes, the women from her country are famous for their beauty. Moreover, it is not just their beauty, you cannot deny that she moved very well," Roxana said, without looking up from the stone she was sculpting. "What bothers you so much? That your brother was mesmerized, or that not even Raiko could take his eyes off her?"

"It does not matter to me whoever Raiko looks at and my brother is old enough to wipe his own dribble," Adhara said angrily as she lay down on the bed and covered her head with the sheets.

Even the captain of the guard had an unusual night. He had received precise orders to double the security and to permit absolutely no one, especially none of the guests, to enter the quarters of the slaves.

He took his position in front of the heavy door that gave access to those rooms like any other night. He was ready to pass another peaceful evening. Two lines of men watched the long passageway that gave access to this part of the palace, and all standing upright, they were carrying out their task with competence.

The night was long, heavy, and boring. The captain began to inspect his nails and, as he was cleaning them with the point of his dagger, the door opened inexplicably in front of his eyes.

He looked from side to side, checking that there was absolutely no one there. He shut the door again, as he had done

256

earlier this same night at the start of his guard shift. Although he checked absolutely everything, the locks, the passageway that connected to the rest of the building and the accesses to the garden, he could find no reason for the curious opening of the door.

Moreover, a line of soldiers positioned in the corridor attested that no one had passed through there. At the lack of any logical explanation, the captain shrugged his shoulders and prepared to continue the long night fulfilling his duty.

Zarin was lying on her bed. She had been afraid that tonight she would receive the call to the bedroom of the revolting master. Fortunately, the master still had some strange ailment and he had not sent for her. The doctors had recommended two more nights of rest.

She had been imprisoned near her home, very far from here. When they saw how beautiful she was, they did not rape her as they did with the other girls they had captured, since they knew that the price would be higher if they kept her a virgin. Since she had arrived, they had kept her confined in her quarters and they only let her out to the main hall to dance for the pleasure of the master and his guests.

That night she had danced once again, as she had done since the day she arrived. But that night was different, that night she had seen a marvelous creature in the crowd. Her eyes had met with those never-ending golden eyes that had left her marked forever.

The night was warm and she could not fall asleep. She got up from the bed and went towards the window that was completely guarded by a wooden lattice. Through the small openings the smell of jasmine entered from the gardens and, wrapped in its aroma, she closed her eyes for a moment.

She felt a presence by her side, arms that wrapped around her waist and lips that pressed breath on her forehead. Invisible fingers began to stroke her face. She opened her eyes, frightened, and did not see anyone by her side. She left her room and ran down the long corridor that led to the entrance of the slaves' quarters. There, in front of the great door, was the captain of the guard, protecting the door in a firm stance.

"Has anyone entered these quarters?" she asked.

"No, my Lady. Have you seen someone?" the soldier asked, nervously.

"No, nobody. Goodnight." Zarin bade farewell.

She walked back to her room slowly. Her face still felt the caresses that she thought she had received. She blamed the heat and the thoughts that wandered uncontrollably through her head.

However, when she entered the bedroom, a red rose was waiting on her bed.

CHAPTER FORTY-SIX

The sunlight beamed through the windows, illuminating their thoughts. Servants entered their rooms, bringing breakfast and the news that their master had a proposition to put to them.

After eating, they went to a hall, smaller than the one from the night before. There, they saw Innoel Hammorib, accompanied by only a few servants.

"I have given great thought to your offer and, as you know, I am a noble man who looks for equal benefit for all," He looked at his servants for signs of support for his words. "As you will understand, it is very difficult to discard a document of such importance and such meaning to my family. My proposal is the following: choose a person from your group to whom I will pose three questions. If you answer the three dilemmas, the book is yours. If you are wrong in even one of them, I will keep the manuscript and the two talents of gold, which I will use as alms for my subjects most in need. May this turn into a joust between gentlemen of wisdom."

Heptos accepted with a nod of his head. He already knew this would be the reply, and that was why he had warned Adhara about her role in the negotiations.

"We accept your challenge and the person chosen by us is Adhara, the granddaughter of King Pilomenes."

Hammorib could not hide a smile of satisfaction. The idiots were putting all their hopes in a woman, and a young one at that. He was already relishing the thought of his fortune growing with the two talents of gold.

"Excellent decision," Hammorib said. "We will meet at dinner time to resolve the first enigma."

They met for dinner in the same large room as the evening before. The enclosure was full of people that Hammorib wanted to use as witnesses to his joust. Once the dinner was over, Zarin was again called to dance. Just like the night before, she

259

captivated the audience with her movements, and Raiko had to keep Dromeas in line, as he could not hide his attraction to the dancer.

When Zarin left the room, Hammorib coughed affectedly to impose silence. The whole audience was aware of the proposition that he had made to Heptos, and they anxiously awaited the outcome.

"I have here one of my wise men, charged with posing the first question," he said, gesturing at a middle-aged man wearing a yellow tunic. The wise man took his position in the center of the room and as though he were reciting a psalm, he reeled off in a monotonous voice:

"There are seven houses, each one of them has seven cats, each cat eats seven rats, and each rat eats seven seeds. Each seed has produced seven sacks of grain. What is the total number of these objects?"

When he finished speaking, the hall was steeped in silence. Hammorib addressed Adhara and said, "You have until the same time tomorrow to give me an answer." He had a content look; he did not believe that a young girl like this would be able to answer one of the questions from his wise man. He, in particular, would not have known how to respond.

Adhara had listened to the question, sitting on a chair they had assigned to her and that was positioned directly facing the wise man who recited the question. From the satisfied smile on her face, her companions understood she knew the answer.

"I do not need so much time, my Lord. The answer is 19,607, or equal to the sum of 7 houses + 49 cats + 343 rats + 2,401 seeds + 16, 807 sacks of grain."

Everyone present began to applaud; the girl's response had been perfect. Hammorib turned red with rage and looked at the wise man by his side with murderous ire.

"Very well solved. I will make sure my next questions are not so easy. We will meet again tomorrow in this same place," and after he said this he left he room, spitting with fury.

In the privacy of his chambers, Innoel Hammorib ordered that his group of scholars come immediately.

"I cannot allow myself to lose this book and I want the money," he barked at the terrified men, "and even worse, I cannot lose because of a woman. You will not sleep until you have come up with two riddles that are impossible to solve."

Adhara had gone to sleep very happy. The look of approval from Heptos, and especially the one from Raiko's eyes, had comforted both her soul and her pride. As she fell asleep, she realized that Roxana was no longer sculpting, on the contrary, it seemed as though she was talking to someone. Nevertheless, the exhaustion of the day was more powerful than her curiosity and she drifted into slumber.

Zarin, too, had fallen asleep. In her dreams, she saw the face of the young blond man whom she had seen once again that evening in the hall when they had called her to dance. She could see his anxious eyes and his strong, bronzed arms. She was asleep, but again it seemed she was feeling a warm breath on her face, like the night before. The breath got closer to her face and she felt a soft pressure on her lips. The kiss awoke her.

She opened her eyes but there was no one around. She sat on the bed, confused, looking to both sides. With dreaming so much about the young blond guest, had she imagined the kiss? She had never experienced such a real dream. A current of fresh air swept through the door. *How strange!* she thought. She was sure she had closed it tightly before going to sleep.

She started to feel fingers caressing her face, tracing it. Again, she felt the warm breath close to her head. Hands took hers and made her get up from the bed. She felt the pressure of arms around her waist and, one more time, other lips against hers with warm, sweet kisses. She was awake. What was happening? What strange magic was this?

However, the caress was so soft and delightful that Zarin allowed her dreams to kiss her all night long.

CHAPTER FORTY-SEVEN

The slave carefully opened the door, afraid of making a noise. She slowly approached the large bed where Rikae slept; her feet did not make a sound on the soft carpet. A small boy was rhythmically moving a large fan of ostrich feathers to ensure the Princess slept in cool temperatures, and the incense burners stayed lit, sending out their heavy aroma of frankincense throughout the chambers.

The slave went towards the Princess who was asleep between the silk sheets, and whispered in her ear, "Your Majesty, wake up, please." There was fear in the girl's voice. Rikae was in a deep sleep and was upset by the manner in which she was awoken. With half-open eyes and in a bad-humored tone, the Princess asked, "What is happening? Who dares to wake me at this hour?"

"An emissary has arrived from Mysia and he says he has an urgent message for you," the maiden said, respectfully.

Angry at having her rest interrupted, Rikae answered, "Can he not wait until tomorrow?"

"The messenger says it is related to the young ones you are looking for," the girl replied.

Rikae immediately came to life.

"Have him come in," she ordered.

A man entered the room. He was still wearing his riding attire and it was clear that he had neither bathed nor changed clothes before presenting himself in front of the Princess.

"I did not want to make you wait, my Lady," he said with a smile and an effort to be respectful. "The ones you are looking for have shown up. They are guests of my master and he wants to propose an arrangement that I am sure will please you."

Rikae was suddenly wide awake, and she began to listen attentively to the proposal.

CHAPTER FORTY-EIGHT

The next day the sun rose as usual, chasing its traditional journey to its highest point; at dusk, it made way for the moon, and another night arrived. They were all gathered in the great hall, having dined and enjoyed Zarin's dance performance. Everyone was ready to hear the second riddle. The same man in a yellow toga stood in the center of the room, and in the same tedious voice, he began to recite:

"Next, four dwarfs, their heads covered with turbans, will enter the room, two of them have black hair and always tell the truth, the other two have red hair and always tell lies. You can ask one question, and one only, to two of the dwarfs. From their answers, you must guess the hair color of each one of them."

Adhara nodded, accepting the challenge. Then, at the clap of the wise man, four beaming dwarfs entered the room. As he had stated, their hair was covered by turbans made of a dark cloth.

The dwarfs began to leap and do acrobatics in the presence of all. They succeeded in standing one on top of the other, until they created a vertical line that was taller than the wise man in the yellow toga. Making funny faces, they ridiculed him, showing that in this position they were taller than everyone in the room. At the conclusion of their lively dance, the four dwarfs stood in front of Adhara, waiting for her questions.

The girl stared into their eyes. It seemed as though she were trying to guess the color of their hair from their expressions. The dwarfs looked at her, impassively, with a completely neutral look on their faces. Adhara turned to the second one.

"If I ask the first dwarf in the line, 'What color is your hair?' how would he answer me?" She asked.

"My hair is red," the second dwarf replied, and immediately pursed his lips.

Adhara looked over the line, analyzing whom she should ask next. The air was tense. Had the girl asked the right question? Only one answer separated her from solving the problem.

Adhara turned to the third dwarf. It was her second and last question.

"What color of hair do the first and second of your companions have?"

"The first has red hair and the second has black hair."

Adhara turned to the wise man who was looking at her nervously.

"The problem is very simple," she said, proudly. "The first dwarf has black hair, the second dwarf has red hair, the third has red hair, and therefore the fourth has black hair."

The dwarfs took off their turbans in front of the audience. Everyone was able to confirm that Adhara had correctly deduced the hair color of each one. A round of applause broke out in the room. The young woman was truly amazing.

This time the applause was stopped in its tracks by an angry gesture from Hammorib. Flushed with ire, he got up from his ridiculous throne and left the room, leaving everyone there in consternation.

The wise man, although alarmed, trying to demonstrate that Adhara's triumph was down to chance, said to her, "Please explain to the audience how you arrived at that conclusion."

Adhara let out the deep breath she had been holding in her lungs and said, "If you had asked the first dwarf directly what color his hair was, the answer would always have been, 'my hair is black,' since the dwarf with black hair would tell the truth, and if the dwarf had red hair he would be obliged to tell a lie. The same if I asked, 'how would your companion reply if I asked him the color of his hair?' I could discern whether the second dwarf was telling the truth or a lie. The answer was 'my hair is red,' which I knew could never have been an answer; therefore, I reasoned that the second dwarf was lying. With this information, I was sure that he had red hair. With my last question, I had to decipher the rest of the enigma and, because of that, I asked the third dwarf, 'What color of hair do your first and second companions have?' When I received the response, 'the first has red hair and the second has black hair,' I understood that the one who was speaking was a red-haired dwarf, since it did not coincide with my reasoning that the second dwarf was lying.

Therefore, as this dwarf was also lying, the first had to have had black hair, the second red hair, the third red hair, and it was easy to deduce that the last dwarf had black hair."

The wise man nodded in silence. The girl had won the second battle fair and square. They retired from the main hall and Heptos signaled that they should meet in the sitting room assigned to Roxana and Adhara. He closed the doors carefully, making sure there were no spies around. With a smile for Adhara, he said, "I congratulate you, Adhara. You have given a perfect answer. But you should not look down your nose at the challenge. It offends the one who proposes it. A little humility would be valuable the next time," Heptos said.

"You don't know how hard it is for my sister to hide her triumphs," Dromeas said jokingly.

"That's what happens when such an arrogant woman has our destiny in her hands. You may be very intelligent, but I don't believe this numeric ability will protect us from arms, if Hammorib doesn't stick to his side of the bargain," Raiko said, worried.

Adhara gave him a hateful look.

"You say that because you are not capable of answering the most basic arithmetic question," Adhara challenged.

"Calm down! I know what you're saying Raiko," Heptos said, "but Adhara is the only weapon we have to obtain the manuscript. At least doing it this way, it is a duel in the presence of his subjects and he will have to honor our victory, even if for a brief moment. Let us go, rest, and prepare for the last enigma."

Following the old man's advice, they all retired to bed.

Adhara tossed and turned in bed, unable to sleep. She was still upset by Raiko's and Dromeas' comments. Those two seemed to be very close recently and she did not understand what they were plotting.

Adhara heard voices coming from Roxana's bedroom once again. Curious, she got up and went to the other girl's room.

"Who are you talking to?" She asked.

Roxana showed her the figure of a tiny man. She had sculpted him from the stone that Heptos had taken from the entrance on the day of their arrival. It was small enough to fit in the palm of her hand. The features on the face were freshly formed, and the only parts of the body recognizable were the trunk, the arms, and the legs. With a voice that resembled two pieces of flint being struck together to make fire, the little man said, "Hammorib sent a messenger to speak to Rikae, Mithridates' daughter-in-law, in the court of Sinope. From the outset, he has been suspicious of why Heptos is here with all of you, and he immediately recognized you and your brother. Since you left, the Princess Rikae has created a web of informers who have been asking about your whereabouts." The tiny stone man was able to pass through the whole palace without being noticed, and Roxana was using him to find out what her host was scheming. "Hammorib is furious with you Adhara, because you have beaten his wise men twice, and he is trying to prevent you taking the manuscript in any way possible."

"How far away is Sinope from here?" Roxana asked.

"I don't know," the tiny man replied. "But the messenger left the night you arrived with a letter in Hammorib's handwriting, and they have still not received a reply."

Adhara and Roxana looked worried. How much could Rikae, Mithridates, or his army know of the mission they were executing?

"Hammorib's chambers are in a fluster. He has all of the wise men in the region there working on the last riddle so that they can triumph over you." With a look of complicity on his strange little face, he continued, "there is not only excitement in the master's chambers; there is also some activity in the slaves' quarters. I saw one of your party leave there not long ago. I don't know how he managed to trick the guards and enter the rooms."

"Who was it? Dromeas? My brother?" Adhara asked.

"No, it was the other one. The one with the mocking smile, I think his name is Raiko."

A stab of jealousy pierced Adhara's heart. If he liked pretty faces with no brains, who knew how to dance, what did it matter to her? She lay down on her bed, but although she tried, she could not sleep the whole night.

CHAPTER FORTY-NINE

Finally, the evening that would decide the contest arrived. They were in the great hall for the last time. The atmosphere was uneasy; Hammorib's subjects could sense how much he loathed his guests. It was not just a manuscript and two talents of gold that were in jeopardy, the pride of the Lord of the house could be the victim of a fatal blow.

The slaves served the dinner, but hardly any of the guests tasted a bite. That night, Zarin did not come out to dance, there was no party, no rejoicing; only heavy silence in the antechamber. As the slaves were removing the remains of the feast, Innoel Hammorib took a package that had been resting by his side during the evening. He pulled back the two pieces of linen that were on top, and showed it to a curious audience.

"Here is the manuscript that has caused this pleasant encounter. I believe I have sinned, having been too benign, and I have posed very easy questions. This time we have a just accord. After the reading of the enigma, I will turn this sand clock upside down, and before the last grain falls, you must have given a reply."

Adhara nodded and accepted the challenge. *I dedicate this to you, my dear Pappous, who allowed a woman to study under your roof,* the girl thought silently.

For the third time, the man in the yellow toga stood in the center of the room and recited the riddle in his monotone voice:

"Two friends meet, happy to see each other after such a long time. The younger asks the older one:
'How are your three daughters? What are their ages now?'
To which the older man replies:
'If you add their ages, you will find the number of years we have known each other, if you multiply their ages you will obtain the number thirty-six.'
The young man did some quiet calculations and then said:
'You give me little information.'

269

'You are right,' the older man said, 'I forgot to tell you that the eldest has blue eyes.'

Answer before the last grain of sand falls. What ages were the three daughters of the older man? Remember you have to explain your reasoning so that we are certain your reply is not a product of fate."

The air could have been cut with the blade of the dagger Ammos always wore on his belt. Cruelly, to create more expectations and to somewhat punish her own, Adhara waited until the last grains of sand were about to fall. As the last grain was falling and with a triumphant sparkle in her glaucous eyes, the young woman replied, "The oldest daughter is nine; she is followed by twins who are two years old. You did not ask me, but the number of years they have known each other is thirteen," she said, unable to avoid her sarcasm.

"The reasoning I have used is the following; the problem postulates that there are three daughters whose ages, if multiplied, will give the number 36 as a result. Taking this number into three factors there are various possibilities, however if you add them together they each give a different total, except for the combinations 9+2+2 =13, and 6+6+1 =13. If the information that the sum was equal to the number of the years that the two friends knew each other did not clarify the problem, it was because the number of years was equal to thirteen and the young man needed another clue. On clarifying that the oldest has blue eyes, it tells us that there was 'one' oldest and therefore the proposition 9+2+2 is the correct answer."

An exclamation of shock erupted from the room. Hammorib had lost!

A dark shadow clouded his face. He stood up slowly, and handed the manuscript to Heptos.

"I hope that I can extend my hospitality until tomorrow," he said and, without another word, he left the hall. Heptos accepted the book with a nod that met with Hammorib's back that was leaving the room. His movement did not show defeat. Hammorib did not know how to lose, and he was surely plotting something out of the ordinary.

They met again in the little sitting room. Heptos was carrying the manuscript close to his chest. When they were sure that they were alone, he gave it to Ammos and Roxana, who once again held the manuscript in their palms. But this time, they opened their lips imperceptibly and soft whispers emerged. The others looked left and right; they feared their host and they did not want to attract his attention.

However, the same game of lights that had formed the other times filled the room where they were enclosed. The sparks hit the roof and the walls confirmed that Ignatius was right; in this manuscript, there was another one of the clues to decipher the Word. In the darkness of the little room, the playful rays of light wrote the phrase:

A rich and powerful king had one son and six daughters, but the prince could not be king for fault of one of his sisters.

The whispers had not disappeared completely when the tiny man that Roxana had sculpted came running into the room. Roxana grabbed him to lift him off the floor and into her palm where everyone could see him. He started to speak. "Hammorib has received an emissary from the court of Sinope in response to the message that he sent. It appears that Mithridates wants neither Dromeas nor Adhara to live, because he fears that Pilomenes will declare them his heirs, and other kings will view this as an affront to him. Rikae, the daughter of Pilomenes, and daughter-in-law of Mithridates, has negotiated an agreement with Hammorib. He will hand you over and he will be left with your two talents of gold and with the manuscript, under oath that they will never bring his betrayal to public knowledge. You must leave immediately. The troops from Pontus will be here at any moment to capture you and take Dromeas and Adhara before Mithridates."

"How can we leave without being seen?" Adhara asked.

"I will guide you; I know every stone in this place." He said, chuckling at his own joke.

Once again, Raiko immediately took control of the situation.

"Adhara, Roxana, Heptos, prepare yourselves for the journey. Ammos, get the horses ready. We will meet in the stables. Dromeas and I have a matter to resolve." As he was walking away, he turned and said to Ammos, "Take an extra horse, we have another travel companion."

"Who?" Adhara asked. The word had barely slipped out when she bit her lip, she did not want to appear so keen to know Raiko's secrets.

"Zarin, the dancer, will run away with us."

CHAPTER FIFTY

They gathered up the few belongings they had brought with them and they followed the tiny stone man through passageways, nooks and crannies in that labyrinth of bad taste that was the home of Innoel Hammorib. The tiny man led the way as they moved from one room to another, to ensure that no one was following them.

Hammorib, very full of himself, never imagined his guests would have discovered his plan. He was waiting for the arrival of the soldiers and dreaming of the manuscript and two talents of gold he would receive for his treason.

Following Raiko's orders, they met in the stables where Ammos awaited them with horses saddled and ready to leave. A few minutes after Adhara, Roxana and Heptos arrived, they watched three figures appear from the darkness. They were Raiko, Dromeas, and Zarin. On seeing how beautiful she was, her head covered with a red and gold scarf, Adhara wanted to cry.

Zarin looked around for Adhara. Once she recognized her, she went forward, timidly.

"You are the most intelligent person I have ever known. You have given this thug a lesson for which he will never forgive you," she said, trying to ingratiate herself with the young woman. Adhara answered with a dry *Thank you* and, together with the rest, she gradually began to walk, leading her horse by the bridle.

They walked away slowly, trying to make as little noise as possible. When they reached the boundaries of Hammorib's lands, they mounted the horses and began a quick gallop, guided by the moonlight. It was after midnight and, with a little luck, they would reach the *Aphrodite* at dawn. Raiko took the lead, followed by Heptos, with Ammos closing the line and watching the rearguard.

As they rode, Adhara noticed that Zarin's horse was always in close proximity to Dromeas' horse. They exchanged sweet smiles and Dromeas went very near to whisper in her ear, while Zarin blushed at his words. It was more than obvious that there was love between them.

Raiko slowed down, letting Heptos and Roxana take the lead, and he positioned his horse next to Adhara's.

"Did you know about this?" she asked, confused.

"A blind man would see how infatuated your brother is with the girl," Raiko said. "All I did was help a little."

"How did you help?" Adhara asked, elated. Here in the dark of the night, after finding out that Zarin was not for Raiko...

"Your brother just needed a push and a little hustle. I lent him the Helmet of Hades, a useful artifact that I obtained in your company. When he put it on, he became invisible, and he was able to trick the ferocious guard that Hammorib had put at the entrance of the slaves' quarters. Once inside, poof!" He waved his fingers. "Love did its magic."

"Was it Dromeas roaming around those rooms? The tiny man told me it was you that he saw wandering around there."

"I only went the last night. Hammorib is not stupid, and he realized something was happening between the two of them. He ordered a strict watch on your brother. I went in his place the last night and I made the proposal to Zarin to leave with us, which she accepted without even blinking."

Adhara felt a warm sensation of relief in her chest. The oppression in her stomach had disappeared, the green-eyed monster that had stalked her in recent days evaporated in the certainty that Raiko was not interested in the dancer. She heard Raiko's voice ask, "Why were you talking about me with the little stone man? Perhaps the proud Adhara was jealous that women, not as intelligent as her, would accept the attention of someone as rude as I?"

Adhara lowered her head in consternation. She was saved from having to answer as Roxana, who was riding in front of them, slowed down her horse, and jumped to the ground. She got down on her knees and put her ear to the ground. Everyone stopped their horses and stood around the girl.

"It is a message from the tiny stone man we left behind. He has sent a communication through the stones on the path along the way, one after another, that has been repeated until it reached us." And in a grave voice, she said, "We left too late! Mithridates' army arrived a few hours earlier than predicted; they

274

discovered that we were gone and now they are following in this direction at a fast pace."

Roxana had barely finished speaking when they started to hear horses' hooves closing in on them. For a moment they froze, petrified, not knowing what to do.

A swarm of arrows began to fall on them. What was most alarming was that they were not coming from Hammorib's side; on the contrary, they came from the direction where they wanted to go.

CHAPTER FIFTY-ONE

Xanthe was sitting on Hippolyta's throne in the inner chamber of the Royal Palace. There was a full moon, but no ceremony of Amazons meeting with male soldiers would take place.

She looked at the empty temple, distraught. The whole community was asleep, but the land of dreams eluded her. Today was the seventeenth anniversary of the day she watched Lisipe and Zoe leave. Her mother and her best friend.

"Make me proud of you," Lisipe had said, as she bade farewell with a tight hug, pressing her to her chest. She held back her tears; an Amazon never cried. And so, with an expression of sadness that she was unable to disguise, she watched her mother, together with her best friend, leave in the royal caravan that would take them far from there.

Hippolyta fulfilled her promise and made Xanthe her successor. It was not hard to do, since the girl was without doubt an excellent Amazon, even better then Hippolyta in some ways.

Xanthe looked at the Palace with sadness. She was queen of a dying nation. Since Mithridates had decided to take over the region and declared himself an open enemy of the Amazons, fewer and fewer kings were offering their soldiers for encounters with her warriors. Each year there were fewer men who came to procreate with them. They were afraid of the retaliation they might suffer by being associated with women who openly defied the sovereign Mithridates.

From a window, she looked, devastated, at the buildings where they conducted their training. There were more teachers than students. The encampment was full of older women with no students to train. Many of the young women had not had the opportunity to reproduce, even she had no descendant. If Hippolyta were alive...

Xanthe stared at the large statue of Artemis, the same statue that Hippolyta had turned to in search of advice. This time it was the moonlight that came in through the openings in the roof, lighting up the statue.

A soft breeze blew, moving along the clouds that partly covered the stars. The moon, in all its splendor, shone high in the sky, and streams of light began to dance around the effigy. Amid the magical sparkles, the statue took life. There, in front of Xanthe, the Goddess Artemis appeared. Beautiful, fiery, in hunting attire, with her bow on her shoulder and her face shining in the moonlight.

"My Lady," she said respectfully, bowing in front of the Goddess.

"Adhara, the daughter of Zoe, is being ambushed. It is your duty to save her. I will guide you there," Artemis said.

Adhara, the daughter of Zoe, her best friend, was in danger. Adhara, the one who would save the Amazon lineage, was at risk.

Xanthe took the Sacred Horn, the same one that Hippolyta had sounded in the forest with Pilomenes, the same one Zoe had refused to sound, and she went out to the terrace of the temple. She took a deep breath and blew the horn with all her might. In the silence of the night, the sound disseminated quickly, waking warriors from their light sleep.

Women started to emerge from the dwellings, anxious and curious. The horn had not sounded for so long that it sounded strange to them.

A group of Amazons appeared in front of Xanthe and, in a deep voice, she addressed them, emotionally, from the steps of the temple.

"Amazons! Of course, you remember our Queen Hippolyta, a woman who served as an inspiration to many of us and who took our race to great heights. The Goddess Artemis has informed me that Adhara, Zoe's daughter, granddaughter of the great Hippolyta, is at risk of death," she paused, then continued.

"It is our duty to fight to the last breath to save her! Prepare for battle! Today we will probably fight our last war. But if we save her, we save all of us. In Adhara, there is part of every one of us. Saving Adhara, we save the Last of the Amazons."

"I want you to go out to battle today and fight like never before. Fill your quivers with all the arrows available, save nothing; you may never have the chance to use them again. Lift your shining shields, in the form of a crescent moon, with pride, since maybe you will never have the chance to use them again. On this night, show how brave and how strong you are. This is your last opportunity. I can no longer promise you a kingdom or a future. But if we have to die, let it be for a worthy cause, leaving the reputation of our race in the highest regard. This will be our last war; we will not die in vain!"

And with a collective cry that came from every throat at the same time, the Amazons accepted the challenge.

CHAPTER FIFTY-TWO

The cry of the warriors resounded in the night, and the horses made the ground shake under their hooves. From behind the cloud of arrows that was flying over their heads, they saw a troop of armed women mounted on spirited stallions.

Heptos' party began to panic when two lines of women on horseback, perfectly formed, separated from the troop, approaching them at great speed. The two lines opened cleanly around them, forming a circle, of which they were the center. A large chestnut horse emerged from the back with an Amazon mounted on it. Upright on her horse, she came right to them and looked around everyone who was there, searching for the women in the group. She got down deftly from the creature, and went to Roxana, Zarin, and Adhara. She looked directly at each one, and recognizing Adhara, she said, "You are the exact image of Hippolyta, but with your mother's eyes," and she immediately put a knee on the ground and bowed her head in respect.

"Long live, Adhara, daughter of Zoe, granddaughter of Hippolyta! I, Xanthe, Queen of the Amazons, salute you." Raising her head and looking straight into her eyes, she went on, "Legitimate heir of Hippolyta, my army is at your disposal and it is our duty to keep you safe."

Realizing that this band of warriors was here to help them, Raiko, Ammos, and Dromeas lowered their improvised weapons and approached Xanthe.

"I am also Zoe's child," Dromeas said proudly. Xanthe raised an eyebrow in a gesture of disdain. Men did not count.

"We must save the three women and the old man," Raiko said. He was not one for formal introductions. "We have horses too, we can fight by your side if you will provide us with weapons."

Xanthe looked him up and down, evaluating him with her glare.

"Agreed. For as long as the battle continues, you can join my warriors. But do not try to give them orders," she said, decisively, "because they will not follow them. I will accompany the women and the old man to a safe place." She pointed to a clearing in the forest that was around nine hundred yards away, "and I will protect them while you try to stall the enemy."

Xanthe escorted Heptos, Adhara, Roxana, and Zarin to the clearing, while Raiko, Dromeas, and Ammos joined up with the Amazon army. Xanthe and her party rode in silence, with the war cries behind them. Soon Adhara remembered where she had heard this name before.

"Xanthe?" Adhara asked, recognizing the name. "It's you, Lisipe's daughter?"

"Yes," the Queen replied, moving her horse to Adhara's side. "How is my mother?"

Adhara bit her lip and wanted to cry, remembering what Dromeas had been told on his journey to Hades. By her expression, Xanthe understood that Lisipe was dead.

"She died with dignity, at least?" Xanthe asked.

"Yes," Adhara lied, not really knowing how Lisipe died. "She died fulfilling her promise."

"And Zoe?" Hearing her mother's name, Adhara could not contain a single tear that rolled down her cheek.

"She died too."

This was more than Xanthe could stand. With a cry that came from deep inside her, she forced her horse to turn around and headed with unleashed fury towards the army of the aggressor.

Meanwhile, the Amazons were fighting a bloody battle. The Pontus regiment and Hammorib's few soldiers, who were counting on the surprise factor to attack a gang of virtually unarmed people, appeared stunned in the face of the rage that was being unleashed on them. It was truly intimidating to see these slight women who molded perfectly to the movements of the horses, with their shields glistening in the light of the full moon.

The arrows coming from the light bows of the Amazons were hitting the faces of Mithridates' regiment. The soldiers raised their shields to their faces for protection, and the Amazons took advantage of this opportunity. With their stallions in a closed line, they rode straight ahead, as they continued launching arrows non-stop, thus breaking up the lines of formation of the enemy's army.

Raiko, Ammos, and Dromeas, supplied with swords and spears, joined the group of Amazons who, with their sharpened hatchets, were now fighting body to body, on horseback, tearing apart anyone who got in their way. In the camp, they could hear the muffled thuds of weapons against shields, as well as the cries and gasps of both victors and losers.

Adhara watched the scene from the clearing where Xanthe had taken them. Something rose up inside her. She, too, was an Amazon, and the time had come to prove it. As she watched them fight, she felt proud to be the descendant of such a noble tribe, and with her spirit uplifted, she turned her horse around and started to gallop, resolved to go to battle.

On the back of her horse, she called out to an Amazon who had lagged behind, asking for her sword and her shield. Armed in this way, she, too, entered the merciless battle that was unraveling.

While she was galloping, Adhara noticed that although her view was clouded, her other senses were growing. In the wild race, she could hear the creak of the bows as they were being tensed, and she could smell the blood of the wounded and the fear of the combatants. She lifted her sword high, as Lisipe had told her to do so many times and, without a thought, she stuck it with all her strength into the chest of the first soldier she met. The sharp sword found no resistance and cleanly entered the body of the unfortunate one. He died instantly, leaving a horse running adrift.

After this experience, a rush of adrenalin ran through her veins and she launched like a Fury against the soldiers who faced her. She felt that she could hear Lisipe's voice telling her, *'Push the animal's rump with your knees! You need both hands free! Cover your chest with your shield!'* She repeated these commands she had learned mechanically as the soldiers fell, defeated by the audacity of her sword.

In the midst of the battle, Xanthe looked up and saw Adhara fighting.

"Hippolyta would be proud of you," she shouted.

Adhara turned around for an instant to hear Xanthe's compliment and then she was distracted. It was only a split second, but enough time for a malicious arrow to stab her in the chest.

Among the soldiers, one of them had a specific obligation. Before the army left to capture the traitors, Innoel Hammorib called his best archer aside to assign him with a special mission.

"I want you to kill that woman who has stained my pride and brought dishonor to my house. I don't care about the other insults, make sure she dies."

The archer had fulfilled his task well. Waiting for the appropriate moment, a mild slip-up, he tensed his bow and shot a poisoned arrow at his victim. He had hit the target.

The impact caused Adhara to fall from her horse, and she remained on the ground unconscious.

"NOOOOOO!" The scream of pain from Raiko could be heard throughout the forest, and it managed to awaken the Gods on Olympus. Hastily, on the croup of his horse, he aimed at the place where Adhara lay in a vain attempt to save her.

But Raiko was not quick enough. From the vast darkness of the night, a huge eagle came down from the skies. His enormous wings reached out over them like a sinister threat. He flew down to Adhara and, without touching the ground, he picked her up with his claws and took flight.

"ADHARA!" Raiko called out her name, while he futilely followed the animal in a frantic race on horseback. But the bird had already taken to the skies and was unreachable. Red with rage and impotence, Raiko stopped on the ground, calling her name incessantly.

CHAPTER FIFTY-THREE

"Adhara, Adhara!" Raiko continued riding behind the eagle's tail in desperation, in a pointless attempt to reach the animal who had already set off in flight with Adhara in his claws. He heard a horse approach him from behind, and a voice echoed in the confusion of the night.

"Raiko, stop!" Dromeas had followed his friend in a desperate attempt to catch him. "You cannot do anything for her now. There is still a war to finish. She is fine. Trust me!"

Reluctantly, knowing that there was nothing more he could do to bring her back, Raiko turned his horse around. They galloped back to the part of the forest where the battle continued. The Amazons had fought valiantly, but the enemy soldiers outnumbered them and the exhaustion of battle was starting to take its toll on all.

The priest and the women were watching the combat from under a tree in the clearing, where Xanthe had taken them at the beginning of the confrontation. The Amazon rode over to them and signaled to Raiko, Dromeas, and Ammos to join them. With a worried look, she said, "I do not know how much longer we can contain them. Take your women and the old man and flee while you can. We will stay here and protect your retreat."

"Thank you," Raiko said, addressing the brave woman.

"Will you give me your word of honor that you will make sure Adhara has been saved?" she asked, with a serious demeanor.

"I promise you," Raiko answered, solemnly.

"You will make sure she fulfills her destiny?" Xanthe continued.

"I will give my life for it," Raiko replied. Xanthe nodded in agreement. Then, with a salute, she bade farewell to the rest of the party.

"Hurry, you don't have much time," and with determination, she aimed her stallion towards the battle.

They mounted their horses and headed towards the sea, to the port were the *Aphrodite* was anchored. Raiko looked back; few

Amazons remained, but they continued fighting in an amazing effort.

A soldier from Pontus noticed that Raiko's group was trying to escape and he called the alarm. Xanthe perceived the soldier's intentions and, swift on her stallion, she reached him and slashed his chest with her sharpened blade. The soldier fell, bathed in his own blood.

However, Xanthe's attack did not go unnoticed by the rest of the enemy army and a trio of soldiers quickly surrounded her. Xanthe defended herself valiantly, but there were too many attacking her at the same time. After a horrific fight, the Pontic swords slit the body of the Amazon.

Raiko witnessed the scene from afar, as he watched the rearguard of the group flee. When he saw Xanthe's body fall, his soul filled with a deep sadness and, at the same time, gratitude. He was sad because the world had lost a great queen. He had gratitude for this woman who had given her life for them. He kept telling himself he would not rest until he had fulfilled the oath he had taken.

The Amazons put up a fierce fight, but at the end of the day, they all fell when confronted with the weapons of the army of Pontus. They were taken prisoner and presented to Mithridates for his judgment. The King of Pontus, with a magnanimous air, offered their lives in exchange for them enlisting in his army and fighting on his side.

The Amazons who had survived without a leader looked at each other confused, unable to make a decision. Their faces turned to Hipsicratea, Xanthe's advisor. The proud Amazon parted the way between her companions, went to the throne and stared at Mithridates defiantly. But when the Amazon and the King were face to face, he fell in love with her, and she with him.

Hipsicratea betrayed her race and married Mithridates. By his side, she fought against the Romans once more, and they captured her at her husband's death bed, where she still mourned the loss of her great love...Once again I am getting ahead of the facts. Forgive me, I will recount this scene later.

CHAPTER FIFTY-FOUR

Adhara slowly opened her eyes. Her vision was blurred and she could not see anything around her. Her chest ached, and breathing was a struggle. She felt strong hands raise her head and put a cup of liquid to her lips.

"Drink this, it is ambrosia. It will help you recover," a deep voice said. It was so deep it seemed as though it came from the depths of a cave and, on its journey outwards, it had grown with the echo of the walls through which it passed.

She drank with difficulty. She closed her eyes again. She needed to rest. She felt the infusion run heat through her veins, injecting delusions of life into her body, and driving the poison from her system.

CHAPTER FIFTY-FIVE

They rode all night through the forest with neither rest nor a break. The journey was difficult since the vegetation was thick, and the roots on the ground abundant, preventing the stallions from going at the desired speed. At dawn, they arrived at the port and found the *Aphrodite* anchored at sea, ready to set sail.

Raiko helped the women dismount while the rest of the men helped the crew with the last minutiae for the departure. He slapped the horses on their hindquarters. *Home*, he ordered. They belonged to Innoel Hammorib, and he did not want to be left with any of his possessions. The manuscript was another matter; Adhara had won it honestly.

"Odon, raise the sail. We must leave here as soon as possible," Raiko ordered.

The faces of the others looked uneasy, one of the party had not returned from this adventure. Adhara had disappeared into the immensity of the night. When he saw their expressions, Dromeas spoke.

"Don't worry about Adhara. Eagles do not fly at night. It was my father who saved her," he said, proudly. Heptos and Raiko exchanged a worried look. Neither of them believed in the existence of the Gods... however, how else could they explain what had happened to Adhara? They had all seen the huge eagle come down from the skies and pick her up in his claws.

Of all present, the priest was bearing the brunt of this. Heptos was feeling remorse, he had taken these young ones on this outlandish adventure, and now he did not know what to do.

"Adhara will meet us again at some point on the journey," Dromeas continued. He spoke with a smile of conviction on his face.

At what point on the journey? Raiko thought, devastated. *I want a more concrete answer. I am tired of manuscripts, oracles, and arguments between Gods. Where is Adhara? When will we see her?*

He had joined the adventure for the money he would receive, but now everything had changed. He could not sit calmly like the others and wait for Adhara to appear by some divine intervention. This woman mattered to him too much and a dull pain burned in his soul at the mere thought that he might never see her again.

"Calm down Raiko," Roxana said. "Trust in Dromeas' word. I too, believe we will see her again soon." And with the peace and calm that she always transmitted, Roxana pacified Raiko.

Raiko was quiet for a moment, as he weighed up Roxana's words.

"I will not rest until we find her."

The *Aphrodite* navigated the Hellespont in the opposite direction, moved by the urgent need to put distance between themselves and Mithridates' army. When they found themselves once more in the blue waters of the Aegean Sea, Raiko decided that they should stop at one of the small islands near the coast of Crete. They needed to restock the ship with supplies, and he hoped that these islands were beyond the boundaries of the war that was being fought between Sulla and Mithridates.

Days passed peacefully, and Zarin was turning out to be a very pleasant companion for everyone. They noticed that she was a happy girl, always disposed to laughter. Moreover, it was clear that was she grateful every day for having been rescued from what might have been her destiny.

"What luck you've had, lion cub," Odon said to Dromeas. "We must sail faster, as I am sure that that nasty type will not accept the loss of a such a flower. I don't understand what she sees in you. You're nothing more than a pale, skinny little boy."

Zarin smiled and buried her head in Dromeas' shoulder.

"Calm down fatso," Dromeas said to him. "We'll find you a whale to keep you company and then you'll forget your jealousy."

Everyone listening, including Ammos, burst into laughter. Everyone apart from Raiko, who continued to look out over the endless ocean, searching for an answer.

The school of dolphins that had joined them earlier was still in tow, and as soon as the *Aphrodite* hit the high seas, their playful squeals could be heard from the deck. Zarin looked at them in delight, under the entranced eye of Dromeas, who never left her side.

The whole crew joyfully watched the unexpected antics of one dolphin in particular. With his whole body out of the water, he stayed upright, moving only his tail in the water, while he clapped his flippers as he mimicked applause.

Two sailors dove into the water. They got on the backs of two dolphins and pretended to be having a race in the sea, like nimble mermen. From the ship, two groups of supporters had formed, bragging about one competitor or another.

The scene had sent Odon, his men and the chosen ones into fits of laughter. Only one person still had a sullen, bad-humored expression, and nobody dared to approach him or say a word.

Roxana looked at him from afar. It was obvious that Adhara's absence was causing him to suffer. For Roxana, it was difficult to understand this feeling of attraction between a man and a woman. She had watched Dromeas and Zarin enjoying each other's company, and Raiko and Adhara doing everything possible to avoid each other.

Love was a sentiment that scared Roxana, one that she preferred to keep at a distance. She knew that it was an irresistible force that she was not able to face. She felt more comfortable with loyalty, it was more in line with her nature.

This was the sentiment that united her with Ammos, and it was the same sentiment she had developed with the rest of the party. They all knew that they could trust her; she was immovable, like the stone from which she had been created.

Raiko was resting his arms on the railings, looking at the sea, when he noticed Roxana approach him. The girl stopped by his side and in a gentle voice, she asked, "You are worried about Adhara, isn't that so?" Raiko looked at her exquisite profile; he felt as though an alabaster statue had approached him. Next to her, he could not pretend, or use his humor as a shield. Next to her, he could only say what he truly felt.

"My plan at the end of this voyage was to take my money and go very far from here. But when I saw the eagle carrying her off into the sky, I tried to imagine what my life would be without her." He took a deep breath and let it out. "And I did not like what I saw. I want this woman by my side always; I want her to eat from my table, to wake up in my bed, to grow old with me!"

An understanding smile appeared on Roxana's face.

"I believe that you call that sentiment 'love'.."

Raiko put his hands on the gift from the Goddess that hung around his neck.

"I thought I was immune to love."

"Aphrodite is only the Goddess of physical attraction, of carnal love. What you are feeling is something else," Roxana replied, and then with a quiet laugh, she said, "The feeling that you have now is much stronger than the rock from which I was born."

"But it does me no good to feel like this," Raiko said with frustration. On the other side of the deck, he saw Dromeas laughing with Zarin. It was the first voyage she had taken by sea and the first time she had seen dolphins. She was delighted with the spectacle. She was smiling and clapping at the creatures' every move. Seeing her so beautiful, Dromeas stole a fleeting kiss and Zarin put her head down in embarrassment. Raiko turned his face towards Roxana and said, "My dreams make no sense, she is an Amazon and there can never be anything between us. And besides, I am not worthy of her; I am nothing but a renegade."

"Is there any way to remedy your past?" Roxana asked.

"No," Raiko replied, abruptly.

Roxana was silent, and her silence served as the unspoken question. Raiko felt that he owed her an explanation and therefore he said, "As Innoel Hammorib stated very clearly, I am the youngest son of a Phoenician nobleman, but I am a disgrace to my family. I can never return to my home country without facing trial for theft and treason. If found guilty, they will cut off my right hand in the main plaza." He was looking at his wrists; he moved his fingers in the air and said, "That is why I fled, because I prefer having two hands to having my honor."

"What happened exactly?" Roxana ventured to ask.

"I don't want to talk about it!" he shouted and then, realizing that he had been rude, he put his head down and said contritely, "Sorry. I should never have answered that way. The truth is, even I do not really know whether I am guilty of the accusations, or not. It is a long story that involves my father, my brother, and a bad woman whom I named the Serpent Woman. I should have fled from her side the moment I met her! But I was so sure of myself..." He allowed the sad memories to reflect in his expression. He put his hands to his face, shook his head, and concluded, "As I said before, it is a long story that one day I will be able to tell...but today is not that day."

Roxana, understanding, answered, "We all have the right to a second chance. You are not a bad man, Raiko. And I believe you are ready to change for her, isn't that true?"

CHAPTER FIFTY-SIX

The ruined city of Dardanos never imagined it would go down in history as the meeting place of two of the greatest characters known to man. Situated south of what was once the glorious Troy, it had never been rebuilt after the distinguished city fell into the hands of the Greeks, suffering the same consequences firsthand.

In the ruins of its theater, a summit had been arranged between Mithridates VI and Lucius Cornelius Sulla, to sign a peace accord that would bring the war between them to an end. Few cities could boast having had two figures as eminent as these two magnificent men as their guests. Two men who would not let their arms be twisted, who would fight to the death, if it were not for the unique circumstances that beset each one of them. This accord, negotiated by Archelaus, the Supreme Commander of Pontus, would benefit the Roman much more than Mithridates. Furthermore, Mithridates had to bow his head and give up all the glory he had achieved.

The recently fought battle of Orchomenus was the decisive victory of the Roman over Mithridates. Once more, Sulla, the brilliant strategist, had annihilated the men that the King of Pontus had brought together on the hills of Boeotia.

For this encounter, Mithridates had called to battle his faithful general Dorylaus to command the troops, together with Archelaus. The two generals could count on gathering ninety thousand men, skillfully disciplined and all trained in the same military scheme.

The battle had unfolded in the marshlands of Orchomenus, on a narrow hill north of Chaeronea. Sulla, following the tactic that had been so successful in the past, ordered his men to dig trenches and ditches to adapt the swampy ground to their convenience.

Dorylaus' troops charged in fury, trying to regain face after the defeat they suffered in Chaeronea. The army of Pontus, which was three times the size of Sulla's army, launched a powerful attack, and the Roman soldiers, startled, began to retreat. Sulla discerned the taste of defeat for a brief moment. Unable to even consider the thought, the Red Commander dismounted his horse, took the Republic Insignia in his hands and, planting it in front of his men, he cried in fury, "Romans, I, Lucius Cornelius Sulla will win an honorable victory here, today, and without you! When they ask where you betrayed your commander, you must reply, 'in Orchomenus'!"

The leader's qualities were undeniable. The exalted speech cast a spell on the men, and they went forward one more time with doubled rage to wipe out Archelaus' troops. The force in the Roman lines was so strong and compact that they formed an impenetrable barrier of swords and shields that moved forward, charging the enemy army. Their pressure pushed the Pontic troops to the marsh, where it was very difficult to maneuver, and Archelaus and Dorylaus watched as their men perished in the muddy waters. Once again, Sulla emerged victorious from circumstances that were not to his advantage.

In spite of his colossal defeat, Mithridates wanted to prove he was a sovereign worthy of respect. He was first to arrive at the summit. He was opulently dressed, and was guarded by two hundred ships under the command of Neoptolemus, the twenty thousand men of Dorylaus who survived the battle of Orchomenus, six thousand men on horseback, and sixty scythed chariots.

In notorious contrast, Sulla wore his military uniform and his escort was made up of only one thousand soldiers and two hundred members of his cavalry. Although he was wearing only his standard uniform, he aroused the admiration of the thousands of subjects of Pontus who had been called to witness such a great event. Perhaps it was his penetrating blue eyes, or his unique hair, that was a very light blond. Few people in these lands had seen a man with such a color of hair.

Mithridates received the Roman with open arms, he then separated Sulla from his body and stayed looking directly into his eyes without speaking. The Roman General withstood the stare, and as the sovereign remained silent, he said, "You should not prolong your silence much longer. It is the custom for the conquered to speak first and for the victor to listen to what he has to say."

Mithridates noted that this was a man of similar height. He was one great man, presenting himself with such a small escort, knowing the force that the enemy had, and Mithridates respected great men. He tried to make use of his excellent skills in oratory, in order to soften the cold atmosphere that was evolving in this encounter.

"My father was a great friend of the Romans, as was my grandfather, and my ancestors. We, a line of kings that goes back more than ten generations, have always had excellent relations with your people, ever since the era when you were only a handful of sheepherders." The educated insult from the King did not go unnoticed by Sulla, who kept the cold gaze of his piercing blue eyes on Mithridates, without blinking. "The Roman Generals in the region left me with no alternative; they invaded my kingdom, allying with Nicomedes. All that I have done has been in defense of my subjects."

Sulla let out a dry laugh and, raising his hand in the air, he stopped the King's speech right then.

"If that had been the case, you ought to have sent an ambassador to Rome and we would have listened to all of your requests. We would have investigated the injustices to see if they were true. You, Mithridates, had this war planned for a long time; you provoked Nicomedes while you were secretly raising an army, allying with the Sarmatians, Scythians, and Thracians. You freed our slaves and pardoned what was owed to us. Not content with that, you murdered eighty thousand Roman citizens by treason, and you did not care if they were women, the elderly, or children. I do not want to hear any more excuses! Do you agree with the terms of the accord that we have negotiated with your general, Archelaus?" he asked, defiantly.

Mithridates looked angrily at the man in front of him. He would never have signed this agreement if it were not for the fact that his army had dwindled and he had lost control of the region. On top of that, the same enemies of Sulla, the *populares*, had reached his territories with fresh troops and he could not handle the war on both sides at the same time.

On the other hand, Sulla was not entirely happy with the state of affairs. He was signing an accord very beneficial to him, but he felt his task was incomplete. He knew that in a short time, once the King of Pontus had licked his wounds and regrouped his forces, he would launch an assault again. But Rome was plunged in a bloody internal war, and the *optimates* needed him.

Archelaus presented a large scroll and put it on the negotiating table. It stipulated that Mithridates must pay the sum of two thousand talents of gold, he would hand over seventy warships to Sulla, and he would withdraw immediately from the territories held by Rome before his invasion: Pergamon, Bithynia and Cappadocia.

Mithridates leaned over and signed the scroll with an ostrich feather. He gave it to Sulla, who also signed it. Once both signatures were registered on the document, Mithridates turned his face towards his enemy and leaned over to plant a kiss on each one of Sulla's cheeks. Those great men looked at each other face to face for the last time.

Ares was watching the scene from afar. He did not like peace treaties, they went against his nature. But, once again, a grim smile appeared on his face. He knew Mithridates too well, and he knew that he would soon go back to his bad old ways.

He signaled to his sons, Deimos, terror, and Phobos, fear, so that they would leave with him.

"Don't worry; we will soon be back in these lands."

Sulla, glorious on his white stallion, left heading towards Rome, leading his troops. He put his hands to his neck, where he found the small effigy of Apollo that he had taken from the bounty of Delphi. He had never taken it off, thanking it once again for his incredible luck.

Before leaving, he had received news from Lucullus. Ptolemy Alexander had agreed to his petitions and had granted him sufficient resources to enlist a large fleet to patrol the Aegean Sea. Now that Mithridates had surrendered, Lucullus would be in charge of making sure the King of Pontus complied in full with all the requisites in the treaty signed in Dardanos.

Together with the message from Lucullus, he also received a missive from Tesseros. The group of seven who were looking for the manuscripts had managed to escape from the Royal Guard in Alexandria. This news slightly overshadowed his victory, however, Tesseros confirmed that he was following their trail and it was only a matter of time before he found them.

Patience. Patience was a virtue that Lucius Cornelius Sulla did not pride himself in, but he trusted in the priest's plot. He had seen immense hatred in his eyes and he knew from experience that hatred drove men to undertake great ventures.

For now, all his thoughts were centered on arriving in Rome and finishing off with the allies of Cinna. Rome would now witness the fury of the Red Commander.

CHAPTER FIFTY-SEVEN

When Adhara opened her eyes again, she felt much better. She looked at her surroundings. She was in a small cave on the highest crest of a range of mountains. The cave had only three walls, with one side completely exposed to the outside. It resembled an eagle's nest. If she put out her hand, she could touch the clouds on the blue of the sky next to her.

Adhara was sitting on a great dark stone, and a very tall man was sitting next to her. He had defined muscles, long hair, and a white beard.

"Where am I?" Adhara asked.

"In the mountains of the Caucasus," the man by her side answered, in that same deep voice she thought she had heard in her dreams.

"What am I doing here?"

"I brought you here to bring you back to life. The poison in the arrow would have killed you if I had not rescued you in time." He halted briefly, and then continued, "Besides, I wanted to give you this," and holding out his hands, he placed a carefully-rolled papyrus in her lap.

"A manuscript?" Adhara asked, still puzzled.

"It is *Prometheus Bound* in the handwriting of Aeschylus. I wanted to give it you here, at the foot of the stone where Prometheus was chained."

"Why this book?" Adhara asked.

"Prometheus was rebuked for having robbed the fire from the Gods and having delivered it to the humans," He hung his head, frustrated, "From that moment on, man lost respect for the Gods; he lost respect for everything divine. From that moment on, I knew that, although I was a God, I was vulnerable. Aside from that, Prometheus had prophetic qualities, and he cried out to whoever could hear that he knew the name of the one who would come to destroy me."

"You did not retaliate?" she asked, curiously.

"Yes, I gave him a cruel punishment. I tied him to this stone," he said, pointing to the rock where the young woman was sitting, "and I had a vulture eat his liver every day. Prometheus was a *Titan*, an immortal being. His liver grew back each night, and each morning he had to face the same torture all over again. But I could never force out of him the name of the one who would come and take my position as supreme leader of the Gods."

There was a long hiatus in the conversation. Adhara looked at him openly. From the beginning, she knew she was in the company of Zeus, the Lord of Olympus.

"Are you really a God?" The question faltered on Adhara's lips.

Zeus let out a bitter laugh.

"A God!" he said, in a mocking tone. "Man is God of his Gods! He creates them, he praises them, and he molds them to his needs. You shaped us according to your image and likeness. We are unfaithful, mendacious, proud, and, above all else, we seek only our personal satisfaction. This is the reason we are dying; we are too human," He said, in a broken tone of voice, "It is a paradox! You created us to explain how you were created."

"Why don't you stop us? Why don't you stop you own destruction?"

"What can I do? I am only a God. We only exist if you believe in us. And I already told you we are dying." He shook his head uneasily. "I wanted to give you this manuscript because I don't want us to be forgotten when we are no longer here. Heptos is intent on saving books that exalt the scientific achievements of man, and he has forgotten about us. We, too, form part of this legacy, this Treasure, that he so stubbornly wants to save. He forgets that we, too, were created in those same minds that he admires."

Looking into her eyes, he pleaded, "As soon as the Word is proclaimed, we will die. It is an irrefutable fact. Would you, Adhara, bear the responsibility of saving this book, so that we do not vanish forever?"

Adhara was touched, and she acquiesced. *How absolute and cruel is death, that even the Gods themselves fear it!* she thought.

Adhara drank two more infusions of ambrosia. She had to be cured completely before setting out on the return journey.

"It is essential that you rest for a few more days. When you are totally recovered I will take you back to the others," Zeus said.

"Are all my companions safe?" Adhara asked, with a hint of worry in her voice. "The last time I was with them they were fighting a bloody battle."

"They are all safe and on board your ship. Raiko as well, don't worry about him," he said, looking her straight in the eyes, answering the mute question the girl had not dared to ask. "However, the Amazons who survived have joined Mithridates' army. Themiscyra has been taken and is in the hands of the King of Pontus. You have truly become the Last of the Amazons," He hesitated, then staring at her, he said, "You have a difficult decision ahead of you. They have placed a very heavy burden on your young shoulders."

CHAPTER FIFTY-EIGHT

Just as they had planned, the *Aphrodite* had docked at one of the small islands in the heart of the Aegean Sea. Raiko gave the crew a free day to rest. He went together with Odon to the village to stock the ship with supplies. They needed to make some minor repairs to the sail, and to spread the hull with tar.

The others decided to look around the little village. Dromeas and Zarin ran through the streets hand in hand in the warm midday sun, looking for any excuse to kiss. Raiko watched them sadly. Seven days had passed with no news of Adhara. Dromeas continued to maintain that she was with their father, and that she would return soon, but for someone devoid of faith it was an argument that was difficult to accept.

As soon as he had left Odon in charge of the arrangements, he had begun to wander around, with disillusion in his step. The island where they had stopped was one of unparalleled beauty. It had been formed from a volcanic eruption. The explosion had created a natural caldera that had been flooded by the blue waters of the Aegean Sea, creating an oval inlet flanked on three sides by the three coasts of the island. The strong, majestic rock jutted out from the sea forming cliffs up to one thousand feet high.

Distracted, and with his head down, he had wandered to a beautiful beach with blue waters. The wind coming off the sea brought violent waves of thick foam that faded away as they reached the shore. A horde of memories flooded his head.

How many years had passed since the encounter with the Goddess! He put his hands to his neck and, in extreme rage, he wrenched off the necklace. He did not want to have Aphrodite's gift. All he wanted right then was one woman. A woman with gray eyes and auburn hair.The woman who was not by his side. Without her, life had no meaning.

With all the strength he could muster, he threw the necklace far into the sea. He kept looking at it, and watched as it disappeared slowly into the waters. He finally felt liberated from the weight that wearing that necklace implied. He was negotiating an accord with his destiny; he was ready to sacrifice the gift of the Goddess in exchange for Adhara's return.

Raiko sat down in the sand, downcast. He did not know that from the heights of a cliff a figure was coming down, circumventing the stones, and watching him.

The eagle had put her down on the highest hill on the island. She felt completely recovered and the manuscript rested in a saddlebag on her shoulder. She knew she had to get down the slope to reach the port where the ship, and her companions, who did not yet know of her return, would welcome her.

Adhara was walking through the rocks to reach the sea. She ambled, absorbed in thought. She had acquired another of the five books. This would put them very close to ending their mission and the end of this adventure. She thought about the responsibility she would face afterwards. What was expected of her? Should she rally the Amazons and convince them not to follow Mithridates? Would they respect her? Would they follow her orders, even though they had never set eyes on her before? *If only Lisipe were alive*, Adhara thought. She felt so alone!

She looked up from the rocky path she was following and looked towards the beach, trying to find the silhouette of the *Aphrodite*. Then she saw him. A handsome man, stopped at the edge of the sea, lifting his hands to his neck in anger and throwing a small necklace to the sea.

This tiny gesture was enough to unleash all her suppressed desires. She saw him there, alone, sitting on the sand, looking miserable and dejected, and she wanted to believe for an instant that he had renounced the gift from the Goddess because of her. She wanted to believe that he felt the same way she was feeling right then.

She ran faster, with the desire to reach his side as soon as possible. Suddenly, the responsibility on her shoulders no longer mattered. She would think about that later. In the name of the Gods! She was only sixteen and she had already touched death.

The future was uncertain, but right now, all she wanted was to be by his side.

She ran as far as the sand on the beach, then she slowed down and started to walk towards him slowly, still unsure of how he would react when he saw her.

Raiko was drawing random shapes on the sand. Engrossed in his chore, he did not realize anyone was approaching. He noticed the shadow that was looming over him and he looked up, bothered by the interruption. His eyes met with a pair of gray-green eyes that looked at him with delight.

"You are giving up your charms? What will happen with the mermaids and all the other women who worship you?" she asked, in a sarcastic voice, pointing at his neck where the necklace had once been.

"Adhara!" Raiko exclaimed.

They stood looking into each other's eyes for an endless moment, until Raiko went to her, and pressing her close to his chest, he kissed her. He kissed her as he had wanted to do the first time they met, as he had wanted to do when they were sailing on this very sea, as he wanted to when she was arrogant... like now, when having found her, he never wanted to let her go.

"I was so afraid I would never see you again!" He said, as his lips searched for hers once more.

They were sitting looking out at the sea; a comfortable silence had developed between them. Raiko turned from looking at the sea and fixed his gaze on Adhara's profile.

"I am not worthy of you, Adhara," he said, sorrowfully. It was strange to see him like this, dejected and sad, the Amazon thought.

"I am an outlaw," he went on, while Adhara remained quiet. "I am prohibited from using my family name. I have no material wealth apart from the *Aphrodite* and I can't even go near the coasts of ..." Adhara put a finger to his lips to silence him.

"Perhaps you don't know that that does not matter?" There was also sadness in her voice. "There can be no kind of future between us. I am an Amazon. When this adventure is over, you will go back to the seas, and I will try to win back Themiscyra…"

She was quiet for a moment, and then she continued in a resigned voice, "Let's not torture ourselves with impossible thoughts, with dreams that will never become reality. Let us enjoy what we have during this voyage and not think of goodbyes… yet."

She settled in his arms, put her head on his chest, and allowed Raiko to hug her again. Tomorrow had not yet arrived, and Adhara did not want to think about it yet.

For his part, Raiko did not want to say anything, but the promise he had made to Xanthe resounded in his mind. *I will devote my life to protecting her*, he had promised the Amazon. It was not going to be that easy to free himself from this thought, and his humorous smile returned to his face.

They walked in the direction of the *Aphrodite*. When they arrived at the port, the whole crew was already on board. Odon was concerned, and he had been mulling over the idea of sending out a party of men to look for Raiko. He was afraid that something bad had happened.

When he saw him arrive, he heaved a sigh of relief and a big smile appeared on his chubby face.

"Look who we have here," he said, seeing Adhara by his side. "I see why you took so long. Welcome back on board, Adhara!"

Dromeas ran to her and embraced her tightly.

"I knew you would come," Dromeas said, filled with happiness, while he hugged his sister just like when they were little children playing together in their grandfather's garden.

"Dromeas, I am so glad to see you!" Adhara said.

Raiko moved to one side with a sad expression in the presence of Dromeas. The boy noticed straight away, and letting go of his sister, he went towards Raiko.

"I do not know what trouble you got into in the past, dear friend, but I want you to know that I am happy that you are by my sister's side," And as he said this he gave him a strong hug.

302

Raiko remained rigid at first, but with the warm reception from Dromeas, he relaxed, and he returned the brotherly hug with unexpected joy.

After they had eaten and rested, the *Aphrodite* set out once more on the blue seas. Adhara recounted what had happened from the time when the eagle picked her up in his claws.

"This is the book that he asked me to entrust to you," and she handed Heptos the manuscript she had received on the top of the Caucasus. "He stressed that I should save it. It seems he did not trust your criterion." Heptos took the manuscript in his hands and rolled it out, allowing his eyes to glance over parts of the text.

"He has plenty of reason not to trust me. I never believed in the Gods and I would never have gone in search of a book that talks about them. It has always seemed to me that their creation was a product of a human weakness."

He looked down at the book again and continued, *"Prometheus Bound,"* he read. "The choice he made makes me hesitate. If this book really belongs to the group of five, I would have to question all that I have believed up until now. Could it be that my desire for knowledge is such that in my search, I passed over something much greater than I? Am I so arrogant that I think I can explain all the mysteries of the Cosmos, using only my limited human mind?" Looking to the ground, he shook his head. "I am confronting the same problem that all the wise man have faced over the years. I think I am getting old and I am afraid of dying."

"Is this a moment of weakness?" Raiko asked, in a sarcastic tone. He had never seen this old man doubt absolutely anything.

"You are right, this is a luxury I cannot allow myself," and handing the manuscript to Ammos and Roxana, he said, "Could you, once again, place your hands on the book?"

Roxana and Ammos stood facing each other, holding the manuscript between their palms. They looked into each other's eyes and their lips opened, but this time there was not a melody to be heard, instead, there were bursts of air. Although timid at first, they gathered force and turned into strong winds. The air began to swirl around them in circles that were getting bigger and faster, until they produced a ring of wind so large that its circumference surrounded the ship. Outside the ring, the sea waters were raging tempestuously and turbulently, but inside the ring of wind, the *Aphrodite* was floating over calm waters, as though she were on a lake.

While the gale continued blowing and roaring around them, humongous flames rose up from the sea, surrounding them. They felt the heat of the flames on their faces and their bodies began to sweat copiously.

As though it were responding to the red flames outside, electric blue tongues of fire emerged from the papyrus. They broke away from the book and climbed into the air above their heads. In a vertical movement, they wrote the words:

At first the God arose, then followed a very long vacuum, and finally man assumed his image and his likeness.

The words hung in the air for just a few seconds. They disappeared slowly, like a fire that dwindled due to lack of oxygen. When the blue tongues disappeared completely, a heavy rain began to fall, bathing them, and putting out the surrounding curtain of fire. The wind no longer howled, instead it slowed down to a breeze that refreshed their perspiring bodies. The waters slowly returned to normal, as though nothing had happened. The seven chosen ones, soaked to the skin, looked at each other.

"Are you sure that the Seventh will understand these confusing statements?" Dromeas asked doubtfully.

"Don't lose faith," Heptos answered. "I, the one who does not believe in anything, have put all my hope in the Seventh."

CHAPTER FIFTY-NINE

It was a marvelous sunny morning, like any other during the summertime on the Aegean Sea. Heptos had gathered everyone together in the cabin. Raiko had asked him for instructions as to which course the *Aphrodite* should take, and Heptos had asked for a little time to think.

"We are very close to finishing our mission," Heptos said, with satisfaction. "However, the Roman army, as well as that of Mithridates, is following our trail, and we still need to find one more book. I am sure that the book that will complete the group is *The Sand Reckoner* by Archimedes. However, this one is without doubt the most difficult feat since we will have to go to Rome to look for it."

"Why is the manuscript in Rome?" Roxana asked.

"The woman who owns the original has a great debt to humanity and she will not hand it over unless I go to her in person. The Roman official who killed Archimedes by accident was an ancestor of hers. This event caused her family to be in disgrace ever since."

In Archimedes' era, more than two hundred years ago, Rome besieged his hometown, Syracuse. The mathematician had devoted much of his ingenuity to the manufacture of war machines to help in the battle. They said that he developed large concave mirrors of light, which, positioned in strategic positions, reflected light onto enemy ships, and set fire to them.

Thanks to the strategies of Archimedes, Syracuse resisted the Romans for a long time. The Romans, in the end, used the most trivial method to take the city. When the whole of Syracuse was sleeping off the ecstasy of triumph, they bribed a guard soldier who opened the gates of the walls for them. Marcellus, the general in charge of the Roman regiment, asked expressly that they bring the wise man back alive. Such a brilliant mind could not go to waste, and there was plenty for Rome to gain if he worked with them. However, during the hunt, the official charged with the order came across an old man drawing circles in the sand. On the order to give himself up, the old man replied, "Do not spoil my circles." The soldier, furious with this blatant disobedience, murdered him, without knowing that he was killing the man he had been asked to bring back safe and sound. It was afterwards, when he saw a papyrus that the man had been working on, that he realized he had killed the great Archimedes. Without saying a word to anyone, he took the wise man's document, together with his own dishonor, and blamed the death on a subordinate.

Archimedes, is, beyond doubt, the best mathematician history has ever seen. Born in Syracuse in 287 B.C., he dedicated his life to the study of mathematics, mechanics, and physics. He is credited with: the discovery of Pi, the relationship of the measurement of the circumference and its diameter, the relationship of floating bodies, the construction of hydro-pneumatic screws, and many more inventions.

My dear Archimedes. Do you know what his motto was? "Transire suum pectus mundo que potiri." -"Surpass yourself and you will rule the world." This quote remained imprinted in my soul from the first day I heard it.

Yes, as you will have already realized, Euclid, Aristarchus and Archimedes were contemporaries, and the three were great admirers of the work of Aristotle. We met thanks to the Library of Alexandria and we developed a great friendship. I was a simple listener, without an iota of the talent they possessed. It was evident that they were very knowledgeable of the Word. Heptos had hit the target. The book of Archimedes would complete the group of five manuscripts.

Heptos kept looking at the faces of the chosen ones.

"Sulla is heading for Rome in triumph, with the intention of destroying his enemy. We all know that he is in high spirits from the victories he has attained and that his ego is large. He believes himself to be invincible. He will do anything to get what he wants, and the Treasure that we are about to obtain is one of his greatest desires." His words sank heavily into the air.

"I cannot force you to go on such a dangerous mission. Only one book separates us from having what we greatly desire, but I can only warn you that you will be risking your lives."

Heptos' words were followed by a profound silence. Six pairs of eyes looked at each other, and suddenly they all started to laugh. Raiko answered for everyone, "After all we have been through we cannot abandon you now. Let's go to Rome and finish what we started!"

CHAPTER SIXTY

The sun was setting on the seven hills of the Eternal City, its rays bathing the valley where it had been founded seven centuries before. Considered *Caput Mundi*, the capital of the world, Rome boasted impressive monuments and public buildings that lined its streets, mainly built of the Travertine marble characteristic of the region. The foreigner who arrived in the city for the first time was left speechless in front of the majesty and beauty of the temples, amphitheaters, and triumphal arches.

At this hour, the owners of the *tabernae* in the Forum were gathering up their wares and preparing to leave. Meanwhile, the restaurants were heating up their cooking vessels and, in the brothels, the prostitutes were making up their faces in readiness for the night's work.

In a house far from the commotion of the city center, Cleantes concentrated on preparing a frugal dinner. In Mysia, when he had returned to the *Aphrodite* with the horses that Innoel Hammorib had sent so that they would accept his hospitality, Heptos had assigned another mission to his servant. *Go to Rome and make contact with Lavinia from the Julius clan. Tell her that you come on my behalf, and that we will soon collect what she promised me.*

Cleantes, with his usual skill, had reached the city in a very fast time, considering the conditions of the road. He had tried to make contact with the person in question. However, he had never been able to meet the lady. A faithful servant had placed him in this modest house and had told him that he should wait for orders. He would have to wait until the time was favorable for the delivery. Cleantes had immediately sent a trusted person to the port of Ostia with instructions to wait for the arrival of a ship named *Aphrodite* and to deliver a sealed message to the captain of the ship on his behalf.

A knock at the door distanced him from his thoughts and he rushed to receive the guest. He opened the door cautiously, thinking that he would finally meet the lady in question. To his surprise, the seven chosen ones were there.

After having decided they would complete the search for the five manuscripts, the *Aphrodite* headed towards the Italian peninsula. The ship continued sailing on the deep waters of the Mare Nostrum and then entered the Mare Thyrrhenicum on the coast of Sicily, following the same route that Raiko had taken many years before.

They passed in front of the same three rocks, but this time no mermaid tried to call the attention of the crew. In truth, the sailors were slightly disappointed, one of the few perks of their arduous work was to look at the beautiful mermaids and dream of them in the shelter of the night... but their captain had fallen in love with an Amazon and all the fun had gone, they thought, disillusioned.

The *Aphrodite* skirted the western coast of Italy and finally docked in Ostia. This port was the maritime entryway to the Eternal City, as the river Tiber that ran majestically along one border of the city flowed into the sea by way of this coastal town.

They tied up the ship at the pier in Ostia, and a few minutes after throwing the anchor, a man approached them and asked to speak to the captain. Raiko received him and the man delivered a sealed manuscript. Heptos recognized Cleantes' writing and they followed the emissary with confidence. He already had a small boat ready that would take them across the Tiber to the Eternal City.

Zarin had stayed on the *Aphrodite,* as Dromeas did not want to expose her to the dangers they might find in Rome. Odon jokingly promised him that he would take better care of her than Dromeas, and with a gesture that meant, *lay one finger on her and I will kill you,* Dromeas said goodbye to the old sea wolf.

The crossing was peaceful, but tense. With a sign, Heptos had ordered them not to speak during the journey. When they arrived, the priest generously paid the man who had guided them there, and he left in silence.

The house they had reached was in a quiet part of the city. The neighbors were artisans and local merchants. It was a modest, but comfortable, dwelling.

When they saw Cleantes in the threshold of the door, they all smiled. Heptos was the first to speak.

"Cleantes," he hugged his old friend affectionately, "How have you been?"

"I have been in Rome for several days waiting for you, my Lord," Cleantes said, smiling. "The lady whom I had to contact has sent me here and we are to wait for instructions."

They spent several days closed up in the house. Only Cleantes went out to the market to buy the necessary supplies to eat, and he brought with him the news that was going around. The capital was in revolt. The latest news that had arrived was that Sulla had gathered an army of forty thousand men on his march towards Rome. He had enough money to contract more soldiers to confront the allies of Cinna and Marius. Nevertheless, after his incredible triumphs, now no one feared the size of the Red Commander's army. They feared the Red Commander, his qualities as a leader, and his military strategy; in the recent past he had demonstrated that he could emerge victorious against armies three times the size.

His men had left the coasts of Greece and it was only a matter of days until they landed on Italian territory. The houses of the great families of one side or the other were guarded and protected. The slaughter of Sulla's followers had stopped, the heads on poles in the Forum had been removed, and many of the undecided awaited the development of the contest. Now, no one considered Sulla the public enemy of Rome. Many could not sleep at night in fear of his retaliations.

A pair of immense eyes watched her. They stared at her. Their size was so great that the contractions and dilations of the pupils, that had the same dimensions of the sun, were discernible. However, the eyes were not frightening; they were warm eyes that radiated affection. They stared at her with kindness.

The image changed abruptly and she saw herself on board the *Aphrodite,* surrounded by all her companions. It was a sunny day and the eyes looked joyfully at how they passed the days on that ship that had become a sort of home. The eyes followed her wherever she went, as if they were watching out for the safety of all.

Suddenly, Adhara opened her eyes and realized that it had all been a dream. She got up from the bed and went to Heptos.

"I already know who the Seventh is," she said, with confidence.

Heptos smiled at her. "I knew that you would discover it at the right moment," he spoke to her with the satisfaction of a teacher. "Now go to your brother and Raiko, and tell them of your discovery. Do not leave them in the dark."

CHAPTER SIXTY-ONE

Cleantes was in the Roman Forum, the heart and the very life of Rome. People gathered there at the market, not just to buy their necessities, but also to catch up on everything that was happening throughout the Republic.

The Forum was buzzing; the latest news was spreading fast. Sulla had disembarked in Brundisium with an army of forty thousand men and he had already defeated the *populares* in three battles. He had advanced to the walls of Rome and his troops had set up camp to regain their strength and rebuild the lethal war machines that had given them so much success in Greece. It was only a matter of time before they took the city.

The Red Commander had sent a committee in his name to speak to the Senate and present his conditions. The parliament remained divided, though many were already wagering on Sulla's triumph. Proof of this was how his emissaries walked the streets of Rome, completely calm. Only a short while back, if anyone even mentioned a link to Sulla, he would have feared for his life.

Cleantes was in front of a stall that sold cloths of different colors. The materials were exquisitely arranged on a counter attended by a fat merchant. Cleantes had orders to go to the market every day and check the fabric stall until he found the sign that had been agreed upon. Then the whereabouts of the meeting would be revealed to him. The servant moved all the cloths with deliberate calm, until he found one of an amethyst color. This was the color they had agreed. He picked it up and attracted the merchant's attention.

"I see that you like the cloak of Syracuse," The man who was selling fabrics said.

"Yes, it is my favorite," Cleantes replied.

"Well, there is enough of this material to dress the Dioscuri who protect Rome, Castor and Pollux, when they lie down to sleep at midnight."

Cleantes took the piece of cloth, paid the merchant, and left. He had understood the veiled message. He rushed through the streets of Rome to find his master and tell him that the meeting

312

had finally been arranged. But the adept servant, who had navigated every type of attack during this adventure, had not realized that a man had heard the whole conversation from the side of the stall.

Cleantes had not recognized him because of his full beard. However, the man had one blue eye and one brown eye and had been a passenger on a ship that Cleantes had boarded some time ago. He had followed the trail, and by making enquiries in a Rome where anything could be bought for the right price, he had found the astute servant. He had set up a stall selling clay pots, next to the fat merchant. He watched him come every day, without buying anything, but today he understood that the oblique dialogue was giving him the information that his own master also desired.

Content with the fruits of his day's work, he knocked over the cart. The clay pots shattered when they hit the ground, but the loss of his merchandise did not matter in the slightest to the phony merchant. The information he had to tell his master would provide for him for the rest of his life.

CHAPTER SIXTY-TWO

The moonless night wrapped everything in its black cape. A group of people was walking close together through the empty streets of Rome. The meeting place had already been determined and today was the perfect day for the delivery, as there was a lack of soldiers to guard the city due to the conflicts that were taking place outside the walls. They could not wait much longer for the hand over. It had to happen before Sulla took the city to allow them time to escape.

The path they had to take was short; the meeting place was very close. They left the house where they had been staying and they went in the direction of the Roman Forum, in the valley between the Palatine and Capitol hills.

When they arrived, their steps followed the *Clivus Capitolinus*, the avenue that all the emperors took on their victory marches, when they returned to Rome triumphant and went to the Great Temple to give offerings for their successes. This was an avenue that began at the western side of the Forum, veered to the right to pass in front of the Temple of Saturn, and then, winding around to the left, started to climb the hill that would take it to its destination, the Temple of Jupiter Capitolinus, on top of the hill of the same name.

They continued walking along the route of the emperors, passing in front of the Temple of Saturn and the Basilica Sempronia. Right in between the Basilica and the Atrium of the Vestals was the meeting place, the Temple of the Dioscuri, Castor and Pollux.

The site had not been chosen by chance. Situated between two large buildings, this small temple was always in the shade of the neighboring structures. The accesses to the side were narrow and dark. It was easy to slip inside the sanctuary without being seen from the main thoroughfare.

Heptos also thought that it was a twist of fate that the chosen temple was that of the Dioscuri. Castor and Pollux were born from an encounter between Leda and Zeus. Although they were twins, both children of a God, Castor was mortal, and Pollux, quite the opposite, was immortal. They were there risking their mortal lives, like Castor, to save the immortality of the manuscripts that they sought with such zeal.

The figures,who walked the streets quietly by night, crossed the portico and entered the main hall. Heptos was trying to move cautiously inside the enclosure, his gaze skimming over the vessels on the ground. He went to one of them, and, just as had been agreed, he found a small wind flute inside it. He softly harmonized a tune.

It was a simple melody, but, for a moment, they all felt transported to the woods of Arcadia, where the nymphs and fauns danced to the sound of this music. A weakness on the part of the priest was that he never believed in creatures of fantasy, and yet it was they who had helped him throughout his mission.

In response to the music, they heard steps getting closer and a man's voice asked, "Who lives there?"

"A friend," Heptos said, softly, "Do not spoil my circles," The secret code was the last phrase uttered by Archimedes before dying.

A delicate shadow, accompanied by a well-built man, appeared in the enclosure. She was dressed in a long cape that covered her from head to toe. She approached the center of the temple and asked, "Heptos?"

Heptos approached the person.

"It is a pleasure to finally meet you, Lavinia."

The person pushed her hood back, and they could see the aristocratic profile of a Roman Patrician.

"Are you sure that no one has followed you?" she asked, softly.

"We have taken all possible precautions. Ever since we took up lodgings in the house that you so nobly offered us, we have not left, and we have followed your instructions."

"Rome is in revolt and there is no one to be trusted. Spirits are high with the war between Sulla and Cinna, and what we are doing is very dangerous." With outstretched arms, she handed him a package swathed in white linen cloths. "Here I bring you what my family has guarded with such zeal. The last work of Archimedes."

Lavinia was a descendant of the officer who had murdered the great wise man; now, almost two hundred years later, the only descendant of that soldier held the manuscript in her hands and she was ready to deliver it to those who had promised to save it. Her ancestor had killed Archimedes, but she would save his work for the rest of eternity.

"Ammos?" Heptos called. Finally, he had in his hands the last book that would help to decipher the Word.

For the last time, the magic they already knew would take effect again. Ammos and Roxana placed their hands on the manuscript. This time there was no chanting. The two figures kept their lips sealed, and the music remained trapped inside their chests. Their bodies shook, supporting the internal force that they suppressed for fear of being heard. There was a heavy sense of dread in the atmosphere, it seemed that even the manuscript feared falling into the wrong hands.

The light, however, could be no less brilliant than the previous times. The swift rays shot into the air and the last clue was unveiled.

Light, darkness, light, darkness, light, darkness and darkness.

Those present read the words one more time, unaware of their significance. However, the light from the words attracted the attention of the guards who were huddled up outside. They entered the temple with loud cries.

"Stop in the name of Lucius Cornelius Sulla!" The playful sparkles had not even disappeared and, in an instant, the hall of the temple was filled with burly men carrying heavy swords. The officer in charge was an envoy of Sulla who had arrived in Rome under cover, as part of the committee that had addressed the Senate.

The chosen ones, Lavinia, and her servant were all apprehended, with two soldiers for each one, taking them by the arms and immobilizing them. Sulla's general addressed Lavinia in a sardonic tone.

"Well, what do we have here? A Roman aristocrat who wants to make a mockery of the orders of her Consul? We are close to

316

the Tarpeian Rock; perhaps you want to pay for your treason in the same way that the Vestal Virgin who betrayed Rome did. Do you remember her punishment? She was thrown off that same stone," he said, with sarcasm.

"Do not dare to touch me," Lavinia replied, in a challenge. "The *Julius* are very powerful and the future of Rome has yet to be decided. The *optimates* have still not declared victory."

The general paused, weighing up his options. He was sure that Sulla would win this war, but if that were not the case, maybe it would be better to act with caution. He did not want to drive another clan of the *populares* against him.

"You will all remain in the charge of the soldiers. You will be taken to Sulla's camp straight away," and with his eyes fixed on Lavinia he said, "You will be tried for treason in due course."

As the soldier dictated the sentence, a figure dressed in a white toga appeared behind him. Heptos recognized him immediately.

"Tesseros, it is you!" Heptos cried. *"Miserable Traitor! You will appear from the circle of seven.* A short time ago, I realized that the traitor the prophecy referred to was not one of the chosen ones, but one of the priests of Apollo."

"You talk of betrayal? How do you dare talk to me like that? It was you who betrayed the God to whom you devoted yourself, not I. They gave you the task of saving the Treasure of Delphi, the gold that we had hidden, the gold that many generations had given us to maintain our greatness, and you used it for your personal gains. With that gold, we would have been able to keep ourselves safe until the war ended, and resume the worship of Apollo. You, on the other hand, spent it on manuscripts that defend the religion that you, only, follow."

"For what purpose do you want the Treasure? To buy a little time? Do you not realize that gold will be of no use to you, other than to live in shadow after having bought the soul of your executioner? Do you not see that the only part of our grandeur worth rescuing is what I have rescued? Our gold will not speak of us in posterity. Our real Treasure was to be who we were, and what we achieved as simple human beings.

317

"Gold does not even maintain the same form of whoever smelted it for the first time. Not even the images on our coins will endure. They will be transformed into the images of others. On the other hand, I have saved our essence, that is more than a Treasure," Heptos said, wielding the manuscript in his hands, "This is a legacy for humanity."

Everyone in the room had remained quiet, listening to the conversation between the priests. Tesseros was silent for a long time, pondering what Heptos had said. Incapable of finding an argument to carry on the discussion, he let out a snort.

"Enough of this nonsense." Pointing at Ammos, he said, "He is the one Sulla has been looking for," he said to the envoy, "He is the Bearer."

On a sign from the general, the soldiers who were holding Ammos made him kneel down and bow his head. One of them took out his sharp sword and put it to Ammos' neck.

"NO!" Roxana's scream filled the entire room. The girl fell on her knees, her face bathed in tears, as she reached out her hands pleading clemency. "Do not hurt him, please!" she implored, while Ammos kept still, kneeling in front of the soldier, exposing the back of his neck.

The soldiers did not stop in the face of her petitions, but the purpose of the swords was not to cut his neck. They slowly passed the blades of their weapons across the top of Ammos' head, relieving him of the locks of his long, thick black hair.

His locks of hair dropped onto the floor in a consistent pattern. Finally, when there was not a piece of hair left, Ammos showed his bald head. On the skin around his cranium that was bleeding because of the small nicks from the sharp swords, they could see the symbol:

It was the symbol that had been written on the skin of his head in that initiation ceremony many years ago. The day when he and the Word had formed one single being, the day when he was consecrated as the Bearer.

Tesseros looked at Ammos' head with a puzzled expression.

"What does this mean?" he could not work out the meaning of what was written. The priest was dismayed; he always though that by catching the Bearer, they would immediately have the solution to the enigma.

With a cruel smile, Heptos answered him, "You arrived late, Tesseros. With this sign, the Seventh already has in his power all the clues to decipher the Word. You cannot stop us! Even at the cost of our lives, these books will be saved and they will reveal the Word to the entire world." His companion's challenging tone came as a slap in the face to Tesseros.

"You still trust in the Seventh? Allow me to laugh at your candidness," and he began to laugh his head off. His endless laugh echoed throughout the temple, resounding long after the priest had ceased the mockery. "The Seventh will not save you. I know who he is, I recognized him from that day when the Pythia proclaimed her prophecy. From that moment, the Seventh was present in our lives, but he has never done anything for you. The Seventh did not even warn you when he found out the Roman soldiers were following you!" In a scornful voice, he said, "I do not believe the Seventh wants to help you."

Heptos' eyes grew dark. Roxana and Adhara contained a groan, and Raiko and Dromeas clenched their fists. From the floor, Ammos looked up and let out a desolate sigh. Heptos cried in fury, "Seventh, is that true? Heptos asked you the question frankly. "Is it true that you will not help us?" he said, looking straight into your eyes.

"Please, Seventh," Roxana said, begging you, she too, looking into your eyes. Hers were full of tears, she was on her knees between the two soldiers who held her by the wrists.

"Please do not let my life have been in vain," Ammos said to you, with his bare head still bleeding, showing the defiant symbol inscribed on it.

Heptos cried at you in rage, "I took these innocent people on this mission because I counted on your help. I always had faith in you. You cannot abandon us now!"

The soldiers were looking everywhere for the interlocutor. They finally understood, they understood it was you to whom the prisoners were directing their pleas.

"The power in my hands must remain until you proclaim the Word. I can live for many more years, but lamentably I am not immortal, please," Roxana said to you, her serenity lost, "Help me fulfill my mission!"

"I have the responsibility of saving a brave race on my shoulders," now it was Adhara who addressed you, beseechingly. "I am the last of the Amazons, if I die, they will all die with me."

Dromeas, her twin brother, presented the weight on his soul to you, "My desire to become an Olympic champion has been cut short. But I still have a mission to complete. I need you to save me so that I avenge the death of my mother!"

"You know that I love knowledge above all else," Heptos once again asked for your support. "I am not asking for me, I am asking because of all those manuscripts that are on the ship and that depend on you to be saved."

"They broke my heart when I was very young and I lost any moral value that a man could have." Raiko was the last to speak, but that did not mean his plea was lacking in emotion. "I do not ask you to save us because of manuscripts, or on altars of the greatness of knowledge. I ask you simply as a man who wants to start his life over with the woman he loves."

Six pairs of eyes turned to you, and imploringly, they said, "Our destiny is in your hands. Only you can decipher it, only you can declare the Word. The wisdom is in you. Save us, please!"

I, Erus Ludus, the Master of the Game, have succeeded once again. I have succeeded in capturing you, dear friend, in the pages of this tale and, in doing so, converting you into one more character. Did you ever imagine this would happen?

YOU are the Seventh, the Discreet Stranger in the prophecy. You were always there, from the beginning, throughout the journey, in the ambush, and you are the only one who, using the five phrases of light and the symbol of Ammos, will be able to decipher the Word.

The manuscripts rest in Raiko's ship, the Aphrodite, where YOU also sailed from Greece to Alexandria, and along the coasts of Anatolia, to Rome. Now, they too, depend on YOU.

"Save us!" is the collective cry of the six characters who have shared this, their story, with you. Six characters who came to know you, and who trust in you so that they may live on. How does it feel to be an omnipresent being, and to have the destiny of the others in your hands?

Only YOU can save us. Will you do it?

AUTHOR'S NOTE

I read somewhere that the Oulipo group created a matrix of all possible crime situations, and discovered that no book had ever been written in which the murderer was the reader.

From this proposition, the idea of making the reader an active participant in the novel was born. However, given my lack of expertise and my limited experience in the art of writing, instead of a story I composed a riddle.

The case is that the reader, who by becoming the Seventh, deciphers the Word, and proclaims it, will become a real character in the next book. In this way, Erus Ludus will be able to continue his story.

If you decipher the Word, send your answer along with the reasoning you have followed to Aenigma.word@yahoo.com or @ErusLudus. I will meet the first person who solves the riddle, and I will make you the character you want to be in the storyline.

Printed in Great Britain
by Amazon.co.uk, Ltd.,
Marston Gate.